YEN

Morgan Wells

Trafford
PUBLISHING™

Order this book online at www.trafford.com
or email orders@trafford.com

Most Trafford titles are also available at major online book retailers.

Note for Librarians: A cataloguing record for this book is available from Library
and Archives Canada at www.collectionscanada.ca/amicus/index-e.html

Printed in Victoria, BC, Canada.

ISBN: 978-1-4251-8705-7 (Soft)
ISBN: 978-1-4269-1768-4 (Hard)
ISBN: 978-1-4269-1767-7 (e-book)

*We at Trafford believe that it is the responsibility of us all, as both individuals
and corporations, to make choices that are environmentally and socially sound.
You, in turn, are supporting this responsible conduct each time you purchase a
Trafford book, or make use of our publishing services. To find out how you are
helping, please visit www.trafford.com/responsiblepublishing.html*

*Our mission is to efficiently provide the world's finest, most comprehensive
book publishing service, enabling every author to experience success.
To find out how to publish your book, your way, and have it available
worldwide, visit us online at www.trafford.com*

Trafford rev: 9/23/2009

www.trafford.com

North America & international
toll-free: 1 888 232 4444 (USA & Canada)
phone: 250 383 6864 ♦ fax: 812 355 4082
email: info@trafford.com

Dear Winchester,

Do you remember me, oh dearest Winchester? I remember you so well from our childhood: Frolicking in the fields of wheat, chill with morning dew, the sun's warm, golden beams awakening the quiet, sleeping houses. I cherish your endearing laughter, and I hear it often. Then, your child's shining face floods my memory, and I am left to drown with only that once beloved image.

I dream of seeing home again, yet I know my ship has set sail under the cover of night's dark cloak and will never again return. You and I, Winchester, are very similar indeed. I have only dusty, faded memories, as you have also. Perhaps, you will never again roam in those golden fields so much like Jane's fossilized honey locks, which in itself is freedom of spirit. I feel a profound pleasure in visualizing your state of mind behind those hard, metal bars with only the notion of sunlit places to sustain your burning urge to escape suppression. Your sustenance will be the very thing to steal your ever decreasing sanity, and this is my sole comfort.

Love always,
Eleanor.

I

Eleanor moved restlessly amongst the protection of towering shelves. Her face twitched twice then returned to its usual seemingly placid, calm aspect. She had worked within the confines of this library for over twenty years, and this was and had become, the sum total of her life experiences. Moving breathlessly from shelf to shelf, she glanced nervously at her watch, trying to avoid the habitual crowd, which usually arrived just after lunch.

The morning had passed with its usual inactivity and predictability. Eleanor's method was systematic like a well-oiled machine. As she rounded the ledge's outer edge, sunlight spilled over her pale cheek, reflected off her lenses, and illuminated a multitude of white hair within her dull brown shade. The sunlight always made Eleanor think of her, and as usual, she flushed crimson in this bath of gold. Retreating behind the darkness of a neighbouring shelf, Eleanor sighed with relief and resumed the task at hand. The smell of books soothed her, lulled her into a world she knew, a familiar place where questions were easily answered and solutions were always within reach. This was Eleanor's world: her paradise and prison encompassing the expanse of her life.

The rustle of clothing made her start for an instant, then standing up, she smiled and greeted the man before her with a very formal, "Good morning, Mr. Gaines."

Mr. Gaines stood still and scowled inwardly at this visage before him. Nevertheless, he nodded in her direction and passed by as was his custom, without uttering a single word. Eleanor relied on this formal acknowledgment, as it had taken them quite a number of years to reach this level of understanding. Mr. Gaines had always held Eleanor in the greatest esteem, and still would have, if it hadn't been for an unfortunate flaw in his character.

Eleanor's thoughts returned to *his* face, always etched so precisely in time, preserved in obscurity before, when Eleanor still could love. She remembered his smile; a kind of light seemed to emit from it and every crevice, every particle of Eleanor felt touched. She could taste it like a bittersweet tea, its sweetness intoxicating, but once drunk leaving you with no other desire but for more. Eleanor made sure she stocked up on this tea. If she had but nothing else to fill her cupboards, ever present was this bittersweet tea. She would sit in the evenings drinking it in copious quantity. Sometimes she'd pretend he was sitting beside her, serving her this extension of his smile, his kiss, his ... then Eleanor's body would begin to move rhythmically, as the tea would trickle down the back of her throat and she would sigh gently, "Winchester, oh Winchester," only to realize the pot was empty and she was and always would be alone. When she was younger this realization would create a torrent of emotion, brimming the pot with bittersweet tears. But eventually the floods ceased, and the necessities and day-to-day drudgery of life made her as apathetic in her conduct as she felt emotionless within.

Jane stood like a bronzed statue, hair streaming in the warm breezes, white lace sundress caressing her sinuous curves. Her hair hung down to her buttocks, shining golden like the sheaves at her feet. With eyes sparkling and perspiration moist lips, Jane looked down at Eleanor who was presently engaged in a long, complicated murder mystery. Jane smiled; she possessed a manner of smile not ordinary in any way, it seemed to light up her face as well as her immediate surroundings. Under that smile lurked a hidden fascination, a sparkle, a kind of ecstatic insight into the wonder of life, not unlike the depths of a fathomless ocean. With this trait, she, like a deviless or goddess, could entice anyone who dared to look into her sherry brown orbs.

She began to leap above the sheaves, in long elegant arcs, a sea creature careening over the waves, one of Humbert's nymphets. She possessed that rare, sought-after poison, and she knew this, as did the eyes of many infected, tormented admirers. Eyes shining mischievously, she dared Eleanor to cease the reading which she had always found to be tedious and boring. It seemed to Jane that Eleanor hardly even noticed the sunlit expanse of field and sky, filled with hidden dimensions of exploration and wonder.

Presently Eleanor gazed up at Jane. Eleanor thought Jane's movements were like an undiscovered prima ballerina, symbiotic with the gyration of sheaves beneath her. Watching Jane, she could hardly breathe so engrossed became her veneration. She knew she could never dance like Jane, and dared not to attempt to contaminate the perfection of Jane's artistry.

Jane's feet curved as a dove's wing might, she shrieked in mid-flight, and fell laughing into the shadows beneath her. Sitting up, breathing heavily, her forehead glistening with what seemed to Eleanor to be opaline droplets, she yelled, "Come on, you lazy bookworm. The summer won't last."

"I was just completing the end of the chapter," Eleanor hissed, irritated at being interrupted from her reverie.

Not liking the response, Jane bounded over to Eleanor, and proceeded to jump on and tickle her, until in complete submission, Eleanor surrendered.

Standing up, Eleanor stretched her tired muscles, frozen from inaction, enjoying the warmth of sunlight passing over her extremities. The summer was waning quickly and soon it would be time for the harvesting of another season. Eleanor inhaled the warmth of the aromatic breezes, and sighing gently, flopped down again at Jane's dirty, callused feet.

"You must be the laziest creature on earth except for maybe the sloth," growled Jane in complete disdain.

Eleanor, not being amused by such keen observation, simply replied, "My activities are more refined which does often reflect a superior intellect."

"Suit yourself," retorted Jane, "But when you become overweight, can hardly breathe, and are nearly blind, I will say I told you so."

This comment Eleanor could not stomach easily. Jane knew Eleanor's intentions were not benign as she pursued her in mad flight. Although Eleanor read more than any other activity in her life, she was by no means a sloth when it came to physical exertion.

Over sheaf they did fly, as the light shifted its gaze in their advance; nearly colliding but never touching were the competitors so equal at this exercise. Reaching out, Eleanor could almost taste the sweetness of Jane's hair, but Jane would only increase her speed ever so slightly to keep the game up. It seemed to Eleanor at times that she felt the same sensation when reaching for the stars or stretching towards that infinite expanse of azure at sunset when the silhouettes stand black and firm in opposition to the ensuing darkness; that same desire for acceptance and unification with something greater than her own insignificance, yet never to be deemed plausible. Jane would recognize a subtle change in Eleanor's expression, and continue to run, yet smile a somber, knowing smile that comforted Eleanor in a way which she could not, and even if she could, would not want to explain.

Jane knew people; somehow she always knew their depths and weaknesses and often, even seemed to be aware of their most intimate darknesses of mind. On occasion, this tendency made the people around Jane nervous and a little apprehensive of her, but Jane did not have any inclination to hide this trait, and Eleanor took it to be as constant as the progression of time.

Eleanor, finally tiring, ceased the pursuit, and Jane looked at her a little relieved for she had also grown exhausted and thirsty. Sitting down on a grassy knoll, Eleanor panted, "I had not realized the extent of my inactivity of late. I have been engaged in these literary activities which are never tiring to one's disposition or mental capacities. I have not found an endeavor which is equally worthy of my time."

"The way your parents are always monopolizing your time, I'm surprised you ever have time for your reading."

"There are many undertakings which are not so easily achieved without a consecrated effort," replied Eleanor turning rather pink.

"That's because you let your parents take advantage. You should only do a certain amount, and then if they ask you to do more, simply ask if they're going to pay you." Jane noticed the influence she had over Eleanor, she always did, but it never prevented her from asserting her judgement, and at times mortifying Eleanor's somewhat delicate disposition. That is not to say Eleanor did not appreciate Jane's input, yet still it occasionally caught her off guard. Presently, Jane began to admire her nails. She had just purchased a new polish dubbed 'Playfully pink', and noticed it was already beginning to chip.

After these words, Eleanor only looked at Jane incredulously. She had never heard Jane speak in this way to her own father, nor was Jane aware that Eleanor knew things about her that no one else did, that Eleanor would never claim to have seen, even if questioned by a powerful authority. Yet Jane would not have cared that Eleanor knew these things. Things to Jane were only facts and facts depended upon the viewer and that pretty much summed up the total of what people thought, talked about, and said. That was that; there wasn't much else at least as far as Jane was concerned.

Jane looked up at Eleanor, with a searching, devious stare that made Eleanor turn away, feeling her cheeks burn in the waning sun. She was glad for the shadow of the tree above, but Jane would not lift her gaze until Eleanor would at least meet the intensity of her glare. Eleanor could not, so she simply said, "The grass is sure dry. But it looks like rain will be coming soon."

Jane laughed a cold, detached, resonating sound that made Eleanor cringe. "Why is it that you can never say to me what it is you mean? If we were actually friends, you would state the topic that weighs so heavily on your weak mind."

"My weak mind? I should have the audacity to tell you what I did see, but I have more taste than to ever even attempt to bridge the subject."

"You're weak and you hide behind your weakness with those words, all those useless words that you think makes you special. Well you are special, but your style of speech is not. You are a wimp. A beautiful, melancholy, special wimp."

"I am not a wimp. How dare you speak to me like that!" Eleanor was now fighting back tears.

"Prove it."

Eleanor stepped forward and could not think of one single utterance which would convey her exasperation at the one and only person who could exasperate her, and this drove her into a state of unconditional frenzy to defend her character. She reached forward and scratched Jane's arm as hard as she possibly could.

It started to bleed almost immediately. Shades of red, pink, deep, dark and running everywhere. Eleanor began to feel dizzy and weak, and heard a strange vibrating sound in the back of her head. She sat down on her knoll before she fell. Sweating, weak in the legs, she moaned, "I'm sorry Jane. I'm sorry... I'm sorry."

Jane laughed at her. "Was that your best attempt? I think you need more practice." Jane smeared the blood onto her hand, and licked it. "Just as I thought, it's sweet."

Eleanor stared in disbelief. "You're crazy. I'm going home now." But Eleanor couldn't get up; she couldn't even move.

"What did I tell you? You should have believed me when I told you."

"I could have scratched out your eyeball, you know."

"I would have stopped you. I am stronger than you. It just amused me to see you so angry."

"I hurt you. I've never hurt anyone before."

"No, you didn't. Don't flatter yourself."

"Now the only way I'll feel better is if you do it back."

"I don't think so. I've got to get going."

When Jane ventured to rise, Eleanor cried, "Do something! Do it!"

"I did. You stopped using all those big words. It's fair." With that response Eleanor was dumbfounded, but Jane smiled, and the truth was that Jane was not hurt. On the contrary, she enjoyed the game and after all, it was all a game to Jane. And somehow she always knew how to get the upper hand.

II

At school Eleanor, Jane, and Winchester were all in the same class together. Eleanor, since she had been an infant, had always been segregated off with the advanced group, and it took a considerable amount of manipulating to finally be placed with the regular kids. Hating the advanced group, as they were all a bunch of overblown snobs who thought they knew more than everyone else, she often enjoyed showing this group up by exceeding them on test scores. It was sheer pleasure to Eleanor to see the look of defeat surface on these miniature, thought-to-be godlike prodigies.

Effie Black deemed Eleanor to be a genius of the finest caliber. She would always ask Eleanor to join her group at lunch, and Eleanor would invariably decline, asserting the unassailability of her relationship with

Jane. The girls in this group thought of Jane as the 'mad girl', who did strange, indecent things, someone to keep your distance from, to pity. No one could understand Eleanor's devotion to this clearly mentally handicapped person. Some of them thought Eleanor was studying this girl to acquire knowledge regarding the girl's special problems. Others thought they were cousins, and Eleanor stayed with this girl out of a profound family loyalty. No one knew the truth, and Eleanor kept it this way. Even her own family was puzzled by her choice of association. But this constant quandary was a sort of relief to Eleanor, who knew that most people never really understood anything, or cared to understand; rather, they enjoyed construing their own negative, sordid details to everyone else's business except for their own: that is, with the exception of Jane. Jane floated in and out of Eleanor's consciousness, and perhaps it was this essential feature which caused Jane to be so compelling.

Eleanor's family was large; there was always much work to be done. As long as she received her usual high scoring, there was never any need to inquire further. But Eleanor enjoyed this. Engaged in either labour or studies, everyone simply left her alone.

The status quo remained until one day Eleanor sickened of the competition, school, and the whole rigmarole. She lost the quintessential desire to compete in this way. It was now necessary to conceive a plan, something subtle. She wanted to spend more time with Jane. She needed to. Jane seemed to help the calm that Eleanor had never felt, a gap, a hole, needing to constantly be filled. Until recently this fissure was temporarily abated by this ongoing competition: Eleanor's scholastic ability which could reduce all others to the subservient position that they already occupied in her own mind. But lately, the fissure had advanced; competition was no longer enough. Eleanor knew that action was required. She was not afraid to do what was needed.

Walking alone by the river, on a wet, rainy day, Eleanor removed her shoes and socks. The green stones felt slippery and mushy between her toes. She began to dance in frantic, disjointed actions. She fell once, twice, and the third time was a success. The pain was strangely exhilarating. Blood gushed from her temple. She staggered, blinked, and fell into the river. Fully conscious, but dizzy, she was still able to gauge her distance from the surface. Contented, she swam to shore and with shoes in hand, traversed the distance home. Her father was the first to see her.

Blood and water ran in little furrowed paths along her forehead and down her cheeks. She looked deranged, and fell into his arms. "Good God, Eleanor. Are you all right? Are you in pain?" her father screamed in alarm.

"Me head pains bad," Eleanor stammered.

"Help me with your sister," he yelled to a younger boy who was engrossed tending the field.

From that day forward, Eleanor frequently claimed to suffer from mysterious headaches, and would then begin to mutter incoherencies, which would excuse her from any activity she was engaged in. Inevitably, her studies were affected. One day, as Eleanor had hoped, her parents were called to the school.

The principal was adamant. "Mr. and Mrs. Wellgrene, I am sorry to have had to call you here, but Eleanor's condition is having a detrimental affect on her work as well as her classmates overall progress."

"We knew you would call us sooner or later," said Mrs. Wellgrene.

"Eleanor seems to have suffered some form of brain damage in her accident, and we strongly feel she should be referred to a neurologist."

"Yes, we would agree, but we simply do not have the money to arrange that. It's very sad what has happened to Eleanor, but she is often able to still work on the farm, and we have other children to feed and raise. Unfortunately, Eleanor would not be able to go on with her studies unless she had managed to get funding. It is very sad for her indeed." Mrs. Wellgrene shook her head slowly. "When we ask her what happened she gets this puzzled look on her face, starts to scream and cry, then finally just stares off into space. She shouldn't have been walking on those rocks in her bare feet. She knows better." At that Mrs. Wellgrene started to quietly weep. Mr. Wellgrene looked accusingly at the administrator, while comforting his wife.

"I'm sorry. I did not ask you to come here to upset your wife. I just needed to inform you that we are placing Eleanor into the regular section of our class environment. Presently, she does not belong with the advanced pupils. Hopefully, she will heal and be able to return in the future. It's such a sad, sad shame. I'm terribly sorry." With that the man blinked slowly, swallowed, and quickly left the room.

After that Eleanor was placed in the regular program, and was classified as one of the greatest tragedies in the history of the school: the child genius who fell and broke her head, and then having to endure her reduced state. It seemed appropriate to many now Eleanor's tie to Jane: the mad girl and the one with the broken head. Eleanor was satisfied. People liked closure.

In the middle of the year, dusty from working in the fields, Winchester was introduced to the class. Already a few years behind his peers, it was obvious that he felt a kind of inferiority to his classmates. Miss Benedict introduced him, "Everyone, I would like you to welcome Winchester to our class. He will be joining us for the remainder of the term."

People just sat there, staring at the oversized, sweaty figure before them. He managed a muffled hello. A few people snickered, but no one said a word. Attending a few months out of every year, eventually boredom would seep in, and returning to his father's farmstead, he was happier working anyhow.

Jane stood up. Her golden hair fell gently over her bare shoulders, and a smile emerged on her face that caused everyone to look to her with a curious admiration. "Hello, I'm Jane. If you'd like, you're welcome to sit next to me."

When Winchester grinned, it became obvious that a few of his teeth had been lost at one time or another. For a moment his self-consciousness faded, only for it to return with a vengeance. His face burning, he became conscious of a hardness emerging from below. "Thank-you," Winchester mumbled. With eyes averted, he hurried to his newly proffered seat.

"Thank-you, Jane. That will do nicely," replied Miss Benedict, trying to return the class's attention back to the exercise at hand. "Now where were we? Bruce, would you kindly pick up where we had left off."

Winchester glanced up at Jane. He had never seen a creature so beautiful. Like a piece of sunshine, she glowed. He wanted to touch her lips, to stroke her hair, to smell her skin... the desire was overwhelming. He had never noticed any girl before. He had sisters, and had had previous friendships with girls but had never noticed anything particular about them. He began to fantasize about Jane, the softness of her skin as a lamb might be to shear, as burnished in tone as a sunflower. A trickle of saliva ran down the side of his chin. Something inside exploded; he lost control of his speech, his tongue was unresponsive to his brain. Jane looked up at him and winked. Winchester bellowed, "Wow, you're beautiful." The class laughed uproariously, and Winchester jumped as though he was not conscious of the words which had just been elicited from his throat. Simultaneously Bruce stopped reading, as Miss Benedict peered up from her book, removing her antique lenses. "Winchester, I realize this is your first day, so I will not hold that outburst against you. Normally, such behavior is not tolerated, and in future, will not be."

With those words, Bruce continued his task, and the class's attention was again redirected, yet Winchester was dumbfounded. He had not spoken those words. He couldn't understand their origin. At any time in his few years of schooling, he had never spoken to anyone in class. He simply couldn't. From what depths had these words come? The confusion was obvious in the contortion of his features.

Eleanor had been observing him from her position across the room. The moment he had stepped over the threshold, she had been enraptured. There was a darkness to his hair and eyes that reminded her of a stormy, rainy day like a canvas she had once painted in all of those private morning sessions. Somehow she could never get the rain to be quite the right shade of darkness and light. The hue was slightly askew; the brilliance or depth always like the work of an amateur. Unlike the copious scenes of wheat she painted with gophers or rabbits or buildings, the shadings somehow perfection, symbiotic with a greater movement, this subject seemed eternally doomed. Eleanor hated amateurs. Here, materializing before her eyes was the hue, something emitted from his aura, his demeanor illuminated the precise combination of depth and brilliance. If only she could transfer this to a blank canvas. Regardless of her surroundings, she began to try.

"Eleanor, Eleanor, it's your turn!" Miss Benedict was on the point of exasperation. "What is the matter with this class, today?" Miss Benedict was now yelling.

Eleanor was reluctantly returned to her present surroundings. "I'm sorry, Miss Benedict. It's just that I have a head head headerache."

"Oh dear, I am sorry. I didn't realize. It looked as if you weren't paying attention."

"Could I be excused, Miss Benedict? I tink I ned some freshed airrr," she whispered.

"Of course, dear. Do you need someone to accompany you?" Miss Benedict was now genuinely concerned.

"No thanks," Eleanor replied, already leaving the room and picking up her imaginary brush. Exiting the school, she walked briskly along the grounds to her favourite tree. The annoyances of other peoples' demands nauseated and repulsed her regardless of the sincerity of Miss Benedict's consideration. Sitting beneath this weeping giant, Eleanor began to attempt the union of color and shade that had only moments before seemed so obvious - the intangible finally had materialized, readily within her grasp. But now her reproduction again manifested itself with mediocre brushstrokes and almost crude shading. Her epiphany had only come to represent the confused vagueness of each previous endeavor. The mood was gone. Yet, as Eleanor tried to recreate the moment, Winchester's image became more and more clearly etched into her consciousness.

III

As summer quickly approached and the golden yolk of life gradually broke upon the horizon a little later each evening, the sounds of crickets would emerge in their eager cacophony from the nearby swamplands. Sometimes, after Eleanor had finished her chores, she would walk over and sit by this mucky residue and slowly sketch Winchester's outline. As she drew, she would grow warmer, her finger tracing along the surface of her skin as she mentally sketched his corresponding body part. There were certain areas she would trace over and over until her own voice would rise and fall with the din around her. On some evenings, she would find her task particularly pleasing and with the emerging stars and warmth of the breeze, she would again commence her illusive canvas. Each time she attempted to free her mind and allow herself to begin the blending, Jane's naked image would obliterate the canvas's inner harmony. After a time, she would stop and decide to enjoy the beauty of her surroundings, allowing her thoughts to be manipulated by more mundane patterns.

As yet, she could never bring herself to actually speak to Winchester. However, she watched Jane laugh and talk to him everyday. Winchester always smiled when he was around Jane. A lot of the boys seemed to when Jane was in their presence. Sometimes, Jane would purposely rub past Winchester, and once Eleanor had seen Jane rubbing Winchester behind her favourite tree, only this time Jane's hand was down Winchester's unbuttoned trousers. Eleanor had felt strangely excited, but she could feel a bitterness welling in the back of her throat. Watching in silence, she would have given anything to have been Jane at that moment. The way he looked at her! Jane's look however was dark and focused. Jane almost seemed angry, but as Winchester groaned, Jane smiled. It was not an inviting smile. But Winchester didn't care. He had the stupidest look on his face that Eleanor had ever seen. That day, on the way home, the tension between Eleanor and Jane exploded.

They had been walking in complete silence and suddenly Eleanor burst out, "Why do all the boys like you anyway?"

Jane laughed. "That's what's picking you. I wondered. Did you see us?"

"See who?" Eleanor couldn't believe that Jane would ask her straight out like that.

"Come on. You could have joined us if you'd wanted. He wouldn't mind if I asked him."

"Why would I want to do that? He's practically in love with you anyway." With that word, Eleanor fell back into their shared reticence.

They walked along for a while like that. The birds were twittering gently in a kind of soothing lullaby. Eleanor realized how tired she actually felt. Today, she honestly was suffering from a headache, and seemed to have an ache in her chest to match. Jane looked at her searchingly, and then smiled. Her sinister expression had vanished. The birds continued in their reverie. Jane's hand fell gently upon Eleanor's forehead. As they treaded the dusty road, Jane stroked Eleanor's temples until Eleanor felt the dull throbbing in her brain very slowly ceasing.

Jane was the first to interrupt the stillness. "Love? I wouldn't call it that."

Eleanor had almost forgotten the subject at hand. Thoughts again flooded the confines of her mind, but this time, the pounding had somehow disappeared. "Well then, what do you call it? How many boys do you do that to?"

"I've never counted. A lot. Not all boys either," Jane's eyes twinkled mischievously.

Eleanor stopped. She bellowed, "Are you so stupid that you actually don't get it?! Maybe, they are right about you! Maybe you are retarded!"

Jane sneered. Scowling at Eleanor's fierce countenance, Jane retorted, "You know Eleanor, why do you always make everything so complicated? You're so romantic. You live in your own world. That's what I like about you. Tomorrow, we're going down to the river. Come." With that last word Jane's expression changed and she began to walk away from Eleanor into the green fields just beyond.

Eleanor was dumbfounded. Why was it that she could never get one up on Jane? She didn't think about this too long. She was satisfied that Jane had invited her, and was already thinking of the shape of the water droplets running down Winchester's broad torso.

IV

In the dawn the smell of the fields and the warmth of the soil teased Eleanor's nostrils. Folds of pink like ripe watermelon tinged the blue slate of sky. A few birds, strokes of contrast in the distance, flew like black seeds blown from a huge, caverned orifice. A time of in-between, a time for thought and reflection with no quandaries from the voices constantly accosting her below. Her time to paint on the canvas she kept hidden apart from the world outside, a canvas of thought to mix and blend and blot off the excess, whatever she felt the need to create.

The rising sun, now emerging from the horizon's edge, caused Eleanor to painfully squint as it began its gradual ascent. Sounds of the awakening household drew her from her silent reverie back to the reality of duty and chore. However, the notion of possibility continued to permeate her consciousness as she began her chores in eager earnest, the sole purpose being their earliest feasible completion.

Jane remained true to her word. They met on the old road and went down together to the stream by the river, to bathe and revel in the soothing coolness. Sometimes a fish would pass, shimmering silver in its progress, down, down where sound was suspended and Eleanor would descend into this realm, its fishy eyes staring at her mermaid-like little face. In this quiet she would remain until the fish had left with only the sounds of its whish, whish, whishing falling into a dull, opening roar in the distance. After this Eleanor surfaced in an explosion of water, a whale from the deep.

"How can you stay down for that long? That's longer than any girl I know." Winchester spit these words at Eleanor like a sweating snake.

She watched his mouth form them. The way his lips moved over and around the words creating them with his pointed, long tongue as they caressed his soft, moist lips in their departure. Eleanor wondered what it would feel like to touch those lips.

"Well? Cat got your tongue?"

Eleanor's eyes responded, and filled with sharp, hot tears. It was obvious her presence was not wanted. She rose from the water, her mermaid tail disappearing into the hidden depths of the strong stream. "I'm leaving, Jane. See you tomorrow."

Jane looked up from the bank, her dark face suddenly alert. "Where are you going? What's the matter?" Jane was confused and it showed in the contours of her features. Eleanor was leaving. She would not say another word. As she left the tears began to fall slowly, silently, then more strongly. Eleanor did not cry often.

Jane's colour changed to a darker shade suffused with crimson. "Come here." Her command was heard by Winchester who obeyed at once. "What did you say to my friend?" Jane's voice was deeper, not to be ignored. Even the stream slowed its progression to heed her waxing anger.

"Why do you always bring her, anyway? She's stupid and has nothing to say."

"She's my friend, and you hurt her feelings," Jane's voice was almost a whisper of perfectly formed rage, a bubble of intoxication, that transfixed her observer. "What is it you want?" Jane smiled.

"Do you have to bring her every time I ask you to swim?" Winchester retorted.

"I asked you a question. Do not answer me with another question." Jane's power was increasing; like blue blood it coursed through her delicately formed limbs.

Winchester was aware of a warm tingling steadily growing. "It's just that sometimes it would be rather nice, if I could see you, just you," Winchester's voice was becoming a whine. He knew he had offended, but not how to seek forgiveness.

She approached him more closely now, barely touching his quivering frame. "What is it you want?" Jane's voice was barely an audible moan, her eyes seemed an infinite pool of softness and light.

"A kiss... a kiss..." Winchester stammered. Again, as on the first day of class, the truth had been elicited without any knowing on his own part. Effortlessly the syllables escaped his constricted throat.

Words had ceased, only the wind could be felt as Jane pressed heavily into the contours of Winchester's body. She could feel his whole being quaking under her, and the sensation filled her with a wild, ravenous desire. Pressing her lips slowly to his, she began to eat them like the field strawberries of summer. One after another the desire to eat became reckless and crazed. Winchester, consumed by the softness of Jane's lips, sucked back harder and harder as his damp body began to writhe uncontrollably. Out came his long, pointed instrument, and Jane met it with hers. Tangling and untangling, Jane became aware of the growing stiffness in Winchester's tightening suit.

Jane, wielding her weapon skillfully, felt the hard surge in his trunks. Simultaneously, she bit as hard as she could. His blood trickled down her throat and it tasted bitter, but the bitterness was as sweet as all of those strawberries rolled into one huge fruit. She held more deftly now, blinded by the sweetness of the experience. Winchester had begun to moan in muffled screams, indignantly pushing her away, eyes of mad terror. Jane sucked and sucked and Winchester began to beat her with his fists, but Jane's ecstasy was too great. She had become Medusa, queen of the snake people, and he her humble servant, and it was his duty to serve her needs. Presently, she let go, blood running everywhere: covering him, her, and filling the stream. He screamed insensible accusations at her like a mad, hissing water snake. The silvery fish laughed from its distant lair, and the wind echoed the sound.

Jane grinned, and began to disrobe watching his growing disbelief. The blood was beginning to pool at his naked toes. Jane, fully unveiled, dove down into the deepest reaches of the moving stream. Winchester looked at his feet, and realizing how much blood he had actually lost, ran, howling incoherencies, and leaving a trail of dripping defeat all the way home to his incredulous parents. No matter how much they coerced, threatened, or pleaded, Winchester would not confess the name of his victimizer, and he never did. Although the wound eventually healed, he spoke with a lisp he reviled the remainder of his days.

V

The morning had passed with its usual bustle as Eleanor had completed the remainder of her chores before joining Jane in their habitual hiding spot. The wheat was high, waving in its majesty in the fields, and as school had come to its annual end, this left them with time to spend together. Winchester often asked Jane if she wanted to go swimming or just take a walk, but since the incident at the river, Winchester seemed of little interest to Jane. Eleanor, however, wondered why he no longer participated in their afternoon rendezvous.

"I thought you were going to ask Winchester to join us today. What happened?" Eleanor's brow furrowed in concern.

"Yeah, well... I don't know. He sounds so stupid now when he talks," Jane plainly stated as the sun bore down on her tanned legs.

"Of course he does. You nearly bit off his tongue. You are a very lucky young lady that he never told on you," Eleanor preached.

"Firstly, if you're speaking to me, I am not a lady. And secondly, I would say that your appreciation is severely wanting." At that, Jane snickered.

"I didn't ask you to bite off his tongue! The thing that I cannot understand for the life of me is, after everything, he still wants you... that is, to see you," Eleanor stammered.

"Well, he should have thought about that before he insulted you. He's a creep, and I would have bit off something else if I could've. Lucky, he only wanted a dumb kiss."

"It must have been some kiss." Eleanor had started to laugh. She couldn't stop herself.

Jane felt the breeze blow up her skirt. She liked the feeling of wind.

She liked the way it tussled Eleanor's hair. Eleanor had the softest hair like the moles that burrowed deep into the earth.

Eleanor sighed, "Are you ever going to invite Winchester again?"

Jane could hear the exasperation in Eleanor's voice. "No," Jane replied. "Is it that important to you?" Jane looked up at Eleanor, and by some subtle alteration in her shading Jane knew her answer.

Jane's eyes darkened from their sherry brown to a kind of blackish brown like the chestnut mane of a horse in flight. Eleanor had immediately begun to blend the hue: a hint more black, a tad more brown, no, no, no.... it's not quite right. She could never adequately appropriate this exact shade. Suddenly, the canvas was obliterated by Jane's approaching dark red lips. As they embraced hers, Eleanor could feel a strange electrical current pass between them. For a moment she allowed herself to suck in this briny taste. Then she felt herself stiffen, and turned away.

"I didn't want you to feel left out. That kiss was considerably better than his, and I didn't try to bite off your tongue." Jane smiled as she said this, but Eleanor was still dazed. "What's wrong? Didn't you like it?" Jane's mouth was now beginning to turn down at the corners.

"I just didn't expect it, that's all. I didn't say that I liked it or did not like it," Eleanor replied as she rose to her feet, dusting herself off.

"Let's go swimming at the hole. I'm dying today." With these words, Jane bolted away, as her averted eyes filled with stinging, molten tears.

At the hole, the water would feel cool and serene. Eleanor needed it to soothe the burning of her hands from the laundry she had been doing earlier. It had been some time since Eleanor had soaked. Since they hadn't planned it, they weren't wearing any suits. Jane had raced, stripped and dove in. Jane was never inhibited and floated on her back pretending to swallow the clouds passing overhead. Eleanor watched her. She loved the way Jane's hair and skin were variations of the same shade, her eyes and lips arresting contrasts.

Jane's penetrating gaze caught Eleanor off guard. "Why is it you like to gawk at my naked body so much, but you never want to touch it, and when I kiss you, you pull away?" Jane's stare intensified.

Eleanor became embarrassed and realizing that she was now fully naked, except for her left sock, looked down. "I'm sorry," she muttered.

"Why? You're beautiful. You have nothing to be ashamed of." Jane pronounced these words as a breeze blew up in apparent acquiescence.

"No, I'm not. Why are you lying? You're the stunning creature that all the boys desire. They've never even noticed me. No one has. The only thing I had was a past scholastic reputation that didn't mean anything."

"I don't want boys."

With those words Eleanor could feel Jane pulling her into that sphere of darkness and light. A sphere in which Eleanor could be exactly what she was, nothing more, nothing less. Eleanor reached Jane as Jane gulped in a huge breath of air, and entered the obscurity below. Eleanor felt herself, as an automaton would, follow the lead.

Once below, Eleanor could see her streamers of golden hair trailing to the fractured, lit surface just above. The tanned visage neared as Eleanor noticed a kind of glow all around them. From within the outer gloom, Winchester's naked form seemed to materialize. As he swam toward her, his figure and loins so familiar just as if she were playing her tracing game, she could feel an energy surge through her system.

Pressing up to Eleanor, the kisses fell like heavy water balloons all over her heaving torso. Again and again, hands and their accompanying tongue caressed the outline of her submerged flesh. All at once, she felt an object advancing between her legs. She began to move with this new sensation until a deep, resonating sound contained within an immense air bubble ascended to the surface, and noiselessly exploded.

The need for air had become so great Eleanor erupted a little blue and unable to breathe. Almost simultaneously Jane surfaced, immediately exhaling and rapidly drawing in deep breaths, while coughing slightly. Unexpectedly, Eleanor's state became visible to her. Swimming over in a few, hard strokes, Jane reached for her. Eleanor was struggling and choking heavily now. Helping her to the shallow end where the float was situated, she lifted Eleanor up, where she began to vomit water and bits of lunch. Jane held her tenderly, yet firmly, and when she had finished, told her to lie down.

Eleanor was somewhat incoherent, and definitely lightheaded. She slumped down on the wood acquiring a few splinters due to her feebleness. Jane began to gently wipe away the debris on Eleanor's face. She was cold and Jane's warmth felt reassuring beside her. Jane began to kiss her face, her forehead, her breasts. She was aware of Jane's repeated, sensual touch and the feeling was so intensely calming, Eleanor began to relax and finally fell into a deep sleep. Winchester never surfaced.

VI

The coolness of the night air refreshed Eleanor and her shaking slowly began to diminish. It had been the usual argument tonight, always about money, how her family was going to afford shoes for the coming school year. Eleanor had always hated the realities of life, the mundane, insane patterns of banter, and its inevitable recurrence. Eleanor could have cared less if she'd had shoes for the coming year; she would have gladly gone barefoot than listen to the constant bickering. The funny thing was that Jane often came to school without the comfort of shoes. Her father had the money to buy shoes, but she also knew about Eleanor's poverty, and how much it bothered her to have to endure the rigmarole.

On the first day Jane had come to school barefoot, Eleanor couldn't believe it. But in that strange way that only Jane could produce, Eleanor felt oddly, yet completely, comforted. This was only one reason in a long list why people thought Jane was deranged, especially since it was, at that time, the middle of winter. Jane's feet had turned blue from the walk to school in the snow. But at school, she had wrapped them in a blanket, then had somehow convinced one of the older boys to carry her home. Or rather, she had given him the privilege of carrying her. Eleanor, to her amazement, had often heard him offer. Jane had always thanked him, nevertheless repeatedly declining. That day though, she'd accepted graciously.

Eleanor smiled to herself thinking of this now. Jane had done a lot for Eleanor. And Eleanor was always conscious of Jane's sustained effort to make her feel like an insider. The ensuing darkness was beginning to engulf her, and she now felt more relaxed. The fields seemed to beckon her, and like wading through the cool density of an ocean, the murmurings of the wheat evinced their own patternings. Closing her eyes, she could feel the undulation of Jane's movements all around her. This was not unusual for Eleanor because the wheat often caused her to feel this holistic aspect of Jane, but tonight the sensation was so intense, as though the wheat seemed to swell and ebb with a frantic oscillation. The perception unnerved Eleanor. Yet, the silence of this space reestablished her reality, and suspended the heaviness of such an impression. Listening to the surging eventide gusts, again she had begun to relax. Barely discernible was the sound of an owl somewhere in the remoteness as if it might fall off the edge of the earth. Without warning, from the previously agitated corner of her mind, the perplexing consciousness again accosted her.

Distraught, Eleanor's eyes popped wide open, and surveyed her surroundings with one swift glance. Reoriented, she sighed, the second heavy sigh that the evening had produced, but she couldn't shake the unease. The soft, whishing of the breezes through the sheaves lulled her for a moment, and she again closed her eyes. The day had been filled with heavy chores. She had been too tired to engage in the canvas she had been gingerly working on for the last week. The warmth of the air was pulling Eleanor into a region of thoughtlessness where she often unconsciously tread, pallet in hand.

This would not have been the first time Eleanor had fallen into an exhausted stupor in the fields, but no one ever really noticed, as long as she returned in time to feed the hens. Suddenly, Jane's father's face was above her, lying on top of her. Moving in and out of her, he was moaning, "Yes, yes, that's my girl." She moved rhythmically beneath him, pulling him closer. The sensation was uncontrollably pleasurable and she didn't want it to stop. She awoke and cried out from the vividness of the image. Sitting up, she furtively looked around her, but no one was there. Eleanor felt her body to see if she was still dressed. Everything was as before. Fervently searching the adjacent soil, she found nothing but her own small treads. It must have been a dream. Eleanor did not know what or how to think. She had no idea of what time of night it was or how long she had been asleep in the fields. She simply knew that she must see Jane.

Running through the fields, she was panting and crying. They had often used this as a shortcut to get to Jane's house. Eleanor knew she would reach Jane in minutes. Her mind racing, she wondered if Jane might be sleeping in the barn as she often did. Eleanor could never figure out why she did this when she had a bedroom of her own that Eleanor could only dream of. She felt cold drops of sweat cascading down her spine, and simultaneously as she ran, was attempting to devise a plan to get past the inevitable run-in she would have with Jane's father, if she happened to be sleeping in the house tonight.

Still crying, and panting harder, Eleanor could see the barn in view. There was a light flickering in the window. She was close enough now to actually make out movement from inside. Suddenly a wall seemed to emerge in front of her like an invisible barrier. Eleanor collapsed before it by the edge of the field. Winded, she could just barely catch a glimpse of movement within the grey boarded structure. Eleanor's eyes widened as she became aware of Jane's presence inside as well as someone else's.

The need for her own silence and stillness became fully apparent to Eleanor, as she became cognizant of soft moans and a steady groaning, growing slightly in volume. The night was alive with the sounds of howling wolves, humming mosquitoes, and bats locating their distant prey. A damp earthy scent rose from hidden depths, and Eleanor wanted nothing but to go to Jane. Only she couldn't move. A candle wavered in the barn's grimy window, its flicker steadily projecting two images onto the farther wall.

The images moved in various positions like a display of liquid jigsaw pieces. Around and around each other, the pieces seemed to engage in a kind of dance, then endeavor to eat the other. This excited Eleanor and it reminded her of the episode behind her favourite tree. However, this seemed to occur in a set pattern, then the pattern would repeat itself, forming a set of extraordinary, silhouetted successions. Eleanor began to writhe and fall with the movements of the pieces until the candle abruptly went out, and Eleanor again collapsed into the wet field, gasping. Always though, it was the piece with the long tendrils of tentacle-like strings which pulled the other back to her, initiating the frantic, oddly-sequenced interaction.

VII

Winchester, Jane, and Eleanor lounged motionless in the still field. Jane and Eleanor lay in prone position beside one another, while Winchester was lying on his stomach at their feet. Perspiration moist from the enduring heat of the past two weeks, these eager onlookers subconsciously awaited the sky's imminent purging. Jane's eyes narrowed as the darkening clouds began to gather and approach from the horizon. The image of an advancing buffalo stampede appeared, as Jane became hypnotized by the power of this psychic manifestation. Equally entranced, Eleanor lay transfixed by the unfathomable capacity of nature's blending, strokes upon strokes of color, texture, and shade, although if attempted by human hands the culminating effect could only be crude and gaudy. These were Eleanor's moments of greatest inspiration and deepest despair.

Winchester's mind was racing. He had finally gained the pleasure of Jane's company. Why had she accepted today? He had to remember exactly what he had done, precisely what he had said, and how he had said it. He recalled the condescension on Jane's face, but even though she hadn't exactly said yes, she hadn't refused and after all, wasn't that a sort of victory? I mean he was here, and if he had managed to do it once, chances were the opportunity would again present itself.

Jane and Eleanor had been walking along the road chasing each other laughing, when suddenly they had spotted Winchester. It was customary for them to pass this way, so he often made it a habit to tarry here in the early afternoon. From his father's fields, he could see them walk by the outer gate. Two figures skipping and jumping in the distance, he always made out Jane's strong frame and wild, cascading hair. Sometimes he would drop whatever he was doing and wave frantically trying to draw attention to himself. Jane would always look in his direction but invariably a scowl would slowly overtake the muscles of her face, then she would stick out her tongue and yell, "We get to play and you have to work!" Winchester would only grin with an inner kind of longing as he observed Jane's bratty tactics. Eleanor, on the other hand, would always stop and stare, slowly raising her hand in greeting with that smile that somehow reminded Winchester of a wounded animal, but he never knew why and didn't bother to give it much thought.

Today, Winchester didn't have to help. He had injured a muscle in his arm. So just before their usual arrival time, he sauntered down to the gate, and began to wait. Kicking up dirt for a few minutes to distract himself, he soon began to feel a coolness steadily emerging in the previously stagnant air. He could see by the sky that a rainstorm was brewing and wondered if they would still show. Without fail, like a mirage in the distance, two figures began to approach.

Squinting, Jane recognized his repulsive form at once. Yelling she said, "Farling, what are you doing here? Shouldn't you be helping your daddy?"

The sound of her voice sent a shiver of expectation and yearning along his backbone and caused a mysterious twitching in his tongue. However, he managed to stammer, "Nah, my arm needs some rest, so Dad gave me the day off. Would it be all right if I joined ya two loverly ladies?" With those words he looked down not sure of the response.

Jane began to answer, but Eleanor, at the thought of being what Winchester meant as a 'lovely lady', burst out ahead of Jane, retorting, "Why of course, we'd love your companionship." But the look on Jane's face had become so searing, portraying such an air of revulsion, initially directed toward Winchester, then due to the affirmation and genuineness in Eleanor's response, toward Eleanor.

Eleanor, horrified by Winchester's facial reaction, realized the source at once, and in that characteristically didactic manner, scolded Jane. "Don't you think that the pleasure of Winchester's company would be much appreciated, Jane?"

"Whatever you say, dearest," Jane slyly rejoined.

At that, Winchester reddened further. He had hardly noticed Eleanor or her words, but nevertheless, with head bowed, took up the stern of their procession.

Feeling invisible, Eleanor scowled back at Jane to which Jane promptly exclaimed, "What? You wanted him, not me." At those words Winchester fell further behind, but like a dog that had been kicked, continued to follow regardless.

Presently, Winchester glanced up at the two figures beside him. He could not help but notice the strange, glazed over look in Eleanor's eyes and the way her lips moved as though she was carrying on an inner conversation. A trail of drool suddenly ran down the corner of Eleanor's mouth, which caused her to become aware of Winchester's eyes and abruptly, she wiped it away. Winchester, revolted, promptly averted his gaze. As he turned his head away, all at once he became mindful of Jane's peculiar state. Her skin had acquired an underlying pallor, and the muscles of her arms and legs appeared limp and lifeless. It startled him for a moment, but then he noticed a slight movement of her lids which seemed to connotate thought. What was she thinking? Did it involve him? Was she glad for his presence or did she only wish that when those perfectly formed slits opened he would have disappeared? With that last thought his heart sank.

A clap of thunder in the distance unnerved Eleanor and Winchester as they both sat up and thought about finding cover. Their eyes met and Eleanor felt her stomach drop, and smiled. Winchester only stared, then looked down at Jane hopeful for some sign of life.

But Jane only continued motionless listening to the approach, eager for the pellets of liquid to hit and bounce off her bronzed skin. Floating in a sea of drowning wheat, hair knotting in sheaves as they ripped and tore at skin that had just begun to leather from a merciless sun, Jane reclined in her catalepsy. Eyes effortlessly chiseled by golden sculptors until sightless the smell of her own blood and the feel of the cutting would be all that connected her to this physical space... here.

The rain began. Like tiny beads of glass, Winchester and Eleanor both winced at the intensity of the sensation. In mounting horror, they looked at Jane waiting for a response from this seeming cadaver, but transfixed they could only stand helplessly above. The storm was approaching its zenith as it swayed in strange formation overhead.

Jane could feel the vibration beneath the heels of her upturned feet. She could smell the rising earth and taste the moisture at the edge of her parched lips. She could hear the distant thunder of their hooves and from within this fury a voice rose and fell. A chant, an ancient song to herald the coming of the buffalo. She couldn't hear the words, but the intonations continued unabated. Leading the pack, snorting, at full tilt, brown fir hanging in tufts of dirt and hair, Jane awaited her opportunity. As its head nodded in assent, she began to run beside it, and found, just as she knew, it slowed its progress to heed her advance. Just then, she leapt with as much force as she could muster, and away. Feeling the wind against her skin, the soft silky hair of the beast lying in folds along her inner thighs, she could discern the flying spit of the lesser creatures splattering against the tissue of her exposed back and neck. Her body began to bounce with the gyration of this great force, as the sound of the wind and the chanting became one.

No matter what they did, nothing would rouse Jane from her stupor. Eleanor had begun to shake and as she shook, she had simultaneously begun to yell. "We have to get out of here! The storm is directly overhead! We're in a field! Do you want to die?! What's the matter with you?!" Eleanor had repeated these same words over and over until her throat ached from the sheer exertion. With this last effort, Eleanor began to sob. She looked at Winchester for help, but his mouth only gaped open in disbelief and fright. Dread caused him to assume a statuesque air, and between cadavers and statues, Eleanor felt as if she were in a sort of immense, all-encompassing museum.

All at once, Jane bounded up. Her eyes blazed with dark liquid fire as she focused directly on Winchester's frame. Her approach was deft and stealthy. A bolt of lightning danced above, as Jane jumped toppling him to the ground. Her sundress, soaked from exposure clung to her child-like cleavage and underparts. Hair, now plastered to her face, outlined the perfection of her sculpted, clay-like form. Up and down, she rode her buffalo as the rain's belting fury only drove her on. The prolonged rubbing action of Jane's supple near nakedness combined with the wearing thinness of Winchester's trousers drove him into a state of unconditional frenzy. His fright, as he watched Jane's movements which seemed to correlate to the rhythm of the dancing light above her, only added to his near ecstasy. He began to moan, softly at first, then more loudly, verging upon gratification.

Jane could see the cliff in the distance. She hung on with greater tenacity for a brief moment, as if for only a fraction the possibilities seemed unbound. Blinded and bloody, she leant down and softly kissed the beast, that had, for a fleeting interval allowed itself to be possessed. The ledge approached rapidly as the ground turned to scree. She knew then that the ride was almost over, the game nearly up.

She propelled herself off, as the roar, chant, and wind ceased concurrently. Deftly and purposefully she kicked in her dismount, and as she rolled in the fragments, she could hear the already distant cries of her buffalo, as he tumbled down, down to his unburied rest.

Jane bounded off through the fields. Eleanor could see the foam coming from Jane's mouth, as if she had suffered a kind of seizure. Eleanor could only stare at Winchester with shaking hands covering quivering lips. His cries seemed to come in primal barks.

Finally, Eleanor spoke. "Can I help you?" But Winchester didn't answer. His eyes were fixed and filled with hot liquid, which now began to overspill. He kind of hobbled to his feet, and reached out his arm, which Eleanor, of course, took at once. Through driving rain, lightning, and wind, they stumbled and, a few times, fell, but in each instance, Eleanor would aid Winchester to his feet, and with face red, and grunting hard, they would continue the long walk to the Farling's farmstead.

When they arrived, Eleanor was quite tired and sore, and in the process, as both of them had become more than a little muddy, Winchester's parents looked accusingly at Eleanor, yelling, "What happened, here? Did you do this to him?"

Eleanor had not even considered this response, and was at a loss for words. Winchester was attempting to mumble something, but no one could quite make it out.

Finally, after a few awkward moments, Eleanor ventured, "No, I just helped him home, sir." Then Eleanor began to sincerely cry.

Winchester breathed something at Eleanor, which sounded to her like a muffled 'thank-you' to which Eleanor only nodded her head in quiet acceptance.

His parents still looked at her with accusation in their eyes, but not knowing what else to do, and with the awareness of the last incident ingrained in their memory, started to help Winchester inside, and once in, vehemently slammed the screen door.

Eleanor could only blink back tears. But a thought had been generated and began to grow. Would Winchester now start to see her in a new light - one of softness and caring, instead of the bitter jealousy he exhibited towards her relationship with Jane? Would he appreciate her act of kindness with no regard for her own well-being? Was this too much to ask or could it be? Eleanor grinned to herself just as another bolt flashed above, then dashed madly home, jumping in puddles all the way.

VIII

The previous night's storm had only temporarily quelled the dizzying heat. Today, it had again returned. As Eleanor tromped across the fields, intent upon her target, she expected Jane's usual apathetic response which almost always resulted from their occasional confrontations. Eleanor's teeth were clenched and her jaw was set in that same predictable way that her mother employed when going to the general store to buy something on credit. Her mother only used this tactic when it was needed and thus reserved this expression for such dire circumstances.

The wheat parted easily and loudly due to the force of Eleanor's stride. This was their habitual spot of retreat and Jane was nowhere in sight. Eleanor fumed. Where was that strange, selfish, deranged girl? She whisked around thinking she had heard someone approach, and expecting Jane, bellowed out, "Where are you, you selfish, egotistical, wanton girl?! How could you? That was so deviously unfair! I just came to tell you that I no longer wish to associate with you. That is all." But after this pronouncement, there was no reply. Yet still, she could discern a faint sound coming from the far pasture. Focusing on what seemed like someone lying down in the tall, shimmering grasses, Eleanor's eyes narrowed and she again began to stomp towards this irregular landform.

Jane could feel Eleanor's arrival at hand. The undulations had been continually increasing and all at once they desisted. The agitation of Eleanor's voice had also ceased, which pleased Jane immensely.

The scene before Eleanor shocked her. In wonder and awe, she felt the weight under her legs give, and found herself sitting cross-legged a few feet from Jane, staring in reticence. The smell of warm honey rose, inviting the furry creatures to partake in the delicacy at hand. Clumps of white violet clover, heavy with untouched pollen, filled the expanse of field, yet the nectar of Jane's offering compelled the airborne magistrates to temporarily dismiss the mundane nature of their customary dealings. In droves, they seemed to hover above Jane, seemingly not in random chaos as one would dive and delicately sip, its black and yellow robe now covered, then leave this divine cleft, gyrating still from the force of its waggle-dance. Another would follow in grand succession as this odd feeding continued unabated.

Eleanor's veneration only heightened as Apollo slowly began his decline from the earth's outer orb. Jane writhed slightly in apparent acquiescence to the needs and desires of the finally receding swarm. Now the jar of honey, exhausted from applications, gaped open empty at the onset of dusk.

Eleanor's anger had left her, and she rose from her reverie fatigued and overwhelmed, as she made her way homeward in the lengthening shadows with a number of Jane's buzzing companions in tow.

IX

Eleanor sat solemnly in the center of the field. A rising wind temporarily caused her to shiver as she pulled her knees to her chest and yanked her dress as far down as she could muster. She had not seen any trace of Jane for seven consecutive days and each day was beginning to fade into the next in a somnolent succession which left Eleanor dazed and slightly nauseated.

Eleanor scanned the horizon and as she did a figure seemed to materialize from the debris of the fallen golden sculptors, rising up slowly, bouncing along, twirling and approaching, then for a moment, like a phantasm offered by demons, disappeared into the vortex of wind and scourged soil.

Eleanor strained, but as on previous days, nothing seemed to reappear. Eleanor closed her eyes and tried to commence the canvas which had been occupying her all week, only again to have it fade into a grey, nondescript obscurity. Strokes brushed against her consciousness but once applied, lost their luster and vitality. The effort itself was ill-fated not unlike another earlier venture. Eleanor considered abandoning this particular work; she was exhausted. Usually her canvas served as her salvation from the boredom and dullness of reality as she knew it, but this canvas lacked an essence, a being, an independent existence which was the difference between the creation of art and color splattered chaotically across a white expanse invariably condemned to exist within its respective solitary state on the visible spectrum. Eleanor's eyes filled with tears from concentration, tiredness, and frustration.

Upon opening them, a blur of refracted light and pigment blended, in an instant precise strokes of discrete tincture imbibed a unified impression with the detail which Eleanor could only achieve by a consecrated effort over a period of weeks or even months. When her eyes eventually focused, standing before her was Jane, smiling wholeheartedly.

Eleanor started. "Where have you been?"

Jane flopped down. "Here and there. Thought you didn't wish to associate with me anymore, anyway." Jane popped a raspberry into her mouth which was heavily stained from her afternoon endeavors.

"Oh, that. I was just upset. You really hurt him you know. He could have sustained some real damage."

"Yeah, maybe. I assume you probably helped him home."

"Well, a lot of good that did. I thought he would have liked me at least a little more after that episode but I don't think he has any desire to ever associate with me. I've seen him working on the farm, and walking on the road, but he just looks up, and when he sees me, he doesn't even smile or wave back."

"What did I tell you? See if you ever listen to me anyway."

"So where have you been all week?"

"I've been down at the river. Trying to get the last few swims in before school starts."

"Oh, I thought it would have been too cold."

"Come on, I'm the one who goes to school barefoot in the snow, remember? You should come down tomorrow. Last swims of the season."

"Maybe. I wanted to finish a book I'm reading."

"You know what they say. Too much studying makes somebody a dull girl."

"You know what they say about not enough, or shall I remind you?"

"Have it your way. I guess I'll see you when school starts then. Bye."

Eleanor sat up. "You're leaving already? You just got here."

"There's berries to be eaten. Soon they'll be rotten."

With that last phrase, Jane rose, and with crimson-stained tongue, teeth and chin, promptly gave Eleanor a belated 'raspberry', and ran off laughing to the multitude of berries awaiting at the white expanse of river.

X

The day had commenced in a glorious effusion of light only to be hooded by the onset of a malicious cloud cover. Eleanor had managed to escape the monotony of continued chores, as she completed them in dreary succession. As long as she was present, the requests continued and she had finally eluded their persistent petitions by employing the now overused tactic of muttering incoherencies with a quiet, yet shrill tone. This usually would cause her father to hesitate and eventually stop whatever he happened to be engaged in, and sent her mother off in a fit of tears. She only used this tactic when, after exhausting all other means she could contrive, the inclination struck her.

Eleanor would be in the middle of washing, cleaning, scrubbing, feeding, or baking, and the demand would invariably come: always another appeal from her mother, father, or one of her copious siblings. Eleanor predictably assented but after hours of requests and due subjugation, a feeling would strike, like a spark, and her consciousness and reality would be overcome, as if a smooth glaze had been applied, colorless, almost without hue or pigment, the texture negligibly altered, the difference nondescript, but the wash would cause her to pause, and reassess her surroundings. From a closed region within the ember would ignite, and a rage would begin. Subtly, without definition it would build, and Eleanor would twitch unconscious of this manifestation. When she did become conscious, in this interval, all became as if washed in a delicate rose, the purest form of this hue, unadulterated, complete.

Birds twittered from the roadside. Scents of near grasses made Eleanor's nose quiver in eager anticipation. As this would be the end of their summertime adventures, she had decided to take up Jane's offer of swimming and join her. A warbler started Eleanor for an instant, its song seemed strained and erratic instead of the customary sweetness of its lofty tones.

Yen

Eleanor yielded to look up at the source of this unusual, uneven melody, and as she did the little sonorous creature plummeted to the hard earth and landed at her feet. She bent down and gently prodded its delicate breast only to elicit the absence of any response. It stared straight out as if at a radiance at once gentle and incomprehensible, entire unto and of itself.

Eleanor leaned over and carefully scooped the carcass into her out-stretched hands. Its tiny body had already begun to cool. By the road-side she sat, rocking back and forth with brushstrokes falling deftly on her consciousness.

In a kind of chasm she painted a feathered tunnel. Layers upon layers of plumage, soft and warm against the harsh coldness of the tru-est black, a circular abyss of texture and depth, lacking any emphasis of light. As she stroked, the clouds began to steadily build. In a few minutes, the rain would begin.

Eleanor began to feel the growing coolness of the late summer air, and remained still for another moment. Looking to the sky, she noticed the white heaviness. She jumped up, realizing all at once that, in these conditions, Jane would not be at the river for long.

Glancing down at the dead bird she was still holding, she became aware of the stained aspect of her palms and fingers. However, there was no time to ponder.

She rose and lovingly placed the tiny vessel into her once sunlit-yellow bathing suit, and ran, as fast as her spindly legs would carry her, down to meet Jane.

XI

She could now see the winding stream, although it was veiled often by vegetation covering its occasionally sparse banks. Raindrops bounced off the hard earth. Through her thin, threadbare suit she could feel the moisture absorbing into its tiny frame. She only cradled it closer.

She had almost begun to yell, 'Jane, Jane, are you still here?', when the crack of a twig and the motion of leaves, caught her eye.

Ducking down, she managed to extinguish a rising giggle. Jane was probably hiding in the foliage. Two could play this game. Eleanor crept along, in amongst the riverside grassland. She always enjoyed the wispy softness against her parched summer skin.

A tree towered a few feet in front of her, and the leaves continued to stir in their seeming rhythmic motion although the wind had died. Two sets of feet greeted her gaze, and at once the smile departed her withering lips.

Jane tugged at Winchester's pants, and once they were successfully removed lapped her tongue up and down. Eleanor could just see the tips of her wispy strands from her present trajectory. Suddenly, Jane forced Winchester to the ground just as he began to pant. In full view, Winchester was sprawled before her. As he gyrated his hips, with eyelids closed, but quivering, he yelped in sheer ecstasy. Eleanor was so close she could smell the sourness of his greasy hair.

All at once, Jane looked up, deeply into her startled eyes. Jane ran her tongue along the tip as it seemed to throb, undulating. Eleanor's eyes became sheer horror, as she gagged back tears of revulsion and jealousy.

Suddenly, Winchester burst out, "Why today? Why did ya decide to today? Harder, harder, it feels so gooo... gooood." Jane said nothing, only continuing to stare at Eleanor, running her tongue in long slow circles. Suddenly, her eyes closed, as she seemed to dive in, sucking feverishly. As Jane sucked, Winchester's moaning was approaching the agitation of a near howl. Consequently, Jane withdrew her offering, raised her skirt, exposing her nakedness, and then began to pant as she rubbed herself between his legs. Suddenly, Jane would mount, thrusting in and out as Winchester sweated heavily, his moaning intermingled with what to Eleanor seemed like the sound of a raspy hissing.

As Eleanor watched, it appeared like an odd sort of ritual which had been rehearsed and re-rehearsed. Unaware of her surroundings, Jane's eyes had acquired a glaze, a lusterless somnolence. Again Jane was riding her buffalo from a place long gone. But as their bodies tensed and contorted, the unification of something, a shade, no something more... a light, so white it almost possessed a kind of blue, a piece of divinity... yes, the unachievable, rationality's opposite... yen, yen, yen. At that, Eleanor's eyes spilled over with tears, at what she could never create or possess, yet to witness and sacrifice to such a force, a voyeur of something greater, as if she could have the power to create such a masterpiece.

Yen

She despised Jane. How could she? How could she?

As Winchester convulsed, Jane simultaneously jumped off. Without a moment's hesitation, she nimbly kicked him, and without further glances in Eleanor's direction, galloped into the grasslands beyond.

XII

A chillness had begun to permeate the air as Eleanor huddled her tattered coat more closely to her hunched shoulders. School was beginning and Eleanor had never been less interested in participating or attending for that matter. As she tarried, Eleanor could hear the ringing in the distance. But she did not alter her present progress. Rather, she continued in the same aimless fashion.

Panting, Jane dashed up to her from behind. "Hey, where have you been all week? I haven't been able to find you anywhere."

"My parents needed more help this week."

"I like your new shoes."

"Thanks."

"We shouldn't be late on the first day. Mr. Dorset won't be very happy. We'll both get the strap for sure."

"Maybe."

"What's with you? I don't see you for five whole days, and all you have to say is one-word answers? Come on."

"I believe we did exchange a glance or two this past week if you recall."

"So you're mad at me, that's it? You don't want anything to do with someone so gross and disgusting?"

"You said it, not me."

"So now you're better than me? You should try it sometime. You might enjoy it."

"I don't think so. I think, at the very least, you should consult your Bible. That is, if you have one. I'll pray for you."

Jane gasped. "When did you start going to church? If you confessed to the priest, he probably liked it quite a bit. You never know."

"You should not speak so disrespectfully about our representatives of God. Father Peters is a good, Christian man."

"And what would you know about the good, Christian priest? You've skipped church every Sunday with me. You don't even believe in God, and you know it! Don't give me that holy Christian attitude crap! You go for one Sunday and you think you're a Christian."

"What would you know about the character of our priest? Your family has never attended service!"

"Why don't you quit being such a ridiculous wimp and tell me what this is really about, that is, if you aren't chicken!" Jane emphasized the last word between clenched teeth, and Eleanor's eyes widened in fury.

"Whore." Eleanor spoke this as she withdrew, backing up, yet still facing Jane.

Jane's skin became suffused with an underlying pallor, and as the ashen tone deepened, Eleanor could not help but being transfixed at what she had created. She filled with satisfaction: an insatiable desire had just momentarily been quelled. Eleanor flicked back her hair and continued towards the school without looking back. The bell had stopped chiming for quite awhile, and she was not certain of the reaction Mr. Dorset would have to her tardiness.

XIII

Eleanor crept in, trailed a few minutes later by Jane. Eleanor attempted to take her customary position, but as she did, a voice bellowed, "What is the meaning of this?"

Eleanor timidly looked up, and as she did, a grey-haired man with tiny glasses seized her arm, hauling her in one swift movement to the front of the class.

"I am sorry, sir," she attempted, but before she could say another word, Mr. Dorset produced his dulled-leather belt.

"You're the smart girl who had that accident. Well in this class, ill-mannered people have no place and will not be tolerated. Place your left hand on the desk, now."

Eleanor hesitated, but the blunt obstinateness of his thick features asserted his unassailable nature. Five heavy raps were administered on both hands. The wounds immediately turned crimson and began to swell. Eleanor felt the sharpness, but the pain quickly ebbed as she looked up and was met by the most sneering, odious expression she had ever been witness to.

Jane, reclining at her desk, arms crossed, legs sprawling open, exhibited such a look of sinister satisfaction, Eleanor immediately felt her face begin to burn with a loathing she never before knew she possessed. How could she sit there and gloat like that? Didn't she know what she had done? Did she not comprehend anything? Eleanor began to wonder about the actual possibility of Jane's retardation. She had given up so much to spend her time exclusively with Jane. She had lost the respect of the other scholars in the name of their friendship, and Jane's indifference had escalated from a mild irritation to a searing hatred that seemed, like a kind of genesis, to germinate seeds of madness.

Eleanor had nearly forgotten the discomfort in her hands. Looking down at the abrasions, the swollen flesh reminded her somehow of dead fish, bloated as they rose to the surface and decayed. Her eyes welled with water of partial pain and pleasure: A realm, unbeknownst to her, had been uncovered, and the choice had already been made to explore this opaque domain.

"Return to your seat, Eleanor. In future, hopefully you will think better of your actions." Mr. Dorset's eyes gleamed with dark, feverish delight. He motioned for Eleanor to sit down. As she made her way back to her seat, with head bowed in supposed submission, she eyed Jane briefly, and grinned depravedly at her. Jane's eyes stared back, apparently emotionless and unremorsefully still.

Suddenly, Mr. Dorset's holler broke the intensity of the moment. "Jane, come this way."

Jane promptly rose and assented to his request.

"Place your left hand on the desk, first."

She smiled, and before complying, made her way over to Mr. Dorset's right ear. For a moment, his brow furrowed in anger and confusion, but then a blush imbued his beige complexion with sudden life.

"Be seated, Jane," he uttered with a slightly harsh although hesitant tone.

Eleanor was dumbfounded but managed to suppress her heightening exasperation. Jane, with head held high, strutted back to her assigned position. As she passed Eleanor, she bestowed a look laced with a smugness of such intensity that Eleanor felt a bitterness welling up in the confines of her stomach. As the bile rose, she sensed a burning in her throat, that suddenly manifested in a taste of unconditional revulsion that caused her to gag on the excrement. Just then, Jane smiled with gratification and nodded in Eleanor's direction, but Eleanor could not meet her gaze. Abruptly, she looked away, her eyes filling with tears of searing hatred and remorse. The wrath spilled over, soaking into the wood of the small, child's desk she was now seated at.

At lunchhour, Jane was nowhere to be found.

XIV

Effie Black stood, mouth agape, pupils dilated in sheer astonishment, "But how could she have?"

Mr. Dorset nodded solemnly. "Yes Effie, we were quite amazed at Eleanor's apparent um... scholastic return."

Effie couldn't believe the news. "Are you sure? This isn't a misunderstanding of some sort?" Effie's eyes scrutinized Mr. Dorset's countenance.

"No, Effie. I checked the percentages, myself."

"Maybe, that Jane-girl is a bad influence. Since she stopped being her friend, Eleanor has started acting like her old self."

Mr. Dorset smiled, but remained silent. "Well, in any case, Eleanor is back to achieving outstanding results."

Beaming, Effie turned to leave the schoolroom. She wanted to catch Eleanor before she left the main road and continued the rest of her way home.

Effie was breathing hard as the cold air filled her lungs. Treading the snow at this pace was tiresome, but she needed to make up the time. She could just see Eleanor's form nearing the fork.

Increasing her speed, Eleanor could hear the heaviness of the oncoming footsteps. Eleanor breathed rhythmically, pondering the algebraic expressions that earlier had seemed to elude her. Her regular heartbeat, and the sobering coldness of the air, gave the computations a novel clarity which the classroom, with its dusty, dull interior, intermingled with the waxen cadaverous aspect of the aforesaid Mr. Dorset, had understandably obscured.

All at once, Eleanor decided to halt and check who indeed was approaching. She and Jane were the only ones who usually took this road after school. Unexpectedly, obliterating her calculations, a force smashed into her, sending them both sprawling into the fresh, roadside drifts. Eleanor surfaced from her bath of soft ice crystals, irritated and yet puzzled by her pursuer. A pale, freckled face bordered by red frizz, blinked and coughed in her immediate direction. Eleanor's brow furrowed with displeasure.

A voice, broken by rasps, emerged. "Eleanor, I wanted to congratulate you on your test score! You must be thrilled!"

For a moment, Eleanor could not identify the timbre. Then, she remembered the constant petitions for her own company that she used to receive from this girl. She never thought much of Effie or her crowd, but now that Jane was no longer in the picture, things were different. Eleanor, recognizing the veneration on Effie's face, was able to recollect this same sentiment expressed back then.

Rising, and simultaneously dusting herself off, Eleanor replied, "Yes, thank-you Effie. I was very pleased and hope to do even better next time."

"I simply would not know how that is possible! It's simply marvelous, Eleanor! Do you feel different now? Is it easier to think?"

"Yes, Effie. I believe it is."

"Would you like to lunch with us? That is, if you do not have standing plans with that Jane-girl." As Effie said this, her eyes seemed to darken.

"Who? Oh, no. We no longer lunch together." For a moment Eleanor looked down.

"So, until we meet again," Effie stepped back, smiled and bowed in submission.

Finally, Eleanor giggled. "Yes, until we meet again."

XV

Eleanor made her way along the frozen pathways, catching snowflakes on the rounded tip of her distended tongue. The whiteness seemed an endless canvas of countless prospect, yet these days Eleanor only scowled at such trivial notions. Hearing the sound of laughter a few feet in front of her, Eleanor saw the two of them, their hair and lashes powdered heavily.

Jane threw the first snowball which hit Winchester, but he only grabbed and tackled her to the ground in a mirthful manner. Jane shrieked, but upon spotting that spying figure, kissed Winchester heavily. Winchester froze; the snowangel he had been creating became suddenly deformed and, as he rose to touch the preciousness at hand, thus made permanently incomplete.

His hand brushed her frozen cheek, and for a moment the piercing mien thawed. Then she leaned over and whispered something quickly into his ear all the while motioning in Eleanor's direction. He smirked and yelled with boyish delight.

Eleanor stood motionless, snow gracing her brows and hair. She felt not the cold nor the elements but again the yearning grew. Their individual breaths, conjoining, ascending, a myriad of shapes and light hues pervaded the giant canvas, which seemed to waver and alter with a unique symmetry that Eleanor felt she could mimic with the correct combination of glaze and coatings. The enlightened canvas breathed, and Eleanor was satiated like all of those other times.

Winchester bounded towards her. His smirk seemed almost devilish, and at that instant, Eleanor hoped more than all else that she would indeed be asked to join. He turned his back, dropped his pants, and a sound departed his pursed cheeks, that was at once repugnant and nauseating. Eleanor was dumbfounded and fell over in the roadside slush. Winchester hastily pulled them back up, and ran after Jane, who was already dashing all the way to the ringing that Eleanor could faintly hear in the distance.

Eleanor choked back tears, but instead of crying, she cackled in disbelief. That slut! He could have her. They deserved each other. He was a dunce who would never achieve anything, and she was practically a retard, but not any retard, a retard slut - quite a profound combination. As well, Mr. Dorset, for that matter, was definitely enjoying himself. After all, she couldn't always have blackboard duty.

Eleanor's eyes narrowed, and the wind picked up, chafing her skin, and seemingly reproaching her. She looked forward to the strapping she would soon receive. She would think of Jane's daily efforts and Mr. Dorset's slightly broader smile and lighter gait after every lunchhour. The deliciousness of her thoughts was causing a considerable wetness to emerge from below. She wondered in sheer ecstasy how Winchester might receive the conveyance of this pertinent matter. The conception of this strategy made her so excited that she found it necessary to stop behind that tree, which Jane and Winchester often used, to rub her finger along her own sticky residue.

Crossing the threshold, Eleanor immediately saw Mr. Dorset's grimace. She lowered her head and approached his desk. "I am sorry, sir. I deserve any punishment which you deem appropriate."

"Do you look forward to my strap then, Eleanor? This is the second time in a single week in which you have displayed excessive tardiness. Do you have anything to say for yourself?"

"I am sorry, sir. I fell down and hurt my ankle on the way and the snow made it even harder to make any sufficient progress." The words had been elicited without any prior knowing on Eleanor's part. They had simply emerged, complete and total fabrication. Hermes had waved his Caduceus and Eleanor heard the captivating summons. She blinked sorrowfully at Mr. Dorset.

"You have been doing exceedingly well, I must admit, Eleanor, and since your father is sick as well, I will let this incident go this time. Try not to do this in future."

"Thank-you, Mr. Dorset," Eleanor beamed and curtseyed.

Making her way back to her seat, a sinister smile crossed her lips, and she nodded purposefully at Jane. Jane leered. Eleanor had to suppress a rising cackle. She bent down and murmured, "Enjoy him at lunch. Winchester should really be told, now don't you think?"

Jane looked appalled. Eleanor winked. Mr. Dorset glanced up, "Now, what is it this time, Eleanor?"

"I was simply asking Jane to borrow her spare pair of stockings, since mine are soaking wet," Eleanor fibbed.

Jane disdainfully uttered, "Why I'm sorry, Eleanor. I didn't bring any today. How cold you must be!"

Eleanor finally seated herself. But regardless of the slight chill, she did not mind at all. The game was up, and she had finally won her first round.

XVI

In the pinkness of the ensuing glow, flakes swept in their ever-downward motion, as the two figures manipulated the frictionless surface at hand. The blades shone, catching the light upon their just-sharpened, serrate edges. With each incision, jagged crevices were crudely hewn from the glistening iridescence.

Suddenly Jane screamed out, "Winchester, we have an unknown visitor. Please, welcome our guest."

Eleanor stood there in reticence, not realizing that either of them were or could have been conscious of her clandestine positioning.

"Jesus, I didn't see you there. How long have you been there, anyway?" Winchester remonstrated.

"Why, that is no way to treat our guest. Come on dear, show her in," Jane persisted.

"For God's sake Jane, *she* doesn't even have skates on," Winchester continued.

Eleanor blinked hard at the tone he chose to employ.

"Well, if you refuse to be civil to our visitor, then you leave me no choice in the matter," Jane retorted eagerly.

"Okay, okay, come in, um... I forget her name."

"Jill, you dunce! Jill... Jill is here." Jane grinned at the cleverness of her own pronouncement.

Jane skated over to the threshold between ground and ice where Eleanor stood.

Eleanor glanced down to her feet and frowned in confusion. "But I have no skates."

"Not to worry. We'll help you on. Won't we, Jack?"

Winchester's brows furrowed in obvious ignorance. "Who?"

"For God's sake, can't *you* just play along for once?" Jane growled.

"Sorry, yes... um, yes dear."

They helped her onto the slippery surface. Her treads were now rendered useless by the slickery substance.

As she futilely attempted to gain her footing, Jane began to giggle excitedly. Her eyes flashed as if a madness possessed the glimmer.

Eleanor shifted nervously, as Jane's grip strengthened.

"Jack dear, Jill is still floundering dreadfully. What do you suggest we do?" Jane challenged.

"Um, um... I don't know. What do you think we sh... sh... should do?" Jack stuttered.

"You are a moron. You have no original ideas, and are essentially worthless," Jane sternly admonished.

Jack's head bowed in shame at Jane's strong remonstration.

"Jill is here. At least you could help welcome her."

Jack stumbled dumbly, and Jane blurted out, "You imbecile. You are so ineffectual."

Jack did not know what 'ineffectual' meant, but nevertheless, he recognized Jane's displeasure, and that's all he needed.

"Jill is from your blood after all. Is that all you can do?" Jane patronized.

"She is?" Jack's look conveyed disbelief. It was obvious he was not readily catching on.

"Forget it. Why don't you just go home?" Jane rebuked.

Letting go of Eleanor's hand, she skated away cantankerously, whirled in a circle on one foot, endeavoring a spin, then laughing hysterically, plummeted onto the frigid, unforgiving surface.

Jack and Jill stood in awe of Jane's mounting delirium.

"You two look like carbon copies of each other with that idiotic expression on your bloody beaming faces!" Jane cackled as she kicked her feet up and down rupturing the previously intact covering. Bits of debris scattered the ice like tiny, glass pellets.

"Jane, are you all right?" Eleanor yelled in her direction, as she was genuinely becoming concerned.

This only served to create another fit of uncontrollable howling that left Jane speechless for a time. Finally, Eleanor ventured again, "Jane?"

This time a response was finally educed. "Tell Jack to come over to me, dear." The petition was laced with a capricious sweetness.

Eleanor looked to Winchester who was already skating over. Jane appeared to be whispering in Winchester's ear, after which he started unlacing her skates. Jane was still spread-eagled, evidently gaping into the sanguine vastness.

Jane noticed Jack's departure as he whirled over before Jill. Producing the skates with a somewhat gentlemanly gesture, Jill accepted them and the pair began the ritual. Jack led her out to the creek's centre. Jill had never owned skates, hence her progress was stilted and unstable.

As Jane had requested, Jack rotated her in circular fashion, Jill laughed in elation. For a moment, Jack grinned, but immediately becoming self-conscious of Jane's omnipresent scrutiny, instantly ceased.

She bounded up. Eleanor noticed her feet were bare and bluish from exposure. She was stunned at the implied risk of this observation.

"Jane!" Eleanor hollered. "Are you trying to lose your feet and toes?!" Eleanor exclaimed with consternation.

"My dearest Jill, do not worry your pretty, little head," Jane countered as she simultaneously danced back and forth on her chilblained soles.

All at once Jane bent over, cramming Jill's still-new shoes onto her too-large specimens.

Rubbing up next to Jack, Jane's voice vibrated as the purr of a kitten.

Her hand reached down and she started to vigorously pet the swelling.

"Why now? But you never want to anymore. Not now," Winchester pushed Jane's hand away. "Not when *she's* here."

"Who?" Jane cooed. "Say her name."

"What?" Winchester was again confused at her meaning.

"Say her name." Again Jane's hand drew toward its magnetic source.

Winchester sighed at a touch he had been craving like an itch which never diminished.

"Jill... say, Jill." Jane's tone had changed to a hiss.

"Jiilll... oh, that feels goood," Jack responded like a well-trained mongrel.

"That's better. Jill wants to play, too. Don't you Jill?"

Eleanor, forgetting she was present, at this sudden entreaty, involuntarily bit her tongue.

"Ouch," Eleanor exclaimed.

"It's fun. Won't you join us?" Jane whined.

"Maybe," Eleanor vacillated. The protrusion in Winchester's trousers induced a squeezing together of Eleanor's legs in eagerness to participate.

"Okay," Jill finally conceded. The fray had been entered.

XVII

Jane undid Jack's pants exposing the pink, pulsating tissue.

Jack was too overzealous to contain himself much longer. Jack had been reduced to pathetic groveling.

Jane bent down, running her tongue along its gesticulating surface.

Jill towered above, captivated by Jane's lapping, and the lack of shadowscapes which were her usual source of ecstatic distraction.

Jack's back hunched as the guttural utterances emerging from his constricting throat were curious to say the least.

"Come." Jane's head turned to face Jill.

"Me?" Jill said timidly.

Jane nodded in assent.

As Jill approached, a smell, kind-of fishy and sour, permeated her nostrils. She stepped away in disgust.

"What's wrong?" Jane giggled in mock confusion.

Jane pulled Jill towards her. She could see the light of innocence reflected like a soft, green shadow in Jill's eyes.

"Pull up your dress. Feel this."

At the point of contact, the touch of the quivering mass against the liplike division, caused her to tremble at the sensation as it rose from this external area up, up, tickling her temples. Jane's hand continued the stroking action. Jack was becoming nearly beside himself. A bead of perspiration fell to the icy floor beneath, transforming into a gelid droplet in passage, the loss of moisture inevitable in its downward, spiralling flight.

Suddenly, the stroking terminated and the agent placed it again in her moist orifice, moving back and forth in accompaniment to the throbbing undulation of testicular function. All at once, the agent squeezed off the tip in which the object at hand went flaccid and was followed by a cacophony of severe protestations from one very inflamed party. Jack, bolting up, skated over to the grass, swearing, penis in hand. Jill noticed the head had become blue. She wondered if this was from the cold like Jane's feet. Jane followed him and so did Jill. As Jack fell over in agony at the stony hardness of his afore-mentioned organ, Jane commanded Jill to mount. When she refused, Jane reiterated the order. Jane pushed her down, her blade narrowly missing the tip. As the feverish rubbing again began, Jill protested loudly. Jane was holding her on top of him, screaming for Jack to insert... that Jill would like it... something about Daddy's girl would like it. Jill squirmed, but the more she squirmed the harder it became. Jack was now yelling back at Jane, saying how she was going to get him into trouble. But Jane only persisted, issuing an ultimatum to proceed or he would never see her again. Moaning in anguish, Jack's hissing had become heavy and incoherent. Jill struggled, but her po-sition, the awkwardness of the skates, and Jane's full weight upon her shoulders made resistance pointless. The petrified tactility below jabbed just as Jane's golden tendrils softly cascaded the frame of her upturned visage. Jane's eyes were closed and her lips mouthed the same word over and over... Daddy... Daddy.

The soft, golden light bathed her above and the hard, fertile snake hissed from its lair below. Like a portrait which painted itself, the mad-ness of color and shape were arranged in a seemingly-preset pattern. Like a circuit, Jill had become the connection between heaven and earth. The pierce was sharp like a flash of lightning, the storm com-menced. The cadence compulsed her, as she felt herself give in to the consummation of portraiture. Tears fell like rain from the golden orb above. After the earnest beseeching of the two other performers that this must remain ever undisclosed, Jill aimlessly walked home. A san-guine substance dripped onto the tops of her once-new shoes. Jill fi-nally consented to their constant supplications; that is, as had been decreed before, the show must always go on.

One lone observer watched from her dizzying height: Erato ap-plauded this distinctive execution.

XVIII

Eleanor lunched with Effie and her group. Eleanor welcomed the wide-eyed stares and glances she was now receiving from this snobbish cluster. The only pretty girl of them cleared her throat and spoke, albeit with a nasalish tone to her voice.

"Eleanor, how is it that now your cognitive functioning has resumed its usually high-level, all of a sudden, out of the blue?" Apparently, this girl's curiosity had won over Effie's frowns and overall disapproval of reproaching Eleanor.

"Why, I cannot explain it myself. It was as if a curtain lifted, and my usual pathological processes returned to their previous level. As you know, my parents unfortunately were not able to employ a licensed practitioner, so the actual regenerative processes will probably remain obscured." After this pronouncement, the group was silent, the muffled giggles had ceased, and the only noise was the sound of rattling paper and chomping teeth.

Eleanor munched delicately on her apple and noticed Effie's obvious approval. Effie nodded and continued eating her peanut butter and jam. Eleanor was however distracted by a dark figure who was eating in the corner as usual by himself. As she bit down, the pulpy material touched her retracted lips and the tantalization of her ponderings deeply enthralled her. Unexpectedly, he glared right at her. Her eyes briefly widened. What would he say? What might he think?

Eleanor finished her apple and walked over to where he was ravenously stuffing slabs of cheese and bread down his gullet. He swallowed heavily and looked up.

"What do *you* want?"

"I was just observing how strange it is that Jane never eats lunch with you or any of us for that matter. I was wondering what you think she might be doing."

"You know, as well as I do, that she has blackboard duty every lunchhour," Winchester growled.

"And why might that be? Can no one else ever take a turn? Even Jane does not misbehave that often." Eleanor's sneer widened.

"What is your point? Mr. Dorset likes Jane to do the boards. So what?"

Eleanor neared the blankness on the visage before her. Her voice became hushed and deep. "Meet me behind that tree which Jane and you so often employ down by the river after school."

"Why? Is this a trick?"

"Well, if it is, you can always leave."

"What for? Jane might get upset."

"I want to try something that Jane likes to do. She told me that I might like it."

"What?" Winchester's eyes receded in suspicion.

Eleanor became quietly indignant. "My tongue... um, you know... licking it. I'll pucker my lips as tight as I can. Jane said that you really like that. Just meet me there, okay?"

Winchester only gawked flabbergasted. Jane had actually told her about that afternoon. He remembered it, every moment of it, how he'd wished she would do it again, but at no time did she. She never mentioned it, although they didn't talk much. He wondered what Jane would think. Before, when Jane and Eleanor were still together, he remembered Jane telling him that, one of these days, Eleanor would play as well. But then the split occurred, and after that Jane never mentioned Eleanor. If she did, she would always say *that* girl I used to know or *that* girl I used to play with, then a lethargy would overcome her, and she would look away and blink hard.

Eleanor was evidently waiting for some kind of response. Observing her eagerness, he realized that she still resembled a wounded animal, but there was something else to her countenance now, a flicker in the eye that gave him the impression of a slight rabidness. He recalled the day of the storm when she had selflessly helped him home. In his relentless anguish, he hardly noticed her. Winchester knew what Eleanor was propositioning. At only the recollection of that day, he could already feel a stiffness forming. Eleanor however discovered it almost immediately. She giggled and ran back to her new-found clique.

XIX

Nevertheless, as Eleanor had requested, Winchester appeared at the scheduled time.

"I didn't know if you'd come."

"Neither did I," Winchester muttered nervously.

Yen

A wind picked up. "How many times has Jane... you know?" Eleanor pointed at Winchester's swelling trousers.

"I don't know. You're the one who she used to tell everything to. You won't tell her we did this, will you? I mean if she found out, that is, if anyone found out she might be mad at me. You're not gonna tell, are you? Um... yeah, maybe we should forget the whole thing." Winchester turned to go.

"No! Wait. I'm not going to tell. Please, don't go," Eleanor pleaded.

Winchester really did not require that much convincing. His eyes glittered ominously. He began hastily unbuttoning. Eleanor's mouth gaped open in evident alarm.

"Well, what did you expect? Come on, are you gonna, or not?"

Eleanor, still dazed, bent down before him. She ran her finger along its shiny surface and it quivered in response.

"Hurry up, while it's hard. Jane's much better. Are you sure you know what you're doing?" Winchester was clearly uneasy as his words came out in loud, erratic succession.

It tasted awful. The slime lined the membranes of her orifice and she began to choke in displeasure. Winchester was obviously indignant. "You're not doing it right! Jesus, you've never even played with one before, have you?!" Winchester pulled away and began raising his heavy woolen trousers. She could see the exasperation carved into his contorted features. He had never felt this way or said those things to Jane. And the expression which emanated from his eyes! What utter contempt at her ineptitude!

Eleanor's eyes swelled with tears. "I can do better. Show me how."

Winchester, not yet fully buttoned, rapidly unfastened his pants. Again, Eleanor tentatively approached, but Winchester's irritation at her pleas, and his growing discomfort, made him impatient. As her lips again began to ingest his specimen, Winchester grasped Eleanor's head, moving it back and forth to a rhythm that she apparently could not easily rationalize. "Squeeze your lips tighter... the tip, that's right."

Eleanor was becoming more nauseated all of the time. Jane always seemed to be enjoying herself regardless of the intensity. Eleanor wanted to pull her head away and spit out this increasing distaste. However, she persevered as she had agreed. Winchester was beginning to wail. Gripping her head more tightly, he moved it more briskly. Eleanor, eyes wide in horror, remained true to her task. The taste and smell were becoming atrocious, and her neck was beginning to ache from his sheer force.

"Yes, that's it, Jane," Winchester cried.

Eleanor could not believe the word which defied her ears. This sense suddenly had become like a cruel enemy, and she would no longer trust its scheming manipulations. Eleanor's torment froze her motion as her heart fell to her stomach. Trying to pull away was no use. She felt his part slide down her throat and as it did he climaxed. The abhorrent seed filled the capacities of her now swollen cheeks. Dizzy from exhaustion, she flopped lifelessly into the soft, consoling grasses. She managed however to successfully rise to her knees, as the world quaked convulsively to and fro.

Winchester chortled. "Not bad. You showed real improvement."

Choking violently, and still on her knees, she turned her head, and vomited heavily in the high grass.

"Cat got your tongue? Boy, that sure pissed off Jane when I said that to you that day."

Eleanor was still gagging. However, she soon caught her breath. "You called me, Jane," Eleanor sputtered.

"What? Oh, did I? Must have slipped out. Sorry."

Eleanor did not reply, choosing to sneer instead.

"Now, you're not gonna get all pissed off. I don't need this. You're not gonna go tell Jane, now are you?" Winchester's face was growing redder.

"Maybe." Eleanor spat.

He walked over to her, grabbed her arm and yanked her hair. "You lying, whore! You said that you wouldn't tell. What's your game?! What do you want?"

Eleanor cringed. Between his rising fury, her tender stomach, and ensuing nausea, she quickly uttered, "I simply wanted you to say, 'Thank-you, Eleanor'. That is all."

With such a direct assertion, and the sudden realization that he was constricting and confining a girl, and fellow classmate at that, his head bowed, and he said quickly, "Thank-you, Eleanor."

Although just before leaving, he raised his head and uttered, "You better be as good as your word and not breathe this to a living soul."

Eleanor's eyes glistened as she wiped her mouth off. "And whom might I tell? I have no intention of telling anyone else that I am a slut just as Jane is."

"Jane isn't a slut! She's my girl! Don't say that about my girl." After this vehement declaration, Winchester stomped his feet like an enraged child.

"She may be your girl. But she also belongs to a lot of other men, and yes, boys too... Mr. Dorset for instance."

"What are you saying?"

Eleanor approached this dunce. He was even more senseless than she had ascertained.

"I'll give you an example to illustrate. The action that I just performed for you? It is highly probable that Jane does this while cleaning all of those blackboards."

Winchester's forehead wrinkled in confusion. Then a lucidity overtook his usually clouded aspect. "What did you say?" he glared.

"I believe you heard me as clearly as I heard myself, thank-you very much."

Winchester felt the gush of ire. He had only felt this sensation once before and anticipated the culminating frenzy. "Take it back."

"No," Eleanor retorted defiantly.

Striking her down in one blow, he kicked her twice in the stomach, and becoming cognizant of her sobs, desisted and now wailing himself, bolted for home.

XX

Eleanor beamed from her now esteemed position as new top student. Scholastically, she had recovered. Even though she was in possession of a black eye and a number of deep bruises on her abdomen, she had evaded suspicion by claiming a severe fall on an icy patch.

Mr. Dorset motioned for Eleanor to rise, as he wished to present her a wooden plaque engraved with the words, 'Meadowlark's most improved pupil'. Eleanor strutted to the foot of his desk. Mr. Dorset looked solemnly up.

"Congratulations, Eleanor. You've made quite a remarkable recovery. I hope your progress continues this well in future. Please go sit on the other side of the room with Effie and the others."

Eleanor glanced down at Mr. Dorset's unzipped trousers. As it was just after the lunchhour, Jane would have grazed her daily domain and Eleanor wondered if his offering was superior in tang to Winchester's unsavory variety. Eleanor blinked demurely, and Mr. Dorset's eyes widened as he shifted uneasily. Jane's advances never elicited such a peculiar response.

Eleanor noticed the smirk crossing the crevices of Jane's olive complexion, and hastily she looked away, not wishing to meet the cunning discernment of her stare. With flaming cheeks, she scrutinized the workmanship of the crudely whittled symbols. Her fingers ran over the smoothed surface, between the spaces where the grain could be discerned and into the chiseled contours, where she suddenly felt the prick of a cultrate sliver. She winced as the sting penetrated the skin under her nail.

"You may be seated now, Eleanor."

As she made her way towards the other side of the room, her fellow classmates clapped in proud unison for her seemingly astounding achievement. Neither Winchester, nor Jane accompanied her deferential reception. They sat there in their various casts of darkness and light, and suddenly to Eleanor they seemed like two clowns in a much grander performance. Eleanor, as always, was the ordained audience.

Mr. Dorset cleared his throat and asked Jane to begin the assigned reading exercise. Jane became suffused with crimson, and to Eleanor's disbelief lost her composure. Mr. Dorset had never asked this of Jane before. In fact, none of Jane's previous teachers had imposed this task upon her.

Jane's mouth fell open in obvious defiance.

Mr. Dorset smiled sadistically. "Did you not read the assigned passages, Jane?" he inquired, unsuccessfully attempting to suppress the mounting eagerness of his tone.

Jane only stared blankly in resentment, culminating in apparent disgust.

"Did you not hear me, Jane? I asked you a question." His tone was adamant.

"No, I did not," she replied in a flat voice.

"Why is that? When you are assigned a piece of material, I expect you to complete it for the following class. Are you so stupid that you did not comprehend my request or did you choose not to fulfill your obligations as my pupil?" He became louder, as he was uncharacteristically irate with her.

Effie leaned over to Eleanor. In a hushed tone, she queried, "Is she just obstinate or is she actually retarded, and illiterate as well?"

Eleanor stared blankly in response. She had never heard Mr. Dorset speak in that manner to Jane. Regardless of her feelings toward Jane, at that moment, she felt a sadness and pity escalating within her. Why was Mr. Dorset speaking to her that way?

Eleanor thought back to all of those afternoons they had spent together and the raw, unbounded energy that seemed to envelope Jane's presence. The way she could use words when she wanted, her technique of fashioning the reaction of others to epitomize whatever mood she fancied, and her ability to somehow control or influence her natural environment stood out in Eleanor's mind. It had never occurred to her that Jane could not read, that she was illiterate as Effie had just postulated. The thought confounded her. Surely, she would have known this if anyone had.

Jane remained motionless.

"Your response is unsatisfactory, Jane. And I will need to see you after school. Also, the blackboards have not been properly cleaned. This must be corrected." Mr. Dorset's eyes glistened feverishly.

Jane's face was set in the most willful expression Eleanor had ever seen. Eleanor was bewildered. She didn't notice any difference in the quality of the just-cleaned boards.

XXI

The snow was whirling in tight drifts of freezing, chaotic patterns. Even though her overcoat was too small, she enjoyed this blinding, rarely-attained peace. Tiny blots of white paint covered everything. Indiscriminately, each animate and inanimate object was delicately buried as if the Grand Master had temporarily desisted for a moment of rest. It was as if all was shielded, obliterated in sheer formlessness.

Ahead of her, a form, almost like a storm cloud, materialized on the frosty road. Just as Eleanor suspected, Winchester was plodding along the icy surface, feet frozen in holey sneakers, bent on arriving home and warming himself before a roaring fire. Eleanor sailed by him, slipping on a section of ice. Winchester continued without even a glimpse in her direction.

"Well, if that is the way you wish to show your appreciation, I think your courtly rituals are severely in need of improvement." Eleanor rose to her feet.

"What do you want? You've already got me into enough trouble. What now?"

"I have only done you favours. I shan't mention them but we both know to what I am referring."

"Well, a lot of good that did. Jane's mad at me, if you noticed."

"No, I did not. It seems that you two are the best of companions. I believe it was just the other day that you, in tandem, performed a most obscene gesture at my expense and for your own amusements, not to mention your other more violent ungentlemanly behaviors."

"What do you use all those bloody fancy-dancy words for, anyway? They give me a bloody headache," Winchester rudely retorted.

"What do you mean she is mad at you?" Eleanor decided directness was much more expedient.

"There are certain things that Jane liked to do that all of a sudden she does not wish to do, okay, Miss Nosy?"

"So, what I did the other day, she no longer wishes to do for your benefit?" Eleanor asked coyly.

"That, not to mention other things, too," Winchester snapped.

"Well, I am not blameworthy for this turn of events," Eleanor snapped back.

"Maybe, but I have nothin' to say to the likes of you."

"I guess an apology is out of the question, then."

"Look, don't get me started. You deserved what was coming. You shouldn'ta said that about Mr. Dorset and her. It wasn't... um... right."

"Okay, I don't think any scholarly awards will be at your disposal. But I will leave you with this poignant point before I depart. What exactly do you think Jane is doing right now? Cleaning boards, Mr.

Genius?" Eleanor raised her brows in evident challenge.

"Don't you get me started again. I got nothin' to say to you. Leave us be. And I'll leave you be."

"All I want is to be your friend. Why are you making it so difficult?" Eleanor's lips were beginning to freeze solidly.

"Go away. Go be somebody else's friend. With all those high marks I'm sure you got a lot to choose from."

"Please, Winchester. Don't make me beg." Eleanor was sincerely affected.

"I can't. I already said. The only way this will be is if you made friends with Jane again, and I don't think that will be so easy."

Eleanor's eyes welled with tears. "I'll do anything. You can beat me, whatever you want, I'll do it."

"No. I said, no. Now, just go... just go."

"I can't. You don't understand. Please."

"Christ. Ya may be a scholar, but ya dumb." With that last retort, Winchester bounded off into the frosted trees, fleeing, frozen feet and all, into the foliage by the fork in the road. The formlessness quickly returned, and it was as if he never had existed at all.

XXII

"Jane, Jane is a retard! Jane's a retard!" Effie was screaming with laughter. The other girls were watching her, neither participating in her antics, nor condemning her, mesmerized by her hysteria.

Effie bobbed in a circle imitating an Indian war dance. "Come on, Eleanor. Wouldn't you agree? Don't just stand there. Say something."

Eleanor was also transfixed by Effie's strange performance. Nevertheless, she was tempted, but, instead of reacting, momentarily stood in silence.

A tantalizing idea seductively played at the edges of her consciousness. Slowly, a diabolical smile crept across her face. "Now Effie, one should not make fun of the less fortunate. It is not the Lord's way."

Jane turned, previously insensate of the barbed phrases being hurled at her. This one, however, deftly pierced the core. Decidedly, she tackled Eleanor to the earth with one swift leap. She began to pound her sides with closed fists, while bouncing up and down rhythmically.

Effie stood, immobilized in fear. The scene before her seemed oddly enacted. Jane did not look at Eleanor as she mercilessly continued to beat her in frenzied succession. Eleanor could only feebly raise her arms in protest. The more she resisted, the greater Jane's efforts became. Eleanor remembered the day of the storm, and how, no matter what she said to Jane, nothing would make her respond. Eleanor's arms did little to fend off the brunt of the attack. Eventually, she surrendered and after a time, became numb to the blows.

Each of the whacks now became paint splattered on a canvas, manifesting in a crude, yet regular rhythm. The colors were bold - mustard-yellows, orange-reds, a hint of purple, dark, the texture uneven - much like the hemoglobin breakdown from a deep bruise. The gaudy texture and overall effect would at once repulse the refined critic, yet fascinate simultaneously. Delight shone in her eyes, which only served to enrage Jane further. The force of the rubbing strengthened, and she moved her fists from Eleanor's pulverized sides to the newly-forming buds on her chest. As she throttled, Eleanor screamed out, "Jane, Jane, stop!" Eleanor's voice vibrated as if speaking before a fan, sounding disjointed like Tarzan's.

More onlookers had assembled. Some laughed in disbelief, but most stood, appalled. None however, acted. Jane noticed not the crowd, nor Eleanor's rising pleading.

The pain had again been suspended. An engrossing sensation gradually arose from her netherworld, below. Again, her omnipresent canvas materialized but this time, unlike the occasions before, she had become the paint, flung in every direction, landing, she knew not where, somewhere in the realm of the intangible.

Writhing, she began to softly moan, the onlookers and surroundings, fading. All at once, she groaned, the tingle passing from head to toe. Effie bounded forward in alarm. "Stop killing her, you retarded weirdo!" She howled in reproach directly into Jane's face. Hauling her off of Eleanor, Effie's rough attempt was conceded to by Jane, who was presently placated. Eleanor continued to lie, numb from the offensive and the chilly ground beneath, yet otherwise, resplendent.

Effie hurried over and eagerly cried, "Eleanor, are you injured?! Can I help you up?"

Eleanor wondered from whose visage such vexatious tones were arising.

Effie bolted off, panicked. "Eleanor's unconscious! Get the nurse!" she screeched.

Eleanor heard this, but cared not to acknowledge currently. The canvas remained incomplete and needed work.

Rushing to her side, the woman propped up her head, and surveyed her eyes which were presently glazed over as if she had ingested a potent drug.

"Eleanor, Eleanor, can you hear me?" The nurse's tone was insistent.

"It was that Jane-girl! She nearly beat Eleanor to death!" Effie wailed.

"It's all right, Effie. Go back into the school with the other students. I can handle this." Gently, she slapped Eleanor's face and wafted smelling salts under her nose. Eleanor coughed in displeasure.

"There, you're going to be fine. Do you feel discomfort or pain anywhere, Eleanor?"

"No, I don't think so. My chest and sides are a little tender," Eleanor mumbled begrudgingly.

"I think you'll be fine. Nothing like that nasty bump on the head you nearly did not recover from. Sometimes, I wonder why they even bother keeping an obviously savage girl in a civilized institution. Would you like the rest of the day off, Eleanor? I think you should go home and rest for awhile."

"Thank-you, Miss Welden. I believe that would do nicely."

After all, Eleanor had a nearly sublime work to complete.

XXIII

Eleanor sat up. Permafrost made the ground hard and frigid against her protracted abdomen. A rustle from the field beyond occasioned her to jerk anxiously. This almost nightly event had replaced the now tedious repetition of her once enchanting tracing game.

A spider's carefully orchestrated movements were revealed through the grimy barn window: a web of delicate mesh like the composition of

Eleanor's retina, images registering and passing, filtering through to the innermost organ of encephalozation - its fixed position a voyeur's paradise or prison encompassing the expanse of its existence. Her breath came out in fractured intervals, her fingers weaving their own unique symmetry beneath the wool skirt and long underwear.

The patterns continued on the far wall, forbidden, like an elixir as she would return each evening for the recurrent performance. The shadowed tendrils hung down, overhanging the floor. Like honeysuckle, Eleanor relished their illicit sweetness. For a brief instant, Eleanor thought she saw the fall of a single opaline drop of her opiate... so sweet, an Elysian potion of incomparable concentration.

The performance was proceeding at a crazed pace. Recklessly, the blessed creatures were dropped to the floor as if someone had unexpectedly let go of their respective strings, unwilling to take the burden for the tragic deeds being committed. The spider shifted to the other side of its web in order to observe the culmination of the frenzied entertainment. To Eleanor's disconcertment, however, the actors were now permanently out of view.

Eleanor, though, was still able to hear the siren's call. The barn's old rotten floor creaked as the mariner, so familiar to Eleanor, but even more familiar to Jane, must have been heaving himself frantically back and forth. Jane's voice rose in plaintive tones responding to his habitual maneuverings. Eleanor gasped as her brain flooded with endorphins. In immediate succession, the siren moaned as she always did with her now-satisfied mariner.

XXIV

Jane scrutinized Eleanor's approach. She wondered what she could possibly have to say. She knew Eleanor was far too proud to ever even consider attempting an apology.

Jane waited.

Eleanor realized that Jane was clearly conscious of her advance.

"Hello, Jane."

"What do you want?" Jane responded tritely.

"I wondered how you did on the spelling test today. That's all."

Rapidly, she was losing her already frail composure.

"Well, we were all informed of your scholastic excellence. I think my performance is essentially irrelevant, now don't you?" Jane's voice crescendoed in order to emphasize her point.

"No, I don't. I didn't know that you could not read, Jane. I never would have guessed."

Jane looked at her as though she may have been performing a magic trick with a sleight of hand which never should be trusted. As Jane reached out, Eleanor thought that she sincerely wanted and needed her help. Eleanor went to say, 'Jane, I'm so glad,' when she felt Jane's grip strengthening exponentially. Her hand began to throb and ache, as Jane applied more pressure. Eleanor tried to free her grasp, initially failing.

"Ouch, that really hurts! Let go! Why are you doing that?! I just wanted to..."

"To what? Help? No, you didn't."

"You will always think what you will anyway. Ouch, let go!"

"You want to teach me to read so that you can feel as though you've helped the less fortunate. Is that not correct? Or, how was it you worded it?"

"I did not know you couldn't read. If I had known, I would have started teaching you immediately."

"Why do you presume that I wish to be taught?"

"Well, I just thought that... well, um, I assumed you naturally would."

"Exactly, as always, you assumed. Consulting me seemed out of the question, right?"

"Well, I didn't like the way Mr. Dorset was speaking to you the other day. That's all."

"Maybe you didn't, but I didn't mind that much. He can be funny that way. If you saw his wife, you'd understand."

"What? What exactly do you mean?"

"Eleanor, when are you going to stop playing 'Little Miss Innocent'? I'm getting sick of it."

"Okay, what do you want then? You have no intention of learning to read. What do you want?"

"I would like an apology." Jane raised her eyebrows to monitor

Eleanor's automatic response.

"I owe you an apology?" Eleanor's eyes widened in awe.

"Must I remind you of the grievous numerous events which have precipitated between us of late?"

"I just can't understand that. How can you not be able to read, yet use all of those words so succinctly?"

"You should know by now that I am no dummy. I learn by example. And my example stands before me."

Eleanor was flabbergasted. She had never considered this possibility before.

Jane demanded, "Eleanor, let us return to the subject at hand, if we could, please."

"Yes, I believe though that you have conveniently reversed the situation at hand."

"I was waiting for you to say that."

"I believe it was you and Winchester who so politely performed an obscene gesture solely at my expense. And it was also you who unquestionably throttled me, unprovoked, I may add, the other day. Now, who may I ask owes whom an apology?"

"You can twist the circumstances any way you deem fit, but it does not change the reality that it is you, as smug and pompous as you are, who owes me what is rightfully due, that is, the justification of your words and actions of late."

"Are you now a member of some official judiciary body?" Eleanor sneered.

"Okay then, I will say this, I'm glad you enjoyed yourself so much the other day."

"What does that mean?"

"I think that we both know what I mean without elaborating further."

"No, I don't think I do. If you would care to enlighten me..." Eleanor's demeanor changed from defensive to enraged.

"Perhaps, not. We have spoken sufficiently to establish absolutely nothing just as I suspected from the start."

"I wish for you to expound on your previous statement."

"Let me put it this way then. You enjoyed yourself as much as you do most nights from your supposed hiding place in the field just beyond the barn. Or, as I would put it, you like to watch us fuck, and I like you watching." At that, Jane snickered wryly.

Eleanor lost her breath. How could she have known that she was observing from the field beyond? She was always so careful to be quiet and still. Eleanor could conceivably understand Jane's cognizance of the spider's presence, but of her own? It seemed surreal. Even if Jane were somehow aware of her presence, how would she know what she was doing at that? After all, Eleanor was only viewing depictions projected onto an old, barn wall. All of this flashed across Eleanor's mind in a fraction of a second, and the horror obviously registered on her face, because Jane suddenly burst out, "Don't look so shocked. It's nothing to be ashamed of, silly," as though the subject matter regarded viewing a movie or something of trivial nature, definitely not something real.

In a choked whisper, Eleanor managed to stammer a single utterance, "Does *he* know I watch?"

"No, he is, of course, only aware of me." Jane's hand reached for Eleanor's, but this time she had no intention of squeezing to evoke pain. Jane only desired assurance of Eleanor's awareness of their shared carnal knowledge. To Jane, this simple gesture would have sufficed, but Eleanor instead chose to flee. The brutal honesty of this undisclosed matter was too great an onus for Eleanor to admit to anyone, let alone herself.

To not only Jane's exasperation, she abstained evermore from attending her once enrapturing evening ritual.

XXV

Eleanor was sickened at what Jane had proposed. Such things were unmentionable and should remain so. Eleanor thought back to Miss Welden's description of Jane as 'uncivilized' and how everyone else said she was retarded and weird except of course for Winchester, but whether he, himself, was retarded and weird was debatable in itself. If Jane wanted to remain ignorant and brutish, the treatment she often received from others was inevitable and there was no other way around this sad reality. Jane had chosen her lot, so whatever befell her was, in a sense, her own doing. A macabre expression seized her features, making her feel strangely dizzy and exhilarated. Yes, Jane was indeed a piteous creature, and after all, she had offered her help, but with that family of hers, and her promiscuous ways, what could anyone expect? Jane was a lost case indeed and Eleanor was secretly gratified. How dare she speak to her in such a manner!

By the time Eleanor reached the schoolhouse, the girls had already assembled. The winter sun caused Eleanor to shiver, suddenly conscious of the nippy air. The day seemed perfect for their scheduled festivities. Effie nodded to Eleanor as she drew near.

"Are you sure she will be there by herself? I hope he won't be with her. It would greatly complicate matters, Eleanor." Effie's little face scrunched up in distress.

"I've worked the whole thing out myself. There is no cause for alarm or concern," Eleanor boldly uttered.

But from the indication on Effie's face, her insecurities were not assuaged.

Eleanor became irritated at Effie's want of valour. She eyed Effie, and in a patronizing voice exclaimed, "When we plan a feat, and we agree upon the execution, one is expected to keep one's word. If you are confused in this matter, speak now, otherwise hold your peace."

Effie shrank from Eleanor's mounting wrath. "I'm sorry, Eleanor. Of course, what you say is true. Forgive my ineptitude."

Eleanor acknowledged this plea by saying, "Are we ready, then?"

The girls began in their progression to the river. The air was fresh and a breeze gently stirred the surrounding vegetation. A man on his tractor passed by on the road and nodding in greeting, smirked to himself at the idea of such young, lovely ladies being the bearers of such serious faces. A winter rabbit froze in mid-stride, sniffing the air in response to the ground vibration of the troupe, only to bolt off, startled, into the dried, decaying grasses.

Effie glanced up nervously at Eleanor's beaming aspect. She dared not speak in case of offending the depth of Eleanor's seemingly decreed silence. Eleanor knew that Jane would not be expecting them: They would both be down there by the tree.

Just as suspected, she could see the tree vibrating with movement in the distance. Eleanor smiled with sheer delight. Unexpectedly, the procession slowed and suddenly halted.

"What's wrong? Why are we stopped?" she challenged Effie, with blatant animosity.

Effie fidgeted, uneasily. "They think it's a wild animal, and are afraid to proceed."

Eleanor stated loudly and frankly, "There is no need to be alarmed. The motion you see is not a wild animal. I will prove this by leading the way. Follow me, but don't hang too far back, or all will be in vain."

Just as Eleanor conjectured, pants bordering his ankles, eyes closed, hips gyrating to what Eleanor thought must have been a previously negotiated rhythm, Winchester was softly 'hiss-moaning', while Jane's mouth became, as always, the pleasure-designated receptacle.

Eleanor, who was standing erect, self-righteous, and seemingly pious, yet covertly heavily aroused, stopped before this disgraceful display of vagrant lust.

Eleanor nodded solemnly. As the procession caught up to Eleanor, Effie stood in horror, while the rest of them either cried out or giggled mischievously.

When they both realized that they were accumulating a considerable audience, Jane ceased her actions, glaring defiantly at Eleanor and her entourage. Winchester was hoisting his bottoms, while attempting to flee, exclaiming as he did so, "Jesus Christ! It's a fucking church picnic!"

Jane sat still and naked, her golden skin blending agreeably with the rotting grasses. She did not speak, preferring to wait for Eleanor to act.

For a moment Eleanor hesitated, feeling a profound pang of shame.

Effie broke the awkwardness with her shrill, rising tones. "You said *he* wouldn't be here! You gave me your word, Eleanor!"

Eleanor had forgotten Effie's presence and those of the others, as well. "Well, he isn't here now, you babbling imbecile."

Effie jerked back, obviously wounded.

The retort departed Eleanor's lips before she realized the meaning conveyed. Right now, she could only think of the form before her, the way the hair of her underarms and privates may have been spun of gold wire.

"Effie, I'm sorry. Leave us, please."

Effie, albeit still hurt, conceded the order.

Jane only looked grimly at Eleanor. Still, she refused to speak.

Eleanor was becoming more and more agitated.

Finally, the silence was broken, as Eleanor blurted out, "Well, do you have anything to say for yourself?"

"I see you are the judge and jury here. I believe you should be more familiar with that commandment than I, Eleanor."

As always, Eleanor was now infuriated. "What commandment is that you are referring to?" Eleanor barked.

"Judge not lest ye be judged," Jane replied.

Eleanor pulled at the grass, impatient and deeply disturbed.

"I believe it was you who was doing all the judging the other day. Do you have anything else to say in your defense?"

"I didn't realize I was on trial." Jane tersely asserted.

Eleanor saw that the girls were dispersed aimlessly across the field and on the roadside. From behind the tree, their positions were temporarily obscured. Eleanor approached her criminal.

Jane smiled, while taking her hand, but this time Eleanor did not resist. "Have you passed judgement, as yet?"

Jane placed Eleanor's finger between the woven gold strands, until she could feel the division of the caverned wetness. Jane breathed in a heavy, intoxicated slur, "Do I have any final requests?"

Eleanor stared, transfixed, yet horrified.

Jane used the digit as though she were employing a chiseler's implement, carefully, thoroughly, deeply, burrowing out an inside passage to the other side. Eleanor hypnotically channeled as bade to in the temporary hush. Flesh as her canvas, sight failed her as the usually smooth surface had become an interior region as altering in texture as in moisture. Only the use of her tactile sense befitted her charge. As Jane proceeded to increase the cadence, Eleanor heard the quickening of breath, rising in pitch, only to become painfully cognizant of the fact that the expiration was indeed her own.

Her sudden and acute consciousness struck her momentarily deaf and dumb. A colossal wave of shame and self-reproach washed over her, and pulling away, she lost her balance, stumbling backwards.

Jane sat up. "What's the matter? *Cat got your tongue?*"

Jane's scathing remark smoldered. But, Eleanor could only gawk in disbelief at what had just transpired.

"Well, this time you appeared to be enjoying yourself to say the least."

"Shut up, you retarded pervert! You're disgusting and so is that illiterate, uncivilized family of yours! It's no wonder! Effie! Effieee..." Eleanor hollered in hysteria.

Effie appeared from the other side of the tree, her face red and cast downward. "Yes Eleanor, what is it?"

"Where are the others?" Eleanor stammered as she attempted to gain back her composure.

"They're by the river. Shall I call them, now?"

"Yes, now Effie, now!"

"Okay, you don't have to yell at me."

"Just do it!" Eleanor screamed.

Once the girls had assembled, Eleanor noticed that Jane was beginning to shiver frightfully.

"Get dressed!" Eleanor dictated.

Jane only looked up incredulously. Apparently, she had no desire to move.

"Get dressed, I said."

Jane remained stationary.

Eleanor did not want to be responsible for Jane's hypothermia, so she ordered Effie to dress her.

"Why me?" Effie whined.

"Just do it!" Eleanor persisted in the same abrupt, uncharacteristic manner.

"Okay, okay," Effie finally conceded.

Once she was dressed, the procession picked her up by her arms and legs, dragging her down to the frozen rill.

Marching down and out onto this frozen rivulet, this intended body observed as Eleanor began her carefully-crafted diatribe.

"Jane, today I have assembled myself and our fellow classmates in order to show you the 'right' path. You have sorely strayed from this path of righteousness which all of us to some extent are meant to take, and if no one else will be the voice of reason, then I, alone, find it thus necessary to elect myself this duty. Your behaviour with one Mr. Winchester Farling is not, I repeat, not in any way acceptable, and for your own good, I cannot allow such behaviour to persist in future.

Therefore, you must abstain from any contact with the aforesaid Mr. Farling and any family relations in order to redeem yourself in the eyes of our Lord and Saviour, Jesus Christ. If you are engaged in any other behaviour which is unacceptable, distasteful, and therefore ungodly, this must be stopped at once, as well. For the previous unacceptable and thus ungodly relations with the aforesaid Mr. Farling, the fair and lenient sentence of ten exposures to this here ice will be administered at once, without further ado. Do you have anything to say on your own behalf, since there is no representative here to speak for you?" Eleanor was calmer now.

Jane said nothing, glancing up briefly to exchange a look of profound animosity towards her trier.

"In that case, proceed with the meted punishment." Eleanor prompted the assembled mass.

The girls lifted Jane's dress, pulled down her undergarments, and prepared to carry out the said ruling.

Like a giant peach had left its imprint on the frosty surface, the girls, as per Eleanor's counsel, ceased. The punishment had been exacted. Eleanor felt giddy and oddly vindicated. Waving her hand, she proclaimed loudly, "That will be all girls. Your work was greatly helpful in the righting of Jane's aberrations, and I, on behalf of the Lord Almighty, thank you." Eleanor bowed. Jane lay there gaping into the omnipresent whiteness and glare of a spiteful winter sky.

When everyone had left, Jane got up. "Do you actually believe that shit that sprang from your lips, today? Or, do you have at least some sanity remaining?"

"Of course I do. And I hoped that you would take my condemnation seriously, but I can see it is to no fruition."

"To no fruition? Is the Lord Almighty now channeling through you or some such ridiculous thing?"

"Well, I can see what your attitude is anyway. So, why does it matter? Obviously, I cannot help you."

"I specifically did not ask for *your* help," Jane's voice was waxing, and as she advanced towards Eleanor, whose stance was pious, and condescending, intending upon shoving Eleanor's face into the gritty frozen residue, the ice beneath her caved in, leaving a jagged, chiselled perforation to the underworld below.

Eleanor, awe-stricken, heard her shriek as if she had been injured in passage, as she entered this iridescent world. Hades had his most desired visitor.

XXVI

Darkness arrived like an unwelcomed visitor: the persistence of deepening shadow, intangible shapes and figures that seemed to shift from under the frozen shallows. The hunt had begun. Beams darted erratically from behind the sparse undergrowth of the banks and along the stream's sometimes sleek covering. Broken in patches, the rivulet could not support the weight of the gathered attendants. A few boat lights glimmered, in the reach, on the undulating surface at the river's mouth, in anticipation of the small, golden spectre to be exhumed from the stream's gloomy clutches.

Eleanor was beside herself. After Jane had broken through, her only thought being how the entirety of the incident had been, and would be, her fault. She was a murderer. Guilt sunk its tentacles deep into her receptive epidermis. Eleanor had again become mute, not germinated from wrath, but this time longing, and in turn, repentance.

Tearstains marked her frost-bitten flesh. Jane... Jane... she could almost hear her distant calling... almost indiscernible, but in the chill midwinter silence, sound had been stifled, as if a hard boot had kicked a child's ear, shattering the drum... yet the pitch was unmistakably hers.

Eleanor's mother came to her, placing a well-worn sweater over her bony shoulders. "Oh, Eleanor. You both should have known better." At the sharpness of her words, Eleanor resumed her muffled sobbing.

"Stop it, Eleanor. What were you two doing out here, anyway? Didn't you know the stream was breaking?"

Eleanor could only stare helplessly at her chosen admonisher. Suddenly, a light flashed across her field of vision, blinding her. Her sight was bleary and her eyes sore. However, she could not protect herself from further violation of the light. Roving flashlights lit up the dried shrubs and grasses. The flawed ice reflected the beams, glistening as if spotlights heralded the arrival of tonight's performers.

"Eleanor, Jane's father will be asking me. What happened today?"

she prodded mercilessly.

"I... I... tink I ned some water... please." This time Eleanor was not fabricating. The disjointed words were regurgitated from her consciousness, and Eleanor was rendered powerless in their passing.

The woman's left eye narrowed and she looked to her daughter in consternation, mingled with the conception of a seeming mistrust.

Eleanor had never seen this particular look present on her mother's face. For an instant, she started back, and then was bombarded with such an unmitigated deluge of shame and guilt, that she burst into a spasm of absolute blubbering.

Her mother, being surprised at this outpouring, went to get the requested sustenance. Upon returning, Eleanor had plunked herself down on the decaying foliage and was still blubbering disconsolately.

"Eleanor, you must act more your age. You've always been oversensitive. Be still now. Get up." Reaching down, she attempted to help Eleanor to her feet.

At this unwanted disclosure, Eleanor glared adamantly at the chastening's source, all the while obstinately pulling away.

"Okay, stay there. But don't give me any of that gabble. I won't have it," her mother reproached.

Eleanor's head sank in despair. She had nothing to say to such an unsympathetic sermonizer.

For a moment, a look, unused, discarded, and nearly-forgotten, crossed the tired woman's visage, and a sound emerged, almost resembling a coo.

Eleanor, in anticipation of something she recognized from long ago and far away, instinctively responded, and a gentle smile filled the contours of her heavily-stained cheeks.

Then, as if snapped from this trance-like state, the woman curtly retorted, "It's okay. It's not your fault. Simply tell me what happened so I can tell that father of hers."

As the intended meaning struck her reasoning capacity, she became all too aware of a twisting sensation, swelling her innards. Abruptly, she vomited into the surrounding vegetation, and as if this purging had released the miasmic substance which had suppressed her faculty of speech, the logical patterning and generation of words returned to her.

"It is my fault," Eleanor loudly asserted. "That is the problem. It is so." An eerie calmness now seemed to pervade her dissertation.

Shock registered on the woman's usually expressionless countenance. "Don't say such things! Someone might hear you! Be quiet! There is no need to say such things!"

Eleanor scrutinized this now-garbling figure before her. Her words only pounded against, reverberating off the shore of her mind. Her mother's life had been a monotonous endurance race of babies, work, and more babies, like so many that came before and would come after. But if their bond had genuinely meant anything, it seemed to be severed in the use of this apathetic spiel of offensive gibberish. A nonsensical being stood before her, uttering meaningless commands that signified nothing. All of her endless labours had brought her to this placelessness, the arrival of the orphaned in the land of nothingness.

Eleanor blinked. "Yes, you are right, mother," she articulated in apparent acquiescence.

Her mother could only stare blankly at the pale form before her, vaguely wondering at the implied meaning of this unexpected affirmation.

XXVII

Eleanor remained with the rescue party even after all the others had gone home. They had been searching for nearly five hours and nothing, no sign of her, had been unearthed.

Lights continued to bob, twinkling on the far-off surface. The illumination of foliage had ceased, and the remaining participants gathered at the mouth. Eleanor was alone. A gentle breeze rose and the scent of a pervasive sweetness, like all of those other times, beckoned her. To go where? Why? She could feel the hole, so vast and trackless, like the charting above, the inscrutable, impenetrable darkness.

Eleanor rocked within the blackness, her knees resting against her chest. The cold had numbed her haunches, but the numbness was all she desired. Time was frozen, and shattered with the breaking stream. The darkness was her only true friend now and welcomed like the soft, hushing voice of a stranger.

A rising mist obliterated any further efforts of the party. If only, she hadn't... the price of everything, the value of nothing. Only darkness remained. The prism had been broken. The canvas unfinished. The knowledge of ignorance. As if a primary color had been stolen by an achromatic thief, grown weary of his state, and willing finally to sell his soul to Mephistopheles for only a moment... only a moment of God-given light.

The mist had captured form and without form, substance vanished, leaving only memory... like the collective unconscious, it persisted and replaced grief. Memory, being that which it is, a function it is meant to serve, a grieving and a simultaneous celebration of life and life's identical twin, death. Eleanor wondered how she would live without this divine spirit, which always knew what her true purpose was, meant, when she could not admit this truth to herself... And now it was gone. And the only one she could blame was herself. She had destroyed her creator. The ultimate sin had been committed and in the circular net of blame, she had been caught.

The bone-chilling effects of the mist were now being felt, yet Eleanor refused to acknowledge the trivial nature of this harsh, physical reality. She welcomed the pain. At least the numbness had been replaced by something, something other than grief... physical pain was a worthy competitor to serve as a substitute for psychic affliction. Her hands and feet were the first to acknowledge this sharp throbbing. But before it could advance further into her extremities, she felt a little tapping on her shoulder.

There, standing behind her, eating pomegranate seeds, was the spectre of Jane, the likeness uncanny, translucent except for a golden aura surrounding its small frame: a mist creature, who had been summoned by no other than Eleanor herself. She repented at the unconditional forgiveness she knew she could never have deserved, weeping at the omnibenevolence of the Creator. Reaching out to touch Jane, a current of watery, red liquid spilt out of Jane's mouth and ran down Eleanor's outstretched arm. She retracted in terror thinking this spectre may have arrived to avenge its slayer. Fatigued from grief and cold, Eleanor saw the approach of another of these mist beings, and at the implication of what this could mean, blacked out, becoming again part of the assuaging darkness.

XXVIII

Eleanor's mouth foamed. Colours combined in erratic, undisciplined fashionings, the canvas not even on par with an unrefined amateur's. She bellowed out a continuous stream of inarticulate commentary, trying to condemn the pigments for their mutinous behavior.

Eleanor's mother's brow furrowed with concern. The burden of fever, accompanied by tremors and fits, had expended the remainder of the period prior to the coming of dawn.

Eleanor coughed. The night's rigmarole had proved far too rigorous for Eleanor's weakened constitution. Pasty herself, she had taken on the image of the spectres of her hallucinations, although they were disjointed, and oddly, flamboyantly attired.

As if a tunnel of obscurity stood between her and the dark, wooden room she recognized as her own, Eleanor vaguely perceived a fixed outline before her and heard the sound of vigorous chewing. Her forehead glistened, proof of the past night's taxing exertions.

"Eleanor, are you going to lie in bed all day, or what?"

The voice was strangely too familiar.

Eleanor's eyes popped open and as she grappled with her deficiency of vision, the gleam of a golden tendril brushed her raw, chapped cheek.

"Is it... is that *you*?"

"If you mean Jane, yes that's me."

"But you drowned. I drowned you."

"No, I swam to where I knew there was broken ice and I scurried into the bushes and went home before I permanently froze."

"I thought you were dead. I thought I'd killed you."

"No, you didn't. Don't flatter yourself."

"Didn't you see me there over the hole, screaming and crying?" With the last word of this statement, Eleanor proceeded to lose her already-weak voice.

"Yes, I did. But I thought you could use a lesson or two, yourself. I did not know the whole town was out scouring land and water for me, until my father went to the store in the evening to find everybody in a state of panic, trying to elect the sorry bastard who would tell him what had happened. It was all kind of funny once it got straightened out. However, nobody knew you were out there. When you didn't come home, your mother came looking for you, thinking you might be with me. I don't know what would make her think that. But anyways, we went out looking for you and found you, half-frozen and quivering, mumbling something about 'mist-beings' or some such fantasy and then brought you here. And I have been here all night, listening to your fits of deliria."

"Jane?"

"Yes, Eleanor."

"I'm tired now."

"So am I."

"Thank-you, Jane."

At that, Jane smiled and continued to munch on her once thought-to-be phantom pomegranate seeds.

XXIX

Peter stood ready for his opponent's advance. Fisticuffs were a regular occurrence, except Peter was not wont to engage in such skirmishes. Today's offender had provoked his opponent by affronting the untainted reputation of the aforementioned, Effie Black.

"I know what you two did in the bushes yesterday!" the offender blared. "Effie's a tart! Effie is a tart!" he sang out the brutish melody.

Effie's eyes stung from hot, angry tears and in exasperation she looked to Peter for reinforcement.

Peter remained, bobbing and weaving, ready for his grimacing counterpart to take the first swing.

At wit's end, Effie implored, "I am not the word you so callously use to ridicule me, and I do not care for the inference." At that, Effie burst into a convulsion of tears.

Peter, helpless to alleviate Effie's torment, became increasingly incensed and continued to bob and weave, although more quickly, to which his opponent responded by an infuriating guffaw that shocked and repulsed the injured party as well as the onlookers.

Turning to leave, the offender, thinking Peter to be as impotent as he appeared, was jabbed on his left temple. At once, the blood spurted and started to pour. Peter, still bobbing and weaving, was ready for more, but the boy lay, unconscious of the spit which promptly landed on his eyelid.

Effie, enamoured, dashed to Peter, who had not yet stopped his now-preposterous stance.

"Peter, my hero," Effie gushed.

Peter, who looked as pale as a ghost, nodded and said nothing.

Jane, who had been one of the observers, let out a giggle of suppressed amusement. Effie glared malevolently at the origin of this unprovoked outburst.

"If you have something to say, be out with it, or hold your tongue," Effie's words were cautionary.

"No, I have nothing to say," although Jane's leer belied her assertion.

"If you have something to say, say it or go away," Effie advised, her tone ever more sharp.

"I was just contemplating that you are not the sole benefactor of his alms," Jane's smile became at once demure, yet sly.

"What are you trying to say? You're not making any sense, although I don't know why that surprises me." Effie turned again towards Peter, dismissing the 'retarded girl's' peculiar and seemingly-nonsensical claim.

Jane, herself, spun around to leave. As she did, she called out, "Ask Peter, if you're wondering."

Effie dispelled the odd form of her rhetoric.

Peter was suddenly overtaken by the most bizarre aspect that she had ever seen materialize on his considerably handsome physiognomy, in all of the years which the two of them had known one another, as his hazel leer followed Jane's Epicurean movements, as she languidly departed the schoolyard.

XXX

It took a good week for Eleanor to surmount the bacterium which had invaded her still-weak system and a week after that to sufficiently thaw out. No one, except for Jane, wanted Eleanor to hurry back. Everyone was hoping that the just-recovered child prodigy would take her time to get well, realizing that Eleanor could easily revert to her previously diminished mental capacity if pushed to return too quickly. Two weeks later, still apt to fits of coughing, Eleanor was again faced with the task of choosing her lunching compatriots although she knew, within her psyche, that such a choice did not actually exist.

Eleanor positioned herself in the lunchroom in her customary spot, next to Effie Black, who currently paid no attention to her regular lunchmate, Eleanor's presence apparently no longer required.

"Well, that's sure a nice greeting after two whole weeks!" Eleanor scolded.

Effie sideglanced her, and speaking awkwardly from the corner of her mouth, said, "Can't you see I'm busy? Peter just walked in and he's looking right at us!" As the lunchroom buzzed with the crinkle of wax wrappings and unfolding paper bags, between this, the sound of munching, and the din of rising voices, Eleanor barely heard Effie's caustic reply.

"Good grief, Effie. You're acting juvenile... positively juvenile."

"Suit yourself, Eleanor. You're such a pious priss anyway," Effie retorted.

"A what?" Eleanor, flabbergasted, inquired.

"You heard me." Effie's sideglance momentarily became a stare.

"I thought you may have missed me, but apparently I was sorely mistaken," Eleanor swallowed hard at the unexpected impact of this attack.

Suddenly, Peter winked at Effie, who became so agitated she shifted back and forth nervously on the wooden bench, not to mention acquiring a few stabbing splinters in the process.

Refocusing, Effie glared at Eleanor, boldly asserting, "Well, Patricia scored at least as high as you have in all of her subjects, and besides she's nice to me and doesn't order me around as much."

"Congratulations to the two of you, then. I hope you will be very happy together. Good day." After this dissertation, Eleanor promptly rose, lunch in hand, and traversed the distance to the other side of the room, stopping purposefully, yet momentarily, at one winker's table in order to convey a few spontaneous, though well-placed, syllables.

Bending down, she breathed, "Meet me after school, behind the building."

Peter's look conveyed astonishment and confusion.

"You'll understand why later," Eleanor nodded.

Peter, shrugging his shoulders, replied, "Okay, Eleanor. I'll see you then."

The green-eyed monster fumed from across this short expanse of space. Phase one was successful. Effie and Patty were in for a surprise or two. If only they knew. Soon, they would be enlightened, too.

XXXI

Peter waited, hopping back and forth, playing an imaginary game of hopscotch. Eleanor recognized her chance and when his back was averted, made her approach. Tapping him gently on the shoulder, Eleanor observed him visibly flinch. He was somewhat of a wimp for someone who could 'sucker punch' if the need arose.

"Geez Eleanor, I didn't see ya there."

"Well, here I am."

"What was it ya want to tell me?" Peter's eyebrows knitted together, becoming one extended brow.

"I don't know." Eleanor feigned modesty, lowering her head. "I wanted to ask you something, but I was afraid you'd say no," Eleanor maligned.

"What?" his tactlessness was obvious.

"Can I whisper it in your ear?" Eleanor blinked.

"I guess." The innocent expression persisted, unaltering.

Yet as Eleanor delicately proposed the undertaking, a look of shock and curiosity, blended like any of Eleanor's Promethean hues which may or may not endure.

"Eleanor, young ladies don't do nothin' like that!" Peter's reproachful glance was adamant, although Eleanor was piqued by his lesser reaction.

"I never said I was a lady. I am a scholar, but sometimes, contrary to popular opinion, the two do not coincide."

"Eleanor! If anyone heard ya, ya know what they'd say?!"

Peter was sincere in the attempt, even though an irksome sensation had begun to grip his loins, but Eleanor could not easily be waylaid.

"I am a tart, simply put." Eleanor bowed at this avowal.

Peter's mouth gaped, and for a moment a sound emitted giving Eleanor the distinct impression of a vast and gargantuan vacuum.

Eleanor took the lead. "This contract will go undisclosed as long as you choose not to reveal it, and it is for your pleasure only, which means that you may terminate it at any time of your choosing."

The innocent expression lingered and suddenly abated.

"Why are ya offerin' me this? And no one will know? Is this a trick or somethin'?" Now, suspicion mixed with irritation at this new possibility.

"It is no trick. I wish to prove a point. That is all. The choice is yours. Take it or leave it. I only ask you to decide, now."

"And it's my choice?" Arousal had defeated suspicion, respectability and, the greatest vice of all, innocence.

Eleanor beamed. "Shall we?"

She led him into the surrounding thicket, although his liver never properly grew back.

XXXII

Peter, head pinned between brambles, looked as if the crown-of-thorns graced his acutely reclining pate.

Pants adorning his ankles, hips swinging wildly, Peter was in his own self-created Eden.

Birds twittered eagerly in the thicket, responding to his mounting ululation. Finally, he groaned.

"Wow, that sure felt great! You're even better than that smart girl ya used to buddy around with. Are you sure I don't owe ya or somethin'?"

After Jane had swallowed, her usual smile disappeared. "No. What girl I used to hang around with?"

"Gee whiz Janey, I wasn't sposed to say nothin'."

"You mean, Eleanor?" Jane insisted.

"Yeah, that's her. But ya won't say nothin', will ya?"

"No. I just never would have guessed, that's all. I wonder what

Effie would have to say about all of this."

"Effie? Why? You're not gonna tell 'er are ya? I mean Effie's respectable and smart and besides, she really likes me." A look of vexation abruptly distorted his usually-inviting features.

"Don't worry your balls off. I'm not gonna say nothin'. There's just one thing you could do for me, though." Jane's eyebrow rose seductively.

"What?" Peter's trousers still stood agape.

"Give my lips one more workout. They're just a little on the tight side today."

Peter smiled and winked at his chosen possessor.

Like a spell of deja vu, golden tendrils shone, undulating in the dusky afternoon light, all the while the ecstatic twittering recommencing, as the much-foraged-for nesting matter caressed the loins of one already-moaning recipient.

XXXIII

Jane madly licked the tubular vessel before her. Kneeling, she awaited the stream of succulent sweetness to emerge, spewing down her itching gullet.

Today, their usual afternoon occupation brimmed with freakish urgency. Brambles bent and snagged in their ardent fervor. Practically climbing atop her head, in escalating gratification, he yanked formidably on a trailing tendril, which instantly broke Jane's concentration, causing her to extort a loud and easily discernible, "Ouch, that hurt."

Peter, unaware of his action, albeit all too readily perceptive of the cessation of Jane's delicately moist applications, discharged a vehement whine.

"Geez Jane, did you have to stop right then?"

"I wouldn't have stopped if one brute hadn't pulled out a clump of my hair. Look, stupid."

Beneath his feet was the said clump, laying in a long arcing mass of radiance.

"Geez, I'm sorry. I didn't mean to," his apology was sincere, yet Jane was not appeased.

Jane's cheeks suffused with a bright red cerise, and prepared to impart her protestation, stopped in midstream.

"What? Are ya okay? Can I do somethin' to make it up to ya?" Peter bumbled.

"Come here." The gentle afternoon breeze quickened.

Not ready for what might ensue, Peter still advanced, his hardness becoming undeniably more obvious with each successive step.

Gnashing at his trousers, her tongue lapped the protrusion as if she were attempting to consume the monstrosity.

Rocking back and forth as if possessed by a daemon, the heightening pleasure becoming a keen and ever-present agony, he again grabbed her head, this time forcefully pressing it repeatedly towards his tumescent masculinity. Uncontrollably moaning, nearing the greatest bliss he had ever known, he bellowed wildly, "I love ya, Janey."

Jane's ears burned as the words vibrated within her drum, their deafening reverberations piercing her brain. The utterance seemed vaguely familiar... but she could not recall their derivative. The itching of her gullet suddenly waned, and all at once, the profound depths of an abysmal and impenetrable sadness overtook her. Their present, trenchant usage unleashed a tribe of cannibalistic daemons. Jane, sucking frantically, her orifice engulfing the entirety of the corpus as Peter mashed her head into the engorged, fleshy matter, keenly and deftly bit, as his daemon elixir cascaded down the interior of her receptive gullet. Eagerly swallowing, still chewing and sucking, the taste of the sanguine sweetness was exhilarating to the deprived palate of her many possessors.

Screaming in agony, Peter beating her, ripping at the source of the golden tendrils, cried out, "Ya bit it off! Get off! Get off!"

As his fists gripped, wrenching the locks from their follicles, they continued to extract the warm, salty distillate from the carnaged mass. Birds chirped madly in the consuming darkness, as the blood-bespattered-ground was now littered with priceless, golden tresses.

Dizzy from terror and anguish, Peter's eyes rolled grievously, as he proceeded to land bitterly on the ground, striking his head on a protruding rock as he plummeted. Blood gushed from this wound as they licked at the fresh fountainhead. Removing her dress, Jane proceeded to imbibe the required sustenance until they, finally satiated, were allayed.

Then, in the subsequent seraphic silence, she rubbed the butchered structure along the interior of her thighs and lips, until covered in blood and dried come, she wailed continuously in rapid succession for an extended duration, never attained before, nor to be after.

Tears flowed from their unleashed ducts, sealed from disuse, mixing with the gore and torn fibers strewn over this scene of sacred plunder.

XXXIV

Movement could be discerned within the bushes, then a rising giggle escaped.

Effie clasped her small hand over her little mouth, on the verge of laughter.

"Can I play with it, again? Pleease, Peter." Effie batted her eyelashes in mock entreaty.

"Well, I really do like ya, Effie. It's just that it doesn't... well... uh," Peter grasped for the hidden explanation.

She grabbed at it anyway. "Peter, oh Peter. I missed it so much," Effie breathed.

Peter pulled away.

Effie looked devastated.

Starting to cry, the customary tone entering her speech, she implored, "Peter, don't you like me, anymore?"

"I like ya more than anybody. Really Effie, I do. It's just it had a little accident and it's real sore now. Honest, Effie. I wouldn't lie to ya, honest." This time Peter's look was beseeching.

Quieter now, Effie queried, "What happened to it?"

"Well, it sort of well, got, well..." As Peter grappled for the truth, his face became ever redder.

"Well, what?" Effie, exacerbated, insisted.

"It got... hurt... ya that's it, hurt." Peter was satisfied.

Effie looking all the time progressively more muddled, finally incensed stated, "That's obvious Peter. How did it get hurt? I assume a tractor didn't run over it."

Peter was momentarily perplexed that Effie hadn't been placated with his initial response, but nevertheless, attempted a second time to vindicate himself.

"Well, that's just it, Effie. Yes, that's it."

Flabbergasted, Effie exclaimed, "A tractor ran over it?!"

Peter, realizing his second attempt had also failed, was now rendered speechless.

"Peter, let me see it, for God's sake!" Effie screeched.

Peter, annoyed at himself for his lack of fabrication tactics, and at the level of Effie's shrill tone, finally at wit's end, declared, "Jane did it, okay? Jane..." As Effie's eyes widened, Peter became silent yet again, and chose this time to say nothing.

"Jane, what did Jane do?" Effie screeched in shock. The bushes vibrated from the sheer intensity of her pitch.

"Jane, um, Jane.... ya know," Peter mumbled.

"No, Peter. I don't know. Show it to me."

At the idea of such a divulgence, Peter shuttered. Needing to appease her, somehow, he alleged, "Jane attacked me. She just came at me and kicked me a lot in the nuts. Pardon me, Effie. And no, I won't show ya Effie, 'cause it's way too gross for no young lady to see."

Effie was horrified.

That Jane-girl was not only retarded and perverted, she was violent as well. Such an individual should not be present in a classroom. Just as she suspected, Jane was more animal than girl. A primitive nature, indeed! The idea of a girl savagely beating a boy's privates! How malicious! How repugnant! How embarrassing for Peter to have to convey to his sweetheart. A thought momentarily interrupted her outrage, but just as quickly, she dismissed its logical relevance.

"Something must be done or said about this problem," Effie descried.

"I have an idea," Peter ruminated.

"A good one, too," he stressed the poignancy of the utterance.

"What is it?" Effie earnestly inquired.

He whispered the peculiar plan into Effie's awaiting canal.

"You're definitely no genius but that just might work, Peter," Effie endorsed.

Winking at her, he kissed her sloppily on her freckled cheek.

Yen

XXXV

Peter, his limp self-evident, scowled at the distant creature before him. A few had enlisted with the help of Effie's persuasive tactics. In turn, they were each in possession of an entire pack of unopened Marlboro's. Although no one, especially Effie, was made privy to his involuntary circumcision, they each, in turn, had their own reasons for participating. Anyway, a pack of smokes wasn't a bad swap. All they had to do was hold her down. Peter said he'd do the rest.

Jane always knew when she was cornered. Two larger boys came up from the rear, the other two advanced from the fore. Jane vaguely recognized these smirking faces. She remembered one of the boys asking her if he could walk her home. She recalled his hands being perpetually dirty and constantly rubbing his genitalia as though he had fleas.

Jane fiercely proclaimed, "What is the meaning of this? I know none of you personally. What is this all about?" Jane, however, was more irritated than scared.

"You'll know soon enough," the dirty-handed boy retorted as he scratched his privates fervently.

The schoolyard was empty except for two approaching figures. The sky was white with the promise of snow, but as the warming trend had already been initiated, perhaps, as usual, rain would serve as spring's harbinger. One of the figures limped badly and the other appeared to be attempting to help. Instant realization hit Jane like a thunderous wave.

Peter, smoking, stood directly before her, blocking her view. Leaning in, he stated, "Jane, I guess ya know what this is about. Now, don't ya?"

"I'm just sorry it ended up happening that way. I like the way it tasted. A lot better than most," Jane grinned.

Effie could not believe her ears. "You're nothing but a hussy, and not just any hussy, a mad one at that!" Effie screeched, like a demented gull.

The group cringed as her inflection assumed the tone of this shrieking bird.

"Honey, with a voice like that, you don't have a hope," Jane sneered.

Peter, like most of the others present, neared laughter, but upon further reflection, desisted.

Finally tiring of the charade, Jane inquired, "What are you going to do with me? And by the way, Peter, did you tell her how many times you came with me? Bet it was more than she could ever hope, that is with the handicap of that voice and all." Jane had gathered her bearings and reveled in the present omen of a storm. The weather hadn't been much interest of late.

"Can I suck it some more? Let me make it better. I can." Jane's voice lilted.

The assembled party was slightly bent in their midsection due to the erotic quiver permeating her voice, like a snake charmer, enticing arousal. The flea-infested youth seemed to flay frantically.

Effie on the other hand, stood in horror at what Jane was proposing. Could it be? It seemed much more credible than the idea of a strapping youth beaten by a slight, albeit mad, girl. No, she could never believe this maliciousness. It was precisely what she wished her to accept and she would not be a part of her charade. How dare she infer such falsehoods about her chivalrous Peter! The gall of that disturbed girl was more than she could withstand.

"Hold that Jane-girl down, Peter. She's going to pay. You won't do this to me ever again," Effie fumed at the top of her lungs.

At such a caterwaul, Mr. Dorset looked up from his final task of the day and saw to his elation, what seemed like a ruckus involving Jane.

Effie repeatedly kicked Jane in the groin. Her shoe was making a grubby indentation in Jane's white frock, and the pain was beginning to shoot in every direction. Peter, felt a brief sensation, and a temporary stiffening, but it stung, and quickly shrunk.

Peter, after watching Effie's foot repeatedly pound this fleshy area, wondered why she had not quit.

Jane began to squeal, and finally giving up her pride, begged her to stop.

Mr. Dorset had been watching enraptured from the schoolroom window, one hand anxiously jerking the agonizing swelling below. Hail pelted his window, adding a dramaturgical touch. At the sight of Jane's blood, he realized it was time for him to intervene.

Peter had become terrified at Effie's mania, but could not bring himself to act on Jane's behalf. After all, it was his idea, and what if Effie believed Jane's lies?

Blood connotated that her genitalia had been reduced to pulp, the agony being so great she could no longer move.

Mr. Dorset seized Effie, removing her.

Effie now became hysterical. Sobbing in fits, Peter offered to accompany her home, to which Mr. Dorset readily consented. The other boys, who had been smoking while the assault took place, had vanished into the storm.

They were alone at last. No bells, or pupils, and even better, no other teachers to interrupt with their constant, ill-timed disruptions.

He carried Jane back into the class, shutting and locking the door.

Anxiously, the hardness becoming all the time more pronounced, he proffered his aid, "Let me clean the wound. I know a little about first aid," he contrived.

She, in an obvious inarticulate stupor, consented to his maneuverings. When he had cleaned the wound sufficiently, he could no longer bear the sight of the pulpy purple plexus, and begging Jane to pose herself for only a few precious moments upon his exposed lap, she in obvious discomfort, snickered.

He, taking her response as an affirmation, positioned her there almost immediately, piercing the raw flesh, as she screamed in evident torment. The cry, like an aphrodisiacal substance, drove him into a state of unconditional frenzy. Thrusting in and out, the protuberant tissue spasmed momentarily, in order to not prolong the agony anymore than was required.

The surging current stung the exposed tissue acutely. Jane yelped from the strength of her suffering. Looking at her present victimizer she curtly stated, "So, I hear your fat, ugly wife is expecting again, sir."

Mr. Dorset fastidiously tucked in his shirt, calmly buttoned his trousers, as apathy mixed with gratification on his blunt, discolored aspect. "You shouldn't fool in other peoples' matters. Effie made that clear, and she's quite bright. You should listen to her." At this last statement, he picked up his wool coat, adjusted his glasses, patted her ailing cunt, and left the stale and rather odorous confines of the room.

A shadow seemed to pass by the keyhole. This storm shade blackened, suffusing the hidden dimensions of the adjoining doorway just past Mr. Dorset's. Eyes glistening, flashes of distant thunder, suggested a particular raising. Cain's wrath was not far from the slit being slashed by this lone observer's fixed gaze upon one certain victimizer's throat.

XXXVI

Standing, beaming in Patricia's direction, Effie proclaimed, "I have something serious which has, and continues, to aggrieve me considerably, and until I communicate this particularly vexatious matter to the class, I will have no peace. May I proceed, Mr. Dorset?" Effie earnestly entreated.

Although the class had been interrupted from their silent reading, Mr. Dorset's curiosity was piqued by the uncustomary manner of such an address. "Yes Effie, do indeed. Proceed."

Effie rose, prepared to impart her meticulously-phrased dissertation, "It has been brought to my attention of late that one presently unnamed individual has maliciously committed a grievous act against one of our fellow pupils. Being the intent was to severely injure a certain party's unmentionable regions, it has come to my attention that this culprit has no place in an institution of learning as their savage, malevolent, and inhumane behaviour necessitates their expulsion from such an institution, and as the injury sustained may have permanent side effects, I could not in good conscience allow this act to go without redress and hopefully, without disciplining the said offender." Effie seating herself, glared pretentiously at Jane.

Mr. Dorset, engrossed by Effie's allegation, an inflection of sadism permeating his tones, asserted with mock concern, "And who may this said offender be?"

Effie quivered in anticipation as her manipulation had evoked the desired response. Effie, head-held-high, pointed to one golden-haired muse, who was apparently dumb to the present proceedings.

Mr. Dorset nodded, trying to suppress a rising smile. "And the alleged victim?"

Effie and Patricia both in unison exclaimed, "Peter is, sir." Bobbing their heads in identical fashion, they looked at each other, then in tandem again asserted, "A most grievous occurrence, sir."

"Is that your official deposition then, Effie?" Mr. Dorset scrutinized his first character witness.

"Yes it is, Mr. Dorset," Effie stressed.

"For the said purpose of modeling a court of law, you will refer to me for the duration of these proceedings as, Your Honour," Mr. Dorset dictated.

"Sorry, Your Honour," Effie timidly amended.

"What Effie is proposing is known as hearsay. It is indirect, based only on what Peter said to Effie in confidence," Mr. Dorset addressed the class.

Turning his gaze to Peter, and looking at him from beneath his steel frames, he ominously uttered, "Is this so, Peter?"

"Yes it is, sir," Peter fidgeted uncomfortably, unsure if he would have to produce the evidence in question.

"Your Honour, Peter," Mr. Dorset impatiently admonished.

"Oh yeah. Sorry sir, Your Honour, sir," Peter attempted to redress.

Effie and Patricia looked to Peter sympathetically, then nodded emphatically.

In preparation for a spontaneous oration, and never tiring of his own didactic, yet stern, monotone, Mr. Dorset cleared his dry, parched throat. "In a democratic society, punishment is meted out by our judicial system in accordance with the verdict reached by a jury of the alleged criminal's peers. I say alleged because in a democracy, a person can only be tried under the law for a crime once, and he or she is presumed innocent until proven guilty. Now, in this case, what Effie is alleging is called circumstantial evidence, as she was not present at the actual incident and we have only her word of mouth to evaluate the ascertained 'facts'. Sometimes, once a verdict is reached, an appeal is made and the case is taken to a higher court. In this case, Peter is the plaintiff and Jane here, is the defendant. Jane, have you, acting here as your own counsel, considered how you will plead?"

"Guilty as charged, Your Honour." Jane's legs splayed, as she conveyed her plea.

"That is the correct procedure, Jane. Good. Do you see how she addressed me, promptly and with an estimable degree of respect?"

The class was silent.

"On behalf of Jane's plea, and the limited, circumstantial evidence presented, I wish the class to act as representative of a jury of her peers, that I momentarily alluded to, and decide accordingly. This will illustrate the institutional practice of democracy in action."

Everyone in the room voted guilty as charged, except for Winchester and Eleanor.

Winchester, aware of the ruling's corrupted purpose, could not bring himself to condemn Jane. Eleanor, also, sensed the corruption of institution.

Mr. Dorset conveyed a look of underlying fury at these two, sole dissenters.

"Well, normally when we have jury members who are not in complete accordance with one another, we have what is called 'a hung jury'. However, the judge can use his power to make the final decision in certain instances as I am electing myself this position and will adjudicate, as I see fit."

Polyhymnia had taken yet again another heinous blow. The class again fell silent.

Clearing his throat and raising his voice, he bellowed, "Jane, you are guilty as charged by the findings of this court, and will be sentenced to blackboard duty every day after school for the remainder of the term. Quite a lenient sentence, if I do say so myself." After this tirade, the adjudicator carefully adjusted his tightening trousers.

Astraea, conquered and rendered sterile, groped within the ensuing darkness for her now overturned scales.

XXXVII

The darkness of silence encompassed Eleanor like an impenetrable lair. Scratching crusty bits of dried tears from her cheeks, Eleanor sighed. In the scope of things, today had definitely been unusual, and as far as Eleanor could deliberate, unbearable was the only adjective she could deem appropriate. The current picked up, and she threw a tiny pebble into its eddies, which disappeared instantly within an emerging spiral.

The slight chill of the stirring wind caught under her skirt and she shivered from the sheer exertion of the day. She could not believe Effie Black's audacity at such a blatant proposal. Who did she think she was? A queen? Closer to a wood imp than any royal personage she had ever seen. What a bunch of idiotic, sniveling sheep, all following a hedonist's and a scorned girl's lead! A yellow-bellied, good-for-nothing bunch of inbred country bumpkins! If anyone had asked, Eleanor would have vented her waxing fury, except, of course, for Winchester. He had stood up for what was right and just. He would not be dissuaded by that pervert's rhetorical tactics. He knew what was morally right.

After the lecture, Jane had scurried out of the class, hurrying home. Today, the only time he would, he let her go, and did not call her back. She would have to learn that a harlot's behaviour entailed a harlot's life, and who better than he to teach her all he knew? And his knowledge on the subject was quite extensive indeed.

Eleanor rushed to Winchester before he could divert paths to his farmstead. "Winchester please, wait for me!" Eleanor beckoned.

"What do *you* want?" he growled.

"I just wanted to say, I thought your stand in there for Jane was highly commendable, that's all," Eleanor meekly imparted.

"Yeah, well I didn't do it for your praise. I did it 'cause that bloody old pervert can't wait to get his dirty paws on her, although she'd probably like it and all." Winchester said the final clause with head bowed.

"That's disgusting! You should be ashamed of yourself!" Eleanor preached.

"Yeah, what would you know? You're the one who told me in the first place that they were doing it. And I thought you were making the whole thing up to make me jealous. Turns out you were right. And I hate ya more than ever for that." At that, Winchester's lip curled with vicious intent.

Eleanor started to cry. "It doesn't matter what I do for you, you hate me anyway. You've always hated me, and all I ever wanted was for you to like me just a little."

"Yeah, I always knew you was a cry-baby. Cry-baby! Cry-baby!" Winchester chimed.

"Well, so what? She still does it with you, so what are you complaining about anyway?" Eleanor wiped her cheeks hard.

"That's what you would think. Since she started spending time in those there bushes with Peter everyday, she has no interest in me. That guy must squirt bloody honeysuckle or somethin' the way she gulps it down! Between Mr. Dorset and Peter, she doesn't give me the time of day. I'm lucky to get a few words out of that puckering little mouth before she's off again! That whore!" With the last word, Winchester started to weep. A soft, hissing sound escaped as the tears brimmed over, silently flowing, seeping into the parched earth. Gasping for air, Winchester reached out, and Eleanor instantly responded.

He may have hated her, but she would have done anything for him at that moment. It was as if the storm cloud was purging its hidden, spiritualistic drops.

"Winchester, can I do anything for you?" Eleanor inquired.

"Get Jane to like me, again," Winchester retorted bitterly.

"You know I have no power in the matter," Eleanor stated softly.

"Yeah, I know," Winchester nodded. "I just wish sometimes that she... that she... I dunno."

"Winchester, do you really hate me that much?"

"I dunno, I guess you're not so bad. I've never thought much about it."

"What about that time when we were all skating? When Jane... when we... what were you thinking?"

"Oh that, I don't remember too much. I was watching Jane's fingers as she touched her um... uh... body. I like watching Jane do that a lot."

Winchester didn't see the look of unmitigated torment cross her face.

"Oh," Eleanor breathed. She couldn't say anything else.

"I have to go now, Lenora. Bye." At that he rose, and left.

Eleanor sat transfixed by the name. Lenora, Lenora... it was a pretty name. She remembered a distant cousin having that name. Her mother had once mentioned a letter from a girl named Lenora. Suddenly, she wished she had paid more attention. In that moment, she had never hungered to be in possession of something with such intensity, such fervor, at any time that she could recall. Jane, Jane, Jane... maybe Effie was right in her condemnation. Hatred mingled with the previous purity of her reflections. Suddenly a graphic image of Mr. Dorset's cock penetrating Jane made Eleanor squirm with freakish delight. Winchester could have her. When he looked at her, he saw nothing. She may as well have never even existed. To him, she was formlessness itself, a blank canvas, utterly devoid of meaning, inspiring nothing in no one. Jumping to her feet, she ran down to the river, and sat on the bank in austere silence, hoping to fade into the diminishing radiance, or be carried into the current never to be found again.

The current, returning to its usual lackadaisical pace, temporarily arrested its incessant coiling. Formlessness slowly pervaded all. The shadows mocked this metamorphosis by their fluttering transformations. In the distant din, she could hear the sound of the gratified mariner beginning to climax. She too began the quickening finger cadence which occasioned the psychic palette to yet again saturate with chroma.

XXXVIII

He stood in the penumbra between the shadowed outer edge of the faded structure and the illuminated expanse of yard beyond. The hour's external stillness made the interval unbearable, as beads of sweat formed and trickled down his sticky brow.

Eyes temporarily averted, he returned to the scrutinization of the room's dull exterior, acutely conscious of the illicit performance which was undergoing its usual execution behind the institutional, dusky blinds that Mr. Dorset daily implemented to conveniently block the light. Pupils fixedly penetrating the boards of this deteriorating structure, teeth gnashing in choler, feet moving uneasily from side to side, he would remain in this aggravated state until he could see Jane's lithe form discharge from the confines of dilapidated frame.

Presently, she materialized. Emerging from the musty enclosure, she affectionately rubbed up to Peter, kissing him most seductively on the lips as if the malicious beating had never even occurred. Oddly, Peter had become the proverbial hall monitor, curiously on duty both during lunchhour and after school. She gave his trousers a swift grab, to which he momentarily winced as if not sure of the intention, after which she reached immediately in and began to rhythmically caress her finding. Giving in to the sensation, Peter grabbed her hand and began to vigorously pump until satiated, then sank resplendent into the soft grasses. Unfurling her tightened fist, she began to lick the substance from her outstretched palm. In veneration, Peter pulled Jane on top of him, to which she giggled and proceeded to bound off into the remaining sunlight.

From this vantage point, Winchester could see all of this, as he also saw this same repetition most days, but today, seeing her lick that stuff off of her hand in that characteristic way in which she could only employ, made the rancor begin to unfold.

Skipping like a child, Jane found her time in the sunlight always too short. It seemed to her that she hadn't really played since... since she couldn't remember. All of her time was now spent in a perpetual state of gratification for herself or others. She missed Eleanor. She missed their afternoons when she would listen to Eleanor's description of some long-winded tale she was currently engrossed in. She missed the way Eleanor would scold her for this or that, or the way she would become enraged with a well-placed phrase that Jane knew would exacerbate her to no end. She missed the way her hair would fall onto her forehead when she was pondering some philosophical enigma, or as Jane would say, absurdity.

Winchester, previously invisible but on her heels, suddenly overtook her from behind.

"Aren't you afraid of catching something?" Winchester snarled.

Jane, unaware of her pursuer, started and then grinned at the implication of his inquiry.

"It tastes good, that is, Peter's does anyway."

"What about, Mr. Dorset?" Winchester's pupils dilated sharply.

"His tastes okay, I guess. Better than yours does, anyway." Jane's grin widened.

Winchester twitched at the unexpectedness of her barbed words. For a time, he said nothing. Then, meekly, he began, "Nobody asked you t'swallow now, did they?"

"I like to swallow."

To this response, Winchester was baffled at what he could say in return, so again he became mute. Jane enjoyed the ensuing moments, observing Winchester's countenance besot with an expanding crimson.

Finally, she interrupted the silence of his ponderous struggle. "Do you want me to?" Jane advanced, her grin replaced by glistening, just-wetted lips.

The curious contortion of feature vanished, and eagerly he ejaculated, "Ya mean it, Jane? Y'actually want t'now?" His rising soprano gave one the distinct impression that Winchester had just reached puberty.

"Of course. I wouldn't tease about a thing like that."

Directing him to the side of the road, behind a rather slim tree, Jane began her ritual. She began with his inner thighs, and he wondered why she was prolonging his agony, when clearly the extent of his swelling indicated he was more than ready. However, he had no intention of offending his server as he had only just won back her previously alienated affections.

After a longer interval had passed, which in his precarious state, seemed an eternity, exacerbated, meekness forgotten, he impatiently queried, "When are ya goin' t'lick it? Hurry, pleeease..." Winchester implored, but his insolence was more of a whine than anything which could be construed as wrath.

Jane, her grimace wider than ever, looked up and innocently blinked. "Lick what?" she simpered.

"You know," he retorted irritatedly.

"No, I don't. If you'd care to explain, pleeease," Jane mimicked.

"My dick! Like we used to. What?! Have you forgotten how? You shouldn't have with all your practice," Winchester growled.

"I haven't forgotten anything, as you so rudely point out. I just do not care for the taste of it. It simply has a substandard flavour. However, Peter's, or Mr. Dorset's, I could suck all day. That is, if he, Mr. Dorset if you're wondering, didn't have to return to his wife."

Winchester was appalled. Again, he was rendered mute.

"I like to suck them, before we do it. It's fun, but I'm sure you probably don't remember." Jane chortled at the look which had just materialized on Winchester's face. Before he could move or say another word, Jane bounded off into the afternoon dusk. A sudden wind having risen, Winchester was sure he could hear Jane's echoing laughter as she made her way through the drying, sea-like grasslands home.

XXXIX

Eleanor could hear the grating of blades maneuvering the thinning surface. Interrupted from her present task, her progression momentarily impeded, she wondered briefly at the source of the sound. Her eyes were filled with crusty particles from the exhaustion of relentless chores. She brushed the matted hair away from her face, attempting to again mentally refocus on the mathematical equations that remained unfinished in her workbook. The weekend had passed without any interim period for endeavouring homework. There was perpetually too much to be done and too few capable hands involved in the venture.

Eleanor paused within the white glare to ponder a more intricate expression, biting her tongue as she attempted to visualize the correct application. This time laughter permanently suspended her cerebration, aggravating her already touchy disposition.

On the crystallized body before her whirled the two of them. Jane, as always, performing; Winchester likewise, enthralled. Surprise registered on Eleanor's soft features, as she again removed the tangled mass which obscured her view.

Jane skated frantically around Winchester while his mouth moved erratically, his hands appeared to be attempting to convey their own foreign tongue.

Jane stopped suddenly, approaching him like a stalking animal. All at once, he seized her forcing his fingers up her panties and into the dark, moist caverns of her recesses. Jane's eyes closed, while his other hand hastily unbuttoned his inflated trousers and began to tug violently on the engorged structure.

They were still not cognizant of her stare. Jane's head fully reclined, like a heron's taunt silhouette, as Winchester's face scrunched in apparent agony. Eleanor could barely make out his mounting ululation. As his moans crecendoed, the avis's silhouetted leg rose and struck in fierce and deft repetition. The reiteration of cries penetrated the vast expanses.

Yen

Crashing to the ice, hands suspended from their previous purpose, they now groped in sheer horror of further anguish at the imminent prospect.

Jane, standing over the hole which had only just swallowed him up, noticed how the region he now occupied had taken on a much darker hue. She was rather partial to this contrast. Surfacing and flailing, his body simultaneously stiffening as it froze in those icy depths, Winchester shrieked, "Help me! I'm gonna die! Help!"

Jane was enjoying the splashing and primal ruckus he was creating, but of especial interest to her was the achromatic nature of her beast. She began to rub her genitalia and hum a single tone repeatedly.

Winchester presently abandoned his struggling and stared in disbelief. It was as though she could not even hear his cries. A keen definable rage filled this nearly gelid creature. "Ya mean bitch! Whore! How could ya?! Ya know I'd help ya! Help me, for God's sake!" His voice was weakening.

Circe was already beginning to moan from her quickening finger cadence.

In the background, he thought he could make out a still figure in the shrubbery. He motioned, knowing it to be his final chance. "You, over there! Help! Help!"

Her monotone resumed permeating the empyrean.

Eleanor frantically grabbed a tree branch, dashed onto the thin ice, madly thrusting it into the frigid hole. Wrapping his hands around it, Winchester attempted to heave himself up, but his strength was not sufficient to support the weight.

Observing his lethargy, and realizing that time was of the essence, Eleanor turned to Jane for help.

"Jane, for God's sake! Winchester's dying!"

She only smiled and took the pointed stick from Eleanor. Eleanor, relieved at Jane's aid, grabbed the branch and prepared to heave. However, she only grimaced at her intruder and yanked it away. Flabbergasted, and knowing that their time was growing ever shorter, Eleanor began to shake from escalating shock and fear. Beginning to stir the arctic liquid, her eyes glistened in frenzy. As she circled the outer edges of the crack, always just beyond his quivering grasp, she would laugh, then jab in the direction of his now shrunken testicles.

"Jane! Jane! Jaaaaaaane!" Eleanor squealed, at wit's end, brutally shaking her.

Apparently arisen, and evidently witnessing the dire nature of their present circumstance, seemingly aroused from mania, she joined Eleanor, and together they began to hoist the frozen mass onto the exposed surface.

Shaking and hissing due to hyperventilation and a good degree of hypothermia, Winchester, crying, swore vehemently in Jane's direction.

"Ya could have killed me... ya fuckin' whore! How could ya poke at me while I was drownin' like that?! What kind of a creature are ya anyway?! This time ya won't get away with it! I'll prob'ly get real sick and die or somethin'!" Winchester wretched convulsively.

She could only stare at her whining embryonic creation. He was lucky that she permitted the birthing.

However, Medea was satisfied in her present attempt.

XL

Mr. Dorset's eyes narrowed as he shook his head in apparent disapproval. Eleanor's head bowed, and she fidgeted uneasily.

"Well, Eleanor? What do you have to say for yourself?" Eleanor recognized the nature of this reprimand.

"I... I don't know. My thinking isn't as clear as it was before. I don't know why. The headaches are a lot stronger."

"Do you think that would explain your poor performance on the last few examinations then, Eleanor?"

"I really don't know, Mr. Dorset," Eleanor's eyes momentarily met his as she attempted to placate him with a response that would ease his insistent and escalatingly bothersome inquiries.

Covertly, she wondered if his tasted different than Winchester's since she knew it was considerably bigger. She had often noticed the protrusion when he was assisting Jane at her desk. However, as she would subtly glimpse now and then, no protuberance seemed imminent.

For a moment, she allowed her legs to splay as she had seen Jane perform countless times to which Mr. Dorset would respond with a fervid leer, as he knew better than anyone that Jane only did this when she was not wearing any underclothing.

Mr. Dorset's soliloquy was finally culminating, coming to its usual and readily-welcomed close. "Are you paying attention, Eleanor? You don't seem to be listening to a word I'm saying," Mr. Dorset condemned.

Eleanor, believing she had discerned a slight stiffening in his lower extremity, was paying even less attention to the didactic nature of this elongated spiel.

"Eleanor, this lack of respect will not do. Today after school, you will fill Jane's position, and clean the blackboards."

At the idea of filling Jane's position, Eleanor almost broke out in a full smile, but realized that such action would be foolhardy, and abstained.

"Yes Mr. Dorset, you are right. I am sorry."

"Well, in any case, I will see you after the final bell." With those words, Mr. Dorset rose and left the small chamber designated for such purposes.

For the remainder of the day, Eleanor was beside herself with anticipation. At lunchhour, Winchester as usual remained aloof from the general populace, eating in fragmented edacious stages, but always looking up in the direction of the presumably still classroom's waning exterior.

Eleanor customarily sat eating her apple knowing what perpetually preoccupied Winchester's psyche.

Getting up, gathering the remains of her lunch, she made her way over to him. "Winchester, would you like the rest of my apple?" Eleanor timidly attempted.

"What? Oh, na, na... I don't want it. You're in my way. I can't see the room. Move." Winchester didn't even look at her. The words just seemed to escape from moving somnambulistic lips. Dark circles emphasized the glazed nature of wearied eyes.

Eleanor, exacerbated at his lack of response, exclaimed, "You know just as well as I do what is going on in there. Why do you continue to sit and torture yourself day-in and day-out?"

"What? What do *you* want, anyway? Can't you see I'm busy?" he snapped, his gaze not having shifted.

"I know you don't like me very much, but couldn't we just have a conversation for a couple of minutes?" Eleanor, in an obvious strategic dilemma, her voice becoming a near whine.

Suddenly, Winchester exploded. "Leave me alone! You're ugly! I don't know you! I don't want to know you! Get away!" Finishing this irate outburst, a raised arm forcefully pushed Eleanor out of the way, as she hadn't yet heeded the initial request.

Eleanor fell, scraping the side of her temple. Just then, the dark blind rose, and Mr. Dorset's frame emerged, his trousers still noticeably agape. In shock, from the sheer force of the shove, Eleanor began to cry, "You brutish freak! I was only trying to be nice. Next time, I shan't bother."

Her remonstrance did not even appear to be heard. The glare remained unrelentingly directed towards the previous distraction. Eleanor, unable to ascertain precisely what deserved such undivided attention, turned to see Mr. Dorset's figure calmly and fastidiously buttoning his beige trousers. Looking up, he presently smiled at the two of them, obviously finding something comical in their temporarily suspended skirmish.

"That bastard! He doesn't even care if we see them, for Christ's sake!" the form before her vented.

As he moved away from the window, Eleanor was now fretting that due to her newly acquired gash, he may not permit her to sample his foreign delicacy. They could both make out the small halcyon figure in the backdrop, partially exposed and still. Winchester got up, and yelling and screaming at no one in particular, carried on this way, hissing all the way home. Eleanor, from this vulnerable pose, could observe all of this: Winchester's violent departure, and the look of apparent disgust which had just manifested on Mr. Dorset's pocked face. Winchester vowed to never return and he never did, not within school hours anyway.

XLI

Eleanor had keenly observed for the duration of the afternoon the unfettered nature of Mr. Dorset's bottoms.

Yen

Its unleashed character had caused her a hyperbolic fixation regarding the quality and diversity of foreign aliments.

She wondered if it would taste like anything she had imagined. She had always wanted to sample even a single bite of the savory, foreign sausage meats that could be seen hanging in the window of the delicatessen every Sunday after church, and once, the butcher had smiled at her and offered, but her mother invariably politely declined, saying sharply to her afterwards, "We don't need others' charity. Don't look at me like that, Eleanor. I'll slap your face."

Today, finally, the moment of discernment seemed at hand. Unexpectedly, Mr. Dorset's bellow interrupted Eleanor's ruminations.

"Did you not hear me, Eleanor?! Move to the other side of the class! Now." His voice had become a snarl.

Not wishing to displease the meter of her approaching delicacy, she practically ran to the other side of the room, plunking herself noisily down beside Jane, to which Jane, sincerely beamed in greeting. Mr. Dorset, annoyed by the disjointedness of her actions, shook his head in displeasure, but this time, said nothing.

Eleanor saw this censure, but hoped it wouldn't affect their after school engagement.

The smell of the chalk excited Eleanor, and she squirmed nervously feeling an uncustomary coolness from her uncommon bareness. At lunch, she had removed her underpants, and even though the air had lost its chill, the fact that she was not used to such a state made her flinch at the slightest breeze.

Applying the shammy to the surface, chalk dust filled the stale air of the closed room, as Eleanor continued in her scheduled charge. She wondered when he would make his advance. Finally, from behind she heard what seemed like the downward movement of a blind, and in anticipation, felt a moisture slowly anoint the tops of her legs. She waited for his hand to seize her crevice, and pierce it forcefully and repeatedly from behind as she had so often witnessed through the keyhole in those supposedly covert lunchhour sessions, when Jane would moan softly until finally he would grunt, withdrawing so that Jane could quickly lick up her mess. Everyone knew Mr. Dorset hated messes.

In the process of boiling, the casing must eventually rupture, releasing its savory essence. For such a divine sampling had been too long awaited. It was finally within seizure.

However, regardless of her level of anticipation, she only heard the sound of an approaching chair being scraped precisely and purposefully along the floor. Perhaps he wished to sit in ease while she performed the seething. Suddenly, she heard a wrathful voice incarnated from behind.

"Turn around Eleanor. I wish to convey a piece of information to you which gives me considerable displeasure."

In all of the times she had managed to bribe Peter with the warm and supple environment of her fleshy, moveable muscle to which he always hastily attended, in exchange for which he had given her access to the best seat in the house, Mr. Dorset's exposed frenzy had never involved the use of discourse, except of course for his usual repetitious obscene monosyllabic commands that he daily employed. Otherwise, no words, other than guttural utterances, were exchanged.

Eleanor turned, but to her disappointment, his trousers were unfortunately tightly fastened. At the direction of her stare, and the appearance of a sudden sullen temperament, Mr. Dorset's brows furrowed in bewilderment. However, preparing to speak, he cleared his throat.

"Place your left hand in front of you first, subsequently followed by your right," Mr. Dorset ordained.

Eleanor, presuming he wished to employ her hands as his implement, graciously conceded. Nevertheless, when he produced the readily polished strapping device, Eleanor again swiftly recoiled.

"Do not disobey me today, Eleanor. I haven't the time nor the patience to endure your theatrics," the authoritative voice predicated.

Eleanor, afraid, meekly conferred.

Ten lashing were administered in all, the only moaning the result of dolor. After the infliction, the prolonged and dreary discourse commenced.

"I guess you're bound to be ordinary like most of the unrefined creatures this school has produced. It looked as if a scholarship was on the horizon for you, but I assume there's no chance of that materializing, now. Consistently, you were surpassing Effie on each consecutive exam, but now it's as though you no longer possess the drive, almost as though you're not the same girl who made such a miraculous recovery.

Whatever has become of your desire Eleanor, it no longer appears to exist. I guess you won't be competing for the district scholarship, and I can't say I'm not a little perturbed about the affair as I, myself, recommended you as a promising and gifted candidate. I do not appreciate playing the fool, Eleanor. I do not. Is that clear?" Mr. Dorset's eyes glistened with malignity.

"Yes, Mr. Dorset. It would not be my intention to tarnish your good name. If I have done so in any way, I sincerely apologize and I appreciate your attempts to redeem me, and humbly thank-you for your leniency and in so doing beg for your forgiveness, as it seems clear to me that I have in some way offended your reputation among your fellow colleagues." After this, Eleanor bowed her head solemnly, curtsied, and began to sincerely cry.

Mr. Dorset was somewhat taken aback by this unusual use of candor, and for once, was rendered speechless.

However, he quickly regained his composure and uttered calmly, "It is eloquence like that which causes me considerable astonishment and displeasure to observe the extensive plummeting of your grades. However, finish these boards and that will be all Eleanor. I doubt if improving your performance now would do you much good. It is a sad shame Eleanor, to go from such promise as a scholar to a mere simpleton in such a short time frame. And to be rather uncomely as well. So unlike that little golden-haired treat who used to accompany you everywhere. A pity... yes, such a pity..." he was now ruminating to himself.

Eleanor looked unblinkingly ahead as his face had become a sneer, and then he laughed hotishly through his blunt, undefined proboscis.

"However, I must depart. I think we have finished here. My wife, Lenora, is expecting our fifth child and she is due any day now. A precious woman, tends to my every need. Her only severe fault is her ghastly close-set features and rotundity. But there are always ways of overcoming such shortcomings. You will have to find a way, Eleanor. Strange, your names are quite similar, and so is the general uncomely appearance, but Lenora did not possess any intellectual predilections. Good-afternoon." With that last word, he seized his coat and vanished into the shadow of the doorframe.

Eleanor could hear the name Lenora echoing in her mind. She

had heard that epithet somewhere before, yet she could not seem to remember where. Lethe's waters gently took from her the association of this reverberating appellative. She felt weary and tired now. She, who was not desirable; she, who was no longer a recognized scholar; she, who could not even appeal to Mr. Dorset, let alone Winchester. Winchester, yes Winchester, who hated her for her keen observations which he would have rather denied. She could only appeal to Peter, and Peter, who was devoid of his liver, would gratefully and eagerly accept any proffered ministerings.

As she smoothed over the granular surface, she could feel her hands becoming covered as if by a fine mist. She felt as if she were the Pythoness of Delphi, sanding away time by the slightest application of frictionless technique, the molecules the only tangibility between her and infinity. Molecules, ordered, never random, ordained by Apollo himself and she his only desired counsel... his only desired counsel.

XLII

The air was calm and moist, yet a slight warmth infused the placidity of the night shade. The chill of the water was still prevalent though it soothed her burning throbbing. The day's demands had proven too exhausting as her rift shone raw and bloody.

A firefly skimmed along the still surface, an electric pulse above the effervescent shallows. Jane's bare image emerged, sparkling from stardust fallen from the ether. Her bronzed tone turned ashen and seemingly petrified due to the slight luminosity of a hovering, crescent-shaped moon.

Jane, fevered and weary, again submersed her corporeality into the soothing radiance. She had been there ever since the moon had risen, stars lacing the midnight hue of sky. The elixir, in its effervescent incandescence, was like a molten liquid spewing from Poseidon's buried den. Jane, immersed in this scape of effulgence, had no desire but to hear the distant sigh of wheat fields, stirring as they steadily grew under the guidance of starlight.

They gleamed above her, tiny pieces of stone like the kind she had heard the Queen wore, the crown's priceless collection. The constellations glimmered as if she had never before looked up, in their majestic progression never charted nor before seen, even though she knew that such was not possible... scientifically anyway.

A trail of rising bubbles obscured the surface, coruscating as they languidly rose. In this dimension, wholeness seemed within her grasp, her golden scales sloughing off, becoming one with the etiolation. A thin matrix pervaded the shallows like a web of intoxication drawing her nearer its vast networkings. The appetence for breath seemed far, removed from the compulsion of the moment. Like an elixir, she drank it in. The heaviness was beginning to fill her like an empty cup, its sweetness intoxicating but once drunk leaving you with no other desire but for more.

Suddenly, a tangibility seemed to materialize from the outer realm. Resenting such an intrusion, for a moment, she chose to ignore this Cimmerian form. Lethe had filled her now with that of her perpetual beseeching. In desirelessness, she would not rise.

Impetuously, a hand pierced through the dull radiance, unfolding in its descent. An offering emerged from without, and within the numinous spring, it appeared waxen and dull as if it existed wholly of itself, a divine prop although sourceless in origin. All at once its pair pierced the periphery, and Jane, enlightened, recognized the source.

Within Poseidon's den was the darkness of eternal night, as somehow she was protected in his womb. The hands were tempting in their lucent supplication, but night's cloak, although worn and holey, possessed a familiarity of smell and texture, that seemed to elude any other desire.

Jane's consciousness became aware of the suspended state of the fourth dimension, as if a point never existed, yet at once, perpetually did. The burden of this moment began to seep through her membranes as the contaminating elixir spread in its due course. Night approached and as her eyes began to close, wholeness was upon her, the final realization was ever nearer in its culmination: Yen, what is always desired... yen, what can never be attained... yen, the necessary perversion of the material sphere... yen, the perpetual quest to know... yen, the illusion.

The yellow light nearly extinguished, but ever so much closer to the blue-white shade that requires no sensory apparatus to perceive the infinite majesty of its unmediated entelechy. The heaviness becoming unbearable in her lungs: the descent began.

Poseidon had gained his most precious possession: Aphrodite was now within his clutches. The desire to possess and be possessed had finally been appeased.

XLIII

The hands vanished, and Jane no longer curious as to their source, gladly conceded their departure. As an illicit intrusion into her placelessness, she had resented their unwelcomed emergence. Seeming more of an ignis fatuus, she dismissed the possible meaning of their appearance.

Suddenly, they reappeared, but this time they were accompanied by a familiar figure. She knew the face, but in the heaviness, signification remained obscure. She was conscious only of a rising sensation and a firm grip around the hollowed region of her spine. Limp, it overtook her. Reaching the surface, light reflected off their watery epidermis, their skin glittering with the sheen of a thin glaze like that often applied to a Renaissance piece.

Dew bespattered the long grasses like tiny white polished pearls. Water streamed off her face as if she was somehow being eviscerated from the liquid itself, only to feel the burning, pernicious surge of oxygen. She knew who ministered to her ails, although she hadn't remembered calling on this pale, minuscule knight. Her eyes opened for an instant and in the haze, the sky laced with orbs of infinite light, while the grasses twinkled from their aqueous indulgence, their surroundings became as if they were floating in Elysian splendor.

As the air filled the expanding sac-like structures, Jane coughed spraying a fine mist of blood over the smooth, receptive surface. The ailing mistress was being held firmly, yet gently. Hemoglobin's hue continued to wash the periphery, as well as the visage of her petite paladin.

The Cimmerian form continued in its resuscitative efforts. Darkness obfuscated all but the manifestation before her and the soft glow of moonlight. She could feel only a hard coldness beneath her and the up-and-down motion of her own respiration, but nothing more.

Sightless, deaf and rendered mute by a dull throbbing in her larynx, barely perceptible was the narcotic breath upon her aching clavicle.

Gathering, the drops of blood materialized into a gelid mass floating above the effervescent provenance. Initially, the mass could only be expressed as an unmentionable gore, but slowly as if chiseled from a divine fire, Hermaphroditus took form.

XLIV

Everyone knew old Mr. Graves. He lived way out on the old Graves' lot, and he had a peculiar, uninviting odour. Eleanor, however, enjoyed this scent as she had some idea of its origin. He had the largest wheat fields, and tended honeybees. Their dull bumbling drone could be heard for miles. Everyone loved Mr. Graves' honey, especially Jane. Jane was a regular client.

Eleanor often followed Jane out to the lot. Jane never appeared aware of her clandestine pursuer, but Eleanor kept her distance nevertheless. She could see Jane bound up the steps and as usual Mr. Graves would greet Jane by swooping her into his arms as he sat down on the creaky rocker on the porch, pulling her onto his lap, all the while talking to her about the bees and current status of the honey, simultaneously stuffing his hairy, heavily-wrinkled hand down his tattered overalls, and his other hand up her cotton-stained dress.

From this angle, she could see Jane's head fully reclined and as they rocked she would moan. The exposed, filthy nature of Jane's feet always made Eleanor snicker from her caverned recess, but she had to remind herself of the constraints of her response due to the obvious potential for echo. While this was being enacted, she usually attempted to make herself comfortable in the slime-filled shaft only to slip and slide mercilessly on the verdant mire.

Eleanor knew Jane must have been spending too much time eating berries, as she was not normally tardy for this appointment. She knew Mr. Graves despised tardiness. The sun having already been high overhead, rather than waiting for Jane to appear, Eleanor had decided to make her way without her. Mr. Graves was in a state. His face was red, and it looked as though he had been drinking for quite a number of hours. He kept coming out onto the porch scanning the horizon for any sign of her. Then he would curse loudly and slam the screen door. Eleanor was afraid for Jane. Mr. Graves was drunk.

From her cool, obscured realm, she was protected from the harsh caprices of the sun. She needed some time to think, something she hadn't done much of lately. She hadn't even done any serious reading. The only consistency was the incessant demands of the farm and her siblings, as well as this Sunday rendezvous. A thought flashed, but quickly dissolved into her consciousness: maybe she could replace Jane. The idea was tantalizing. How would she explain that to the old man? He hardly talked to anyone anyway, and besides, Jane would know. But she had to do something.

Deciding a warning was greatly needed, she ran across the dusty field, past the mounting humming, to the steadily moving figure who had just graced the horizon. Jane was approaching.

Panting and out of breath, Eleanor ventured, "Jane, how are you?"

Jane, flabbergasted, exclaimed, "Wow, are you lowering yourself to actually speak to me?" Jane's sneer was becoming all the time more evident.

"Jane, now is not the time. I have to tell you something. I would not visit Mr. Graves. He is in a state of total inebriety." Eleanor lowered her head, not able to meet Jane's fixed gaze.

Jane appeared not to even hear her. "I thought after the other night at the swimming hole, we would begin talking, but you continue to avoid any contact."

"Jane, didn't you hear me?! Mr. Graves is drunk! He could hurt you, okay? Don't you get it?"

"Oh, he's drunk. Oh, that's what inebree... whatever is. I didn't know what you were talking about as per usual." Jane, however, continued to walk directly towards the old man's rickety shack.

"Jane! You're going to get hurt. Stop!" Eliciting no response, Eleanor was becoming all the more angry.

"For your information, Miss Wellgrene, I am not going to get hurt. He might be drunk, but he's old. A little more force would probably feel better with that limp thing. If you let yourself, you might even enjoy it. You never know."

"Jane, that's disgusting! You shouldn't speak that way. It is unbecoming."

"For Christ's sake Eleanor, why don't you join us for a fuck instead of hiding out in that stupid, shit-filled well?" Jane's sneer was becoming yet ever-greater.

Eleanor just stood there shocked at Jane's words. She had known all along that she had been down there. How could she have known this?

"Suit yourself," Jane said as she turned and continued towards the dull drone.

The idea was intoxicating. She wondered how Mr. Graves would react. It was much bigger than Winchester's and much hairier and stinkier, too. But the idea of being involved in the transaction... the thought of being given a batch of honey all for her own consumption was presently too taxing to refuse.

"Wait, Jane. Can I come, too?"

"I hope so. That's the idea," Jane shrugged, then laughed.

Eleanor didn't get it. Her brows furrowed in complete confusion.

The screen door banged repeatedly in the distance.

XLV

Mr. Graves bellowed at Jane. The words had lost their coherency. Coming towards her on the lot, his pants already agape, he swooped her into his still powerful arms and attempted to lift her dress. Spotting the presence of a rather timid creature, he demanded, "Who's this? What's she want?" He looked to Jane for an answer, as his bulbous eyes flashed madly.

"She wants it, too. You know. It." Jane snickered mocking demureness.

"What? I didn't hear ya. Honey? Does she want honey, you say?"

"No," then whispered something in his ear.

He said nothing.

"You're late. Come up on the porch. Turn 'round and lean on the rail. Hurry up, now."

Unfastening himself, he raised Jane's dress, and began to enter from the rear. The redness of his face became more pronounced and it was obvious by the rank odour that he hadn't bathed for quite some time. Plunging in and out, from this perspective it seemed to Eleanor that it was like watching her mother unclog the drain.

"Hold still. You're movin' too much."

"It hurts."

"Well, that's what you get for bein' late. Maybe, you won't be next time. Besides, your daddy said you was always on time. Are you tellin' me he's a liar?" As he said that he pushed all the harder.

Jane grimaced, but managed to reply, "No, sir."

For a moment he appeared as if he were going to laugh, and then his face turned a bluish-purple as he closed his eyes and groaned.

"That's a good girl. Let's sit in the rocker now, and bring over yer friend there."

Jane staggered as she stumbled over to where Eleanor, paralyzed with wonder and fear, was standing. Jane brushed the hair away from Eleanor's clammy forehead and gently took her hand. Eleanor, however, shook her head and remained fixed.

Mr. Graves rose and, leaning on the banister, laughed at Eleanor's timidity.

"What's your name, girl? You ever done that before?"

Eleanor, sweating profusely, just shook her head.

"It's okay, I won't bite. Won't do no virgin." He laughed again.

Eleanor relaxed a little.

"Your friend's not the mouthy kind, is she Janey?"

"No, sir. Not at all, sir."

"Okay, Janey, you and I will rock for awhile and then I'll do what you asked, okay?"

Jane smiled and nodded.

To Eleanor's amazement, the 'limp thing' had again hardened and was ready to reenact the transaction.

Jane hopped onto his exposed lap, and proceeded to rock for the next half hour 'til he again moaned. Jane, today however, appeared to relish the cessation.

"Okay, it's your turn. She looks a little like my late wife. Too bad, she was a sick little thing. Not much good for this kinda thing."

"What's your name, Little Lady?" the old man smiled. Suddenly, his face had become almost inviting.

"Eleanor, sir. Sir," Eleanor's voice nearly an inaudible whisper, "may I go home now, please?" Eleanor's paleness belied the smile she attempted to feign.

"If you want, you can. But I wasn't gonna hurt you or nothin'. You can do as you please."

"Thank-you for your kindness, sir." As Eleanor turned to leave, she felt a sudden grip on her arm. Her stomach sank.

She looked up to find Jane shaking her head. "You're not leaving, yet. That last one was for you. He won't hurt you. It's okay."

Eleanor looked at the old man who was still smiling, but somehow she did not feel constrained by the nature of his demeanor.

"What do you want me to do, sir?" Eleanor could not believe the words which left her very own lips.

"Take off your undies and sit up here on my shoulders, if you want."

"Why?" Eleanor's brow again furrowed.

"Just do it. You'll like it. You'll see," Jane urged.

"Get the honey, Jane," the old man ordered.

Jane nodded and obeyed.

Taking off her underclothing, Eleanor could feel a burning steadily rising in her cheeks.

"No need to feel embarrassed."

Presently, Jane returned.

Before Eleanor knew what was happening, she had ladled out an amble portion and proceeded to smear the cool, sticky glaze along Eleanor's underparts.

Eleanor squirmed from the odd sensation.

The old man's outstretched arms beckoned her and as he lifted her little frame onto his shoulders, she felt it drip down, landing between the middle of his eyes. Out popped his tobacco-stained organ and as it began to consume, Eleanor could only feel the warm, repeatedly applied pressure of this wet, apt muscle. The sensation was beginning to cause her breath to come in spasms.

The drone of bees was steadily becoming more removed and Eleanor hadn't even noticed that her own contortions now mimicked the rapid swaying of the chair. Eleanor's eyes remained fixed on the outline of a dike in the distance. Imperceptibly, a mirage, as if the result of sunlight blended with water, had suddenly manifested itself. The sensation was intoxicating. His soft, furry beardtongue graced her labia minora and majora as if he, himself, were a honeybee eliciting the essence from her stamen.

Eleanor began to scream in ecstasy pressing her steadily-convulsing-muscles heavily into the furrows of his wrinkled face. Wishing the sensation to continue forever, as the mirage had attained the magnificence of a kind of superior reality, Mr. Graves found it necessary to interrupt her reverie.

"Wow, she can sure holler, can't she, Janey?"

Looking to Eleanor, he said, "You was starting to suffocate me, like one of those octopussy tentacles." At that he laughed. So did Eleanor. And to see the sincerity of her pleasure, Jane did as well.

Jane smiled and that golden light, as always, emitted from her source. Grasping her hand, Eleanor ran with Jane into the diminishing radiance. Overhead, a great blue heron, too far inland for one of its kind, flew.

XLVI

For the last few evenings, Jane had been coming out to the old man's lot at highly irregular intervals. For this time of night, the image of his still rocking figure seemed strange indeed. And even stranger was the fact that on each consecutive night, he had been sitting in the exact same fashion on the porch. A few days back, Jane had asked Eleanor if she wished to accompany her and Eleanor had accepted, but of course on the condition that she remained relegated to her usual place in the well.

The incessant flicker made her recess appear all the more eerie and removed from the scene being performed before her. The dank odour accosted her nostrils, yet she was too spellbound to actually notice its rankness. The candle before her was nearly out, yet the usual performance seemed hardly to be finished. The rocking chair's frantic movement had manipulated her attention for the last hour or so.

As she forced herself back and forth, culminating finally in shrill howls creating a peculiar discord with the squeaking of the chair, she jumped off beckoning to Eleanor as she had on each night, but Eleanor who was sweating profusely, trying to support her own weight without slipping in this constrictive dungeon, had one hand anxiously stroking the only flower within this slime-filled crevice, while the other held the rapidly dwindling wick.

The wax in running down the sides of the candle had formed the curious images of what looked to be either the obscene, exposed form of Jane's utter nakedness or rather, Mr. Graves' oddly-hued epicanthic fold of readily available and strangely rigid tissue. Eleanor, practically beside herself, and irritated from the particularly difficult nature of trying to maintain somewhat of a vertical position upon an undefined slope, suddenly saw Jane jump off the pendular frame just as her candle was extinguished and a delicate moaning had begun to rise from these hidden recesses. The shock of sudden and complete darkness made her flinch and immediately a trail of scorching wax contacted her exposed upper legs and privates. The pain shooting out in many directions caused her to shout in momentary exhilaration, then abruptly in keen and distinct anguish.

A wash like the aurora borealis that had so often filled her with an intense and unabatable desire, covered her consciousness and the fields of Elysium seemed so near, almost within touch. The ejection of charged particles played within and without of the seeming confines of her mind - her finger and flower now at rest with only the slight indication of burning flesh in her private and discrete crematorium.

Opening the jar of honey that she had just produced from the cabin's interior, Jane continued to signal from the porch. Eleanor, too curious and hungry to refuse the invitation, emerged a little sweaty and somewhat unsteady on her feet. As she approached the porch, a gentle breeze blew up and a peculiar scent caused her to abruptly stop.

"What is it? Don't you want any? Best honey around. I always get some after we do *it*," Jane smirked.

"Yeah, I do... I do," Eleanor stammered.

"Well, I'm not gonna wait all night," Jane retorted irritatedly.

Eleanor could not take her eyes off the figure on the porch. "Doesn't he want any?" Eleanor's brows furrowed in mock concern.

"He's got all the honey and more. This is for you and I. Come on."

Eleanor now heard the old planks squeak eerily beneath her feet, and wondered why she could never hear them from her recess. They seemed to reverberate inside her head as the rocker often would when she'd shut her eyes.

Jane groped at her privates, attempting to yard down her pants, but Eleanor jumped back in mounting disgust and alarm.

"What are you trying to do?" Eleanor angrily stated.

"Playing hard to get are we? You'll miss all the fun." Jane laughed maniacally as she pulled down her own underclothes and applied a good ladling of honey to the receptive flesh. As she turned, she jumped on the exposed figure and began the steady rocking.

The creaking of the planks was the only sound which could be heard clearly in the culminating darkness. But after awhile, she began to sing.

The lilting tones floated in the expansive adumbration.

"Hush little baby, don't say a word, Mummy's gonna buy you a mockingbird; if that mockingbird don't sing, Mummy's gonna buy you a diamond ring; if that diamond ring turns brass, Mummy's gonna buy you a looking glass; if that looking glass gets broke, Mummy's gonna buy you a billy goat; if that billy goat don't pull, Mummy's gonna buy you a cart and bull; if that cart and bull turn over, Mummy's gonna buy you a dog named Rover; if that dog named Rover don't bark, Mummy's gonna buy you a horse and cart; if that horse and cart fall down," Jane's pitch rose uneasily.

"... Papa's gonna buy you a *rocking chair*," her pitch became suspended, but the rocking motion continued relentlessly.

Eleanor slumped down in the corner of the porch, and silently but surely, the tears began to pour from her, soundlessly trailing into the surrounding formlessness.

Jane dismounted, and approaching Eleanor gently gave her a kiss on the forehead as she emphatically stated, "Your turn to play horsey while I watch."

But this time Eleanor was not shocked.

Rising, Eleanor began the application. The honey felt sticky and dripped into the singed tissue of her upper thighs. Mounting the form, darkness had obfuscated any remnant of detail from the scene at hand. It felt cold and hard and its size was more like an obsolete farm tool.

After awhile, as she rocked, the sheer warmth from her own body heated the slippery implement, and the initial reciprocal diversion became a keen and honed pleasure. She wondered briefly why Mr. Graves did not move or say anything to encourage or discourage her performance, but the ecstasy was too great to question such trivialities for long. Her breath came in quick, successive gasps as the squeaking of the planks increased, then just as quickly, abated. Her arched dorsum slumped like the still propped figure before her, and as she breathed in the ensuing warmth of the night air, an advancing figure giggled from behind.

A lit candle unexpectedly illuminated the form in front of her. Cadavers and wax figures again filled the space. Suddenly, her eyes became an owl's wide gaze as the presence of the grimacing, open-mouthed cadaver manifested before her. Wide-mouthed, pants agape, Mr. Graves remained stiffly propped in his rocker in apparent obscene and grotesque splendor. The grasses stirred gently. The swelling breeze caused an offensive odour to rise from this still mummy. Eleanor, still naked, stepped back and silently bowed her head, humbled as if awakened from a prolonged dormancy.

XLVII

The sun had risen, a momentary and grandiose spectre. Eleanor waited patiently along the river's banks. They had agreed to meet here this morning after last night's gruesome discovery. Eleanor's eyes, caked with dried mucus, had not actually been properly closed since a certain object sat heavily on her conscience. She had arisen before the beams awoke the still houses in order to be able to meet Jane before her usual daily chores.

She could see her figure approaching. Her walk was unusually gay and quite light for the nature of last night's unearthly finding, but Eleanor was relieved to see she had chosen to attend.

Jane was carrying something in her left hand. Arriving, Eleanor noticed the bareness of her filthy, dew-bespattered toes. Reaching out to Eleanor, Jane offered her the red object that she had been carrying. "Want one?" she smirked.

Eleanor was hungry, but refused. "How can you eat at a time like this? Don't you know what we did? That man is... is no longer of this earth."

"Good grief Eleanor, you were finally enjoying yourself for once. I really don't think he minded, and if he did, he wasn't complaining," Jane giggled.

"That's disgusting. What we did was a... a... a..." Eleanor became mute and her aspect at once exhibited a strangely transparent hue.

Jane approached her face and whispered, "But it felt so good, and who would ever know, that is, unless you tell."

"Jane!" Eleanor hollered, "That is not the point. God knows... He saw us and we know. Isn't that enough? Well?" Eleanor was more than adamant. She was quite beside herself.

Jane, irritated, looked away and biting into the apple, chewed and spit the bolus directly into her unyielding and staunchly puritanical expression.

"You liked it," Jane breathed, her eyes twinkling as she took another, this time rather large, bite of the apple meant for one considerably irate Eleanor.

"What did you say?" Eleanor's look hardened as she wiped away the moist residue.

"You heard me. You're more worried about someone finding out than you are about sinning against 'Our Father who art in heaven' for all the preaching that comes out of that good-for-nothing hole in the middle of your face. If there were no constables and no one could find out how much of a slut goody little Eleanor really is, just like her freakish friend, you'd go back again and again till that other hole was just as loose as mine is!" With that, Jane took a gigantic bite of her apple, and at the look which had just manifested on Eleanor's face, began to heartily laugh, her volume increasing audibly.

Eleanor stood there as if petrified, made somehow impenetrable. She rose her hand and slapped that freakish, blond, blasphemous creature as hard as she possibly could, only she did not stop at one slap. She kept on slapping until she made Jane call out. When she saw the blood dripping on her toes, she realized that Jane's nose was bleeding.

"Stop! Stop! Stop it, Eleanor! Please stop!" Jane pleaded.

Something in her had been unleashed, and if she hadn't heard the pleading, which almost did not even sound like Jane at all, she wouldn't have desisted.

After that, for a moment, Jane said nothing.

Then a strange and profound presence seemed to entrust Jane into its confidence and, like a supernatural being, jumped on Eleanor. Eleanor, who had now been awakened from her internalized state, attempted to defend herself, but her resolution and innate strength seemed now more than Eleanor could successfully fend against.

Her kisses fell heavily and the tendrils, like a deft and penetrating smothering, simultaneously obscured the brightness of Apollo's mighty glare. She seemed possessed as if a daimon had risen to the surface and was making its presence felt. The smell of honey covered Eleanor like a blanket and at once a kind of peace overtook her, soothing the startling revelations of her previously sinful conduct.

Suddenly, Eleanor felt a tangible and odious wetness trickle down the top of her thigh, and at once, she experienced a sort of cramping grip the bowels of her stomach. Resisting, Eleanor tried to plead with this daimon, but her voice only came out in tiny gasps of barely audible moans. All of this wriggling was making this creature all the more eager in its progress, and just as Eleanor managed to raise her leg slightly to kick it adroitly in the groin, a hand pierced the boundary of her undergarments and fully embraced the precious wetness. Eleanor found this sensation more than she could bear, and as she struggled suddenly felt a cold rodlike hardness rub along her privates. The nature of this peculiar caress made Eleanor think of a soft, sheath-like covering, like a... a... a sort of giant, mushy thumb. As the engendered friction was applied along the surface of her vulva, it produced the most oddly pleasurable contraction. She began to wonder what it could be when suddenly the object began to burrow itself inside of her. She resisted, but it was unrelenting in the singularity of its intent. Eleanor, her chords again vibrating within her larynx, heard the imperatives ring out, "Stop! Stop! Please stop!" But the daimon continued furiously, ravenously burrowing into its newfound moist and soft den. Eleanor felt herself labouring against this pervasive force, as she attempted to physically repel this nearly completely burrowed body by fully thrusting her pelvis with spastic contortions. However as it reached the deepest realm of her interior, the presence of a distinct tissued wall preventing its continuance, it rapidly retracted with the abruptness of an ebbing tide.

Eleanor, having finally grown accustomed to the sensation, was beginning to feel a keen sensibility arising from the nature of its forceful advance. The rashness of the removal evoked such an odd sentiment of simultaneous relief and disappointment that Eleanor felt an uncanny change in her disposition. The daimon rolled off and remained, humming its strange rhyme which became absorbed into the flowing susurration of the nearby river, while Eleanor lay paralyzed by the intensity of her own response.

XLVIII

Shame had chiselled its irrevocable earmark upon Eleanor's brow and as Jane repeatedly hummed the lullaby, Eleanor rose and looked at the spread-eagled creature before her. The daimon finally satiated, Jane lazed in the engulfing grasses and let out a ghastly belch.

"What? You've got that odd look on your face again. Penny for your thoughts?"

"How can you be so cavalier? Don't you have any sh...sh...sh," Eleanor stuttered on the word. It could not be elicited.

"Shame," Eleanor whispered, her eyes overflowing with tears. She could no longer stand Jane's lack of feeling or empathy, her general sense of apathy for all.

Eleanor ventured a word or two, "Is there nothing in *there?*" she seemed to look directly through Jane as though she were burrowing a hole with a torch right into her centre.

Jane, who was now sitting up, felt her face unexpectedly flush and stared at her accuser blankly, but as Eleanor cried, Jane felt a growing sense of malice overtaking her senses.

Eleanor, exacerbated by her seeming lack of emotion, turned and began her retreat. Her feet felt heavy beneath her and the consciousness of a distinct and lugubrious doom seemed to hold her down like a dead weight had been all at once attached to her ankles. She had to get away from the inevitability that Jane seemed to impose upon her wearied consciousness. Her legs clomped along one after the other in dreary succession and her mouth felt dry from its previous exertions.

The severity of these subtle infractions would not be tolerated. As though in possession of winged feet, she flew after Eleanor. It would have been easy to tackle her at any time. But the moment was not right. It must be waylaid. The river was rapidly nearing, the bank a mere twenty paces distant.

They both reached it simultaneously as Eleanor grabbed her hair in hysteria. "Why won't you just leave me be? I've done nothing to you. Just go," Eleanor pleaded.

Jane shook her head. Always the deterministic flicker in her molten lit pools.

"What is it you want? What do you want from me? What?" Eleanor's voice reverberated off the foliage and shrub-like vegetation of the banks, but in response, Jane would only shake her head in ominous rejection of Eleanor's persistent and cloying pleading.

She began the approach and the further she advanced, the wider her grin became. Eleanor, in reaction, began to retract. Her head shook from side to side in obvious terror, and as she retreated she wept, beginning to stumble uncontrollably.

Jane's intention glittered in the depths of her sherry-stained orbs, Medea making her occasional, yet official rounds. Just before the final stumble and subsequent splash, Eleanor's last plaintive tones could still be heard, "Please. Please. Let me be. Let me be. Please."

Then the plash and flailing as Eleanor attempted to surface. However, the branch of a laurel was being repeatedly applied to her now bloody skull. A vital essence escaped into the surrounding effulgence. Fragments of spectra dwelt in the apparent heaviness of this realm. Like the precise mixture of countless glazes reapplied and allowed to dry and blend into each other... a kind of miniaturized, contained perfection. The intrusion of this escaping sanguine hue into the undulating radiance added a pyretic element to the gloriousness of her canvas, and as it continued to permeate her aesthetic, she became choleric to the supposed origin of this intrusion. A figure floated within the spectre of the canvas and as it was tangibly red, and as it appeared to have no mouth, Eleanor decided to address it regardless, "Would you kindly remove your presence from the boundary of my creation?"

It bubbled its response, red and oozing as it blurred the region around the cranial space, therefore preventing her from seeing almost entirely. "It is not your creation." And with those words, everything faded into an all-encompassing blackness. However, Eleanor was glad that the red being had finally vanished.

Daphne, present throughout the entire execution of the attempt, remained victorious on the river's mossy bank.

XLIX

Eleanor awoke. The faint smell of sulphur could be discerned on the breeze as the sky had become overcast and dull. Eleanor choked, spitting up regurgitation and phlegm. She couldn't remember surfacing, but all at once she had arrived.

Her skin felt cold as she shivered and blinked. Her eyes were bloodshot from the strain of passage and hair stood out in small tufts on her head. She unclutched her hands and let out a gentle coo, surprising herself by her own nonsensical utterance. Again she coughed, but this time with her spine curved, her head bowed forward, and her arms and legs pulled in towards her chest. She broke this position and rose stretching outwardly as she did so. A rainstorm was approaching and suddenly Eleanor was acutely aware that she had not completed even one of her daily chores.

At this realization, she momentarily wondered where the time had gone, as she tried to run but stumbled as soon as she began. The burden of her own drowning resurfaced in her consciousness, and startled, she balked at the familiarity of the memory. Where had she gone? What had saved her? Fragments converged within her conscious mind, as the tale spun, intersecting and diverging simultaneously. The nonsensical nature of the episode repeatedly presented itself, as she distinctly remembered the adamant intrusion of the red being into her sacred realm. The fragments remained and nothing seemed to dispel their relevance or their discontinuity. Eleanor was simply and profoundly baffled.

She looked a fright to behold, and decidedly took the forest route home as it would be faster. The profoundness of her state of mind deepened and a look of abstruse anguish contorted her small, pale features. A rumble could be heard overhead, and Eleanor again shivered from the chill of the prevailing elements. Rasping, she considered running, but abandoned the thought as she realized just how weak she actually had become. Reaching the denseness of the overhead canopy, she could see the field where Jane had performed her frantic and much-needed ritual. Eleanor shivered for the third time at this thought.

Arriving on the threshold of the field, she could feel a revitalizing surge of energy pass through her body. The rain had begun. The musky smell of warm earth permeated the expanse, and Eleanor, regardless of the lateness of the day, needed to stop for a temporary, but much-needed tarry. Again, like before, she blinked hard trying to focus as the rain beaded down the miniature folds in her forehead. Her vision seemed somehow inaccurate for in front of her lay the strangest object she had ever discerned.

Its cylindrical shape and spongy texture could barely be distinguished within the downpour's dominion. She thought for a moment that it might be an odd sort of field mushroom. Curiosity gripped her as she approached, but upon discernment, she sunk away in horror.

"It couldn't be!" Eleanor heard herself exclaim, and then looked furtively around to make sure no one else had heeded her strange retort.

The mushy giant thumb lay in the field fully exposed to anyone who might happen to pass by, as raindrops bounced off of its fleshy, glistening exterior. Its rigor made it somehow extraordinary, yet its delicacy due to the vulnerability of its present state, could not be denied. The idea of the severing made Eleanor gag on what little food remained in her stomach. The knowledge of where it had been and what it had been used for caused the nausea to accost her in vicious and relentless waves. Another crack of thunder reverberated. Thank God no one was there to hear it. An idea was rapidly germinating. The rational intent of the blending began.

Someone would find it. No matter what she did with it, someone would dig it up and know exactly what it had been used for, and exactly who had used it for what purpose. They had special advanced ways of finding out these things. Eleanor even knew the term, 'Forensics'.

She thought of tracking down Jane for help, but what would Jane do? Probably take it home to use on a regular basis, and show up with it at the dinner table, saying, "What, what are you all staring at?" No, that would never do and Eleanor realized that no matter what, Jane would surely never take the blame... solely. Eleanor knew she would be held just as accountable. Jane would make sure of that. She was no martyr. She may be a lot of things, and presently Eleanor could think of quite a few. The idea of a penal sentence was not particularly pleasing to Eleanor's sensibilities. She knew what needed to be done.

The woods were near. Eleanor was glad for their sanctity. The moment had arrived and the time for action was now, regardless of higher consequence. The fire was not hard to build. She found plenty of dried twigs under the larger branches that were damp from the storm. Although inexperienced, she commenced the building. It did not take long. Even though the air was not cold, the heat from the flames helped ease her intense shivering. In silence, she uttered a small prayer asking forgiveness for what she was about to undertake.

Once the smoke materialized, she pierced it on the end of a stick which she had sharpened for this distinct purpose, and began. Simply incinerating it would not be enough. That could leave evidence. The embers rose as the juice dripped down into the flames of the crackling blaze. Eleanor's mouth dribbled slightly at the sides, and ashamed, she wiped away this wetness. A sweetness could be distinguished in the dampness of the breeze, and Eleanor now curious as to the origin of this scent, decided that as she wanted no trespassers, the entree was successfully prepared.

Its texture felt rubbery along the palate of her mouth, but the taste was not undesirable. It seemed to be permeated by a honey-glazed flavouring, a marinade that Eleanor could only guess at its apparent origin. Juice ran down her chin, as the stick remained, charred and bare under the thickness of the shadowy glade.

L

Winchester half stood and half crouched as Jane leaned heavily on his shoulder. He had found her semiconscious and nauseous by the well. It had been abandoned and a roughly erected 'For Sale' sign had been placed on the property.

Winchester, not sure what to say, ventured a few words. "What ya doin' out here, anyway? They found old man Graves few weeks back, dead's a doorpost. Nobody'd even went to the funeral."

His look remained inquisitive.

Jane grimaced, the jab of a sharp abdominal cramp, and retorted, "I like it here okay. If you must know, I enjoy the hum of the bees."

"No bees now. Some guy came up here and took 'em all away. Same guy put up that sign there."

"Okay, okay, what are you so nosy for anyway?" Jane countered in apparent anguish.

Winchester, regardless of their history, was legitimately concerned. "Geez Jane, are ya sick or somethin'? I mean I could go home and get my... "

Jane didn't let him finish. "No, no, I just need to rest for awhile. That's all. Let's sit down here."

As she plopped herself down on the roadside, Winchester noticed the sweat rolling off her pale cheeks and soaking her underarms. "Jane, ya sure..." Winchester broke off as she had grabbed him by the shorts, and was attempting to tug them off.

"Jane, what ya doin'?" He could already feel it readily hardening. "Everybody'd see us here. Can't... ?" Momentarily tense, he broke off again as she finally managed to get off his shorts, locating, and slowly swallowing the elongated swelling.

Winchester couldn't believe his luck. She had been nearly half-naked by the well. Before he had woken her, he had thought how good it would feel to go up from behind and put it in before she was conscious of his advance. It was already so hard and it had been a very long time since she had even desired to speak to him. It would only have taken a few minutes. He had even gone so far as unbuttoning his trousers, but when he approached, he had seen the most ungodly sight. It even had a kind of rotten smell to it. At first he thought it was the entrails of some animal, but then upon further investigation, he had no idea of what the gory mass could be. Jane however, who was slumped over by it, seemed unconscious of its closeness. Regardless, Winchester had stepped around this sanguineous mound, rousing Jane from a pronounced and seemingly arduous slumber.

Jane did not want to hear anymore of his questions. She couldn't stomach more inquiries. The coroner had had his own, and she had handled it her way, as she was handling things now. Another pang violently gripped her and as he began to moan, it slid out of her mouth and she lay unresponsive to Winchester's incessant petitions on the side of the road.

He quickly did up his pants, and lifted up her wearied, bedampened form, taking her down to the river, where hopefully the resuscitative flow would relieve her ailments.

Jane did not awaken as yet. She lay sweating and foaming a little at the mouth in apparent fever and discomfort. Winchester cradled the lithe object in his arms as she murmured incoherencies into the elongating shadows. Gently he stroked the golden tendrils, so soft like the fur of a kitten's. Her breath came and went in tiny gasps, but as she slept gradually she grew calmer and embraced him in the entirety of her grasp. The pain appeared not as pronounced and Winchester was glad for her momentary relief. He had hoped he wouldn't need to fetch his mother, as he knew Jane would probably refrain from conversing with him permanently.

The heaviness of the dream was upon her. She could see his form as he descended into the opaque realm. She had not even permitted herself sight, nor sound. His shrieking cries and beseeching grasp were not witnessed by her. Medea was intent upon her premeditation. Down, down... he had sunk into the vagueness of the nebulosity, hardly a splash had even been discerned. Only now did the articulacy of a name form, the betrayal departing her parched, split lips.

As her fever broke, and the articulation of a quick succession of nonsensical words echoed from her throat, did Winchester think he could distinctly make out the oddity of a repeated and muffled appellation. It sounded strange and peculiar and something like 'Zagreus'.

LI

They walked hand-in-hand. Eleanor felt something slimy well up in the back of her throat. The fields were filled with newly brandishing stalks and Winchester, recently-satiated, laughed genuinely and uncharacteristically sweetly. Jane's thin summer dress inadequately disguised the fact of her near nakedness. She seemed to laugh demurely as though insensible of all else.

Yen

Eros dwelt in their realm. Reaching for her hand, Winchester winced as Jane pulled hers away, giggling as she did so. He, seemingly irritated, grabbed her waist, causing them both to fall head first into the knee-deep grain.

How could they? How could he after everything that the little tramp had done to him, and yet he still wanted... Eleanor choked on the realization. Her stomach began to churn and her head spun simultaneously, as she could not seem to successfully orientate herself any longer.

Streams of colour began to come at her from every direction. Eleanor, unconscious of their landing, felt as if they soundlessly would descend into her, diffusing her now-permeable opaque membrane and entering, but never finding any point of contact. The colours spun in their glorious movement... a movement of light she could never attain in all the ecstatic fervor of her attempts. The element became hers, as if she possessed it... for a moment like the onlooker often feels in viewing a Turner, like the one she'd seen in Mr. Dorset's book on great painters that she would look at over and over.

Eleanor could see the swirling of the detailed strokes, the deep storm shade upon the golden hue within the shooting streaks of a deeper shade interspersing the contrast of these two pigments. So much white, the ultimate reflection of undisturbed space within this apparent flux of movement, captured in an instant... the illumination omnipresent, never uniform. These shades would never intimately come to know this rough creamy weave so often the possessor of Eleanor's fancy. The grief became overwhelming.

Suddenly, the shades separated and the colours all-at-once absorbed into each other, hues that were foreign to the speculations of this canvas melded and became one as Eleanor, finally-satiated gave in, and lost consciousness.

LII

Jane approached Eleanor, as a sly smile slowly made its way across her face. "How are you Eleanor? I believe you fainted the other day."

"Yes, well I hardly believe that you would have had much interest since you were already previously engaged in other activities."

"Oh, you mean Winchester?" Jane smiled fully.

"Yes, you could say that," Eleanor retorted dryly.

"Well, we were wondering if you'd care to join us for a frolic or two this afternoon. Do you think you'd be available?"

"Why on earth would 'the two of you' want me along? If you'll recall, Winchester can barely stand the sight of me."

"Eleanor, don't do yourself a disservice. Winchester does not hold such petty grudges. If he did, do you think for one moment that we would be together?"

"It's funny that you should ask that. Exactly why are you together, anyway?"

"That little green monster is showing its ugly head. I told you before, you're more than welcome to participate."

"That's truly vile. Please directly answer the question, Jane, if you would." Eleanor's voice broke on the last word.

"Well, you know yourself that my dance card is more than a little empty now that poor Mr. Graves has left us. Something to fill the space, you could say." At this, Jane laughed.

Eleanor sneered at the tart before her.

"Tsk, tsk, Eleanor. After everything I've done for you, you haven't learned the lesson yet."

"Everything that you've done for me? What would that be, Jane? Trying to kill me, causing me to be seen as an idiotic parallel to the retard you are, and above all else, making sure that the one person you know that I need feels nothing for me... absolutely nothing!" Eleanor was screaming at this point.

"Is that what's eating you? To answer your first question, I like the presents *Windy* gives me."

"*Windy*? Is that what you call him?" Eleanor's brows furrowed.

"Well, you know, he farts a lot." Jane giggled.

"You are truly amazing. Only you could lead a conversation away from its rightful direction by your stupid and inane attempts at diversion. Why don't you just answer me? Answer me for real, for Christ's sake!"

"You should not be taking the Lord's name in vain. It might affect your chances. You know, the pearly gates and all." Again, the sly smile surfaced.

"You think you're so smart you stupid, little, conniving whore!" With these words, Eleanor pounced on the vile creature before her.

"Eleanor, for a supposedly civilized specimen, you're rapidly degenerating."

Eleanor, momentarily rendered impotent, rolled off in a state of utter despair. "Just answer the fucking question, you bitch," Eleanor's hands grasped at the tendrils of her now-matted, dull brown shade.

"Okay."

At the calmness of Jane's reply, Eleanor was stricken mute.

"Blaming me for your lack of scholastic status is untrue. That was clearly and decisively your own decision. As for Winchester, how he feels for you is out of my hands. It is only because I loathe him completely that he desires me. If for one moment, I decided that I cared for him, his fancy would almost instantly disappear. Part of the black magic of human nature, Eleanor. You, of all people, should know that."

"But you do admit that you indeed did attempt my demise?"

"Attempt your demise? Yes, I do admit that."

"Why would you wish to end my life, Jane?"

"Why? Why not?" On these last words, Jane's voice softened and the look of utter despair transferred to Jane's aspect.

"That is not an answer." Eleanor was no longer enraged.

"Because you possess everything that has any meaning at all to me." With those words, her voice broke, and she vanished into the formlessness of the sheaves in the field beside the road's edge.

LIII

There were two place-settings at her woodland table service, yet no plates nor utensils. The canopy provided the perfect gathering-place for her and her guest. At first she hadn't known what it could be, but felt strange from the abdominal cramping. It could have been something she had eaten which had been spoilt, but somehow she knew otherwise. She also knew her presence would be missed. There were always so many tedious chores, never-ending and gruelling. The morning, resounding with the tweets and cheeps of birds, was still cool, as she had only just finished the milking.

Bringing a single bowl, some matches, a few bricks of precious charcoal, which she realized her hide would be more than a little-tanned for, a bit of snuck milk, and the crust of some dried bread, she had made out for the covered recess of the nearby woods. Arriving she sat down, glad to be out of direct sun, as the heat would soon arrive. The smell of earth and grasses, as well as the buzz and hum of the birds and insects, allowed her to rest, momentarily unconscious of the slight cramping and heavy tiredness.

The sweating had already begun, as had the waves of nausea. Removing her undergarments, she started to heave and push, struggling to rid her body of its mephitic element. Its landing, soft and primal, a bath of milk which it would never get to drink, was beneath her. Contracting her uterine muscles with all of the might she could muster, and biting into the stick she had sought for this dual purpose, finally something gave way, a tiny sac aloft and free, then floating in this bath of life-giving substance, only to sink into this glandular secretion at her feet.

The birthing over, Eleanor lay, effete and supine, the next task suddenly too much to even conceive of in the present. Panting, she became an extension of only her breath. Inspire, expire, she became the rhythmic movement as of the tide, whole and fully-formed, by the subtlety and the majesty of this life-affirming movement. Now her guest would finally feel welcome.

This sensation of not being alone gave her the necessary strength which was needed. Taking the stick in her left hand, she began to beat and beat until mangled and rendered formless, in this scrambled state, it seemed to scamble and cramble, and could not escape. Burrowing the end of a multi-twigged-branch into the soil, Eleanor made sure it was secure, hanging the bowl from the bark of its projection. Skewering the crust on the other twig, her repast was ready to cook.

Arranging the rocks in a circular fashion close to the branches' base, she chucked the bricks into its centre, and realizing how hungry she had actually become, quickly lit them. Sunlight passed over their surface, and the golden glow upon the purity of the black hue, made Eleanor fill with awe at the perfection of this rendering.

They grew warm rapidly, then hot, turning red. The fire was quick to become a small blaze and the mixture immediately began to harden. Removing her toast using the unwashed stick as her lever, she placed the unsavory coagulate upon her half of the piece, and did the same for her guest. All at once, she thought she saw the belated-being-blink, then where its tiny mouth would have been, the space opened and the most pretentious sounding vocalization she had yet heard to date emerged: "Meaning without context is epitome of form." She wondered what this could possibly signify, especially since unborn, preformed fetuses did not speak, blink, or breathe for that matter.

Mangled in this way, she could not see its form, and it became as if it were Scotch woodcock, piping hot, a crust of carbonation its crowning ornamentation. She had had it once before. If only she had some savory anchovy paste, it would have been impeccable. Biting into her own form of ambrosia, she consumed the inconsumable, but felt her guest would not be pleased. Penitent, she sat, the last vestiges of the fire still sizzling and popping under the shadow of the canopy above. She did not have to wonder why he hadn't eaten his portion. She knew he could never eat the thing which she had just consumed.

Burping, and nearly gagging on the mutilation, she sat solemnly, again alone. She may not please him. He may shun her presence, but she could still cultivate his five ways:

Silence...

Purification...

Openness...

Response...

Time.

LIV

"Lenora! Lenora! Lenora, answer me!" Winchester was calling from quite a distance.

Eleanor, with her back averted, did not realize that the beckoning was meant for her.

"Lenora, didn't you hear me calling you?" Winchester, out of breath, finally caught up to the still retreating figure.

"I didn't realize that you were calling me. My name is not Lenora," Eleanor sullenly replied.

"It's Jane. We was playin' in the field when she went into one of her states an' ran around believin' she was a buffalo or somethin'," Winchester was anxiously spitting his words.

"I see that you haven't sustained any injuries this time," Eleanor snickered.

"Okay well, she fell down and I guess ya don't care or nothin'. See if I ever carry *you* home again," Winchester's face suffused with a distinct redness.

"Do the two of you ever notice that the only time you actually speak to me is to either put me down, or when you want something?" Eleanor's brows raised.

"I never thought much about it. Lenora, are ya gonna help or what?" Winchester's face wrinkled in desperation.

"I already told you. My name isn't Lenora," Eleanor bluntly reiterated.

"I got to get back to her. She's not well. She's not, Lenora."

"I guess she chose that for herself, didn't she?" Eleanor's mouth had become a tight little fissure in the middle of her face.

"*You* mean, Lenora. *You* just plain mean!" Winchester hollered as he turned and ran back to where he remembered Jane was situated.

Themis had spoken. Her cornucopia hung depleted at her left side.

LV

The wind picked up. Eleanor scudded her feet along the ground in quick, whisking motions. Dust blew up as the wind carried away the suspended particles. The last few weeks had been more or less of a blur of chores as the summer passed by in dreary monotony. Lately, she hadn't seen them anywhere and as the solstice had already passed, there wouldn't be many more chances before school resumed.

The sun felt soothing on her skin and feeling rather lackadaisical, not truly caring whether or not she missed lunch, she flopped down into the long, soft roadside grasses. The birds hummed musically from their lofts as Eleanor watched an overzealous baby bird being fed a worm by its insistent mother. Stretching, she yawned and began the arduous blending of stroke after stroke of brown and bits of Indian red to arrive at just the right combination of bird, branch, and mutilated worm bits. Her usual morning rendezvous had now often given way to a deliberate and rather debilitating dedication to her chosen field. Instead of the copious hours she would spend with her psychic palette, this had been replaced by a careful and scrupulous reading of the Bible. Eleanor had decided she was going to be a theologian, and if she could not preach the Word, she would settle for the Puritanical, highly-venerated role of a nun. She would make sure that her previous actions with that Jane-girl did not corrupt her chances, regardless of Jane's undignified and blasphemous attempts at debauching her earnest endeavors. She would not be dissuaded. God would see the truth of her convictions. Jane would get what she rightly deserved, and if anything, Eleanor simply felt pity for her ignorance and the ungodliness of her chosen course.

She had not shared this epiphany with anyone. For the time it was private, her own newly-conceived being, and she would keep it this way until the moment was right to disclose her chosen course and then, she would leave... to become what she was always meant to be... and God would see her resolve... He would understand that she could only love him... Him in his infinite wisdom... in His infinite love... Him in His infinite... His infinite... what was it?

She could feel her mind giving way to a drowsiness that suddenly overtook her and as the wind picked up she could taste the grit from the road which landed silently upon her dry, parched lips. She laid the Bible she had hid under her dress upon her chest and slowly began to mentally recite a psalm, when from without, all at once, she heard piercing screams. Startled, and abruptly vertical, she saw that just beside her the once-satiated baby bird had fallen calamitously to the hard, unmerciful ground. It was screaming in pain for its mother as it had obviously broken its wing. Eleanor did not know what she should do. She knew it was suffering and would soon die. She closed her eyes and recited a little prayer for the quick departing of its tiny soul. She stood for a moment unwavering, seeing herself cloistered in a habit, her veil trailing down her back, sweating from the searing heat of the day, towering over an ailing child comforting his ails. The image transported her there to that place, away from this, from the dreariness of it all. She wished she could be there now, saving his life, infusing her life into his. From her reverie, she was again roused, but this time violently, by the screeching creature's mother, as its repeated, sharp pecks pierced viciously into her soft, pale skin.

Dropping the Bible, she began to beat at it wildly, uncontrollably, as it deftly started for her gaping eyes. Her pupils dilated as she cried out, "Get off me!" Her face was bleeding and the bird's acidic defecation burned into her derma, staining her clothing as well. It would not desist, and seemingly in the distance she could hear the cries of its suffering offspring. Eleanor's desperation increased, as suddenly she thought she could discern two very distinct voices laughing in unison at her. As the godforsaken beast's blows tore at her epidermis, again approaching the vicinity of her eyes, she became mad with fear. A single thought had conceived itself and repeated its visionary peal: stricken blind, she would never paint. Never stood out, defined, undulating, ominous as an inscription would upon a stone tablet. Thoughts seemed to cease, and choler like a red flood bursting illumination suffused the now-dull movement of previous thought. What would she do? What could she do?

She began to beat more vehemently, a defiance fed upon sheer bits of disemboweled rage entered her blows, and she beat the thing away, but once it had fallen helplessly to the earth, she continued until she had stomped the life out of the godforsaken thing. Near its mutilated form lay its baby, shrieking all the more, beside itself with pain and anguish. With one sharp blow of unmitigated fury, Eleanor's foot deftly and permanently put it out of its incessant misery.

Again the silence defined the space, and Eleanor, bloody, covered in mites and fecal matter, could taste the bitterness of her appalling covering, and slumping down beside the Bible, dissolved into a fit of tears.

LVI

Eleanor knew there would be no shoes for the coming season. This year wasn't looking good for entertaining ideas of such frivolity. She looked down at her present pair with their gaping holes along the toe and soles. Sighing, she shrugged in apparent apathy. Nonetheless, she knew Jane would have a pair, probably of the newest, nicest variety. For a moment, her color deepened, then decidedly she again shrugged, remembering that she hadn't read today's assigned verse.

The river was especially high for this time of year, its usual lackadaisical idling had become much more like a surging current. She could hear its roaring from the cover of the forest glades. Leaning up against the bark of a nearby tree, she brought out the Bible and sat it on her lap. Looking up, as was customary from her position she could see a break in the trees, seemingly opening a porthole to the fields beyond. As she began the passage, she suddenly noticed how sore and tired she actually felt. Since she had lost her status as scholar, they seemed to expect more and more from her at home, and no one really paid her any attention except Peter once in a while, when he wasn't pretending to pursue Effie, but really engrossed in Jane. Jane was beautiful to him, not just beautiful, but "wow wee, look at that puss!" Not to mention the golden locks that always seemed to frame it so well, as a halo frames an angel's crown. Effie, on the other hand, was the newly-toted top scholar, she was really nice... yeah nice, well no... not nice, but smart, very, very smart.

Although there was something about Eleanor that he really liked. A kind of unique strength. Besides her obvious benefits, there was something about her. He wanted Jane, he respected Effie even though he knew she could be considerably cruel and more than a little vindictive, but he actually liked Eleanor. Eleanor was somehow always well... Eleanor, and he liked that.

Just as Peter drifted in and out of her thoughts, there before her, in the fields beyond, he suddenly materialized. Sitting on top of a girl with the prettiest bows on her shoes she had ever seen was a figure identical to Peter's, with his pants all but removed. But how could it be? Only one girl she knew wore shoes like that.

Always barefoot, except on the first day of receiving a new pair, Jane's feet were sheathed in a fine covering of supple, buttery leather. Eleanor thought Jane had forsworn others for her sacred bond with Winchester. So, nothing had changed. She was still the same Jane. Eleanor smiled from her elevated stance. Winchester already hated her or at least didn't take any notice of her. She had nothing to lose. She knew he wouldn't be pleased.

She leaned back to enjoy the frantic thrusting of this twin. He employed an urgency to his stroke that she had never experienced in all of their relations. Sweat glistened off his face and neck, and then the show was terminated, and he lay prone upon Jane's quivering breast.

Eleanor, as she deliberately began today's chapter, was simply and wholly grateful. God, in His mercy, had granted her a sacred and long-coveted trust.

LVII

"I asked you to clean it up! Now do it! Do I have to always repeat myself? Doesn't anyone listen? You're all a bunch of bloody idiots! Good-for-nothing leeches! That's what!" Eleanor's father was beside himself. His speech was nearly inarticulate and heavily slurred.

Eleanor momentarily stopped kneading the dough. Droplets of sweat beaded and ran down her forehead in tiny currents. She could see flames start up from the blazing chamber. The incinerator was ready.

Lately, this was becoming a fairly regular occurrence. Wondering why he was suddenly engaging in such unbecoming behaviour, she ventured to ask him a question. But before the words had left her lips, a look of the strangest character crossed his face. Wrath, torment, anguish passed and she said nothing. The oven grew hotter. It was time to put the bread in before the wood was wasted. Moving back to her kneading board, pygmy faces peered out at her from their hiding places.

Her father sneered, "Thought you might do something with those brains, but you're just like all the rest." Eleanor was tired, tired of divulging the clandestine looks of hidden resent and outright pity, tired of the extra chores, and the innuendoes from peers, parents, and teachers alike of brain injury, retardation, and stupidity. Tired of... But her father only turned and departed, not a word of praise for all her constant daily efforts, or tendings to her copious brothers and sisters.

What kept her here? What was it? She knew what it used to be. Such an old, decaying definition no longer possessing any life or vital flux. What was it? She thought of the Bible waiting under her quilt.

Yen

She thought of the seven deadly sins. One day they would all pay for what she had been through. God would see to that. She knew divine justice must exist, somewhere, not here. She thought of how much she had learned already and it had only been a few months with a precious moment spared here and there when she wasn't being called, hounded by entreaties or actively sought out. Dark circles had formed under her lids and she felt like sitting down and crying and crying and crying. But her ducts were dry and sealed and the idea of sobbing waves of unrelenting grief only tired her further.

The bread had begun to rise. She hadn't eaten and the smell of it made the rumbling in her stomach chambers become audible. Little eyes blinked in front of the stove. Having now emerged, they stood with her, hungry and waiting also. Again she began to stoke the fire. A strange, acrid smell slowly ascended from the embers. Eleanor coughed as she started back. The scent began to permeate the room, and the once anticipant, small eyes smarted and filled with moisture, spilling over and causing a ghastly sound to emanate from tiny, hollowed orifices. The room had filled with heavy black smoke, but Eleanor was puzzled as to the source of the dilemma. The stench was becoming intolerable, as she opened all of the accessible doors and windows. Crying and pulling on the tails of Eleanor's skirt, little bony hands reached up, grabbing and clawing for breath. In this realm, all that could be seen was the whirling, spiraling trails of dark smoke pouring from the rising streaks of scarlet blaze. As the odour of decay rose, Eleanor thought of the seven deadly sins: gluttony, covetousness, pride, lust, envy, sloth, and what was the last one? She couldn't remember it now for the life of her. Simultaneously, she realized that a small animal must have burrowed its way into the pipe and inevitably become trapped in its workings. They would pay for their sins. Tired of the screaming and pulling beneath her, she struck out at the small hands that tore at her dress skirt. A figure tottered towards her bawling out inarticulate phrases. A being like a demon stood and spattered out words garbled and stammering.

"What you doing? Tr... tring to burn down the whole damned house?! Stupid, useless girl!!! You're just like your mother!"

At those last words, she jumped back. Eleanor had never heard him speak of her that way. He looked as if he had even shocked himself.

"I... I... I... damn you! Git the little ones outside now!" He yanked forcefully on her arm and something made a popping noise. The pain was extreme as it shot out in every direction.

Pulling away, Eleanor proceeded to run upstairs, grab her precious cargo and flee from the billowing stench. As she ran out, leaving that babbling demon and all of His Lilliputian sufferers to his bunglings, she thought, 'Am I my brother's keeper?' and in quick succession, 'Cast thy bread upon the waters: for thou shalt find it after many days.' She quickly drove such thoughts away from her consciousness and thought only of the saying 'Cast not pearls before swine', for they did not believe and love Him as she did. For this she knew she would be rewarded. God's wrath would be hearkened and she would serve Him. The Holy Covenant had been entered.

Beyond, Cerberus smiled from the entrance to the sacred lair.

LVIII

The day was now favourable to her in that she found her sought-after spot still uninhabited. Coughing, she attempted to rid herself of the noxious substance, her vestments being smoky. Stretching out in front of the hollowed area she had created in the earthy portion by the roots, the Holy Scriptures open in front of her, she looked up to steady the slight dizziness in her head, and dangling before her on a single, fibrous strand was a large, hairy spider.

It swung gently to and fro on the breeze as a hypnotic trapeze artist would on a thread used to delicately fashion the silver chalice. Transfixed by the pendular motion, Eleanor watched its waverings. Suddenly swinging forward, it promptly and deftly landed on the tip of her nose, and Eleanor, cross-eyed, remained inert.

"Ouch! God-damned, useless one of God's creatures!" As it bit, she smacked it away, jumping to her feet and stomping on its exoskeleton. Bespattered, the earth attained a moist, crimsoned hue.

Instantly, she felt a pang of remorse pass through her. Such an attitude of wanton disrespect would never do for her chosen vocation. Penitent, she repeated a long series of Hail Marys while crossing herself even though she knew to be true to her faith she should visit a proper confessional. Psychically, she could see herself humbly speaking to the Father, cinctured and serene in God's house, serving Him, and loving all of His creatures, alike. The image had become interspersed with waves of psychedelic colour and shape. Her mind drifted out, and she, not recognizing this series of patternings or form, began to mix her palette.

She hadn't painted for what seemed an eternity. But back the old appetence came, unfettered and undiluted in its archetypal form, with all of her instruments intact, awaiting her act of commencement. Involuntarily, she lay back and began. The more she applied, blending color and hue, light and shadow, the darker the outerworld became, and almost exclusively inward she had no recognition of this alien territory. The painting defied form and content both, and in its rendering seemed almost repulsive by the sheer nature of its unconventionality. It merely, by its outright act of defiance, existed. The crudeness and ugly formlessness of its line and structure made her almost wish to tear it into a million tiny pieces and fashion it again from she knew not what. Something in its very nature simply appeared atrocious and nearly deplorable to the human eye, but a certain thing or capacity, invisible, obscured, even remote, seemed to necessarily redeem it.

Sweating from the unmitigated exertion of this taxing necromantic state, Eleanor became conscious of the strange, and even dire nature of her present condition. Supine and unable to move or speak, she lay feeling as if an inert elixir had transmuted her vital flow, turning her very essence to lead. Attempting to move her legs, she found she could only helplessly twitch, and if she decidedly concentrated, grip the roots beneath the palms of her outstretched hands.

In the field beyond, where only a few days before she had seen Peter and Jane in a most compromising position, she saw the image of Jane, but as if out of Midas' nightmarish tale, the entire scene had been fashioned out of this alchemic riddle with the exception of the air, and Jane fully transformed, strode amongst the wheat which bowed and was beginning to collapse due to the exhaustive weight of its luminous stalks; butterflies, once airborne, crashed to the earth as if a blight had felled the entirety of their race; and Jane, crippled by the weight of her lower extremity, stood impotent in this perpetually-sought-after damned panacean realm.

When the weariness of this exigency had passed, Eleanor, damp and cold from fever, shivered uncontrollably, and shakily attempted to rise to her feet. The sun was just preparing to dip beneath the horizon and with its shallow fall, Eleanor remembered again the self-assigned task she had originally set out to do. Opening the Book, she began to repeat the seven sacred sacraments, committing them to memory. As her lips silently formed the syllables, ma...tri...mon...y, Ho...ly Or...ders, con...fir...ma...tion, bap...tism, Ex...treme Unc...tion, and Eu... Eu...Eu...cha...cha...rist, the last one would not permeate. Again she tried, but the word could not be visualized, and would not form.

Eucharist, the unifying principle, the paramount sacrament, above and beyond all others. What was it? The host and wine symbolizing the body and blood of Christ known as.... She could not remember the name of the doctrine. Trans something. Transub.... No. What was it? She couldn't remember anything. The Eucharist. She must learn these sacraments. They were not difficult. Algebraic equations were often much more taxing. Perhaps, she was becoming the dunce everyone assumed she was anyway. What was that damned word? She knew she knew it. Transubsta... she just could not remember.

The debilitation was undeniable, and surrendering, she gave in to this overwhelming sensation, and lay prostrate upon the upper tier of the earth. The ground, still warm, comforted her and she wondered how long she could lie here undisturbed by human hands. The line *Till human voices wake us and we drown* surfaced in her consciousness. He always could convey such majesty. If only her paintings could express a single drop of his genius, and surely the timeless endurance would be attained. No, that was no longer her volition. She was not the Creator. She had decided. Ecclesiastical life was all that remained to her. There was no going back. Suddenly, she wished only to lie here for all eternity and watch the meadow creatures which would pass. She could pray or paint as she liked. There was no judgement here only the omnipresence of the silence, the lulling, sonorous silence of the grasslands and trees, the birds and bees her constant companions. That would be paradise indeed, to meld with the earth and be what? Whole, impenetrable, actualized, immovable... here in this realm, serving solely as an extension of the divine earth, alloyed with the exosphere. That would be her act of volition, if such could or would ever be granted the validity of choice.

LIX

The sun having set, Eleanor, indifferent towards the dreary walk home, remained and lay down yet again on the rapidly cooling earth. Licking her lips, she found that her mouth seemed dry and salty. A hue of blue azure infused the invading blackness. Suddenly, a hare hopped by, pausing to gaze at this alien being which caused its usual dwelling ground to become momentarily terra incognito.

Eleanor reached out to what she could still discern as a textured brown softness and grazing its coat, it jolted and was off, its hind legs seemingly carrying it towards the newly-starlit heavens. Sweeping down with talons fully extended, its wing span so great as to glance her cheek in passing, it ensnared its dazed victim, and briefly hovering, the crimson stain bespattering Eleanor's face and hair, flew off with its limp prey. Uncovering her eyes, she smeared her war mask, and gaping at her blood-washed hands, shrieked as she thought the owl should have. From its vantage point, it tore and ate in bloody bits its evening meal, indifferent to the strange chaos from below. The moonless night had claimed its hapless victim, and Eleanor, tired, feverish, cold, and altogether in shock, could only think of the liturgical element as though this was a lesson He had granted she must learn. The Eucharist would permeate her brain's limited cognition. Clasping her hands, now on bended knee, gasping for air, she crossed herself and began: "Hail Mary, full of grace. The Lord is with thee. Blessed art thou amongst women, And Blessed is the fruit of thy womb, Jesus. Holy Mary, Mother of God, Pray for us sinners, Now and at the hour of our death. Amen." She proceeded to finish this torrent of syllabic usage with the sign of the cross. Again she began, crossing herself, and gagging: "Hail Mary, full of Grace. The Lord is with thee. Blessed art thou amongst women, And blessed is the fruit of thy womb, Jesus. Holy Mary, Mother of God, Pray for us sinners, Now and at the hour of our death. Amen." She followed the prayer again by this final symbol. As she repeated the gospel, she gasped harder, and pupils dilated, she reflected on how He had died for her sins and crying out, began yet again. The creature from above watched the peculiar nature of this strange discord, and bored with the spectacle, hooted thrice and flew off into the engulfing darkness.

Fainting into Hecate's soothing arms, Eleanor lay dormant, fallen away from this Cimmerian realm, and saw, beckoning from the field beyond... Jane. The light of the noonday sun bathed her skin, and joining hands, the notes rose up as if independent of their vocal chords, up, up, into the empyrean.

Ring around the rosie
Pocket full of posies
Husha, husha we all fall down.

As if in a vacuum, the circular motion was maintained, a gentle wind lifting bits of stalk and seed into the warm-currented air. Eyes locked, they circled as if the silence was ordained and sacred to this long-absent ritual. With the lack of all sensory input, a sense of form only was granted permeability here. Morpheus had ordained it so.

LX

Eleanor's sleep was uneasy and permeated by bouts of sporadic coughing, due not only to the smoky environment, but also to a certain incidence of pneumonia stemming from the other night's heavily taxing ritual. Restless, Eleanor wondered who had brought her home. She knew she had not walked herself. The house was silent and peaceful, but her temporarily granted state of lucidity did not come without expense. Her forehead wrinkled with concern as she, at this moment, felt she should again begin the act of penitence. How else would He know? He must know that her contrition was genuine, and she would have to make the necessary sacrifices. Kneeling, her body felt weak, and trembling, she nearly fell over. Her impregnable will kept her upright, yet she was doubtful as to how long she could maintain this stance. Sweat began to surface along the span of her arms and legs, and wavering, she toppled to the splintery planks at her knees.

Strange shapes overtook her and flying in this land of naught, she could not regain her proper sense of things. Objects with indiscernible form emerged from the periphery of the realm she now inhabited. A being with long tendrils of gold and a body composed of blobs of red and pink materialized. The familiarity of her own form was only granted by the distinguishable features of her face. Here, she had become a blobbish colourless thing which could only be described as translucent. The scarlet being approached and as it did, her own luminous shape bent and attempted to shield itself as it bounced against her. Looking down, she realized that her diaphanous figure was no longer uncontaminated. Blotches of red stained the previous immaculateness of her form. Somehow, the impurity stuck obstinately to her surface. Looking up, she could see a blob of yellowish-white in the sky. Curious, she considered that this shape, although seemingly less vibrant, may indeed be the sun. Effortlessly, as though she had almost no part in the levitation, she began to float towards her object of speculation. The warmth of its rays felt good against the cool dampness of her skin. As she gained in distance, she noticed smoke pouring off of its dull surface. It must be burning up and preparing to extinguish! Somehow, as though she played some divine part in this performance, she knew that she now must act. Passing the sun, she tried to gain speed, and the harder she tried, the faster she flew.

Stars sparkled like diamonds laced into a sky of black velvet. At least, in the realm of the heavens, her expectations of this celestial space endured. Suddenly, the matrix changed and the stars became luminescent crosses enveloping her. Eleanor, no longer a luminous white beam, became simply the form of her previous self, the small shape of a young girl adrift aloft in the heavens. Her speed arrested, she could no longer propel herself, but instead merely float along defenseless in this place. She found that if she concentrated she could kneel within the stardust and pray for the forgiveness she knew that she did not deserve. This she knew. She could see their approach: winged, serpent-like, she-monsters, three in number. She hoped that they would help elicit His forgiveness. They arrived laughing, and Eleanor, confused, simply reached out, and was taken between two of them, and with the speed that had previously possessed her, the third monster led, while they followed.

Again touching the strange ground, it wavered in its blob-like, jellified state like a green-brown coagulation. Still hearing their demonic laughter, Eleanor wondered what they would do. Yet, she feared them not. Again the tendrilled, scarlet shape approached and Eleanor, rendered impotent once more, bent in a paralyzing, quaking fear. The blobbish earth seemed to respond to her state of mind, and too was more unstable than before.

Cackling, they pulled her up by her arm and pointed to the nearing glob. Puzzled as to their intention, Eleanor still looked on in horror. One of the three, reached out to it and shrieking with glee, tore a big, globby bit from one side of the tendrilled mass. The thing screamed out, its tendrils standing on end. Their communication had been conveyed. The sacrifice was necessary and would be made. Angrily, the same fiend strode forward and yanked off a golden tendril. The thing shrunk back in evident anguish. Eleanor, spurred by their mirthful demeanor, too began to join in with the odd chorus. As they ripped at the scarlet thing, its tendrils fell to the ground, now rendered impotent, as Eleanor had once been by them. A mass of scarlet globules lay inanimate, the thing finally having ceased its incessant, gut-wrenching screeching.

Psychokinetically, the pieces rose up and entered their dribbling, gaping mouths. As they eagerly chomped at the substance, still they occasionally managed to let out a peal of laughter between engorged mouthfuls. Satiated, they looked at Eleanor and beams of white light left their divine orifices only to again imbibe Eleanor with the sacred luminosity. The sacrifice had been performed; Forgiveness had been bestowed.

Grace descended upon her psyche and her sleep gained a comfort never before attained. As the Furies slowly faded into the firmament, Eleanor wondered if it had only been a dream. She however, did not wish to ponder this question too deeply. For now, it was enough that such had ever been.

LXI

When Eleanor, due to the applications of continuous cod liver oil and steaming water vapour, eventually recovered, she found that in the course of her sickness of three weeks duration, there had indeed been a serious earthquake. The Wellgrene's barn had been rendered asunder by

Yen

the force, and smaller aftershocks had been felt for weeks. Just as they were beginning to subside, Eleanor roused from the heaviness of her continuous slumber. She awoke however, to quite a state of affairs as these events had left them in more of a financial bind than ever, and of course, this did not improve her father's growing thirst.

During her affliction, her parents had been informed by a prominent family friend that Eleanor's condition, as it had often resurfaced, could indeed be degenerative. 'Mental cases often were, you know.' Personally, Eleanor thought this guy was a quack, but people seemed to possess the utmost respect for the peculiar fellow. A psychiatrist by trade, who never had once set foot in the house, Dr. Woolston's mother was on intimate terms with Eleanor's grandmother, whom Eleanor had also never formally met, but had been privy to many a respectable tale. Nevertheless, the doctor considered himself an expert on Freud's triad of id, ego, and superego. When they occasionally ventured into town on a family outing, he would greet Eleanor's father with a formal, "Good day, Norman." But often that was as advanced as the conversation got, except his eyes invariably narrowed, and a suspicious leer would all at once come over his countenance, invariably cast in Eleanor's hapless direction.

Eleanor was groggy during the first few weeks of her recovery, but soon afterwards, began to return to her usual force and vigor. The smell of wheat hovered in the air, as harvest time was rapidly approaching. Her hands were calloused and splitting from the burden of increased tasks due to her mother, who recently began snapping at her to do this or that. Since her father had begun to drink, quite an unprecedented level of hogwash environed the town. Up to now, the only thing her family had been known for was the largest squash on record a few years back. According to various backstairs sources, Eleanor's father was preparing to run off with the butcher's drunken wife, who had become quite a good companion of his during his nightly taverned escapades.

Eleanor clung tenaciously to her Bible studies. She had made a pact with herself that if anything suffered, she had decided that it could and would not be these. Accordingly, every weekend, depending on what event may have been taking place at the church, she would sit in a back pew, and if the light came through the windows in just the right way, she could manage to barely discern the small, black inscription of her own personal Bible. It was the only possession that actually had any meaning to her. Her grandmother had sent it last Christmas and this fact had given her the impression of a righteous woman who always wore a dark hat with a feather. She never knew why she envisioned her this particular way, probably from a character in some book she had read, but couldn't manage to place. Her name was Mrs. Vivian Edward Norman Wellgrene, and Eleanor, since she could remember, had always referred to her grandmother as ma'am. She never considered this, only that it was, and had become, a matter of course over the years to the point that at Christmas, when Eleanor wrote her, she would always use the following salutation, "Dear Ma'am, Here's hoping the good Lord will bless and keep you well this Christmas and in the coming year." She would always sign this correspondence with the formal closing, "Yours sincerely, Eleanor Wellgrene." This form of greeting had gone on since Eleanor could remember and was now their established usage.

Today, in leaving for the church, the overcast sky glared defiantly from above as if the vehemence of its originator were upon her. She shook off this feeling, and with Book in hand started down the main road into town. It was a fairly busy day. A tall, barefoot man was loading his truck with bales of dried hay, and tipped his hat in greeting as Eleanor advanced. A destitute couple with their young, screaming child in tow was arguing as she approached, the child extending his tongue in her direction as the too-young mother uttered a stern remonstrance.

Eleanor quickly passed all of this hubbub, as she had little interest in these trivial happenings. The smell of cooked food wafted between the buildings leaving a pungent rather odious redolence. The church stood before her, its leaden-glass windows a palette of refined colour. Mounting the steps, she crossed herself, and managed to swing open the cumbersome, engraved, wooden doors. She heard a snug, solid thud as they closed behind her, leaving her entombed in fragrant darkness, the only discernible light from the windows at her rear.

Genuflecting, she slid into the rear pew, and waited. Clasping the Book, she silently prayed, again beginning a long succession of Hail Marys. The space was empty and all that could be made out was the Holy Mother and the pervasive smell of wood. The darkness seemed more severe than usual, and blinking, she could barely make out some movement near the front row. Otherwise, the space was deserted. The silence reaffirmed her, and suddenly weary, she felt herself effortlessly sliding down the back of the pew. Closing her eyes in the darkness, she was enveloped and even though her final enclosure was probably pine and would have leaked, she did not mind. The peace was omnibenevolent and her mind, momentarily, emptied of all earthly concerns. She must have fallen asleep for when she reopened her eyes, the candles had been lit, and involuntarily she reached forward and removed the heavy, black Book from its miniature shelf. Opening it, she turned to chapter eight in the Book of Revelations, and reading aloud, she uttered, "I am alpha and omega, the beginning and the ending, saith the Lord."

From within these sacred pages, like a bejeweled bubble of parchment, it slid and fell into her lap. In its brilliant opalescence, it reflected the glow of the burning tapers. Its delicate gold filigreed edges awed Eleanor's sense of veneration, and she turned it this way and that so that the light caused it to refract most magnificently. The amorphous shape, who had been sitting near the front of the chapel, had evidently vanished during Eleanor's repose, and no one was now in sight. She was alone. She had never possessed a ring or any piece of jewellery, but she had always secretly envied the women at church, who in their Sunday attire, always looked so becoming with their dress and gems.

Suddenly, the priest materialized from within the candlelight, and Eleanor could feel the palms of her hands beginning to sweat. Slipping it delicately into her threadbare pocket, the priest nodded his head towards her in welcome. Eleanor smiled in return. She considered if she should confess her finding.

"Good afternoon, Eleanor. Are you keeping yourself well these days? We heard you had quite a bad spell there with your health." His smile was sincere.

"Yes, thank-you, Father. I have been very blessed regarding the improved state of my constitution."

"Yes, you know Eleanor you should really be more careful. You have been quite a sick, little girl."

"Yes Father, but the Lord has taken care of me."

"Eleanor, I don't want you to misunderstand me, the Lord has and does perform many a miracle, but even the Lord is limited in what He can do sometimes. We must help Him through our own acts of faith and judgement. It doesn't make sense to allow oneself to be exposed to the elements, and then expect not to get sick. That is not exercising our own judgement as we should. Do you understand, Eleanor?"

"Yes, Father. I am an undeserving subject Father, but I assure you, not an ungrateful one." With those words, Eleanor began to cry.

"What's this? I am sure you are both deserving and grateful, Eleanor. Do not chide yourself so." He brushed his hand along her head, and she felt presently, more well than she had for a very long time. This would have been the perfect opportunity to tell him of her find, but somehow she could not bring herself to commit this act. She could still feel the tiny, captivating bulge pressing against her leg from within her frayed pocket.

The Ring of Gyges had been acquired.

LXII

It slid around her finger. It was so large that the collet would invariably end up facing her palm, but Eleanor did not mind. In the sun its matrix shone reflecting all of the colours which could be desired on a palette. Running her tongue along the stone, its smooth coldness reminded her of a divine icecube. Lying back she took it off and ran the perfect smoothness along her legs and inner thighs. Shivering with delight, she thought she heard a sound from the outer fields. Nothing stirred, so she resumed her reverie and turning it this way and that, it caught the sun and reflected a most intense blue from within its inner depths.

Suddenly, she was standing before her.

Eleanor, startled, sat up exclaiming, "Jane! I didn't see you. I mean, where did you... how?" Eleanor all at once realized the ring was in plain sight, and acting quickly, slid her hands into her pockets.

"I mean I didn't see you come up. I just didn't see you, that's all," muttered Eleanor, red as a cherry.

"Well, hello to you too. Is that any way to greet an old friend?" Jane, barefoot, slumped into the shade of the overhead tree.

"No, I guess not. I just was deep in thought, that's all." Eleanor's head quickly bowed.

"I noticed you're not alone," Jane's eyebrow raised.

"What? What do you mean?" Eleanor had no idea of what she meant.

"Your trusty prayer book? The one you never leave home without. I have to tell you Eleanor, it's not doing much for your reputation. No siree."

"Well, I'm not interested in what others think of me, that is, except for the Divine Father."

"Really? Uh-huh... whatever you say, dearie," Jane sneered.

Eleanor hated it when she chose to employ such a condescending tone.

"I've been meaning to ask you something that I've been considering now for awhile," Jane stated directly, but obviously in deep thought.

Eleanor had no idea what this could be, and was praying in the back of her mind that she hadn't seen it, but knew it was hard to pull one over on Jane.

"Let's just say for a moment that you lived in a world, but that world could only contain two colours. What colours would you choose?" Jane looked up at Eleanor with the gravest sincerity and something like reverie.

Eleanor was fascinated by her look and the nature of the query. "Only two colours? Geez, that's a difficult question. I don't know. What would your choices be?"

Jane was hoping she would ask. "My world would be at once the colour of golden wheat and blue azure sky, and in dwelling there I would know what it felt like to be infinitely green." Jane seemed to look through her at some indefinite space beyond.

Eleanor, confused, stated, "That's not possible. Nothing can be all gold and all blue at the same time." Eleanor was offended at this travesty of the spectrum.

"Why not? I can imagine it. If you cannot, your limitations are not my responsibility." Jane seemed legitimately offended.

"Okay. I didn't say I couldn't imagine it. I just said it wasn't possible. I can imagine it," Eleanor conceded.

"Well then, that satisfies as an answer in my books, and after all, it was my question." Jane's superiority again surfaced. "Well, how would your world be coloured?"

"I don't know. I've been thinking, and it's such a shame to be able to choose only two colours even if you could combine them. I mean your world will never know red or orange or purple. Without these colours what could a sunrise or sunset ever mean? Or a summer strawberry? How could there be a mist without the delicacy of a faint purple? It seems like such a profound loss. I can only answer your question by saying black and white. If I had to restrict my world to two, it would be black and white."

Jane stared in amazement. "You mean to say that you would reject colour altogether?"

"Well, I suppose there would be light and shadow, as well as night and day, but even they would be a crude occurrence." Eleanor was beginning to seriously ponder the possibility, when Jane broke in.

"But don't you think that would be awfully selfish?"

"No. I couldn't conceive of a world devoid of one of the primary colours. It would seem almost, well... blasphemous."

"Only you could tie religion into the quandary. Well, I suppose you wouldn't want a world devoid of even one of the magnificent colours in that ring you have in your pocket." Jane's eyes shone.

"What ring?" Eleanor's secret had not avoided her scrupulous detection.

"Now now, Eleanor. I won't let your little secret get out. I do know that Dr. Woolston's mother is sadly missing a ring which looks very much identical to yours. The only thing I want is for you to admit it. Why would I want to take away your precious colour palette? All or nothing." Jane smiled. The slyness had returned.

Eleanor's blood boiled a keen and unmistakable reddish-pink. She could feel the hue pulsing through her vessels, as she sat shaking all over.

"Confess your sin, Eleanor. That will do." The ordinance had been received.

Eleanor's head bowed and taking her hand, begged her not to tell anyone, especially Dr. Woolston or his bereaved mother.

"Kiss my hand, Eleanor. That's better. Now, that wasn't so hard, was it? I forgive you. Now, if you're lucky God will too."

LXIII

Eleanor wondered how she had managed to appear right then. She might have given it back. She just hadn't thought about it that much. After all, she was only enjoying it, and surely after a time, she would have returned it to its rightful owner. Why did Jane have to arrive at that exact moment? Was this some kind of a joke that He was playing on her? And if it were, why would He choose her of all people for His ministerings? She could think of better recipients. She knew that Jane would never have returned it. On the contrary, she would have aptly favoured Dr. Woolston, and the old miser, 'out of the goodness of his heart', would have bought his mother a brand new one, which would have brought tears to the old biddy's eyes! If He wanted that bunch in heaven, by golly, He could have the lot of them! She wasn't going to have any part of it. And she would keep it, just to spite them all. If He couldn't choose a more appropriate subject for His ministerings, why should she do anything for His divine favour, if He was as unjust and whimsical as a spoiled child! How dare He! She would not accept it, not in that golden, spoiled, wanton form! They could all go to Hell for all she cared!

Eleanor had been walking at quite a clip since she had left Jane at the tree. Suddenly she stopped and realized that damnation was impending, and she, due to her own pride, covetousness, envy and anger, had been the agent of her own doom. Upon bended knee, she began the petitioning. Four of the seven deadly sins had been committed in one vile, fiery breath of hate and vengeance. She had stolen the ring, not God, and not Jane. Who was she to condemn Him for His chosen messenger? Remorse passed over her in waves and wholly lost, she did not for even a moment know what to do or what would become of her. Her life was in His hands, and she cried out in grief and actual physical pain. No words came to her, only the profoundness of her sorrow. How quickly she had turned from Him in the hour of her test and had ultimately failed, but not just anyone, she had failed Him, the Almighty, the one to whom she had proclaimed her own faithful and undying love, and why? Her vaingloriousness had cost her everything in the end. She could now see it. She was one of the damned. What else was left for her? She knew that no matter what she could not, and never would, have brought herself to return the ring.

Getting slowly to her feet, she felt as if she were awaking from a nightmare only to recognize that this state was much preferable to her reality. She thought for a moment about beginning a long succession of Hail Marys, but abandoned the notion as futile. There really was no point. She began to weep in long, slow sobs of hopeless despair.

She was totally alone in a pervasively neutral universe, filled with finite reason, mechanistic dictums, devoid of morality, and fundamentally unable to apply a positive or purposeful direction to the freedom of choice she once believed, but now knew, she no longer possessed.

Heading back from the direction she had just come, she knew not what to think or do, and no longer cared. Life passed by around her. She had already ceased to be. Almost involuntarily, she began aloud to recite it.

"The Lord is my shepherd; I shall not want. He maketh me lie down in green pastures; He leadeth me beside the still waters. He restoreth my soul; He leadeth me in the paths of righteousness for His name's sake. Yea, though I walk through the valley of the shadow of death, I will fear no evil; For thou art with me; Thy rod and thy staff, comfort me. Thou preparest a table for me in the presence of mine enemies; Thou anointest my head with oil; my cup runneth over. Surely goodness and mercy shall follow me all the days of my life: And I will dwell in the house of the Lord for ever."

Upon completion of this declaration of her love, she felt momentarily a warm peace encompass her, and embracing it, the fear ceased to penetrate her essence. She was free. And His love was all. He had not forsaken her, and to Eleanor, this was everything she could ever esteem to, or hope for.

LXIV

The riverbank was nearing as the sun was beginning its still early descent in the west. The afternoon might hold some promise yet, and this realization, newly-arrived at, was a sheer comfort to Eleanor, who had just looked over the abyss into the bowels of despair. Atonement was necessary, and Eleanor, although weary, had an idea. She knew that the Hail Marys were certainly relevant, but she wanted to show Him, by an act of such devotion, such utter, undeniable commitment, that He was her All.

The sun's rays felt warm on her skin as she began to disrobe. Her nakedness made her feel whole in an element which if she could, would choose to never leave. Her reprieve, her church, her frolicking grounds all at once, and this is the place she knew she could find Him if she needed His assurance, advice or comfort. She was home, and appropriately so, this is the place she would atone.

The water glistened silver at her feet, and she shivered as its heatlessness contacted her skin. Immediately it swirled at her toes, and for an instant, she thought of turning back, but the notion quickly passed, and she forged on. Flowing in eddies around her waist, the bluishgreen pigment engulfed her. In this world of silver-gray and bluishgreen, the caress of the curves and cavities of her corporeality became like a long and forgotten contact, which once again found, could never be ignored. It alone remained translucent, the only materiality unaffected by these two hues omnipotent power. She smiled and, in need of air, rose to the lit surface above, the now opalescent liquid running from her mouth and nose.

The light seemed blinding and the distance to the shore was farther than she had expected. Crossing herself, she began the washing. Scrubbing her face with her palms, she began to traverse the length of her abdomen and accompanying appendages, terminating with her toes and feet. Floating on the waves, she could feel her sins being washed from her. He would understand the genuineness of her meaning. He would see her washing away her sins. It was the only way. Surely, she could not confess such a deed to Father Peters. Even if he understood and might even empathize with her plight as a sinner, Dr. Woolston would surely find out. This she knew. Therefore, this way was the better one. God had already forgiven her. She had felt the divineness of His love encompass her. She had been absolved and now the cleansing would begin. It was the only way. She knew that He must know that. He must.

As she proceeded with the gravest of countenances, she glanced down at the band of iridescence, and in shock, saw that it indeed, was gone. She looked around fitfully and gasped as she swallowed the first of many mouthfuls. Where could it have gone? It had been there only a few instants ago; she had felt the tightness enclosing her thumb. Surely, the light must have blinded her. It could not be. It mustn't be. It was the only truly beautiful thing she had ever possessed. How could it have simply floated away?! She had purposely worn it on her thumb as she knew it was too big for all her other fingers. This couldn't be! Looking towards the land, she refocused on a gnarled tree near the shoreline. She could make it out distinctly, thus she knew her vision was unimpaired. Her back now to the sun and positive of her visual capacity, she again glanced down at her thumb. It was not there. Thinking of turning back, she knew that she had had it on the sand, and remembered admiring it in those shimmering depths. It must be down there somewhere. She could find it if she could muster the strength. First, she must calm herself. Inhaling and exhaling as deeply as she could, she dove down into the opaque, murkiness below. The previously predominant hues did not dwell in these lower regions, and as she descended, she thought she felt a slimy form brush momentarily against her, which caused her to start, and lose air. In this realm, she could make out only faint whitish shapes. She wondered if this might be His idea of recompense, her black and white world, ready and willing to absorb her. Still, she pushed onward. Her head could feel a steady pressure building and she had not as yet even discerned the bottom. She knew she could go no deeper, and even if she could, this sunless realm would not conduce the use of sight. If she had been a giant magnet, her property of attraction would have been much greater. Feeling as if she may have been rapidly transforming into a heavy, sinking magnet, her negative ions being pulled down towards the positive ones in the abyss below, the desire to surface was abating. Now that it was more difficult to cognate, the reality of losing her most precious possession was rapidly waning into a deep, dark, circular whirling sensation in which she felt if she would only give into it, she could indeed be free of all worry, of all perception, of all... her black and white world was left and the distant sound of chaotic voices as though a chorus had suddenly surged up from the deep.

Ganga's tail had been granted the adornment of a band, patinaed with opalescent radiance.

LXV

Eleanor remembered little. She awoke on the river's bank choking up phlegm and some blood. The murkiness surrounded her, and for a moment she was certain that she had died, and He, in His divine providence had left her in the world she had wished to remain in, devoid of light so that she could not conceive the profoundness of her loss. However, as she surveyed her environment, her optical system still optimal, she was forced to realize that she had indeed surfaced, and from the acute pain in her chest, was fully conscious as well.

Almost immediately, she felt for her thumb, but knew what she would find. It had been lost and she would be forced to be forever conscious of her transgression, that being her finite, but seemingly everlasting penance.

Coughing, she rolled over on her side and spit up more blood and mucus. Even though it was the middle of summer, the night felt chilly, and shivering, Eleanor attempted to rise, but found she could not. She wondered what Jane would do if she were here. But truthfully, she was more curious as to what Jane would say. She always had the most profound way of catching and keeping Eleanor's attention.

The darkness was alive with the sounds of field and forest, and the river was sonorous in its own right, as mounds of tiny pebbles lay at her feet. The storm, which she knew nothing of, had mercilessly flung her onto the shore, also excavating the riverbed. She, however, did not recognize these and wondered as to their source. Quivering, she again tried to stand, but the weakness in her lower extremities was so severe as to render the action purposeless.

All at once she felt a gentle softness beside her, close to her flank, and fluffy. Startled, she called out, but a whine and wet tongue promptly responded, quelling her fears. Nestled beside her, under the stars, with the wave action in calm and regular rhythm, their breathing fell into synchronicity, as the warmth from the beast's flanks diffused into Eleanor's stiff, inert form suffusing her with the breath of life.

St. Nicholas had indeed answered her call.

LXVI

Every day for the past two weeks, her same four-legged frolicking friend had accompanied her on daily outings to the grove by the river. Bible in hand, they would set out, and 'Beast', as she had come to call him, would lead the way.

He was large and his movements were clumsy. Inevitably, his tongue would protrude and Eleanor would initially scold his undisciplined demeanor, but invariably end up laughing and following gaily in tow. Still coughing from her recent near miss, although overall generally on the mend, Beast would bound over, jump up towards her face, whining and begging to be stroked. Not until they had terminated their progress and he had been sufficiently patted, covering her with his overzealous furry-wet sentiments, did he desist. Eleanor would, as often as not, end up flat on her back in the roadside clover with his full soft coat covering her like a warm blanket. Sometimes on these occasions she would fall into a prolonged slumber and not until awoken by his sloppy, wet kisses would she realize the lateness of the day, and scolding herself, hurry home to awaiting chores.

Suddenly his ears perked as though he had heard a familiar sound, and whining softly, turned his head and seemed to listen.

"What is it, boy? Do you hear something on the breeze?" Eleanor cooed.

Beast replied by looking up innocently at her with his round sherry eyes and gentle face.

His moist nose quivered and vibrated keenly as he pointed it in this same direction. A wind suddenly picked up, and seemingly satisfied, he trotted off in the ascertained direction.

Eleanor had never seen him leave before. On the other hand, it had always been she who had been first to depart. Dejected, she called after the retreating figure.

"Beast, Beast, are you leaving me only after we have just found each other?" Eleanor stammered as a genuine note of deep sentimentalism inadvertently entered her mock tone.

Turning his head back, he looked directly at her and barked knowingly. He seemed to want her to follow.

Yen

At once maintaining a brisk clip it wasn't that difficult to keep up with him, although she had to pay attention to his maneuverings as he loped along.

Eventually, she too could hear a noise. She could not discern its exact articulation, but nevertheless it seemed to originate from the ground. At last Eleanor would get to meet Beast's owner, even though she vehemently had hoped he didn't have one. Each day, she had managed to save a portion of her bread and occasionally a bit of the meat she had access to. Now, the idea she had been secretly longing for seemed to be fading into the nebulosity he had indeed materialized from. Regardless, he was taking her somewhere, and at least she would know for certain one way or another.

The call had become clearer and she could just make out its muffled enunciation. "Orestes, Oresteese, Or...ess...teese....."

The rhythm was sing-songy and Eleanor, now that she could discern the utterance, would have known that voice anywhere.

LXVII

Eleanor peered down into the chasm whence emitted the summons. It was a deep, dark hole and she could barely make out her figure. Beast, however, had already entered the cavern.

"He's yours? I didn't know you had one," Eleanor quickly uttered.

"Orestes? Yes, we've had him for awhile. I'm his favourite, aren't I, Orestes?"

The dog whined knowingly and rubbed the side of its muzzle along her leg. As she scratched his left ear, his tongue began to protrude rhythmically.

"He's been keeping me company for the last few weeks," Eleanor looked down at him, suddenly distressed.

"Yes, he's everyone's friend really. I only require his assistance occasionally. But he knows better than not to come when he's called. Isn't that right, Orestes?"

"That's certainly an odd name for a dog. I call him, B..."

She interrupted before Eleanor could finish the epithet. "My name is Electra. This is Orestes and you can be Iphigenia, that is, if it suits you to be."

"What odd names! They are Greek deities?" a tone of nervous tension entering Eleanor's voice.

"For a cultured individual Eleanor, your extent of acculturation is sometimes questionable to say the least."

"Well, where did you hear of these names? I might have heard of them at some point briefly, on a test of Hellenic culture or something, but I didn't take that much notice, and I really don't remember. And further, I don't think that's any reason to insult me." Eleanor was warming.

"Okay, okay, you win, you win. Are you playing or not?" Her posture slackened.

Eleanor, temporarily satisfied, nodded her head in acquiescence.

"Good. If not, I was going to change your character to a Harpy."

"What's that supposed to mean?" Eleanor's back was again up.

"I think it's self-explanatory. Now, are we going to play, or what?"

Before Eleanor could protest, she noticed dangling from her chest on a rope made of wood and vine, was a large, deepish red piece of amber, shining like an alloy of silver and gold. It swung heavily as it rotated on her tiny-tanned-nucha.

Eleanor saw its glisten, and grasping it with her fingers moved it this way and that. Jane, shutting her eyes, began to rock rhythmically and opening them suddenly stammered, "It was my mother's."

Eleanor could only make out the deepish tone of colour and hue as if a shellac of vibrant red had been added to the darkest hue imaginable. It seemed to be on fire. Eleanor found herself smiling at the figure before her, and reaching down groped her pocket in the darkness to find only that to her great dismay, she had lost her most precious possession. Frisking herself, she blurted, "Where is it? What did I do with it?" She looked down searchingly at Orestes and he, turning his head sympathetically to one side, whined consolingly.

"I couldn't have lost it! My grandmother gave it to me. It's very old. Can you help me look? I can't see very well down here. Maybe it's in the substratum."

"The what?" Her voice sounded perplexed. "*What* did you lose, Eleanor?"

"My Bible! I can't have lost it!"

Yen

"We'll find it. It can't be far." Even though the light had almost disappeared completely, Jane's voice seemed oddly empathetic in the darkness. Eleanor didn't know what to say.

On hands and knees, they felt around the hard earth that served as the base of their present dwelling. But, nothing could be found.

"Where the blast is it?" A note of panic permeated Eleanor's usually calm tones.

"We'll find it. It can't be far. You probably dropped it chasing Orestes."

"How could I have been that stupid!" Eleanor was becoming beside herself.

"Eleanor, calm down. We'll find it."

"What would you know about it? You're down here playing your childish games and frolicking about, while I'm studying the Scriptures and doing chores all day, trying to live my life by a moral code of ethics that you could never even conceive of, let alone understand!"

"Now, who's attacking whom? If that is your choice in life, who are you to reprimand me? Are you better than I by your choice? And if you think you are, what do you really know of Christianity, or of anything for that matter?"

Eleanor was rendered speechless. She didn't know why she had said these things. She only knew that she was so very tired of work and endless toil and the nothingness that made the days follow one another in dreary succession with her Bible as her only source of hope or inspiration, or repose for that matter.

Beast was laying flat against the earth, eyes lifted but solemn, watching the two forms oppose each other. Suddenly, his ears perked, as his head shot up simultaneously.

Unexpectedly, they both stopped short in mid-sentence having heard a shot in the distance. Eleanor tensed, but Jane only shrugged.

"Someone's hunting. It's nearly dark. I should be getting back soon," Eleanor mumbled, as if conscious of a foreboding.

"Yeah, you would say that. Are you scared or something? I'm sure you have nothing to worry about, Eleanor. Your divine God would surely protect you after everything you have given Him, don't you think?" Jane's tone was no longer empathetic. On the contrary, it dripped with sarcasm.

All at once, the caverned space was illuminated from within, Jane having lit the candle she had brought with her.

"You mean, you had the candle all this time? Why didn't you light it before?" Eleanor was again warming.

"I only light it once the dusk has hit, and the dusk has hit, now." Jane's face formed a ghoulish smirk.

"If you had lit it before, we would have been able to see that the Bible obviously was not here and we wouldn't have had to look and get our smocks all dirty!"

"Maybe, but that would have been too easy and I would have used up my candle a lot faster. Then we would have been in complete darkness and it would have been extremely difficult to get out of our little recess."

Eleanor ceased to continue the tirade which she could feel mounting. They both looked down at Orestes and noticed his ears were still on the alert. They could faintly hear something in the distance.

"You should be happy. Windy's coming soon."

"What? Oh, I should go. I want to retrace my steps and see if I can find it."

"In the dark? I don't think so."

"Does Winchester always come here to meet you after dark?" Eleanor abruptly asked.

"Yeah, fairly often. He doesn't like to go too long without seeing me. Why don't you stay? C'mon, Eleanor."

"You know he doesn't like me and besides it doesn't matter anymore anyway." Eleanor looked away.

Before Eleanor could climb out, she heard the distinctness of footsteps and Winchester's stutter, "J...J...Jane?"

"I'm down here stupid. Come down."

"Who's with ya?" he called.

"You don't have to yell. A friend. Someone we don't get to see very much."

"That Lenora-girl?"

"Yes, but not Lenora you retard, Eleanor to be precise."

"Oh."

"Are you coming down or what?"

"Is she goin'?"

156

"No, I don't think so. She's going to watch."

Eleanor's eyes widened, but no sound came from her lips. Then, "I... I... have to.. to..."

But Winchester was already down undoing his bottoms. "I can't wait much longer Janey. Is she goin' or stayin'?"

Jane blew out the candle as she uttered, "Stayin'."

Eleanor couldn't see anything except an outline pressed up to the wall and the other gyrating to and fro. Orestes made a sort of sound between a whine and a growl and seemed to settle into a ball for a quiet nap.

Eleanor was sweating as Winchester began to moan and the shadow moved more frantically. "I'm comin' Janey, I'm comin' hard." This utterance was followed by a loud guttural grunt.

"Well that was very quick. You're not improving much, and the way you're going I'm beginning to wonder if there's any real point."

"I been studyin', Janey. Honest, I have."

"Well, if it doesn't show in the performance, then it doesn't matter, now does it?"

From the inflection in Winchester's voice, it sounded as if he was about to cry.

"You're not gonna stop doin' this or nothin', are ya Janey?"

"We'll see," but as soon as she had uttered these words, a booming voice bellowed down from above, "Jane, are you down there? I've been looking everywhere! Damn, foolish girl! How many times do I have to tell you not to..." but as he shone the lantern down into the chasm, his speech stopped short.

Winchester was frantically buttoning up his gaping trousers, but Jane was making no effort to pull down her elevated dress. Instead, she was removing her necklace and throwing it at Orestes. As it flew through the air, Eleanor could just make out the semblance of a miniature statue. Orestes swallowed until the necklace, both statue and rope-wooded vine, was completely ingested. Eleanor could not believe that it had been fully consumed.

"What are you doing down there? Who's all with you?"

"Eleanor Wellgrene and Winchester Farling, sir," Jane plainly stated.

"Eleanor should be going home now, then. As for Winchester, I'd like a word or two with him. I brought you something, your favourite, but now I'm not so sure you deserve it."

He threw down the carcass and it landed in the cavern's center on the stone tablet imbued with the emerald hue. Its neck made a cracking noise as it impacted the granite and a dribble of blood leaked out of the doe's nose.

Eleanor was horrified and began to scream. Suddenly, she felt herself being pulled up and out, as a look of displeasure passed over Jane's father's aspect.

"It's better if you go home now, Eleanor." His cold command seemed to ordain her affirmation. Turning to leave, she felt a cool nose nudge her palm, and slowly she began the long trudge home.

Kind of stunned and in relative shock, she and Beast continued in their preset task, but hearing penetrating screams turned around. In the distance she could just make out what looked like Winchester being repeatedly kicked in the groin. The figure seemed to be attempting to clasp himself to mitigate the blows, but to no real avail.

Edging back, Eleanor made her way along the tree line out of direct sight with Beast in her wake. She was now close enough to make out the words and see the general action.

"Please sir, no more. Please..." Winchester's begging was bone-chilling and yet he did not desist. Winchester's hands were covered in a dark substance. Eleanor could only guess that it must be blood.

Jane stood watching, silent and seemingly menacing as well.

"You shouldn't be doing these things with other people's daughters. I have no mercy. There is no point in appealing."

"My parents aren't gonna like this! They'll get ya! Ya ugly bastard!"

At this, he began to roar, a loud, chilling resonation. Jane who up to this point had stayed silent, now began to snicker as well.

"Take off your pants. That should shut you up." At these words, he began undoing his belt.

Pressing up to him like she had seen Mr. Graves do once before to Jane, he grabbed the bloody gonads and began plunging in and out in faster and faster succession. "Nice and tight. Better fit than Jane. Too bad you're so bloody ugly!"

Winchester could no longer hear anything but his own gut-wrenching screams.

Eleanor, no longer able to handle the sheer horror of the scene, covered her ears and closed her eyes, and curling into a ball, felt the softness of Beast's coat at her feet.

LXVIII

Jane sat cross-legged like a Buddha obviously absorbed in the contents of what appeared to be a small, old book. Eleanor, who had been looking vehemently for her Bible for the last couple of days, could not, no matter where she searched, locate it.

Jane, glancing up, gazed directly at Eleanor whom, up to this moment, had been completely unaware of her presence.

"What are you doing down here? Still scouring? Thought you would have found it by now." Jane shrugged indifferently.

"Evidently, if I am still searching, I have not found it, now have I?" Eleanor barked back.

"Snippy, snippy. What's your problem today?" Jane retorted, engrossed once more in the pages.

Eleanor wondered what Jane was reading. She had never seen her read before as she knew that Jane couldn't read, or at least, couldn't read very well. Her puzzled expression quickly vanished as she remembered the gruesome nature of the other night. "Who's Windy? I mean how's Winchester?" Eleanor was sincerely concerned.

Jane peered up again, but this time blankly. "Who?"

"You know very well who." Eleanor countered dryly.

"Why do you ask? Did you see more than you would care to admit?"

"I... I... I saw. Yes." Eleanor's head bowed.

"Well, I haven't seen him. He beat him pretty bad. I think he managed to stumble home eventually."

"You mean, you don't even know?"

"Should I? He wasn't very good anyway. I don't know what you're so concerned about. It's not as if he's dead or something."

"What? No, but I'm sure he's missing one less important function of his body!"

"Probably. He was always too eager, and so bloody stupid anyway."

"Jane, how can you be so cruel? I'm sure the Farlings could conceivably press charges. Did you ever think of that?"

"Eleanor, you just don't get it, do you? I mean, so what? The guy can't piss for a couple of days and if the thing never works again, trust me, his future girlfriend wouldn't be at a loss." Jane peered down.

Her apathy appalled Eleanor. "How can you be so indifferent? The beating was horrific, but it wasn't just that. It was the other..." Eleanor's voice trailed off.

Jane glared up, this time evidently irritated. "Well, what was it then? I thought the beating was pretty bad actually. You didn't?"

"Of course I did! But the other. I can't even say it, and you stood there laughing! Are you as much of a psychopath as your...?"

But Jane interrupted. "A what? A psycho what?"

"A psychopath!" Eleanor stepped forward and hissed the word at her to which she responded by closing her book and getting up.

"Okay Eleanor, exactly what are you trying to say? The fucking? Is that it? When my father fucked Winchester? I kind of got off on that part. And you have to admit, it was pretty funny to hear him scream like that. He sounded like a rooster for Christ's sake!"

Eleanor almost swallowed her tongue. She couldn't think of anything to say. Instead, she grabbed the book Jane was reading out of her hands and ran as fast as she could away from the sheer Satanic nature of Jane's words. They were beyond anything she had ever heard. She couldn't hear anymore. Out of breath and panting, she stopped behind the remnants of their barn and opened the flap of the book. The characters were indiscernible. The only intelligibility that could be perceived was found in flipping through its leaves. The frank state of strangely clad couples who were engaged in various postures of fornication interspersed the foreign script.

LXIX

The morning promised an unscathed sky, cloudless, and serene. Eleanor walked disconsolately along the path by the riverside. She still looked for them. First her ring, then her Bible. What was next?

The days of summer were quickly coming to a close with only a few

Yen

weeks left before the onslaught of another school year. Her thoughts were temporarily interrupted by the lilting strains of singing coming from somewhere in the vicinity.

It stopped abruptly, and Jane appeared on the bank, still cross-legged in the pose of a Buddha. Although her eyes were shut, her feet were filthy as usual, her light smock as unbecoming as ever.

Opening her eyes, she suddenly blurted, "Did you bring it?"

Eleanor, staring transfixedly at nearby pebbles for any sign of it as they floated up with the tide, did not hear a word of Jane's query.

"What?"

"The book which you so kindly stole from me the other day."

"Oh, right. I guess we both lost one then, didn't we?"

"I want that book back, Eleanor. I know you're not a thief, because if you were, that would make you no better than a common sinner, and everybody knows that you're not me."

"Well, you didn't do anything to help me find it, so what does it matter?"

"I didn't take your Bible, Eleanor. Give me mine back."

Eleanor, seemingly unmoved, slumped down beside Jane.

"What's with you today?"

"What's the point of anything, anyway? I just can't feel it anymore. I'm tired Jane, so tired."

"C'mon, Eleanor. Is it all that bad? You know what they say, it'll all be better tomorrow."

"Jane, that's such a stupid saying! Tomorrow never comes." Eleanor lay back.

"Exactly."

"Nothing ever changes. If it did, there would be far less sinners on this blasted planet."

"And how would you know?"

"No, Jane. How do you know? You condone it, for Christ's sake! You're no better."

"Don't use the Lord's name in vain, Eleanor. It doesn't suit your style."

"Shut up! Shut up! You can shove your witty, little, word games!" Eleanor fell silent. Then, "I don't care about that stupid book. Why do you need to look at a pornographic book anyway? You get plenty of practice yourself."

"That book isn't exactly what you think it is. I need it."

"How would you know? It isn't even in English! It's a bunch of filthy, dirty pictures!"

"It may be that to you, but it isn't to me. I do know and it's enough that I know. I don't ask you to explain your Christianity to me, now do I? You know, and that is enough."

"Some Christian I am." Eleanor's lips pursed, her eyes narrowed, and she couldn't say another word.

Jane's voice softened. "You are a good person, Eleanor. I know that. You can't save all of the people or change all of the things that you see or know about. Even if you choose to keep my book, I still know that. I believe it. And that is enough, it has to be."

Eleanor was looking at her now. "You are not a good person. You aren't, Jane. I believe that, too."

"I know that is so Eleanor. These are facts. You are; I am not. I am what I am though, and that is enough. It has to be." Jane's voice was rising now. "C'mon. Let's go. I want to show you something." Jane took hold of her hand, and first pulling her upright, heaved Eleanor to her feet.

Eblis was waiting.

LXX

Jane had gently taken Eleanor by the hand and they seemed to have been traveling for a long while. Eleanor, looking down at Jane's bare feet which were currently dirtier than ever, finally commented, "Jane, I have to rest. Where are we going?"

The hedge they were walking parallel to loomed large as Eleanor could see nothing beyond.

"Jane? Jane, for Pete's sake, I have to stop!"

Jane whose feet were sore also suddenly blurted, "My feet are sore too, okay? At least you wore shoes. I would have too, if I had known I would end up bringing you here."

"Bringing me where?"

"To see Sir Bifford's place of course."

"Who?"

"Sir Bifford. You remember him, don't you?"

"Oh no. He's not like old Mr. Graves is he?"

"If I recall, you shouldn't be complaining."

"He's not an old pervert, is he?"

"He was. But he was different. My father's old boss. Used to work for him in the off-season."

"You mean, you did it with him, too?"

"I would have. He had a really big one. I mean really big. He liked me to suck it. His wife didn't want anything to do with him. That frigid, old bitch! She was always rude to me when I was around, but I think she liked it more than she let on. This one time I was sucking him off and she walked in, and you should have heard her! Crying and screaming and on-and-on she went. What a racket! But secretly I think she liked it. She didn't like me much though. Before I left that day, she made sure the maid gave me a good beating! I've never been beaten. She probably got off on it. I hated the bitch for that. I told Sir Bifford about it, but he said there wasn't much he could do. It was his wife's money. But he gave me extra money, and a few extra polishes. He used to give me nail polishes from Paris... Paris! He was always good to me."

"If that's where we're going, I don't want any polishes Jane. My parents will wonder how I got them."

"No, Eleanor. You've got it all wrong. He's dead."

"You mean we're going to visit some dead guy?"

"No, silly."

"We're not going to visit his wife?"

"She's dead, too."

"Why are we going there then?"

"I want to show you the old place. I go there sometimes. It's abandoned. Some people say it's haunted. I really liked sucking Sir Bifford. I would have done more, but he never wanted me to. I... I don't know why."

The gate stood before them. Its wrought iron still bore the inscription Sheads' Manor, the maiden name of Sir Bifford's wife.

It was cracked open far enough for the two of them to just fit successfully through. The yard was overgrown with creepers and foliage. From their trajectory they could just make out the old turrets and spires of the place. It was splendid in its dilapidation.

Jane was already hoisting open the front door. Its heavy creaking could be heard from Eleanor's present location within the overgrowth. Jane slipped through the crack and vanished from sight.

The light's angle having shifted glanced the stone facade and the side of the petals of wild roses. Frozen, for an instant protected, as if the shutter had fully dilated then closed recording an image, the scene's spoilage, redeemed from its mundaneness by the nature of the undertaking.

Eleanor, once she had located the path to the entrance, slipped into its labyrinth. Jane sat naked, cross-legged on the floor meditating. Occasionally, small vermin would scamper across the room, but Jane's concentration remained focused and undisturbed. Like a pillar of stone, she sat like one of the priceless vases which had once graced the room with its presence.

Eleanor stood, suspended and motionless, as if she had been transformed somehow by the contemplator.

All at once she spoke, "What are you doing?"

Jane did not respond.

Eleanor heard a wind causing a branch to beat like an incessant knocking on the door.

She decided to assess her surroundings: broken wooden boards, thick grime and dust on everything, essentially no furniture, nothing particularly noteworthy or special about the room except for a fireplace, pale marble with faces carved into its frontispiece: angular and bestial, yet beautiful in its rendering.

Suddenly the still figure, seeing the veneration on Eleanor's face, piped up, "Arresting aren't they? In his latter years, Sir Bifford, confined to his wheelchair, carved as a hobby. He was really quite good."

As Eleanor followed the multitude of otherworldly faces, as their seeming darkness contrasted the whiteness of the marble, Eleanor could only shake her head. It must have been the years of soot build-up which created the impression.

She rose and from behind, Eleanor heard the striking of a match. Eleanor wondered if she were going to ignite a candle as the light was gradually diminishing from the interior of the room. Almost immediately the sweet scent of smoke arrested her nostrils, as she quickly turned around somehow expecting the room to be ablaze. Instead, spirals of smoke departed her lips, dark and perfectly formed in their conception.

"I didn't know that you smoked," Eleanor sputtered.

"There are a lot of things you don't know about me. Sir Bifford always gave me some."

"You like that taste?"

"Well, there are worse flavours. Oh Great Cannabis: the Tree of Life, herself."

"You are right. I hardly know you at all. I thought I did, but really I don't. Who are you?"

"In some ways, you know me better than I know myself."

The wind picked up again.

Eleanor felt a chill pass along her spine. "Do you come here often?"

"Sometimes, when I want to reflect undisturbed."

"So, you don't bring anyone here?"

"No."

"You want to know who I am. I am who I am who I am who I am..." she laughed uproariously as though she had uttered the wittiest remark.

Eleanor looked on perplexed and astonished.

"You want to know? Do you know what traducianism is? I am either a reflection of this principle or of creationism and if I am not any of the above, I could be said to contain the atman or let me see..." she drifted off as her eyes closed and opened heavy with stupor and languid from delirium.

"What are those words? I don't know what they..." Interrupted, her sentence remained unfinished.

"If you must know, my grandfather was a theologian. Bet you didn't know that, did ya?"

She waved the joint around her head. "Come over here, Eleanor. I want to show you something." Kissing her heavily, she wrapped her arms around Eleanor and began to consume her lips, gently and systematically. Eleanor was rocked into the crevices of her supple nakedness and probing tongue. She tasted like a sweet, sweet cherry wine. Her fingers began to explore hidden formations of layer and form. As

Eleanor writhed along the filth beneath her, she noticed to her horror that flames were silently engulfing the borders of the room. Eleanor pointed to the nearing blaze, but she only giggled pressing herself further into her. Eleanor jumped up and screamed at her, "We have to get out of here! The whole place is going to go!" But insensate, she only attempted to pull Eleanor back unconscious of her blared warning. "Come on! Get up!" But Eleanor couldn't pull her up. She was choking now on the smoke and her mounting frenzy at Jane's unresponsiveness was greatly weakening her.

The room was now various shades of oranges, reds, and yellows and even though she could see that Jane was still laughing, she could no longer hear it. The faces in the hearth became as if alive as they reflected and altered in the ensuing glow. The wooden structure was dry and receptive to the heightening advances of the burning. A voice deep and familiar could be vaguely perceived. Yanking on Jane's arm, Eleanor for all of her strength, could not pull her to her feet and Jane, her face still miming laughter, groped at Eleanor lustily. Eleanor could no longer hear her own cries above the inferno. The structure's supports, now mere kindling, hung like stalactites just over their heads. Jane's demanding touch seemed now like the petitionings of multitudes of lost souls, begging in futility for absolution.

Eleanor, now helpless, managed to pull herself away, at once effecting the rift from the seemingly random, ever-changing combination of aggregates known as Jane.

Now disappearing, the manor's invisibility a manifestation of the necessity of protecting the knowledge, Erebus scarred his faithless lover.

LXXI

The enclosure vibrated furiously to a rhythm its ramshackle frame was well-acquainted with. The sheer force and fierce snorting however were highly uncommon as were the gasps and quick, short breathing of the weary recipient. Black, silkily clad with clambering hooves, the creature's gesticulations were punctuated only by its occasional grunts and growls.

Yen

Pressed into her tiny corner, her matted, dull, golden tufts, once-precious tendrils, hung lifeless and limp. Scaling, red masses covered her face and arms as well as descending towards the small of her back. Either lizard-like now or a distant kin to a Gorgon, Jane had metamorphosed.

Enjoying every violent thrust of the beast, due to his manifest size and power, she became keenly sensate of a warm stream running down her legs and staining her feet a dark, sanguine hue. The sensation was ghastly and painful, yet she would get her fill. Tucked neatly into the crevice of this seemingly inaccessible corner nook, she safely received his enormous projection. Nearly ready to scream out in anguish and unmitigated exhaustion, she howled as his release came, then quickly coming down on all fours and moving away to the farthest end of the cage. The grotesque shadow smiled revealing missing teeth and emphasizing blackened lips.

The beast's stare seemed as if he too were disgusted, turned to stone by the Gorgon-like woman. Bloody and burned, Jane, momentarily satiated, had nearly slumped into a heap of shaking flesh, when an irate and looming image entered into his barn.

With clenched fists, he ordered the shaking figure to rise. Undoing his belt, the extent of his own projection became more than evident and a look of relief swept over the still-shaking-figure's countenance. Pressing the figure against the panels, he began to thrust more and more violently until even the bull turned away seemingly humbled by the eerie reproduction. Finally, moaning and then beginning to speak, the figure simpered, "I thought you'd never... It has been so long. Thank-you... thank-you..."

But the look of contempt was so severe, and his facial muscles unmoving, that the speaking desisted. Removing himself, he began to fastidiously do up his pants, and once this task had been completed, picked up his hardened black leather belt made from the last bullock's hide and began to beat the already scarred figure into a senseless and increasingly bloody state. Never touching her face for fear of it flaking off in its entirety, he kept repeating the same negation, "No child of mine... No child of mine... No child of mine."

Theseus, nor his clew, were nowhere to be found.

LXXII

Black hordes swarmed over the sheaves in throngs. It could hardly be conceived but befell them regardless. They hissed and swayed and as the dusk set in, everyone in the crowd alike, save for small children, anticipated the fall of night and the burning of torches. Sweat beaded off farmers' brows as the realization set in of the now-foreseen hardships that awaited them in the coming year. It hadn't been that long since the last infestation, so everyone had assumed that the way would be clear to a year of good fortune and plenty. Exhaustion carved caverned impressions into the already withered faces of the men and women who were one and all swatting violently with any implement available at the diligent feasters.

Their collective vigour was now slowing due to the little progress that was actually being made. As if in slow motion, moving to a strange and soundless rhythm, the somnolent beings continued in their action, seemingly purposeless, pervaded with a kind of eerie dread, as if the knowledge of the following year were too much to bear.

Eleanor watched the scene, but she too hadn't been herself since the manor fire, as Jane's injuries had been sufficient enough to warrant hospitalization. Eleanor had not slept much since the incineration, and the little sleep she got was infrequent and haunted by gaudy combinations of color that possessed not a shred of harmony, nor decency, nor even taint of class. Invariably she would awaken, disoriented with a sense of lugubrious dread, as though the spectrum itself had altered and everyone knew and had accepted this transformation gladly save herself. These dreams not only penetrated her hours of supposed repose, but also effectively quelled any ability to compose even a rough textured canvas with vague outlines of color for which she was apt to find herself attempting more and more often of late. The inability to express something which usually had come so naturally to her made her restless and agitated. Dull muddy browns, mustard yellows, and diluted reds with pale, translucent hues seemed her only choice of palette. At first, she had cried out, sobbing in intervals at the reduced and pathetic state of her art, and then, tiring of this action, she too had assumed the trudge of the somnolent figures as a morose acceptance of the inevitable crept into her gate.

LXXIII

The fire's roar like an angry sea rose as the crackle of chaff sent sparks up into the abysmal silence above. He, like Cronus, stood towering over the gluttonous devastation. Burlap sack in hand, the beating had begun.

With chiseled aspect and dark contour he stood in fierce defiance of the advancing current. Seized by fits of foaming rage he slew any detectable vibration, felling all and sundry. His movements were frenzied and any scrupulous onlooker made sure to keep their distance. Against the noise of the blaze could be heard the repetitive thwacking like an odd sort of rhythm as if sound itself had revolted leaving him the sole sphere of the lower frequencies to dominate. Undaunted by his futile dallyings, the tide only roared more loudly and he, the realization of near-defeat registering in his consciousness, bellowed as his powers waned. The sound, like a wave, carried swiftly by the hot currents, made its way to the sleeping ear of one badly-beaten and scaled cherubim, as a smile covered her newly-acquired scars. In the distance, Hephaestus tended the flames as they rose and fell like the beating of a bird's wings.

Phoenix was not far off.

LXXIV

Jane sat near the pond within the ensuing darkness listening to the various ribbits, croaks, and trills of the marsh's animal life. Eleanor, nearby in the darkness, thought that just as Jane had become a sybaritic, bespeckled frog due to her excessive scarring, her voice had gained a slightly croaking tonality to it as well.

"Jane, Jane, can you he... he... hear me?" Eleanor's voice quivered.

"Yes, I can," Jane's speech came in waves, strangely, almost inexplicably, like soft, sibilant croaks.

"Jane... Janey... why? Why didn't you come with me out of that fire? Why did you insist on staying? Why didn't you just come... for God's sake! Why does everything have to be such a tragic performance

---

of the first degree?!" Eleanor had lost her composure as the tears started to flow.

"Are you so sure you are crying for me? Let's be honest for once, you're crying for you. Boo hoo hoo." Jane's laugh, like a dry, buried cough, caught in her throat causing her to choke.

"I'm losing you. You must hate me. You must..." Eleanor could think of nothing else to say.

"Hate you? What is hate anyway, the absence of love? No Eleanor, you've got it all wrong like you always do." At that, Jane sighed.

"Games! Games! Games! Speak plain! Speak plain!" Eleanor bellowed, the echoless silence reverberating nothing.

"Plainly, Eleanor. Plainly. Mind your adverbs." Jane uttered with perfect composure.

Eleanor sat, looking on, stupefied. "Jane, please. Please, Jane." Her sobbing was now filling the silence.

"Eleanor, why are you crying? Why cry? If you don't understand Eleanor, I cannot help you. This you have to do on your own." Jane's voice broke off, the heaving cough returning in spasms.

"Did you ever love me, Jane?" Eleanor's tone was pleading, yet merciless.

"Love, Eleanor. What is love?" Jane's eyes danced in their sherry perfection, untouched by the flame's hands or by life's merciless beatings.

"How can you be ever so cruel? Have you no heart?!" Eleanor cried out.

"A heart, Eleanor? Spirits have no hearts. Even you should know that, Eleanor. Sometimes, I think there's so little hope for you. Eleanor, really." Now Jane sounded like her own mother, a bona fide whore whom she had never met.

"Please don't die Jane. Please don't..." Eleanor's voice fell off.

"Do you think that's the worst thing that could happen? An end to all of this beauty, madness, suffering?" Jane's voice had resumed its customary timbre.

"Yes Jane, I do. I do." Eleanor was adamant.

"Who are you trying to convince? Me or you?" Jane seemed to want to giggle.

"Jane, I'm being very serious! Don't mock me!"

"I'm not mocking you. I'm still trying to make you see. Don't you see, it would be a gift. It's a gift, Eleanor."

"Jane, I'm not ready. Please, I'm not ready." Eleanor's voice was almost a whisper.

"I know. I know, Eleanor. But I am, and it isn't your choice, just as it isn't mine. Do you see?"

Eleanor, flabbergasted, yet still softly sobbing, asked, "Are you saying it's His choice, Jane?"

"Something like that, Eleanor. Something like that." Her voice dropped off. Quietly, she uttered, "I'm cold now, Eleanor. Would you help me home, please?"

"Of course, Jane. Of course." Helping Jane rise to her feet, as she supported her frail, bony body, she hadn't realized just how light Jane had indeed become.

LXXV

This time Jane's injuries were more obvious. The side of her mouth was slashed and a good deal of bruising covered her torso. The doctor had even been called. Apparently, Jane had been diagnosed as epileptic. The seizures when they came were still comparatively mild for the extent of her lacerations.

Jane would have to remain inside at lunchhour and after school unless someone could be provided to aid and walk her home. Jane's father had actually come up to the school to deal directly with the situation. Mr. Dorset had even offered to see Jane home. He, himself, had examined the extensiveness of her bruising and as her face was a good deal mashed up, wanted at all costs to prevent any further disfigurement. However, they had both agreed that Eleanor would be the pupil most suited to the task, and the situation was promptly dealt with.

Mr. Dorset called Eleanor back into the classroom at lunch. "Eleanor, are you aware of Jane's newly diagnosed medical condition?" Mr. Dorset queried.

"Yes, vaguely, but I'm not sure what this has to do with me," Eleanor tersely retorted. Being eager to return to a novel she had only begun, she hoped whatever formality he wished to see her regarding would not take long.

"Well, due to her condition, it is necessary for her to have an escort to see her home and, as it would not be appropriate for Winchester as I'm sure you'll agree, Jane's father and I were wondering if you would graciously oblige us and consent to a few minutes of your time, slightly off of your beaten track." Mr. Dorset nodded insipidly.

"Well, actually it's necessary for me to return home immediately after school as I have many chores to do around my parent's farmstead," Eleanor quickly uttered.

"I was hoping you might show a little more courtesy for myself, whom hopefully you regard as a respected authority, and as Jane's father is also one of the more outstanding members of our small, but humble community, that you might have conceded to such a slight imposition. Do I have to remind you that the two of you were, at one time, inseparable?" Mr. Dorset's tone was firm and impermeable. It was obvious that he was not willing to accept no for an answer.

"Jane and I no longer associate outside of class, but if it would please you, I will concede to your request," Eleanor's head bowed in acquiescence.

"Very well put, Eleanor. It is that kind of eloquence which causes me considerable pain to see your potential as a scholar in such a diminished state." Mr. Dorset's countenance darkened.

"There are only one or two more points to settle before I dismiss you, Miss Wellgrene."

Eleanor thought she noticed a tightening in his trousers, but dismissed the perception as highly implausible. Shifting awkwardly in his chair, he fidgeted as though an itch which, in the name of propriety, could not be scratched plagued him.

Clearing his throat and lowering his tone, he began, "Often it is necessary for Jane to stay for a prolonged period after school. As you probably already know, she is my blackboard attendant, and her father and I see no reason for this state of affairs to change. However, this will require a little patience on your part, Eleanor. I hope this will not pose a problem." Mr. Dorset evidently expected a response.

"No, sir. I will have to somehow incorporate it into my daily schedule," Eleanor dutifully agreed.

"There is left to us only one outstanding matter then." Mr. Dorset again shifted position.

"I have often seen you, how should I say?... perform certain... should I say?... rituals, upon a certain, should we say?... boy, outside of this very classroom on certain afternoons. Some people might find this information highly disagreeable, although I cannot say that I am one of those people. However, if such information found its way to a Mr. and Mrs. Wellgrene, they would certainly not be amused, and I could not say for certain what might befall the young girl sitting very prim and proper before me now."

Eleanor had presumed that Mr. Dorset, since his back had been turned on all of these said occasions, never saw her. How could he have known? Unless Jane had informed him of her presence. But why would she do that? Why would he care what she did, anyway? He had not cared if she had seen his exposed state before. All of those times at the window. Why would he now?

"What is your point, Mr. Dorset?" Eleanor's face was red, yet more from ire than embarrassment.

"My point is simply this. My wife has been out of town for the past week. She has been quite ill and is staying with her mother for a few days. Jane, well you have seen the condition that she is in, is incapable of performing certain expected duties. I was hoping that you might bestow some small favour that you have so generously and often allowed Peter, and in turn I will say nothing to the previously mentioned parties. As you can see, I am in a very bad way." The protrusion was more than obvious.

Eleanor couldn't believe her luck. She had waited she had thought in vain to be the object of Mr. Dorset's attentions and now that the moment had actually arisen, she was beside herself and knew not what to do.

Quickly unbuttoning his trousers, Eleanor could not believe the size of the thing at hand. It was nothing at all like Peter's or even Mr. Graves'. It was huge and, not only that, it was ugly. Mr. Dorset stared at her suspiciously. In a commanding and impatient voice he ordered, resuming his guise as a despot, "Kneel and commence."

Eleanor could only stare in disbelief. His eyes were closed and he seemed to be waiting for her to act. When she remained motionless, he opened them again and, raising his voice, venomously uttered, "Well, we don't have all day! Get going!"

Eleanor only continued to stare in apparent shock.

"Okay then, have it your way." Pulling her down onto the floor, he bent her at the knees, positioning her awkwardly but firmly there, and repeatedly began to thrust her neck at his privates each time commanding, "Open your mouth wide," as his father had done so often in his dental chair.

Finally, like a doll, she responded, sucking madly and frantically unaware of her surroundings or reality. To Eleanor, it was like drowning, a slow, laborious, magnificent suffocation only to be awakened by a surge of bitter fluid, like eating her own vomit as she simultaneously and unwillingly regained a consciousness she had grown ever so tired of enduring.

LXXVI

Mr. Dorset's back faced the class as he wrote in elaborate cursive on the chalky-surfaced board. Since Jane had not been able to clean them, they remained dirty now most of the time.

His script read, "Alexander the Great."

"Does anyone know who this man is?" Turning around to face the class, his posture now assumed its customary arrogant pose.

As no one immediately responded, he took this opportunity to listen to the frequency modulation of his own timbre by commencing with much ado and intensity, "There were ungodly ways and acts committed in this heathen's time," his head cocked to the side as he prepared to deliver the sermon.

From somewhere in the room, the dreaded question was issued, "What is a heathen, sir?"

"A heathen! A heathen is an enemy of God, an unbeliever, a conspirator to the devil, representing the Dark One himself. Alexander the Great was a conqueror who ruled a mighty and vast empire. He is indeed a powerful, historical figure and that is why we are now going to study him and his conquerings, but it is still of utmost importance to remember what he was. He murdered on a mass scale! He was not a Christian in any sense of the word! And for those of you who are familiar with this usage, he was a homosexual! Ungodly, evil, vile ways he followed, but if everyone will turn to the map on page twenty-three, you can see for yourselves the extent and magnitude of his empire."

Eleanor, bored by this diatribe, blinked to keep herself from falling asleep and glanced over to where Jane, who had just today returned, sat.

Tufts of dark hairs stuck out of her head; her red, blotchy face was heavily scarred; and looking back at Eleanor, attempted a weak, sad smile.

Eleanor looked away, her eyes filling with hot, burning tears.

Mr. Dorset observed this exchange, and interrupted from his narcissistic tirade, paused to scrutinize these two victims.

"Are you two paying any attention at all to what I am offering, or are you both in your own little world somewhere?" Mr. Dorset maliciously queried.

Jane sat up and blatantly stated, "We are in our own little world as what you say or teach has little or no relevance. A different perception of what constitutes religious veneration, sexuality, and bloody, strategic acts of battle cannot be construed as ungodly, evil, nor vile as these societal definitions simply did not exist. They did not. Do you understand?"

Eleanor, observing her quiet candor and composure, smiled, as her words seemed to issue from a source she knew not what.

Mr. Dorset's eyes blazed as the choler built in his throat and nearly snarling, he went to move forward, and suddenly halting and obviously distraught, became overcome with what seemed to everyone present like... grief.

Turning around so that his face was averted to the scrutiny of the class's gaze, he seemed to momentarily spasm, and then temporarily regaining his composure uttered, "Regrettably, I forgot an appointment that I must keep with my wife. I must leave at once. Class dismissed." Picking up his coat and case, back still averted, he left without another word.

Oddly, everyone present remembered that his wife had miscarried her fifth child.

LXXVII

The implement had been raised. It struck repeatedly. A dull throbbing reverberated in Mr. Dorset's skull. The tarrying figure looked down upon his hapless victim and smiled fully, denoting the existence of pure satisfaction.

Mr. Dorset groaned which could only mean that the creature was still alive. Throwing the trowel on the floor, the clanking echo could be heard down the confines of the small hall. Although irrelevant, as this perpetrator had indeed made sure that the school was now empty of any potential witnesses, it was still a necessary procedure.

Undressing it so that the complete exposure of its fleshiness was all that remained, for a moment the odd discoloration and sheer ugliness of the thing made him wonder if he actually wanted to carry out the scheme. Dragging it by the ankles over to the wood stove which was now cooling down due to the time of day, he proceeded to stoke the fire by adding small bits of kindling and shoots of green saplings he had collected for the purpose. All the while his actions were slow and methodical with that odd, freakish grin plastered on his face. Tying the hands together, then to the stove's opening, nearly any movement at all would cause the grille to fly open in the creature's face incurring bad burns as well as temporary blindness from flying embers. Bending the feet underneath the body, he proceeded to tie each foot separately to an individual iron leg of the stove, criss-crossing the hemp rope so that too much fidgeting would surely result in the whole structure landing on it at once searing its entirety. Last but not least, he stuffed the dirt-filled rag into its mouth.

As the thing remained unconscious, its head slumped down on its hands, its feet tucked under it like a small infant which could not as yet walk, it looked almost sympathetic. Sitting down at the back of the room, he began the waiting. All he could think of was her, the perfection of her hair, her permanently-tanned face and body, her tiny rosebud lips, the softness of her skin, and the rough playful texture of her feet. Her perfection was the only divinity he could or would ever know.

He heard it move. He heard it struggle for breath. He knew if he left now the whole thing would eventually pass: that is, he could turn back. It was fidgeting and making awful noises. The stove's door blasted open, a shower of sparks shooting out. It screamed. He got up and went towards it. Swinging the grating closed, and speaking in slow, deliberate tones, he began to utter simple commands.

"Shut up. See what happens if ya don't."

Slowly the thing responded. Its head moved up and down, showing it understood.

The darkness had filled the room's cavity, the only glow being red light from the stove's interior.

Undoing his trousers, momentarily he felt self-conscious and nervous, but in an instant it passed and he felt a rapid hardening. Approaching the thing's face, he ordered, "Blackboard duty. Suck it off."

The thing looked confused and bewildered. He pulled the rag out of its mouth. "Who is that?! I can't see anything! I need a bloody doctor! Get me a bloody doctor, you brute, freakish bastard! Let me go! What do you want from me, you faggot?! Go find some of your own kind!" By this point he was bellowing.

"You can call me Alexander, Alexander the Great that is. I think ya know him. I heard ya speakin' it the other day from just outside that window there. Good view from those there windows. I hate repeatin' myself though. Don't like talkin' much neither, but just to keep it straight and all I said, 'suck it off' like the little, blond whore ya made suck yours all bloody day long!" His order was louder and more menacing now.

"What?! You want me to... what?"

"Get goin'!"

Thrusting his penis at the thing's mouth, it seemed to engulf a tiny bit of its head only to bite down with chompers fully drawn. He screamed out but managed to pull back. It bled as a tiny piece of the head was missing.

The thing was laughing, as it spit furiously. "My wife will realize that I'm gone and the first place they'll check is here, and they'll catch you, and put you away for the rest of your natural life, you bloody, devil-loving fool!"

Tiring of his bellowing, he stopped the orifice again with the dirty rag and replied, "Is that the best ya can do? Don't say I never gave ya the chance to bite it off or nothin' cause ya had your chance and ya didn't even hurt it or nothin'. Jane nearly beat it off with a stick when she was real mad, and her daddy near kicked it off with them boots of his. That near did me in. Anyway, your wife won't know nothin'. No one will hopefully 'til Monday morning. Ya usually visit your wife's sister and all after school, now isn't that right?"

The thing only looked back at him unblinking in apparent shock.

"See, this here is okay. You hardly hurt it. It's near hard again."

The creature's eyes became rounder and the muffled vocalizations sounded oddly like begging.

"What's that you're there sayin'? Can't hear ya. Better speak up. Wait a sec though. Got to stoke this here fire."

Releasing the opening, the flames danced high and leapt out at the countenance close-at-hand. It turned itself away as best it could. After stirring up the contents with the poker, he eyed the implement ponderously.

The creature whined adamantly. As he deftly pressed the tool between its legs applying it thrice, the screams were blood-curdling. The stove shook uneasily as the creature attempted to flail, the incinerator door flying open, yet again burning its face and eyes.

He laughed. "Lucky, nobody's around here. Lookie, it's hard again."

Now holding the thing's gonads, he played with them while it whined most wretchedly.

Beating against the thing with his lower parts, slowly at first, then more forcefully, he managed to prolong the agony. Suddenly, it was all over, and momentarily satisfied realized that he was only devoid of one thing: a prize.

The thing was crying most grievously, and annoyed with the constant barrage of such a sound, he got his hunting knife, reached around, and promptly proceeded to hack it off. The creature spasmed in apparent seizure, and Winchester, who calmly saw what was about to happen, moved hastily out of harm's way. The crash and sound of searing flesh was strangely devoid of any struggle or scream.

LXXVIII

Wearily, Jane arrived at the old Graves' lot. The sign still stood in its place, undisturbed except for a swarm of wasps which had claimed the wooden posting, gnawing and tearing at its interior portions. The throng's activity was so engrossed in its devouring endeavor, they hardly took notice of her arrival. Purposefully, a wasp flew off with its mate's still intact carcass, anxious for the awaiting consumption.

The site remained vacant in its dilapidated, yet to Jane, still magnificent state. The bees were long gone, yet oddly Jane could still hear the humming. Positioning herself near the well, she shut her eyes in the warmth of the noonday sun. A cool breeze had arisen, a preliminary sign of fall's arrival. Her hands shook, as she took out her last cigarette.

Lighting it, she watched the curling tendrils of smoke writhe and twist in the currents. She loved this place, and oddly missed those afternoon rendezvous with old Mr. Graves. She butted off a long stream of smoldering ash. The hairs on her flesh responded still even to this tiny, enkindled form. Deftly taking its lit end, she pressed it firmly against a scar on the side of her leg. For a moment, she sensed relief.

She could hear the approach of her customary gait. Right, left, short pause, right, left, short pause... it was like a nonsensical, rhythmic discord.

With eyes still shut, she uttered, "Is there nothing harmonious or agreeable about you, Wellgrene?"

"What?" Eleanor hadn't realized that she was aware of her advance.

"Oh. I was attempting to approach without disturbing your reverie or slumber, of which you were partaking, I could not be sure." Eleanor simply stated.

"What do you want?" Jane retorted, irritated by the interruption.

Looking at Jane's state of physical degeneracy, she knew that now was not the time for trite responses.

"I merely wanted... wanted... um... um," she bowed her head in shame.

"I do not know why I came," Eleanor softly muttered.

"I do. But this cannot be a long visit. I'm expecting company soon, and I think it would be best if you were not present." Jane's eyes were still closed.

"Okay. If you don't want me here, I will leave."

"Sit down, Eleanor."

"I just wanted to ask you a couple of... of... things."

"Yeah," Jane took a long drag of the butt, before a pronounced exhale, and said plainly, "Having problems with that third ear of yours, are ya now? Don't know what to do with it?"

Eleanor's brows furrowed in apparent confusion, as she inquired, "What third ear?"

"Don't you mean the one between your legs, Eleanor? Isn't that what all this is about?"

Jane's comment bit smartly, and Eleanor fed up, wryly retorted, "Jane, I don't want to play anymore games. I'm tired Jane, so dreadfully tired," her timbre nearly a whine.

"Mr. Dorset is a problem that will take care of itself. What did you always used to say? What was it? Divine justice? Yeah, that's it."

"Mr. Dorset? How did you know?"

"Mr. Dorset's a pain in the ass," after which words she laughed in spite of the seriousness of the moment, "and an insult to his much renounced and heavily repressed hero, one Alexander the Great."

"What?" Eleanor was never more confused by Jane's speech. "Are you feeling all right, Jane?"

"God, Eleanor," Jane's eyes flew open exposing their oddly-hued irises, "For a one-time scholar, you d*uuumb*."

"Jane, your eyes!" Eleanor exclaimed. "Let me help you to a doctor, Jane please!"

"What's wrong with them?"

"They're all wrong, Jane! Something's very wrong with you, Jane!"

Her sherry brown orbs had strange splotches of almost opaque blue.

"Oh, that. Ignore it. Otherwise, leave." With those words, Jane again closed her eyes.

"Jane, you don't understand! You are very sick, and need a doctor! Don't be obstinate. Not now!" Eleanor was now pulling on Jane's right arm.

180

Yen

"Eleanor?"

"Yes, Jane?"

"Fuck off."

Eleanor, for the second time in two, short days, again did not know what to do. She sat down heavily and this time did not start to cry, but sob.

Jane reached over, and cradling her friend, began to softly sing, "Hush little baby, don't say a word, Mummy's gonna buy you a mockingbird; if that mockingbird don't sing, Mummy's gonna buy you a diamond ring; if that diamond ring turns brass, Mummy's gonna buy you a looking glass; if that looking glass gets broke, Mummy's gonna buy you a billy goat; if that billy goat don't pull, Mummy's gonna buy you a cart and bull; if that cart and bull turn over, Mummy's gonna buy you a dog named Rover; if that dog named Rover don't bark, Mummy's gonna buy you a horse and cart; if that horse and cart fall down, you'll still be the sweetest little baby in town."

Eleanor, now silenced, suddenly found herself asking, "Did you ever love, Jane?"

"Yes, once, a long time ago I loved, Eleanor. I loved," Jane cooed. "Did you, Eleanor?"

"I don't know, Jane. I don't. Please don't leave me alone," Eleanor whimpered.

Methodically, and without even knowing why, Eleanor began to tenderly caress Jane's throbbing heels and soles, until Jane, momentarily placated, breathed a long-held sigh of relief.

In the distance, Jane could see his approach. Without warning, she resumed her customary pose decreeing, "Leave now."

Eleanor jumped at the severity of her tone after just having been lulled into a near slumber, but, although unwillingly, obeyed.

LXXIX

The few cornfields bordering his lot remained unscathed by the fire's gluttonous reign. As she approached them, their towering greenness with red-golden tips suggested the potency of divine brushstrokes, as her hand shook with longing.

She could see his advance, marching towards her, unable to hear their words as if they had somehow fallen far away into another dimension, realm, and the only thing remaining were images, naked, scarred, isolated, drowned, shaken, like a culture so infatuated with their form and movement, the content now having no meaning, like the cursive gone-awry as when the hand shifts almost imperceptibly to the left or right, meaning devoid, void of coherence.

Between the ears, Eleanor, enshrouded, felt the sanctity of the towering stalks. Pants around his ankles, he, mad from the shock of what he had done, plunged eagerly in and out of Jane for what seemed to Eleanor an eternity. Jane, spread-eagled across the mortar of the opening appeared for the first time today to be truly enjoying herself. Clearly and distinctly, the intelligibility of the words pierced through, "Ohh... *Bill*, you always could make me come," Jane shrieked in apparent ecstasy with her eyes still shut, William being of course the given name of one Mr. Bill Graves.

Winchester's eyes glazed over, his face becoming blank and pale. Eleanor saw the characteristic dark shade come over Winchester's countenance. Shivering in fear, she dared to momentarily look on, and found that she could not turn away. A change had come over the scene before her like all of those other times, her psychic palette again resurrected with a flourish and ardour which had been nearly successfully repressed beyond all consciousness. The blending began. Shades came to her readily and brushstrokes flew from her fingertips. Perfection of hue, depth, and brilliance filled her metaphysical rendering. The harder she concentrated, the greater the purity of her piece. Eleanor's eyes had become a hybrid of power and terror simultaneously.

Winchester's ears bled, the blood flowing freely and pooling around his feet, like that other time so long ago. Grabbing her face in the palm of his hand, his lips, stricken with echolalia, seemed to repeat her words, "Ohh Bill, you always could make me come," as he spat deftly and precisely in the middle of her forehead.

So long before the odyssey having gone awry, the siren beckoned him on, her once golden-scales now stubble and scars, revealing her tusk-like interior. Eleanor, in consternation, wondering why sound had become nearly unintelligible, touched the cartilage of her outer ear, finding it to be heavily bloody as well, stared at her hand and at the scene about to take place before her in disbelief. Instantaneously and without warning, she too had become an object of her own piece.

Screaming in hysteria, Jane and Winchester, both looking towards the screeching ears, searched for the invisible perpetrator. Eleanor, no longer able to remain in shadow, emerged bleeding and shaken, a formidable sight to behold. Jane, now Lilith's elder, nodded to her followers, both standing helplessly, mouths agape like tiny goldfish blowing bubbles of air as they drowned out of water, and glancing at her reflection below uttered, "The involution begins."

Finally exhaling, she jumped into the molten element at her feet. Thira had been submerged beyond the visual realm.

Jane, now immortalized, swam strongly and deftly, a prism of gold following in her wake. Iris smiled from her cloud-filled height. The message had been delivered.

LXXX

Eleanor could feel the repeated applications of a wet substance streaming warmly over her face. She jerked severely as a muscle spasm seemed to grasp the entirety of her body. From the all-encompassing sensation of sheer coldness, she wondered if the applications arose from a merciful, passing sea sponge and she had soundlessly sunk to the ocean's bottom, carried by the strong arms of the river.

Opening her eyes, focusing was difficult as if they had ceased to function, no longer needed in this dead sea environment. Beast stood over her sodden frame. As she pulled him towards her for warmth, her hand brushed by what seemed to be the pages of a book. Suddenly sitting up, now vertical, there sat her Bible, a little torn and tattered, swollen from exposure to continual moisture. Cradling it to her, she realized that it had been found by one furry and benevolent subject. A gentle wind shook the ears surrounding her and unable to recall what had been seen, she, suddenly uncommonly averted to traversing Mr. Graves' old lot, promptly and deliberately took the long route to town through the corn.

Today, the place was all abustle, the shouting of youth, the whir and chink of small industry, the hush of the bank manager's voice as he passed lankily by with his trail of investors and advisors, the murmur of a group of ladies, obviously heading out for an annual picnic to commemorate some such event or the like. Eleanor noticed little. Her set upon object being one Mr. McFerson's Grocery and meat supply store, the largest and busiest provision outlet in town, she hoped that she might go wholly unnoticed. With Bible in hand, this would give her the advantage of an added pious aspect, and her filth may elicit perhaps a small outpouring of sympathy. This she could only hope for. She knew another Watcher who would not be so forgiving of the action she was about to commit.

On the shelf before her it stood, the smallest sampling of the green fluid, one of her favourite tastes which she only ever partook on those rare occasions when she chanced to visit the priest's family residence. His mother would always provide the most sumptuous delicacies for her guests, which Eleanor had been privy. She recalled the taste of the salad now, its firm, fresh, garden vegetables covered in a pungent cheese, awash with a copious sampling of the green elixir. All they ever had eaten at home was bathed in a spattering of white lard, and they were lucky now to consume even this common aliment.

People in respectable dress glanced displeasingly at the state of her attire and either looked at her searchingly and finally disdainfully or, took pity on her apparent plight, and humbly smiled. She would respond by either averting her gaze or occasionally smiling demurely back. She managed to walk covertly through the store, completing a number of rotations until it became so busy inside that she was required to either act or, if this could not be instrumented, otherwise leave. The clerk was currently overoccupied, and Mr. McFerson, who couldn't help but smile at her himself, was also heavily engaged in weighing and wrapping a pound of beef, when Eleanor figured that now was her one and only opportunity. Sliding the bottle under her vestments, she looked stealthily around and relieved, felt that no one had indeed seen her action. Walking slowly but decidedly for the door, she let out a long-held sigh as she reached the outlet's exterior, yet regardless, promptly increased her gait until she was safely out of sight.

LXXXI

Mr. McFerson's gaze had not been averted. For twenty-three years his gaze had remained fixed yet friendly, and it could safely be stated that in that time frame he had not missed a single unconscionable act. He eyed her retreat from a keen perspective behind the weighing scale. She, not evading his scrutiny, did however manage to stimulate a somewhat measured, although sympathetic, response. He nodded his head in Mrs. McFerson's direction and she, temporarily stunned, nodded back. No one else had suspected or witnessed anything. Save for the shrewdness of one hawk-like stare, Eleanor would have escaped, unnoticed, a tiny bottle of olive oil the richer. He had no intention of mentioning this afternoon's indiscretion to anyone. Mrs. McFerson would take care of that. She always found just the right thing to say to just the right recipient. At the very least, he knew that family had been through enough of late. Yet it was his intention to stem off the source, himself of course being the source, the stem now having acquired a significant crimp.

Mrs. McFerson hurried to the window, just as Eleanor rounded the outer edge of the bend, and let out what could only be described as a strange kind of squawk. Many shoppers ceased what they had been doing and turned their faces towards Mrs. McFerson's only to see her intently observing something from the drawn curtain before her, at length repeatedly shaking her head from side to side. Finally, she rushed to the front of the store to join her husband, muttering all the while, "That poor girl. Did you see how that girl was dressed? God-forbid! In tattered rags like that! Our Milly would never set foot out of the house dressed like that! That family has endured misfortune after misfortune. Now thievery! My gracious! And such a smart girl at one time too!"

And finally involving the said customer in her monologue, "Such a pity Mrs. Woolston. We must pray for them. That is all we can do. We shan't chastise the poor thing! No! But we shan't be taken for the fool. Nothing will be said. By no means! We aren't cruel people, and we are more than familiar with struggle ourselves, but nay, nay, we cannot accept their business in this store ever again."

The customer, being one Mrs. Woolston senior, shook her head forlornly and uttered in a somewhat reserved, nasalish manner, "Yes, I know the family. I didn't see Eleanor. They have had quite their share of hardships of late. More than I dare say. It has been especially hard on poor Eleanor. With all of those chores, and now in such a reduced state after being a one-time scholar, it has been awfully hard. I need not tell you of Mr. Wellgrene's recent alcoholic lapses. I am sure you have heard about them, if not witnessed them yourselves. I pray that they have not been too hard on Mrs. Wellgrene senior, as we have been on intimate terms for such a long duration. She is a very good woman, and it pains me to see her good name tarnished as such. You are a good, Christ-loving woman, I pray let me make up the difference, and nothing more regarding this matter will be said."

"Oh dear Mrs. Woolston, you are a good woman indeed. Do not think that I meant for you to proffer any such thing. But since you offer, and as I can see it pains you so, I and my husband kindly accept your gracious offer. We are all Christians here. And you have been such a sweet, loyal customer! Thank-you."

Mrs. Woolston paid the difference. Quite a sum for the largest and best bottle of virgin olive oil. She had wondered how Eleanor could have fit such a quantity under those 'tattered rags' but made no outward complaint as not to offend the two smiling recipients of her charity. Tomorrow, she would pay a much-needed visit to Mrs. Wellgrene. It had been a while since they had spoken.

LXXXII

The bottle's contents glittered in the dull light of a waning moon. The coolness of the night air bit into her exposed shoulders and collarbone. It would be difficult to balance in such a cumbersome position, but the moonlight had awakened her, and for some reason unbeknownst to her, she knew wherefore she must come. In night attire, she had proceeded from the darkness of the house, as she desired that no one, that is, no little ears would discern her progress and then endeavor to follow. Tonight, as most nights, her father was out engaged in his usual cavorting and revelry.

Rising, she had followed this pale, dull light like a beacon to where she knew not. Shivering, she found it highly undesirable to attempt to traverse the field in these conditions, as it had suddenly gained sharp teeth that bit unexpectedly into her skin like tall, vamping fiends. She could hear a soft slither and rustling as snakes made their way slowly and methodically to their holes.

Lighting the candle, she could just make out the outline of the well in the distance. It drew her, and in her gown, she looked a somnolent walker, devoid of all purpose save the one at hand. Why was she here in the middle of the night when this was the only time she was permitted to rest: repose, the last sacred respite of the weary. But yet, it drew nearer and she was in no position to desist. Peeking over the top of it, she could see something white and floating down the shaft, in the soundlessness below. It resembled a newborn with its lanugo hair, covered in the marks of birth. What ever was it? Was it her child waiting inside the womb, furry and green with the slime of life? Once again, she forced herself to peer over the side. It was a girl child drifting in a sweet, sweet sleep. So sweetly she slept, Eleanor feared that any movement or interruption on her part would wake this celestial cherubim. But yet she was drawn nearer down to it. It needed her. And she would come.

She hadn't forgotten. No. The pages rustled most vexingly when silence was all Eleanor could hope for, yet it served the purpose, the purpose which had no outer shell of meaning, only an inner kind of perfection, of unknowing, of limitless *unmind*. For a moment, she cradled her precious cargo so cold to the gentlest touch. Eleanor shivered. But still she knew. She knew it was hers. This was her child and she loved it so. Momentarily rocking her as she pulled her nearer, she tried a song, a soft, sweet song that would not awaken her sleeping beauty, but all that emitted from her dry, parched lips were syllables, broken, fragmented, disjointed, an eerie, comfortless discord and then she remembered. She knew that she was Echo and she invariably held the remains of Narcissus in her arms. She too had fallen madly and passionately for the reflection in the pond. How could she not? How could anyone not have?

She had begun her labour of Sisyphus yet Jane remained a delicate blue, unresponsive to Eleanor's ardent petitionings. Producing the bottle of liquid, as an elixir of ground peridots, she opened it, all the while balancing on the well's left inner ledge. Dabbing her fingers into the oil, like seeming glossolalia, first touching the damp, stiff hands, then the damp, waxy forehead, she began to slowly recite, "Per istam sanctam unctionem et suam piissimam misericordiam adiuvet te dominus gratia spiritus sancti, ut a peccatis liberatum te salvet atque propitius alleviet."

LXXXIII

Mrs. Dorset strode rapidly about, apparently in some sort of severe agitation as the boards of her front porch groaned defiantly from the great, heaving weight. She did not at all seem ill as she desperately arced indiscriminately back and forth as Eleanor fancied a great wrecking ball may. Eleanor wondered if she had yet resumed her domestic imperatives.

Eyeing her frame, she deftly and slowly made her advance.

"Mrs. Dorset, excuse me, but you looked as if you were in such a state, that I felt obligated as a student of your husband's to ask if you are well."

At first, Mrs. Dorset did not reply or seem to even acknowledge Eleanor's presence.

"I'm sorry. I don't mean to be rude. Something dreadful 'as happened. Something so dreadful!" With those words she began the pacing which momentarily she had ceased.

"Come and sit down, Mrs. Dorset. You look so awfully pale."

"It's your schoolmaster... Mr. Dorset. I have just been told of 'is sudden and tragic passing."

"Oh, dear! You poor, poor woman! I am so deeply sorry. Please sit down, Mrs. Dorset. Let me help you." In her silence, she feigned upset, when unbeknownst to any, she rejoiced, and had to suppress a rising cry of joy.

"How did this happen? It was only on Friday at school that he seemed so well."

"I can't tell you. It is indeed dreadful, the story. It isn't fit for a lady's ears, and they scarce told me too much," her breath was coming in gasps again.

Yen

Her folds of flesh splayed out in odd contorted shapes and dimpled depressions as she sat upon the hoary, wooden rocker.

"I'm sorry. I should not have asked. You have already been through too much. If I am not imposing, I should like to make you a cup of hot tea, that is, if you would fancy one."

"Oh, that would be nice. I left the children with my mother after the visit to the morgue. They wouldn't even let me see 'im. Said the body was in no condition for a lady's eyes. Oh dear, I shouldn't be telling you all this."

"No, please, do not make yourself fret. Sometimes these things happen and we have to believe and have faith that it is all a part of a greater plan that we could never hope to fully understand."

Eleanor could smell the briny offering between her legs, and licked her lips in eagerness.

"Oh dear, and so many children to raise! How am I ever going to..." her voice trailed off in tears.

"Lenora, you're so beautiful," Eleanor murmured as she bent down beside her, gently stroking the hair from her sodden temple. For a moment Lenora started, then as her body seemed to yield to her touch, asked, "How did you know my name?"

"Mr. Dorset often fondly mentioned you, and occasionally, due to the closeness of our forename's, mixed us up."

She looked at Eleanor suspiciously, but then shrugged and said nothing.

"Come now, let me make you that tea."

Holding her arm, they rose together as she delicately massaged the fleshy, creased skin, the warmth of her touch causing Lenora to jerk, then blinking, close her eyes and sway in obvious exhaustion.

Once the kettle was placed on the stove, and Eleanor had skillfully lit and stoked the fire, Mrs. Dorset uttered, "You know I haven't eaten a thing all day. I just realized that now."

Eleanor had just returned from the other room with a blanket for Lenora, and seeing the bread and cheese on the counter, asked if she would like a sandwich with her tea. Mrs. Dorset, heavy with hunger and exhaustion, nodded thanking her. Seeing the dirty dishes which overflowed the confines of the sink, lining and filling the counter, she automatically pumped the sink with water, and began to scrub the crud from each crevice until not a single depression remained soiled.

Lenora could only stare in awe and reverie at the strange little angel who had fallen into her life and aided in mitigating her suffering, when no one else seemed to offer assistance or even care. Nobody had ever done her dishes before, and Lenora could only sit in grateful silence, and now, with the thought of an uncertain future of unseen struggle and unending strife, she closed her eyes and nearly fell over from fatigue.

Eleanor, noticing and catching, as she gently righted the laborious frame, had seemed to have acquired the strength of a deviless or goddess. Hesitantly, but firmly, she helped the grieving woman rise to her feet, and led her tenderly into the near bedchamber.

Once there Eleanor could hear the kettle coming to a furious boil, and helping the limp creature into bed, gently whispered that she would return erelong with tea and the previously proffered sustenance. It nodded unknowingly, but oddly comfortable in its newly privileged state, uncustomarily said nothing.

Eleanor returned, carrying tray in hand, with an assortment of miniature morsels for the bereaved, and now-nearly-sleeping, form.

"Lenora, here dear, have a little something to eat. There's tea, and here, I've made you some sandwiches of butter and cheese," Eleanor smiled reverently.

The woman, never before having been privileged to such doting services, began to cry unknowingly from the cognizance of the strain.

"Oh, you are a dear indeed, attending to me so. I've never had…"

Eleanor interrupted before she could finish her sentence. "Now, now, don't make yourself fret so. I have many brothers and sisters myself. I have so many chores. I scarcely know what to do with myself half the time," she smiled at the woman who seemed to now be breathing in her every word.

"I'm so glad you are here. I don't have anyone to…"

Again, Eleanor interrupted the anxious creature. "Sh.... there there. Have some tea and nourishment." As she began to feed the being, it ate as readily as her ministerings could be rendered. It was obviously hungry, and Eleanor, never before known to this being, had successfully invaded and won over the heavy heart of its lone inhabitant. She smiled darkly with the knowledge of her victory.

"You're so very cold. I noticed that there is no coal in the stove. Shall I add some?" Eleanor graciously offered.

"No, no. I'm sorry. There isn't much left, and I was saving it for the children..." again her voice conspicuously broke off.

"Oh dear, I'm sorry if you are cold." With those words, the woman lowered her head in shame.

"No, no, you're fretting again. My family is quite poor. More so now, and often we have no heat to speak of. I am used to these conditions and often think I have become immune to cold, but you, you tremble so. The tea does not seem to be helping much. Perhaps, I could warm you."

It responded by almost instantly lifting the blankets, and Eleanor, beside herself with mounting hunger and wetness, trembled expectantly. Like a succubus, she dove with the deftness of her kind. Momentarily, the thing nearly giggled as it writhed in expectation.

Beginning with her forehead, she started kissing, stroking its scars of battle. In her dip, she began to run her tongue delicately over the undulating surface. Her necrophilia arisen hands and wet muscle reached out again and again, as the being grew warmer. Lapping, the dark organ, gracious and full in its movements, obviously possessed the deft and subtle powers of rhetoric, unlike a long-gone-priestess as Troy's fall would attest. The creature, realizing pleasure's infinite potential, cried out as Eleanor's chosen instrument again aptly pierced the sacred crevice of its nether realm. A new convert to hedonism, she lay, splayed and innocent, as Eleanor began to recreate the experience anew for her now avaricious mane. Creator heavily kissed creation, and left, joining her sole accomplice Merlin in night's all-enclosing-grasp.

LXXXIV

"Boy, for the last bloody time, what did you say your name was?" the officer bawled as he boxed the sides of the red-eyed freak's ears.

"Well, if I told ya once, I told ya again and again! Alexander! Alexander! Alexander!" the boy bawled back.

"Christ! And your relationship to the deceased?" the officer, now bug-eyed and frenzied, blinked but continued.

"He was the schoolmaster, the schoolmaster, and I quit school long time ago 'cause I couldn't stand the bastard or nothin'. If he's dead, well he prob'ly had it comin'. He liked his girl students a little too much, but maybe they liked it too. I wouldn't know. I already told ya all of this already!" Winchester began to cry. "Now, if I could just go home. I live up on the Farling farm. My father is John Farling. I don't know what ya want of me!" His voice had approached the timbre of a whine, and he fidgeted uncomfortably under the strain.

"You're not going nowhere, you bloody, murderous bastard! Mr. Dorset doesn't get to go home and his wife nor children don't get to see him neither. Why should you be going home? Never mind that there young girl."

"I don't know what ya mean. Honest, I don't." He started to blubber again.

"All this sissy crap! Why are you cryin' now for? Should have thought of that before. Doesn't look like you will never be going home again… boy! But prison life might be fun for your kind. After all, we found a very important piece of evidence in your keeping!" At that, the tarrying officer discharged a dark, sinister laugh, and the other officers glared at the fiend before them as sweat ran and dripped off their foreheads and underarms, as if the thrill of the hunt were too much.

"Did ya like the feel of his nuts as ya ripped them off?! Should have eaten up the evidence for a snack. I've seen it done in a case once I was covering." The officer nearly beside himself, dominated the room, and nodding to the other shaded faces, subsequently they seemingly vanished into the crevices from which they had arisen.

Winchester suddenly started, as the officer approached him, ordering him to stand.

"I must admit, we've never seen something quite like that before. No, indeed, an ingenious ploy." From behind the officer pressed his hardening genitals into the crevice between the boy's cheeks. Winchester screamed, but no one could hear. "Why are you screaming? Isn't this what you did to Mr. Dorset and then lopped it off just for the hell of it, too?! You're going to get a lot of this in prison, you should know."

Winchester's response was nonsensical as the blubbering had removed any trace of coherence from his utterances.

"What? What was that now, boy?"

Again, more blubbering.

"Look, okay, okay. And we still have our clothes on."

He approached Winchester, very close and whispering in his ear asked, "My wife never understands what a good, long suck is. I think you do. Would you mind?"

It was undone and hanging there, and Winchester thought he had never seen a thing so revolting or ugly, and promptly, without further ado, vomited upon the officer's newly-polished shoes.

"For Christ's sake boy, no one would ever imagine you murdering that poor bastard Dorset and that little, scarred girl. What was her name? The beautiful one before the Bifford place went up? J... Ja... Jane. That was it. Jane... what was her last name again?"

At the mention of Jane, Winchester tensed. And looking directly at the man, coherently uttered, "Jane... Jane's dead? No, not Jane. She can't be. No! No! No!"

Throwing a bawling, shrieking fit upon the floor, Winchester kicked and frothed at the mouth, until, in utter exhaustion, devoid of hope or sanctuary, Alexander fell out of consciousness, and had to be carted away, a dead weight under the arms of his enemies.

LXXXV

The air vibrated with talk. It was all over town like the plague. Eleanor could only wish it were. Chatter... here... there... in the streets... in the churchyard... in the hardware store and bakery. It fluttered and filled the windowsill of town hall and bedroom alike as it wove its intricately coloured fabrication.

"A love triangle was it? That poor Jane-girl! What a sad, sad business! She was quite a beauty you know, before all this!"

"And the wickedness of that Farling boy?! Who would have thought? Who would have known? The Farling's have always been such respectable people."

"I knew. I knew it all along. There was something not quite right about him. Did you hear the way he spoke in that queer sort of way?"

"Queer, you say? Yes, indeed, in more ways than one."

"No, no, one shouldn't make light of it. Poor, poor Mr. Dorset. A good schoolmaster at that too, although a stickler for those rules. But rules are rules, and after all, he did his job and was a family man. That boy must pay for those two sad, lost souls!"

"A love triangle, you said?"

"Yes, well she was quite a beauty you know before all that, and she did flaunt it so!"

"Yes, but there's no telling how to read a mind like his. Did you hear what he did to poor Mr. Dorset? What everyone is saying?"

"That boy is sick. Too sick for help. There's only one thing that will do for that. Put the fellow out of his misery with one swift blow! I'd do it. He has it coming and he knows it!"

"Well, you know what I say. 'An eye for an eye, and a tooth for a tooth.' There's no two ways about it!"

"Let some of those criminally insane take care of him! He would think what he's done to poor, old Mr. Dorset was a walk in the park!"

"I'd like to get my hands on him. I'd show him! He'd never hurt no one again. That is, if he ever walked!"

"I'd cut it off! You know I would. All our young ears having to hear such tales as these! Puts bad ideas in their heads! Nothing good can come of it, I say! No, indeed!"

"I would have liked to get my hands on that Jane-girl. She needed to learn a lesson or two herself. Always parading around in that skimpy little dress! I'd show her myself why little girl's shouldn't be walking around like that! My husband knew the girl quite well. She used to come around here regularly. 'Quite a girl,' he used to say. Don't know what he saw in her. He always seemed so happy to see the filthy, little thing!"

"I wouldn't have minded showing her a thing or two myself!"

"I'm sure you wouldn't."

"That's what started all the trouble according to the talk!"

"Her daddy's a mighty rich farmer! Handsome as they come. Keeps to himself a lot though. No wife to mention of."

"I wouldn't mind a taste of him or his riches!"

"Thelma, you wench! You shouldn't speak ill of the dead!"

"I wasn't. I was just sayin' it, that's all. I used to know him when he was young. We went to school together. All the girls were crazy over him. He didn't even notice. He was always too busy with the boys to even care. Some people said he was strange that way. You know. I don't know. He was always polite to me and mine. Never a cruel word from his mouth. Imagine he'll miss her lots, poor little thing."

LXXXVI

A breeze stirred the trees and dried grasses as the old rickety shack moaned in apparent protest. Mr. Graves had been gone now... how long had it been? She couldn't remember the details, but did however recall his tongue, deft and lapping, elicited by no other than Jane's skillful bartering abilities.

The sky seemed burdened by a ripening heaviness, causing an undulation as the barometric pressure wavered. Again the wind picked up, and momentarily, from only the thought, the humidity between her legs precipitated and trickled down, as a single drop ran down her ankle.

The smell of a culminating storm nearing within the vastness of the plain relaxed her wearied muscles and she lay, splayed and humming, down on the rough, splintered planks of the porch. Above her she remembered the plunging image of the kitchen sink as Mr. Graves released his clogging. She laughed, not a bitter laugh, but a sweet, soft laugh. A laugh meant for higher pursuits like the reactions to the joyous cry of a newborn child, or the sight of an old couple gathered round the hearth with the children of their children. Nevertheless, it was a soft laugh, delicately rendered and inviting in its audibility.

"I miss them," she heard herself murmur, and wondered if now she might be together with Sir Bifford having a divine orgy of the finest calibre. As she was divining the lot of the late Mr. Graves, the rocker in the corner of the porch, as though an invisible force possessed it, uncannily began to systematically rock.

For a moment unnerved, and then slowly, methodically the rocking motion without became identical to that of within, and she, also rocking, became the physical manifestation of an instinctual, primordial movement, which seized her, and would not be resisted, regardless of the muffled, yet still *imperceptible*, sounds of inner chaos.

Hidden, the recess accessed, then engorged, the spell had taken.

Growing accustomed to the motion, she began to hum... steadily, surely, the scale: A... B... C... D... E... F... G... only to be repeated, seemingly ad infinitum. The harmony must be educed again. It must.

Rising and beginning to whirl, the gyrations, painstaken and arduous, became circular and repetitious like the previous rocking. The scale, begun again, would be repeated until confused and senseless, Eleanor remained, the toll of the spell evinced on her countenance. She had become a dervish, her energy holy and chaotic, like a sacred spinning, geometric top. The sun, now a giant candle, watched her Pythagorean gesticulations, as she in turn, had also been hypnotized by his advance.

She could scarcely discern the syllables, aurally rendered and a perfect whisper of breath:

Sa...

ma...

Sa...

mal...

I

am

Sal.

Mrs. Dorset, her mistress of the Lenora tribe, Lenora, Len or A, Elan or Nora, Alenor... like Eleanor, nihilus cognomen, awaited.

LXXXVII

The hall was packed with mourners, some of which Eleanor had never before seen. She recognized others though, most notably the figure of Jane's father, sitting solemn and forlorn in the front pew. She had come with her own father, brothers and sisters who were now running about the church making a spectacle of themselves. When Ignius yelled out, reprimanding his sister for whatever the latter had just done, Eleanor could no longer tolerate this display, and storming over to him, boxed the side of his head, and took him back to where she and her father had been sitting. Her father, more embarrassed by the public acknowledgment that he was the guardian of such unruly offspring, looked reproachfully at Eleanor, before averting his gaze from further public scrutiny.

The service commenced and Eleanor, who had begun to psychically repeat the seven notes of the scale over and over to herself looked up and saw her father staring directly at her with the most intense look of contempt plastered on his small, yet menacing features. Eleanor saw this look as well as the varied, yet strange looks of not a few undiscerning onlookers, as she hadn't realized that during the mental exercise, her tongue had inadvertently distended from its orifice, giving her the odd appearance of either idiocy or mental retardation.

Noticing Mrs. Dorset and her four children amongst the mourners, she said nothing. However Eleanor, who inwardly wished her father, brothers and sisters, as well as the rest of the congregation for that matter, might be swallowed up by the bowels of the earth, licked her lips, and noticed Lenora shift in her pew, daintily splaying her legs apart. Her daughter at that moment began to cry, and Eleanor, irritated by the interruption, shot the child a daggered look.

No one had said anything to Eleanor and even if they had, she would not have been able to respond. She had not spoken since the humming had begun, and saw no reason to start now. The service had commenced without Eleanor really noticing and as the minister droned on, the words created a discord of nonsensical vibrations against the membranous labyrinth of inner ear.

Suddenly Jane, apparently the undead, sat up, and asked her directly and outright, "Two-timing me already? I'm barely cold yet for Pete's sake!"

"Jane?! Jane! Is it really you? I thought you were..."

"I am. Let's not get into the particulars of quantum physics, time-travel, and quarks, but hey, cheating is cheating! Now get in this here casket and eat-me-out before I'm forced to ask Windy, our locally-sexually-challenged youth to do the dirty deed instead!"

"What? I barely understood a word of what you just said!"

"Just get over to my cold, frigid cunt before the worms beat you to it!"

The congregation audibly heard the strange and eerie scale which was being repeated by the pale, sickly girl who, rising slowly exited the pew and proceeded to the front, as though possessed by a force which compelled her onward. The minister, baffled and not a little bewildered, asked the strange child if she wanted to say a few words, to which the only reply being a repetition of the eerily reaffirmed, apparently nonsensical scale.

"I'm sorry, I don't understand." He shifted uncomfortably, unsure of her intentions and the seemingly delusional look evinced upon her countenance. "Are you all right, Miss?" At wit's end to appropriate responses, in desperation, he finally petitioned the masses, "Could someone get a doctor, please?"

Having gained the head of the church, the opened casket stood before her. An Oriental silk, red and dark pink like two polishes given her by Sir Bifford, cloaked the extremity of her corporeality. Cocooned, the scents of sweet ginger and something more wooden, earthy... lingered. The scarf betrayed its striations of fuchsia like the exposure of damaged tissue, and red, not of the ordinary variety, but there being a keen deepness to the hue as of Chinese, in intricate, diaphanous folds. Reaching down and gracing it with the tips of her outstretched fingers, the material was so soft and pliable, almost warm to the touch. Jane now lay, a tiny, polished marble visage, followed in tow by a body as lifeless and fine as a delicately rendered leaf, the outline of its veins made manifest by only the encompassing gloom as it floated down the stream, sacrosanct and pure. Unsure if she should climb in and fulfill its aforementioned decree, she tarried, undecided in her progress. Eleanor gasped, and realizing that she was utterly and completely alone, fainted into the abysmal silence.

Murmurs rose from the crowd as time passed. Someone had placed a pillow under the back of her head, and her father, with younglings in tow, had left the church, and was nowhere to be seen. Carrying her to a forward pew, a few of the men had carefully placed her down, while some of the ladies, Mrs. Dorset heading them, fussed over the small, pale frame.

Two bodies now lay, both supine and sleeping, the only real difference to the casual observer being a refined blue hue to the skin as of the presence of blue blood, no other differences readily discernible. The doctor and his aid arrived, and carried out one of the two sleeping forms, while Mrs. Dorset, fussing and fretting, all the time followed, not wishing to abandon her newly-acquired-friend.

The service resumed as though nothing had happened, the minister having regained his composure, and by its close, had nearly forgotten the extended, and somehow tedious interruption. The chamber, resembling shittimwood, was lowered slowly into the ground.

The Ark of the Covenant was now concealed.

LXXXVIII

They glittered majestically, towering over her removed, distant position as if she instead were the far-off star, faintly emitting her first rays of light. The night view of the heavens stretched far and wide as she knew that somewhere there, she would find her. She wondered if Uranus might help in her beseeching. The ground had failed to produce any likeness, so the heavens were her only other possibility.

Beginning the vibratory scale again, the calling began, and Eleanor knew that Jane's ears had always proven superior to any. The silence dutifully received its pure set of notes, in ominous succession, the scale never varied. There above her preceding his chase, she spotted her. Running, running, always running, but only ever content in such a state. She could never catch her. What was the point of trying? She must accept the truth, and be humbled by grace. Whose grace? The grace. The chase was written immortalized above her. Yes, it had been written in the stars. Someone... who was it?... had seen to that. At least she had been granted that odd and fleeting satisfaction, but oh so fleeting...

To be bathed in this starlight, while up above *she* was of it, seemed so unfair, so unjust. But it was her awareness that differed. It only could be that way. She could feel it slipping like a slippery banana, and wondered what that meant, if she were already mad, or indeed the madness was descending. Both or neither, like the philosophers say. How long had it been since a brushstroke had graced the psychic palette? Her cerebral canvas which was always deemed to receive the impressions of either a grotesque rendering or something more suggestive of an enlightened mind. The strokes... the strokes... when had they last come? She couldn't remember, the tiredness being so heavy. Wanting to be free of such heaviness, such burdening weight that had too great a level of intricacy and seeming inconsistency that it was forever to be deemed unintelligible, full of errors, omissions, and contradictions, but Eleanor knew that wasn't the case. She knew. Now, did anything else matter except for this perception, the one and only perception which truly contained the quintessence of value itself? This was enough. It had to be. This knowledge of all, of everything and nothing. Whether or not the search was futile or fertile, it did not matter in the end. All that mattered was contained in the shell of a nut, that proverbial, old analogy for the essence of matter, when the universe had contracted back to its innermost point, a billionth of a billionth of a second before it. What? *No thing.* That is all.

Orion here epitomized the chase, given to the viewers of time immemorial, and Pleoine and her seven followers being, by no mistake, not unwilling participants for all their pomp and show.

Eleanor looked on as the silver grasses shuttered and were humbled by their majesty. Gently raising her forefinger to the sky, she traced the thrice laced belt, and sighed. It had been so long since she had picked up a brush... so much time had further eroded the cavities of thought as the synapses fired their own sacred songs. She wondered if she still could... if that old feeling might again possess her as it once had if she allowed it... if she could only accept herself, and the gift of the knowledge, the truth. It was not a narrow truth, but a universal truth and it was simultaneously her truth. She had been given it not for any reason but just because... just because. Why was the reasonlessness so difficult... so bloody unforgiving?!

The grasses rustled and Eleanor roused herself from whatever gibberish she had been thinking. Gibberish.... kibberish.... brushstrokes now suffused her consciousness as the night's coldness bit unmercifully into her bones.

LXXXIX

"What do you expect me to do with her?" Mr. Wellgrene's eyes widened with anger and resent. "It's hard enough for me to earn a living these days especially with my wife having left. I've got no time for these head conditions or illnesses!"

"We weren't trying to imply that you do, Mr. Wellgrene. We are simply asserting our position, that is all, Mr. Wellgrene. We are not judging you or yours. The case is simply and sadly that in her current condition, she has no actual place at this institution."

"Well, if she isn't in school, and she's never around the farm much to help me anymore, then what good is she to me?" Mr. Wellgrene fumed.

"She obviously needs some professional help and probably some prolonged resting period. We haven't forgotten that your daughter was a one-time top scholar, sir."

"Yeah, some good that is to us now. Those days are long gone." Mr. Wellgrene, his replies having run dry, bowed his head slightly to impart his lack of awareness of what to do or say next.

"Well in any case, we are sincerely sorry about the whole affair sir, but as we have already described, she is not only incoherent, she is also a continual class disturbance, and is insubordinate and obstinate as she persists in continuing when she has repeatedly been petitioned by her teacher to stop."

"Well, I can't say that she was ever particularly fond of singing before. I can't say I ever heard the girl hum a tune, let alone sing a note. But things change. I can say I'm reminded of that fact everyday." Mr. Wellgrene's colour rose for a moment.

"Yes, we are sure that it must be very difficult, but unfortunately can offer no other alternative." At this last word, the principal cleared his throat.

"That's all you people do is 'offer alternatives'. I still have to do the doing. I'm the one that has to come up with a plan of action."

"Yes, this is the sorry fact of the matter. But it is out of our hands, and we are sorry for you, but especially for your daughter, Eleanor. It is sad indeed to see such a gifted youth go awry in the midst of only beginning to realize her promise."

Mr. Wellgrene placed his hat back on his head, and abruptly quit the room before the little assembled group could utter another pithy saying. Those people and all their bloody words! It gave him a headache just to think of it, never mind having to actually sit in a room full of the gibbering monkeys! He set out on the walk home, and thought he might make a little detour to the brewing house to get his mind off all of their gibbering tongues. He had had a full enough day before he was required to show up for their little meeting. It hadn't accomplished anything. It never did. Now, he himself had to plan and take the next step. He hated that part. His wife had always handled the details of these affairs. The soil was his sole task, and what a task it was! He shouldn't be made to handle all these ever-taxing disruptions!

The brewing house being open, he entered its darkened recesses, full of its usual smoke, odours, and talk. It received him gladly without question or judgement with all of its pomp and show intact.

XC

Eleanor loved looking around the guest chamber that was now regarded as her regular abode. It contained a washstand in the corner with jug and basin, a delicately woven tapestry upon the wall, a few crude carvings of woodland animals, a crucifix centered above the frame of her own small bed, and the prettiest antique of pink and red china roses that Eleanor had ever seen. Yet, of more import to her than all of these, was a small, filigreed bullion of the most precious variety which rested upon her bedside table.

Eleanor often fancied a world composed solely of this element. Rendered valueless in such a world, it would no longer control the worth of men, not serving as a relevant contention. Beings made of gold, heavily clad in gilded threads, walking with thudding force down streets forged of *aurum*. The homogeneous spectre would near purity of form, that is, wholly lacking any. This thought was too delicious and she would foam at the mouth as the notes came weakly and spasmodically from what felt to Eleanor like her bowels themselves, after which exertion she would break into a heavy perspiration, ending with the emptying of her agitated entrails, to which her grandmother would storm in, promptly lift the covers and begin to clean up the mess. Eleanor, however, was not conscious of this hapless ritual. She only sensed the bustlings and administerings of the old lady, and vaguely wondered what the cause of the fuss may have been, continuing all the while in her reverie of the paved golden way so appealing in its silent majesty of refined splendor. To be in such a world upon such a road and to meet such a girl as... again she could not remember and the notes would again begin... A... B... C... D... E... F... G... then again, and again like the constant barraging of a mad voice instructor bent on the accompanying perfection and akin madness of pupil. The screaming then would follow in quick succession when the vocalist would come to the dire realization that the transmitting frequencies came forth wholly from her own uncanny vibrato.

XCI

Dr. Woolston remembered the case. Not only did he remember it, he had taken quite a keen and discriminating interest in it. He eyed the girl before him up and down as though he was considering an equation of the most dire seriousness.

"Yes, indeed. Uh huh. Just as I suspected. The case is degenerative and is continuing to do so, and will persist in regressing now and in the inevitable future. Sad, perhaps. Yes, very sad," he added as though he were checking off a box upon an imaginary scroll. He nodded at his own recollections and running his tongue along the surface of his teeth, gingerly but purposely began to clean the impurities from his fingernails.

He didn't notice the girl's advance, but once she had reached her targeted destination, he started, so beside himself from the sheer unexpectedness of her action.

Clearing his throat, thinking aloud, he ruminated, "Yes, you do demonstrate a clear fixation, this is true." Allowing her fingers to tarry a minute longer, he exclaimed, "Your behaviour is unacceptable, Eleanor. Do you know what I am saying to you?"

Shining the opthalmoscope into her eyes, he could see the accompanying shrinkage of pupil as the involuntary reflex took over. However, no other movement seemed apparent.

"Did you hear me, Eleanor?" he reiterated, this time more loudly.

Again the hand rose up and began to massage the shrunken organ.

For an instant the shrunken vessel began to grow, and Eleanor, noticing its still minuscule size and the oddness of its shape, momentarily desisted in her pursuance. Dr. Woolston was no longer fighting off her advances. Instead, his eyes were closed and he seemed unconscious of her touch. Unexpectedly, they again flittered open, and almost menacingly he queried, "Do you know that your behaviour is unacceptable? Do you even know that your name is, Eleanor?"

The figure remained impassive, yet continued in her exertions.

Again he shone the opthalmoscope in her eyes, and repeated the query, waiting for a reaction which would signify some response. When none was forthcoming, he mumbled out loud, "In the interests of science, perhaps this might elicit some form of recognition." Undoing his trousers, Eleanor could now see the ripening of her endeavours. Clearly, the thing had grown. Engulfing it with her tongue, Dr. Woolston at once cried out, but when the intoxicating sensation registered, he quickly drew in his breath so he would not call out. Clearly, and perhaps even subconsciously, he thought if nothing of value came out of her mouth, something of value may be put in.

Their sessions continued in the crevices of the dark leather and polished wood-filled office. Five of them in total, and Eleanor, who left each with a wider grin than when she had come, was profoundly and oddly irritated at the end of the fourth session. Her pupils were broad and Dr. Woolston had noted this expansion in his log, although he could think of nothing which had been different on each of the occasions save for the third.

On each successive meeting, he had asked the girl if she knew her behaviour to be unacceptable and when no acknowledgment came, he then asked her if she knew her own name. When no rejoinder was ever given, Eleanor would initiate the massage, and shutting his eyes, he would undo his trousers, and she would begin. Regardless of circumstance, it seemed to yield to her telekinetic manipulations.

On this said third meeting, Dr. Woolston found he was especially agitated by Eleanor's endeavourings, and as the excitement mounted, became almost beside himself with a kind of frenzy. Hoisting her hind end towards himself, he leant her stomach and pelvis against the rich mahogany desk, and with her ribs and arms prone before him, she became a game carcass laid out to dry. Beginning to bear down mercilessly, heartily pounding away, his frenzy still persisted to mount.

The acrid stench of fecal matter and the reek of warm, decaying epidermal tissue reached Eleanor's nostrils as the distress became too great. She wanted to scream, to yell out at the object of the intrusion, but when she attempted to do so, a sound, high-pitched and vibrating, emitted from whence she knew not. She felt as if a hautboy had been inserted, subcutaneous and splendid, and once again she could hear the purity of her scale, however this time repeated in rapid succession in order to parallel the quick duration of the interludes.

However, Dr. Woolston, once relieved, was unperturbed. He wondered however why it had been so very long since his last... his last... for some odd reason overture came to mind. He had a friend who could provide the best boys available, yet perhaps it had been too long, since his chosen genitalia had changed, yet not the predominance of his focus.

Regardless of all of it, on this aforementioned fourth occasion, her pupils had nevertheless dilated, her face betraying a curious expression of unmitigated contempt. Then unexpectedly, upon the following visit, when Eleanor was at the height of her performance, that is, as they had resumed their previous favoured activity, and Dr. Woolston's back was arching in preparation for his customary groan of relief, Eleanor, deftly and purposefully, bit down as hard as she could, to which she nearly received a great blow to the head.

As Dr. Woolston rolled about the floor, groping his privates, he couldn't help but wonder as to what would have caused this particular effect. Unable to examine her pupils, and too sore to even stand, he suddenly understood the root of the problem, the same neurosis which plagued all females, the only explicable cause of such violent behaviour and invariably, there was no cure: penis envy. Yes, he could always rely on this condition, plaguing all his female patients alike. No cure, unfortunately. Even though he had come to enjoy their visits, he had no other choice but to recommend institutionalization. It was the only viable option.

He had managed to push her out into the waiting room, notifying his secretary that he would not be receiving any other appointments for the day. As the younger and older woman sat staring at each other, Eleanor wondered why she could never make the thing grow enough. It simply refused, and Eleanor, beside herself with vexation, found that she wanted nothing more than to hear her scale. Her muse awaited, but the notes would not be produced as this obstruction prevented their formulation. As its tip vibrated, she awaited the sound of her scale, but nothing materialized. Irritated and filled with sudden and unexpected ire, her pupils dilated, and down she bit.

XCII

The softness of covers felt reassuring and the familiar smell of hot water and suds wafted into her small chamber. It was washing day, and her grandmother had begun even earlier than usual. For the first time in weeks, Eleanor hadn't awoken to that eerily repeated succession of dreary notes. She truly hated waking to this each morning, and had begun to scream uncontrollably when realizing that the sound came from her own throat. However, since this epiphany, she had steadily begun to improve. Each day she did something to assure her observers that her strength was beginning to gradually return. Her grandmother bathed, clothed, and fed her in regular intervals, and even though she had not spoken, she had, on occasion, smiled.

During these several weeks, Dr. Woolston was not in any condition to make his customary appearance and refrained from public view as much as possible. On the third successive Sabbath however, he appeared, clad in usual attire, at one Mrs. Vivian Edward Norman Wellgrene's doorsill. This being his final, formal examination of Eleanor, he planned immediately afterwards to impart the inopportune news.

Upon entering, he took off his hat and coat and handing them to Mrs. Wellgrene senior, nodded in greeting, and promptly asked where the girl was. "Eleanor is in the adjacent room," was the equally prompt answer, although Mrs. Wellgrene senior thought she may have a word or two with his mother regarding the sorry state of her son's manners, even though she knew just how busy his practice was becoming.

After a few minutes he returned, the usual pretension, condescension and artificiality of sadness awashed his features. "I am terribly sorry to inform you, Vivian, that your granddaughter's condition has no real hope of recovery. It is my professional opinion that her cognitive abilities have degenerated sufficiently, and will only continue to do so in future. There is nothing more which can be done. As well, I am recommending the committal of the girl to an institution, where she can be properly cared for." At the end of this diatribe, he cleared his throat, reached for his hat and coat, all the while smiling to himself, and rose to leave.

"Just one moment, Howard. The girl's name is Miss Eleanor Wellgrene. I will have you know that. Furthermore, she was once a well-reputed and highly-gifted scholar, I will have you also know. In any case, I believe that my care is the best that she can receive, and I do not, and will not, believe that my dear granddaughter will never speak again. She needs time to recover. You should have some understanding of this more than others, I dare say, Howard. As well, your mother will hear of this visit, and I for one, do not think she will be pleased. Good day, Dr. Woolston." With those parting words, she promptly herded him toward the entrance, nodded a similarly abrupt farewell as he proceeded to trip over the sill, and promptly clomped the door to, and he was left, his face and lower extremities having taken quite a downward turn.

Eleanor could hear her grandmother, now soliloquizing to herself, "I will not hear such meaningless rubbish spoken in my house. I simply will not," she nodded in self-confirmation, and walked towards the kitchen to proceed with the remaining day's chores.

XCIII

The priest bent down and whispered something into her ear. As his skin brushed against her cheek, she felt a keen and distinct pleasure being conveyed through her body like an access to primordial meridians of energy. His vestments were of such a dark tone, devoid of any hint of light whatsoever save the collar round his neck.

Eleanor felt that energy again fill her and she wished to be inside it. Her world was only an infinite space of the creator's prism, refracted again and again, and here, she was of the light, primordial and knowing in her achromaticity. With her arms and legs splayed about under her bedclothes, afloat in this space that contained the realized desire of these two polarities, which forever rendered her canvas utterly flawed and wholly imperfect due to the sheer nature of the attempt, always a limit of the limitless potential.

Black and white. She had been asked, and it had been answered. Her world would not exist devoid of a single hue! She would not have it! No, no, it was final and set. Now, she was awash in all of its realized perfection. The absorption of all reality within its grasp, by the very definition of its antediluvian nature, the darkness knew and questioned not: knowledge in its quintessence. But here dwelt correspondingly, in the fullness of its humble and redeeming nature, the palest of shades or rather of shadelessness. Reflection itself - Narcissus finally satiated by his own reflection in the pool: Love.

The void of lightlessness and the sacred reflection dwell simultaneously united here, existing as one. The inspiration of the one causing the expiration of the other, although no cognizance could ever figure in which order the seeming commencement would ensue or the pattern take: an equation so divine, any mathematician's dream theorem. But, why? How can they exist simultaneously these two worldviews without breaching, forever breaching the boundary? Perhaps, the grey tone knew. If it did, it never told. She could hear the question but it was not framed in words: it was the scale and this very same seven note scale had become the seven hues of the visible spectrum - sound had become light, and in that fragment, she could see J... J... Jane, that was her name in the light, within the light, of the light, finally out of the cave. Slowly, another figure materialized, and as though, her energy which flowed from him to her had become again pure, there played that other one, she knew so well, who never knew her own name. They were beckoning to her, and wished her to come. Their thoughts were not words to be heard, but forms to be known, to be apprehended for they were within reach here.

She only knew for certain her own reply, and as she thought it, they knew it too and slowly slipped further into the grey. But somehow this slippery place necessarily fell away, and as it did, she heard herself say, "I am of the prismed space. This is where I wish to be."

Her words came out. Slurred and mumbled though they were, yet still coherent and within our frame of reference. The priest sat up, and called Mrs. Wellgrene exclaiming, "Come quick, Mrs. Wellgrene! A miracle has just occurred!"

The old woman, bent with age and toil, after the man explained what had just transpired, exclaimed, "Praise the Lord! It is a miracle!

Thank you, Father."

The man only smiled and nodded in reply, "Yes, the good Lord is gracious."

Crossing himself, he blessed the now heavily slumbering girl, who was weary from passage as she had only just gained back the threshold of mind. Leaving a rosary at the foot of her bed, he gently covered an outcropped appendage, and quietly closing the door, silently left.

XCIV

Eleanor's grandmother's face furrowed into a little withered ball of expression. She had never seen a face do that before.

Her grandmother, appalled at the state of her gift, chastised, "I'm rather disappointed in you, Eleanor. I thought that you, more than others, would have taken better care of such a special gift. It was a family heirloom." The woman's eyes seemed to progressively mist as she continued to speak.

"I'm sorry ma'am, I honestly tried to take proper care of such a highly distinguished item, but the chance to do so seemed taken away from me regardless of my sincerest endeavors." Eleanor uttered softly, yet directly.

"Your directness is an asset to your character, and the way in which you choose to express yourself makes me wonder why you chose to stay here with me instead of returning to your father and the chance for a proper education, but this being the case, it does not change the fact that your irresponsibility is to blame for this sad ruin," uttered Mrs. Wellgrene senior in an unchanging timbre.

"Yes, and no apology will ever make up for the reduced state of our family's treasured Bible. I can only hope in time that my good actions will help to again elevate the esteem of myself in your eyes."

"You could choose a better, more appropriate word, my dear."

Eleanor was puzzled as to her meaning.

"Don't look so befuddled. Instead of 'hope,' simply say 'pray.'"

"I am sorry to admit that it is very difficult for me to use this word." Eleanor knew she wouldn't be content to hear her reveal this.

"Whatever can you mean?! You are a Catholic! You do acknowledge our Blessed Virgin, do you not?"

"Please do not ask me this. I have no answer for you presently," Eleanor's head bowed, as she had only managed to further erode her esteem.

"Oh my dear child, you are so lost! I know that you were a stern believer. Whatever changed your mind so?" the old woman bawled.

"I honestly do not know exactly. I can only tell you that this subject is one which has, and continues to, cause me considerable angst."

"Well, believer or unbeliever, if you live under this roof, you are expected to at least attend church each week dressed in your Sunday best, and also Mass at Christmas and Easter, and especially attend, the three-hour Sunday school class taught by our own good priest. You will learn and hopefully espouse this way of life. Bible or no Bible, it is your gift to wholeheartedly embrace, and I sincerely pray that you will one day come to see that." At the end of such a lengthy monologue, Eleanor wondered if she would bow, but indicated nothing to this end.

"You probably do not understand the importance of what I am trying to convey to you, but one day, you will. I will pray for this day. Will you pray with me?"

"Yes ma'am, I will pray with you." Even though Eleanor knew that she could never pray in the same way that her grandmother would, she smiled and agreed to the request willingly. She desperately wished to please the wizened old lady whom, although formal, always meant well in her deeds, and after all, had rescued her from that place, where she hoped never to return.

XCV

"Sit up straight and finish your dinner properly, Eleanor."

Eleanor, who had characteristically slumped over her mashed potatoes, falling into a near slumber, bolted upright at the sharp reprimand, while at once replying, "Yes, ma'am. Sorry, ma'am."

The old woman shook her head disapprovingly at the girl's profound weariness, and wishing to keep her attention focused on the business of the day queried, "And what did you learn in Sunday school, yesterday?"

"The seven deadly sins, I believe, ma'am," Eleanor mechanically retorted.

"What is this? You believe? You should know. What are they then?" was the brusque reply.

"Avarice, gluttony, malice, lust, covetousness, sloth, and, and, um .... I can't remember the final one."

"Hubris. Does that sound familiar? You should know that one well, I should think, Eleanor."

"Yes, that's it. It slipped my mind for a moment, that's all." Eleanor sighed knowing that she had failed her grandmother's test.

"Yes, yes, yes. And what is your opinion of these seven vices?"

Eleanor, for an instant rendered speechless, simply answered, "This is something which you may not wish to know."

"Well, tell me anyhow. I am perfectly capable of deciding this for myself without the need of your censure."

"Yes, of course, I didn't mean to imply..." Eleanor stammered at the scowl which materialized on her opponent's face.

"Be done with it. Spit it out," was the now customary terse response.

"Yes. I just don't think that these are unreasonable thoughts or actions which should be classified in any way as sins. Each and every one of us commit these acts and have these thoughts, daily. Not to be able to do so would deny us our very nature as human beings, and if we could conform to such strict standards, we would all be saints, and the necessity for religious institutions would fundamentally disappear."

"Perhaps you were right in your initial assertion. For an intelligent girl, you have missed the entire point. These are standards which we aim for, we attempt to live up to, and maxims which are by no means easily attained, but that is what makes them so important, and why we are all sinners!" With this last word, the old woman rose, threw down her napkin, and promptly quit the room, before she would say another word, leaving Eleanor to the quiet contemplation of her pooling gravy. She wished the woman had never asked her this as she knew she could not answer in a way that would ever please her, and she would not lie to her. There wasn't any point in it. But at the same time, her intention was not to upset the nerves of the one lady whom had so graciously taken her in, when there was no one else. She wondered how she might mitigate such an outcome in future, without the need of fabrication.

XCVI

In the distance, she could see the thing, its hulking, limping frame obviously maimed in some way as it hobbled through the drying fields. It looked like a shrunken buffalo, lamed by the scarcity of grassland and through the diminishing of its kind. Eleanor squinted into the distance as the whiteness of sky had created such a ghastly glare of reflection which considerably reduced the visibility of the naked eye. It seemed to be studying her as though it had fixated upon her form, and she started for an instant, alarmed at the possibility of a lone, rabid creature that was suffering from starvation as well as its other ailments.

As a wind had started up, it attempted to gallop in her direction, but as its aim was somewhat askew, she could not tell if she were its desired object or not. Momentarily it fell to the ground, and Eleanor, even from her removed perspective, could easily discern just how exhausted the creature had become. Even though there sometimes appeared packs of wild dogs, rabid and ravenous which drifted into towns and had to be put out of their misery, with an occasional stray hound escaping detection, this particular creature's ill state unsettled her, and she went back to the yard to collect a pail of well water, then set out to see if she might somehow relieve the sickened thing.

As she approached, she could feel the wind again picking up, blowing particles of heavy clay at her face. As she neared the stricken entity, it seemed to cry out, whining meaningfully. Suddenly aware of who it was, she heard herself bellow, "Beast, Beast, is it you?!" This time however, a blast of air nearly propelled her off her feet, and wondering if this indicated a coming storm, she ran to him and gathered the stinking, heavily-panting creature under one arm, his tail now floating in the pail of water slung over its opposite. Shelter had become an imminent requirement.

Walking through the fields, she could hear the wind beginning to whip the drying grasses and knew her grandmother would be beside herself with worry. She shouldn't have been so stupid to venture out when the gusts were already apparent, but she couldn't turn herself away from the lamed animal. And now to find that it was Beast! He had somehow managed to find her. At least if they were to be lost, they would be together... a whirling dervish embodied in a ball of wet, furry, six-legged rage.

The lightning like the veins of a hand had begun. Its luminescence made Eleanor wonder for a moment if perhaps they were not floating in the realm of the sea, a strange two-headed creature banned to that region by Thor himself, that is, as he had tired of her eternal dissidence. A roar could be heard from behind, and Beast, although nearly unconscious from out-and-out exhaustion, still shook with fear. She dared not look to her rear as she did not want to see her fate approaching. She only wished to see what was before her, for here, there was still hope. He must have known she couldn't leave him to the merciless clutches of Providence. She couldn't lose anyone else, not now, not after everything which had happened. The roar turned into the regular beat of a whirring, as Eleanor could barely make out the shape of her grandmother's form beckoning to her in the distance.

Suddenly, from the sky a chariot drawn by two steeds appeared. The charioteer nodded to her while pulling on the reigns, then opening his mouth widely bellowed, "Hey there, quite gusty today, ain't it?" The being, its gilded shield and armour shining majestically even though it had grown quite dark, Eleanor no longer able to discern the presence of daylight, nodded again to her and yelled at the unruly creature, "Whoa there, now!"

He noticed her stare, the way she examined the line and form of his silhouette, how his sinew and shape became a luminescent outline against the onset of darkness. "You are in need of shelter, you and your beast?" he boomed.

"Yes sir, I think I am caught in the clutches of a tornado, and I fear I have lost my way."

Again the unruly beast yanked obstinately on its tether. "Whoa, I say, whoa!!!"

"Why do you no longer paint, Eleanor? It would please us so if you would," he smiled.

"I... I...," Eleanor stammered. At the thought of someone other than herself being aware of her art, she wondered how this could be.

"Well, you see sir, I do not exactly paint the way most people do.

My attempt is merely a cerebral rendering. I have no canvas, nor paints. It is all 'up here.'" With those words, Eleanor with her free hand, pointed to her head.

"Yes, yes, I know that. But this is beside the point. The point is that you have stopped."

"Well... I...," Eleanor still could not fully comprehend the how's and wherefore's.

"Answer me!" the being boomed.

"I am sorry, sir. I thought that it mattered not to anyone but myself. I have not seriously attempted a canvas in quite a while. Something has been flawed in my ability, or motivation, or inspiration, I just don't know.... Something is askew. It isn't right, and I can't..." Eleanor had almost forgotten the storm, Beast, and the significance of the booming presence before her in an attempt to articulate and herself understand why this had come to pass.

"Yes, yes, it's all well and good. But now, now, you must begin again. Do you see? You must." He distinctly seemed to be waiting for some kind of a confirmation from the pondering form before him.

"Yes, perhaps you are right. Perhaps..." Eleanor ruminated.

"No, that is not acceptable. Will you begin again, Eleanor?"

It was clear to her that he expected a response.

"But I have no canvas. No paints. How do you expect me to seriously endeavor..."

Before she could finish her sentence, the being again boomed, "Enough!"

Eleanor, now acknowledging the full potential of what lay before her, shook simultaneously with the creature cradled in her arms.

"Yes, yes, I will, I will, sir!" Eleanor cried, not wishing to upset him further.

"Good. That will please us. The rest will come," he nodded apparently satisfied with her and himself. Watching her he seemed to nearly laugh, and suddenly, just before Eleanor thought he was going to vanish into the thin and ominous air to which he had materialized, asked her if she and her animal would care for a lift home. She quickly nodded her assent, and before she knew, they were borne on the ephemeral clouds of oblivion, beyond and back, her grandmother's homestead, a tiny dot in the distance.

Eleanor could not remember of all they spoke, only that he, more than most, was indeed a sparkling conversationalist, and she enjoyed herself fully. Suddenly the form within became the form without and Eleanor realized that her grandmother again was standing over her, and she and the creature she had managed to save were in the safety of her small, wooden bed.

"Ma'am, ma'am, is the storm over?" Eleanor's voice crackled as though from misuse.

"Yes dear, it is. Rest now." And she felt a warm, soft hand delicately caress her temple.

Beast stirred, and licking his lips, they both gently fell back into the comfort of welcoming sleep.

XCVII

Beast could smell it under her dress. She had managed to conceal it well. The gaseous substance rose up from the sludge, bubbling to the surface in random effluviums. She pondered how long the plant matter must have been fermenting to create such a fertile state. She loved the bog. And it was such a perfect place to play with Beast, even though, as her grandmother put it, that always meant a good dose of elbow grease and heavy lather were to be next on her agenda.

Beast nudged her significantly, but Eleanor was not as yet ready. Sitting down upon a nearby rock, she asked Beast, "What if he was wrong? What if neurosis is not caused by the irreconcilable nature of the conscious from the subconscious, but indeed from the very real potentiality of the reconcilability of the two? Did he ever take that into account?"

Beast only whined and stared back wondering when she would be ready. Eleanor smiled at him and lay back on the flattened rock she now customarily used for this purpose. Reaching over to the sludge, she grasped it, allowing the texture to permeate, oozing through the webbing of her fingers.

"Perfect, it is the perfect consistency! Now if it only came in red, yellow, and blue, we would be set, wouldn't we now Beast?!"

Beast jumped up, bounded forward, then leaned meaningfully

against her still-bony underbelly. "Well, do you want it or not?"

Lifting her dress, he could see its tip sticking out of the hallowed orifice. Looking to her for some kind of affirmative gesture, he could see the distention of her naked lower abdomen. His tongue began to lap, and as it did, the marrow loosened. Very gingerly, in order to receive not the punitive damage of previous instances, the dark pink applicator was applied. As it loosened, finally becoming dismantled, the core was successfully extracted. Its recipient and applicator both satiated from process and product, respectfully, nothing was left to do now except sprawl out leisurely, and observe, as she forced the moist matter through her fingertips, heaving the humus high into the air, blackened dots now aloft, then against clouds of colourless hue, momentarily defining the amorphous interplay of corporeal space, today's sustenance for the hierophant's pursuit.

From below, a loud flatulent discharge was heard, as both participants gaped in sudden stupefaction at one another, not sure of whom the culprit may have been. Bubbles of methyl hydride rose to the surface and plopped. Suddenly a voice could be intelligibly discerned. To these participants, it sounded oddly like this: "Only through the expression of a systematized illusion can a plausible reality be rendered intelligible."

Regardless of its intended meaning, it served to break their respective states, and even though the painting was not complete, at least, it had successfully begun.

XCVIII

Her grandmother was in quite a state when Eleanor returned from her cavortings. She entered, wet and panting, with Beast following in tow.

"Where have you been?" was the initial sharp retort.

"I... We've been down on the bogs. I've been running him," Eleanor replied unaccustomed to the vexed state of her condemner.

"You both look positively filthy, mud-caked at the heels!" The old woman seeing the growing mortification appearing on Eleanor's face, lowered her voice, and stated as calmly as she could, "Put that dog outside where he belongs and give him a bath. Then take one yourself. But before you do," and with these words the tone of ire began to reappear, "do you know what has become of my leftover stewing beef?"

"I... It was nearly a week old. We would usually have eaten it by now, if that is what you meant to do. I assumed that..." Eleanor's timbre was growing weaker.

"Never assume. Always ask. I was planning on serving that up for supper, Eleanor, as I haven't made it into town this week yet."

"I'm sorry, ma'am. I honestly did not know." Eleanor was obviously sincere.

"Well, you'll know it tonight, when you go to bed hungry," was the second curt rebuttal.

"Yes, ma'am," was her sole reply.

"Eleanor, I was under the impression that the meals which I provide are plentiful. Is this not true? Are they so barely sufficient that you feel the need to consume the remainder?"

"Oh no, ma'am. I didn't eat the stew. Your meals are more than apt. Sadly, I was concerned about Beast and how weak he has been looking since he has been with us, and unfortunately, he was the lucky recipient of the object in question." With those words, Eleanor lowered her head solemnly.

Her grandmother's voice rose noticeably as she trilled, "You fed my beef to your damned dog?!"

"Yes, ma'am, he seemed so weak," was the barely audible response.

"That food is expensive, Eleanor. Good-gracious, we have to budget in order to survive. I may be well-off, but as the good Lord says, 'Waste not, want not.' Eleanor, this will not do. Such an indulgent act when I permit you to stay with me out of the goodness of my heart." For a moment she paused to inhale a large, long draught of air.

Continuing the admonishment, she preached, "Well, it is time that you learned the honest value of a dollar. I heard that they're taking on people at the library in town, and I think you should try for it. I realize that you never were able to complete your education, but I'm sure they'll at least be able to find some odd job for you to do. What do you think?"

Eleanor was too dumbfounded to speak, and immediately resentful of the implications this idea entailed. She knew what people already thought of her, and had no desire for further contact.

"What would happen to all the chores that I do, here? I am beginning to increase my workload as I feel ready, and am plenty busy with them. Would you be able to manage without me?" A note of melancholia had oddly entered into her tone. It was more than obvious that Eleanor hoped the answer might not be in the affirmative.

"I think so, Eleanor. I always have managed on my own since your dear grandfather, God rest his soul, passed."

As the response came, the words like bullets pierced her skin. Smiling meekly however, she uttered, "If it pleases you ma'am, I will proceed as you deem fit."

Her tone now freed of its previous burden, she again continued, "I think it would be best for you in the long run, dear. I am not going to live forever, and you will need to manage for yourself one day. You are welcome to stay here as long as you like, but some sort of employment will eventually be necessary. I think you might even be happy in spite of yourself amongst those copious books!" She nodded, uncharacteristically grinning, obviously pleased with her evocation of Eleanor's prospects.

Eleanor was not however, at all, convinced. Nevertheless, she managed to force a smile, and nodding reverentially, mechanically retorted, "Yes, ma'am." Suddenly suffused with crimson, it was becoming increasingly clear to her that she should have followed her initial instincts, catching and gutting a fish instead.

XCIX

The tree stood before her. Its smell, like a mantled grove of warmth, covered her from the bitter chill of night. She wanted to embrace it, stroke something vital, something living. Maybe if she got close enough to its branches, she would indeed become a part of it. Her grandmother had placed candles all over its foliage, and in the blackness, its silhouette had begun to glow, slowly from within, its aroma filling the room.

She could now hear him at the door. Her grandmother never liked it, but she had just bathed him that day, and after all, she had already gone to bed. She could hear him scratching, his claws chipping the paint. Paint, paint, yes... but now? He was at the door, and just for a moment she wanted to caress him, in the candlelight, before she would put them out.

Opening the door slowly so as not to make a sound, she looked severely at Beast, so that he would know her intent. Turning and making her way back to the tree, its light serving as a sort of beacon in the darkness, she sat down, he close at her side. The warmth from his coat made Eleanor conscious of her own tiredness and she, unable to resist the urge any longer, lay back onto the carpet. It felt cool, yet soft like the moss of a forest floor beneath her, and tonight, especially tonight, she could imagine that the ceiling was indeed the sky laced with infinitesimal quantities of star constellations and tonight she would rename them all.

His coat seemed jet black in the encompassing darkness and from the ensuing glow she could make out his outline, as though all of his hair had been edged with a pigmentless hue to define him somehow. No longer able to keep them open, she shut her eyes, and feeling for the softness of his coat, gently stroked his silhouette as though she were attempting to gingerly, but intentionally, blur it. Her mind floated and she wanted to remember it, to commit it to memory somehow before she fell into the land whose shores she was now gracing....

They had returned after the midnight Mass that her grandmother had attended ever since she was a little girl, the procession of candles always bringing a tear to her eye. Eleanor and her grandmother sat in their customary spot next to the priest, Eleanor wearing her new blue velvet dress with a collar of eyelet lace. She had never possessed a gown and the feel of it alone had been enough to make her shiver with delight. Her new patent leather shoes clicked on the floorboards and in them all she could think of was the shuffle-off-to-buffalo that Jane had once taught her.

Peering down at her gift, she reached out to feel the brickwork at her fingertips. What mortar and pestle had crushed, then the mason laying the brick side by side, one on top of another, the friction of their tactility abrading her skin. Rubbing all the harder, she did not desist until she had worn a keen and noticeable tear along the inner surface of her palm. She wanted to preserve this moment in her memory and under *his* mantle, she felt safe, as though she could see everything, but no one could see her.

Before her grandmother had retired for the eve she had produced a wrapped package of what looked to Eleanor like a distinctly rectangular object with a set of paint brushes hanging from it, after which came a moderately-sized basket, containing, as Eleanor was transported into a state of awe, paints, one after another: tubes of crimson, bright yellow, indigo, white and black filled the wicker container. Fondling them tenderly, delicately as though they were Dresden china, she began to cry, softly at first, then with more vigor.

"I never thought... I never thought... anyone would..." she stammered while blubbering.

"I never thought that They would, that He would," she began just as incoherently again. "I never thought..." this time falling into a complete and horrid sobbing.

"Dear child, I didn't..." her grandmother, rendered just as unintelligible, stammered in unison, as though she too had momentarily caught a transmittable disease.

"I didn't mean..." her grandmother, still lost for words quickly regained her composure.

"It can be returned. I hardly wished to upset you so, my dear," her grandmother finally managed to definitively announce.

"No, no, it's not that. It's just that I never knew anyone... ca... ca... cared." Again she stopped. "I cannot tell you what this means to me. Thank-you. Thank-you, ma'am."

She gazed up, her eyes brimming with tears, and managed a faint smile.

"Oh dear child," she gently stroked her forehead, "Merry Christmas, dear. My dear, Eleanor." Then she turned, and slowly made her way, ascending the creaky flight of old, wooden stairs.

"Merry Christmas, Grandmother," she whispered. In a softly venerating voice, she continued, "May you be blessed. May you be blessed."

C

The grimness of the morning caught her by surprise. Somehow, she had expected glorious sunshine, but this was not however the case. Sunday school: her grandmother would not be persuaded otherwise. But strangely today she wanted to go. She hoped to meet someone whom she could talk to about her own matters. She was beginning to get bored of doing everything with her grandmother, and the fire in her breeches was becoming unbearable. She missed Mr. Graves and Mrs. Dorset. Hell, she even missed Dr. Woolston! The itch was ever-present or omnipresent like the cleric was now saying.

"Yes, this is what it means when we say the Holy Father is omniscient, omnipotent, and omnipresent. He is all-knowing, all-powerful, and is everywhere at one or all times."

Finally, she had got the boy with the crooked-toothed smile to notice her, as she crossed and uncrossed her legs suggestively. She wondered if he would notice that she wasn't wearing any underpants.

Suddenly, his centre tooth seemed to protrude further, and even though he was uncouth and seemed vacuous, he was the oldest in the class and the most likely to get her implied meaning.

Grunting and immediately coughing, she knew he had received her blatant message.

"What is it, George? Did you say something?"

"Um... no, I didn't, Father. May I be excused?"

After George had left, Eleanor quickly asked if she could be excused as well.

"You too, Eleanor? You are new here. If you can tell me what it was that I just spoke of a moment ago, you may be excused."

"You spoke of the Holy Father being omnipotent, omniscient, and omnipresent, sir."

"And do you remember what these terms mean, Eleanor?"

"Yes, they respectively mean that the Holy Father is all-powerful, all-knowing, and present everywhere at one and the same time."

"Very good for a novice. You may be excused this time, Eleanor."

Eleanor replied, "Thank-you, Father," as she jumped from her seat grimacing as though her departure indeed connotated an emergency.

Peering through the keyhole, she could see him holding it. It was as large as Eleanor had hoped. What a fine organ! She watched eagerly as he relieved himself. She was hoping that he would be doing something quite different. It would make her task considerably easier, but unfortunately, this again was not the case.

When George exited, he glanced suspiciously at Eleanor who smiled knowingly, and then asked, "Hey, were you watching me do my business in there?"

She managed to appear momentarily horrified and then promptly afterwards, affronted. "No, whatever gave you that idea? But if you don't tell anyone, I would be glad to help you after class in any way that you might like."

"Help me, why? You don't even know me. Why would ya want to help me for, anyways?"

" 'Cause I like you. And that's not entirely true. I know your name is George, now don't I?" Eleanor blinked at him.

"Yeah, I guess. What's yours, then?" George asked blankly.

"My name is Eleanor. Pleased to meet you, George," Eleanor retorted, mocking cheerfulness.

"Okay then, we should be gettin' back to class. Father Flatly doesn't like stragglers much."

"Okay, but wait. Meet me after class behind the church. Okay, George?"

"I guess so, Eleanor. Bye." George, not wanting to keep the good priest waiting, left directly.

After class, Eleanor walked a little ways away from the structure, and noticed in the distance just how sooty the church appeared to be. She tarried long enough for most of the other classmates to make their way homewards, and Father Flatly even asked her if she'd like a ride.

Eleanor, however, had other things on her mind. She could see his lumberous figure in the distance, shifting uneasily from one foot to the other. Approaching him, she could feel the wetness picking up between her bare legs.

"There you are. I was beginning to think you weren't coming. I was going to go home. I'm kinda hungry, you know." He seemed to be a little irritated at her for keeping him.

"Okay, okay. How about we take a walk behind those trees over there?"

"What for?" George was more innocent than Eleanor had hoped.

"I don't know. I want to show you something, that is if you want to see it," Eleanor coaxed, coyly.

"Will it take very long? I want to be getting home before it rains."

"As long as you want it to," she teased.

They walked in amongst the trees and when they seemed out of view, Eleanor lifted her dress, and asked George what he thought. Maybe, she should have asked him if he thought.

He replied by covering his eyes, and repeating, "Geez, oh geez."

"What's the matter, George? Haven't you ever seen one before?" Eleanor placated.

"No, I shouldn't be looking at no girl's bottom."

"I want you to look. Please look, George."

Carefully uncovering his eyes, he appeared shocked and pale, as if he had been terrorized by an alien intruder.

"Is that what it looks like?" George asked timidly.

"Yes, George. Do you want to touch it?" Eleanor cooed.

"Maybe. No, you're gonna get me into a lot of trouble. Is that what this is all about? Are you tryin' to trick me, or something?" George, angered, turned around to see if anyone could see them. Meanwhile, Eleanor took his arm and passed his hand over her moistened labia, fingering herself, as she did so.

"What are you doing?" By this time, his frown had started to fade, and Eleanor, now begging said, "I just want to suck it for a couple of minutes. Can I?..." but she had already started undoing his protruding trousers. The involuntary response had begun.

For a moment, George seemed to be going to jump back, but then he, realizing what he would be missing, began to help Eleanor undo the remaining buttons.

As her tongue lapped, George muttered, but Eleanor could not hear what he was saying. She could only feel the hard, wet protrusion filling her mouth. Just before she thought it would squirt, she asked if he might, if they might, if she might, 'put it in,' but he just stared at her vacuously, now uncomfortable in his newly exposed state.

"I'll insert it. It won't hurt, I promise. It should even feel good. Pleeease, George. Just for a minute."

"I don't know. I think you're going to get us both into a lot of trouble, and besides I don't even know you."

"Tell me one thing, George. Didn't what I was just doing feel reeeal... good?"

"Yeah, I guess. But I don't know about the other. It sounds like a bad idea," George chastised.

Rubbing it back and forth across her wetness, he began to move mechanistically. Pressing him into the tree's hollowed crevice, she hoisted herself atop his obtrusion analogous to the multifarious branches and twigs surrounding them, but soft, like no other barked extension. The exterior of the vascular cambium having been different, George would be an unnecessary distraction. However, unfortunately such was not the casing.

Having only just placed it in, the obvious rhythmic sensation which George could not accommodate himself to, as it kept slipping out, it fell out yet again, this time quickly convulsing on Eleanor's upper thigh muscle. The spilling of the pale yolk like yellow liquid sunshine having not occurred, Eleanor wanted to cry out in exasperation, but at the sight of a tall, lanky, now-grimacing fellow, Eleanor, stupefied, pointed at this gawking, nearly-laughing figure, standing directly behind them.

George, however, began to continuously repeat, "Geez, geez, oh geez," until Eleanor, sick of his idiocy, finally cried out, "Shut up, for Christ's sake!" to which George responded by flushing a bright red-purple, and quickening his repetitive ejaculations. Eleanor stood, interrupted, her dress hoisted above her waist, suddenly engrossed by the hue which George had abruptly turned. And the other only stood pondering, also spellbound by Eleanor's lack of decorum, as though he couldn't figure out exactly what she was and how to respond to this pale creature before him.

CI

Eleanor watched as George yanked up his pants, which currently graced his ankles, nodded reverently to the figure before them, then hurrying along the trail through the trees, the crack of his buttocks prominently displayed, all the while muttering seeming gibberish to himself, and passed out of sight without another intelligible syllable.

Eleanor scowled at the interloper, promptly pulled down her dress, then after being suffused with a deep smear of crimson along the ridge of her cheekbones, stepped back and barked, "Now, what do you want?"

"My friends call me, Chef," was the calm reply.

Examining his long form, and quiet manner, he suddenly seemed to gain an attractive property, that she hadn't noticed until now.

"Who are you, anyway?"

"I'm the dullard's brother. And who are you, anyway?"

"I'm not in any position to disclose that pertinent detail, now am I?" Eleanor again barked.

"If you're afraid I'm going to tell Father Flatly, the town gossips, or your grandmother, think again. I've got better things to do with my time."

"How do you know me?"

"I've seen you around with your grandmother, and besides the congregation did quite a bit of praying on your behalf. Apparently, they didn't pray hard enough."

She looked at Chef, and from the expression on his face, couldn't help but smiling, too. "So, what do you do around here?"

"I tend my father's farm, and watch over my little brothers, even the stupid one, whom you seem to like. We just live over there." He pointed in the direction of their farmstead.

She fell silent, humbled by an odd power his words had over her. Nothing came to mind, and she felt a keen pleasure building as she scrutinized his height and aspect.

A creature slunk up from behind, and rubbing against his leg, meowed twice, soft and high. Reaching down, he swooped her gently into his arms, and asked, "Would you like to hold her?"

But she had already advanced, its black, silky coat like a tiny panther's mane. Now embracing the animal, her companion softly muttered that her name was Bast, "You know like the cat-headed goddess of ancient Egypt?"

She could only cradle her new recipient, and peering back at him, oddly and uncharacteristically, meowed two times.

He only smiled again and replied, "Tomorrow, I am going hare hunting. If you can, meet me here at two."

Handing Bast back to her designated owner, she felt the closeness of Chef's jaw and beard, as she gently purred her assent into the crevice of his neck.

CII

It shone in the sun as a piece of petrified wood, hewn and polished to perfection. Just then, it seemed to jerk sensate of its stalkers. Its pupils dilated, its nose quivering, and with the great power of its hind legs, it jumped nearly five feet straight into the air.

In his venery, Chef hadn't noticed Eleanor's attempt to entice it with a long, oddly-coloured carrot. She heard the whooshing - a tiny, deadly projectile spun, then careened through the interim space. It too reflected a silvered hue, stony and glittering in its propulsion.

The object struck the creature, cutting between its spinning sockets directly, spattering what first seemed as though it should be silver and slithering, a cool, removed colour as of a mercurial calm, the scene devoid of all vibration, then she became sensate of a screaming, only to realize that it was her own voice, and glancing down at her clothing, Eleanor observed an angry, angst-driven canvas, smeared with a textured gore.

Chef came over to her, grabbing her arms and hands which tore at the tufts on her scalp. Now gently holding her, then stroking her forearms, the scene was again slowly transformed back into its previous mercurial nature. Stretching onto the tips of her toes, she strained forward and softly kissed his bare neck. Deftly picking up the carcass, he walked over to a distance of some twenty yards, peered directly into her eyes, to which she responded by indicating her intent to approach, only to have the hunter negate her signal by meaningfully shaking his head.

Eleanor stopped in her tracks. Turning his back, he drew his knife, its blade freshly sharpened, and holding it ably by the scruff of its neck, slit the soft, pliable throat. Eleanor saw nothing, only the darkening pools growing at Chef's feet.

Looking away Eleanor wondered if sacrifice were necessary. All of it forever. If there were a button to undo everything which had been achieved... if there were only a button, would she depress it? A red flashing unit of mass destruction. But if there were also a button on this very same unit which would, could, eradicate all the suffering, for ever and ever, would she press it? Maybe it was one and the same button.

Maybe it was...

Chef presented her with its skin, washed and devoid of all associations, purified in the very act of his ritual. He smiled. And as Eleanor ran her hand over the velvety covering, still damp from evisceration and ablution, suddenly surprised to find the hare's ears a part of the softness of the proffered pellicle, providing a distinct, discrete pleasure to the touch, she wanted to cry out, but all at once knew exactly why she required the offering.

"Thank-you, Chef," Eleanor heard herself retort.

"You're welcome. I wanted to ask you something. Would you like to come for supper on Sunday? Then you can see for yourself what they call me," his head bowed shyly.

"Me? I... I... what would George say?" Eleanor wished she could retract this idiotic response.

"I don't know. I guess he'll be there too. His favourite is stewed hare, you know." With those words, Chef smiled again, turned and departed.

"Supper's at six sharp. Not much left for latecomers," she heard him pronounce as he made his way along the path into the woods, out of sight.

CIII

It bubbled before her. Its hot, grimy stench rose. She stirred it with the stick she had collected for the purpose. When it boiled, it kind of spat at her, disclaiming her intent. Luckily, her grandmother wouldn't be back for hours. It was her bridge-playing day and Eleanor had carefully planned the time allotment.

The surface thickened and again prodding it, she wondered when it would be ready to crack. The vapor was definitely offensive, and teetering over this heat, Eleanor soon gagged in response. She wondered if the addition of regurgitant could make the concoction any more odious. It was nearing the stage when water could be added. But Eleanor's concern had shifted to a matter more demanding of her immediate attention. What could she do to rid the place of this omnipresent stench? Surely her grandmother would notice and Eleanor couldn't help but thinking of Salem. She didn't need anymore incriminating incidents to add to her repertoire. She was already all too certain the poor woman would be unceremoniously divulged of her multifarious exploits. She needn't wreck the house as well.

Eleanor's mind began to race. How long did she have? Even if she found out, she wasn't doing anything wrong, was she? But how would she explain the way she had come to possess the skin? She had fibbed before, one more white lie didn't matter. She could hear herself exclaiming, 'Yes, yes, I met the fellow Chef, yes Chef, while I was f...ing his little brother. Quite an annoying, fumbling mess. Can't blame me for trying though.' And then, 'No, no, you see the bumbling idiot came on my thigh. Good for nothing really. Not a frolic in the park. No, ma'am.'

She could hear it all now. She would hate her. The pilferer of everything the dear old lady held sacred. Maybe she could explain how badly she needed to come, how that was the only thing which would make her forget for a little while... a momentary lapse of consciousness... a repose for the wicked.... Perhaps, if things had been different. If she had only chosen another path, maybe then it would have been all right. But the machine with that dastardly button. What of the...? What of it...?

Eleanor sighed audibly. A heavy, heart-felt, lugubrious sound as the mixture sputtered and boiled up in counteraction. "Double, double toil and trouble; Fire burn, and cauldron bubble," she heard the lines repeating. But who said them? For whence did they come? Was she again going crazy? This time she knew her grandmother wouldn't tend her as before, praying, and calling the priest for his guidance and higher wisdom. She knew what would become of her, what became of all girls who were like her at heart.

Finally, the brew inflated until Eleanor thought the whole thing would overspill, but unexpectedly, it desisted.

She knew it must be time to add the water and as she went about doing this, a thought, from whence she knew not, arose, germinating an idea. A sweet and delicious idea so intoxicating: Soon, she would paint. Regardless of all else, soon the illusion would finally be manifest. A curtain crossed her consciousness, the bleary confusion resurfaced and the question so familiar to her again arose from within: How?

An eye centered and surfaced in the mire, afloat momentarily, somehow so familiar, but she could not place the source. The desired consistency was nearly attained, as Eleanor saw a tiny, familiar face appear in the window. Graymalkin. No, no, that wasn't her name. Mouthing the syllables, she tried to recall it. What was it now? Somehow, she couldn't remember. She felt weary and tired.

Pawing at the glass, she meowed in response. Opening the frame, the diminutive creature squeezed agilely through and cradling it to her, she made their way to her designated room, and lay down on the tiny wooden berth, as her companion purred in acquiescent supine splendor.

CIV

The small jars sat amongst the rows of bottled preserves down here in the cellar. The damp smell of musty earth was oddly refreshing as Eleanor sat brooding in the shadows. Today was Sunday and she still hadn't decided if she would go to Chef's after all. On that said day of the making, she had managed to air out the house, clean the pot and stove, and bottle the concoction, all evidence thus nearly divested, before the scheduled return. She had cut it close though. After awaking, she had to quickly put out the cat and shake off her bedding before starting the lengthy clean-up. Fortunately, she had managed to do it all in time.

"Eleanor? Eleanor? Are you in there?" her grandmother bellowed from outside the darkened burrow.

You would have thought she was in the recesses of the earth with the force being exerted.

"Yes, I am. Would you like anything?" Eleanor asked.

"No, dear. But how long have you been in there?" a note of concern entered her voice.

"I don't know. Do you need me?" Eleanor wondered why she was asking. Maybe something was wrong.

"Come out for a moment, Eleanor."

She could hear the woman's voice lower in decibel, and instantly obeyed.

"Eleanor, what is the matter? You look so pale." Her grandmother gently brushed the hair from Eleanor's forehead.

"I... I was just thinking, that's all," Eleanor muttered.

Her grandmother's face contorted into such a display of genuine worry that before she had really thought about it, the secret came out. "A young man invited me to his home this evening, and I wasn't sure if I should go or not."

"What is his family name?" the woman inquired.

Eleanor felt her cheeks suffuse with sudden humiliation. "I am sorry to admit that I do not know this fact."

"I'm sorry. That's all right, dear. What then is his given name?" her grandmother again quizzed.

"He is known to some as Chef, ma'am," Eleanor replied shyly.

"Yes, I know of this boy and his family. He is a good, well-mannered boy with younger brothers, and good, kind, Christian parents. Some youthful company would do you well I think, Eleanor. Were you invited for supper?"

"Yes, ma'am," Eleanor acknowledged.

"Would you like to go, Eleanor?" she queried for the final time.

"Yes I would, ma'am."

"Good. Then the matter is settled." She shook her head with self-satisfaction.

"Why don't you take a jar of preserves for dessert?" the well-intentioned lady offered. Going into the dug-out, she emerged with what she thought to be a jar of the aforementioned sustenance.

"Here, we are. One jar of preserved pears for dessert." Smiling at Eleanor, she nodded towards the house and replied, "I believe it's time for some little ragamuffin to get washed and ready."

Eleanor couldn't help but grinning in spite of herself.

CV

A candle wavered in the distance alighting the window of the gnarled, wooden structure. For a moment, she thought she saw the furry silhouette of a familiar spider from long ago. She twitched nervously. Approaching, she couldn't see the elevated figures of the three children hidden in the loft. Upon the threshold, she heard the too familiar sounds.

"Eleanor, Eleanor, entrez-vous, s'il vous plait!" the words boomed from aloft.

Sweating profusely, Chef plunged more vigorously. "We didn't think you'd be coming for the main show."

George moaned, breathing heavily.

A voice, noticeably strained, giggled in the shadows.

"Come and join us, won't you?"

Eleanor stood astounded in the doorway, yet she felt a trickle of moisture run down her leg.

"Chef, is that George?" she muttered now again rendered a somnambulist.

Like a divine and whimsical prince aloft with his eunuch, she wondered where they could have gone. Had they somehow been severed since their previous rendezvous? Chef, before answering, began to plunge forcefully before moaning himself, after which he allowed the distended jewels to trail from his fingertips, and Eleanor could see how well-hung George indeed was. George instantly began to sob as Chef pulled away. Their court jester jerked noticeably nearby, obviously the middle brother, tugging furiously on the end of his monkey. A trail of dribble ran from the sides of her mouth as the final moan sounded.

The three of them were suspended above the vat of bubbling stew which graced the centre of their dwelling place. Like warlocks, the two older brothers descended, glowering in their descent.

Eleanor's position had remained fixed since she entered. Chef approached her smiling. "Welcome darling, are you enjoying the show?"

Eleanor found herself still unable to respond.

Chef continued, "This is my younger brother, Spencer," as he reached down Spencer's again protruding trousers. Eleanor could still hear blubbering from the above recesses.

"Your little brother sounds upset. Shouldn't you...?"

"You should go comfort him. Really, Eleanor," as Chef approached more closely, "it's the perfect time to suck his you know. But before you do, my brother was wondering if you'd give him one, that is, if you don't mind too much?"

The other brother, his lower extremities protruding all the

more, howled at Chef's hand gesture, as Chef rubbed it all the more furiously.

"It needs to be sucked," Spencer whined into Chef's left ear. "It's too hard."

"All right, all right, hold your horses." Again they both giggled.

"Well, Eleanor? You haven't said much," Chef retorted with distaste.

Eleanor, responding by sitting down on the log positioned before the fire, while looking at neither the despot nor his inept counterpart, held out her hand, replying, "I brought some preserves."

Chef shrugged, after which motioning above to his youngest brother, to which both elders reacted by proceeding back up the wooden steps ascending to the still blubbering mass.

"Hurry up. I have to finish supper," was Chef's command.

"No, no, no," was the muffled and pleading voice of their youngest member.

"It's too hard, Chef. I thought you said she'd do it," the disembodied Spencer whined.

"Well, he will anyhow," was the wry rejoinder.

"But I wanted her to...," the middle child continued to complain.

"Shut up, and get it over with," was the sharp reprimand.

All she could hear was the nasalized sobbing of the youngest, and the mounting moans of his elder oppressor, while the eldest stood, watching eagerly. Suddenly, the elder shook violently, the youngest shrieked, while the eldest fell over laughing into the bale in the corner, pointing at the hilarity of the scene before him, exclaiming, "You squirted his eyeball! You got his eye!"

Getting to his feet, Chef hurried down, seemingly startled, muttering all the while to himself. "I must see if our guest is well-entertained. I must tend the stew. I'm late... I'm late," sounding oddly like the white rabbit from a very familiar, well-reputed source.

Eleanor, now the privileged courtesan within the divine court, had however rose and left, the only indication of her having ever at all been, the jar of 'preserves' left for the palate of her refined company.

CVI

Sitting awkwardly on the divan in one Mrs. Vivian Edward Norman Wellgrene's parlor, for a moment he fumbled nervously, unaccustomed to his civilized attire. Mrs. Wellgrene had not been expecting him, and wondered why now after so many months would the man arrive upon her doorstep. She had never liked him, remembering his seemingly fallacious blubbering at the trial.

"Well, what is it that I can do for you, sir?" She could not recollect his name, and not wishing to be impolite, did not probe further.

"I simply wished to speak to your granddaughter. My late daughter and she were such good friends at one time."

"Yes, yes, you mentioned that. But, what exactly is it that you wish to speak to her about? The whole ordeal has borne such a weight upon Eleanor, too much I dare say. So you will sympathize, if I wish to know the nature of your inquiry."

"Yes, of course, Mrs. Wellgrene. It is just that your granddaughter is the last living relic of the events which have transpired. She is the only living witness and my only possible access to realizing the truth of those final happenings." At that, his head hung denoting seeming gravity of manner. With a touch of flourish, he added, "It is still very hard for me you know, ma'am."

Mrs. Wellgrene's left eye narrowed scrutinizing the oddly handsome, yet dark figure before her, adding herself now, "Yes, I'm sure it is. Yes, of course."

Nodding more to herself than the man before her, she continued, "Yes, you may speak to Eleanor for a little while, but if she seems troubled at all, or is unable to respond in any way, she must not be forced to answer. She has been through more than enough, and as you know yourself, the courts deemed her... what was it? Unsound in some way. What was it, now...?"

"Yes ma'am, a non-credible witness, I believe was the term," the figure again bowed his head in reverence.

"Yes, that was it. It has been a most difficult road to achieve any degree of recovery, and I will not have you or anyone else fiddle with what has occurred through the gracious guidance of our Lord and Saviour,

Jesus Christ."

The shiver was nearly visible which ran the breadth and length of his spine, but smiling and nodding in seeming solicitude, the good lady was presently satisfied.

"Do I make myself clear, sir?" As usual, her conditions would not be ignored and required some outward gesture denoting assent.

"I understand fully, ma'am. She is a very lucky girl to have such a devoted grandmother. I only wish to speak with her for a few minutes, and if my questions seem at all trying, you have my word that I will discontinue my entreaties." He bowed his head for the final time, and the woman was pleased with his candor and show of civility.

"Yes, please wait one moment, and I will see if Eleanor will come down," she replied and quit the room.

CVII

Eleanor's eyes were heavy with sleep and exhaustion as she was awoken by the gentle shaking of her grandmother. The woman's eyes filled with concern, and almost simultaneously she asked the girl, "Are you feeling all right, dear?"

"Yes, yes, thank-you. What's wrong? Is everything all right?" Eleanor still felt heavy with inertia.

"There is a man here who wishes to speak to you, dear. Do you think you could manage it for a few minutes? It won't take long."

"Who is it?" Eleanor immediately tensed.

"It is the father of... what was her name?... Jane. Yes, that was her name, Jane."

At the mention of this sound, Eleanor felt numb and unsure like the prodding of a distant memory cell, unresponsive to electrical stimulus. She did not want to feel anything. She was so tired.

"What ever can he want of me? I don't have anything to tell him. 'They' already have established that."

"Yes, but he wants some kind of peace concerning Jane's passing, and he thinks you can give this to him. Do you think you could speak to him for a few minutes?"

Her grandmother obviously wanted her to, and as Eleanor herself was curious to exactly what this man expected from her, it was her own curiosity which finally roused her mind.

"Yes, yes, I think I can speak to him," Eleanor stated plainly while rubbing her sleepy lids.

Entering the small sitting area, which was seldom used, Eleanor noticed the way his shadow added prominently to the already shaded corners of this dimly-lit space. Her grandmother closed the doors behind her, leaving them secluded in the chamber, as he greeted her formally with a nod of his head.

"Eleanor, how are you? I have heard that you have been through some more-than-difficult times," his voice was deep like the sounding of a brass drum, and as it reverberated time-and-again booming off of the tiny-recessed-walls, once it became audible enough to decipher, reaching the canals inside her head, finally deemed intelligible, Eleanor nearly could not comprehend the words.

"I am fine, sir." A bead of sweat ran down her forehead.

He could see that she was nervous, and had hoped for a more neutral response, but now able to actually smell her fear, decided that it would be copacetic to get the upper hand.

Shadows danced tangling on the walls, an intersecting geometric snarl of unintelligibility. Was that Mr. Dorset shadowed in Winchester, shadowed in Jane, shadowed in Jane's father? Where was the initial point of contact with the canvas? Suddenly, its three-dimensional nature caused Eleanor to spin effortlessly around its centre, but it had no contact point. Only from her position directly above it could she see that it was not a two-dimensional flat surface. No, indeed! It was three-dimensional, but this was not its quintessence. It was, it was, she dared to look away, but somehow she was ethereal and could see all: It was indeed a vortex.

"I only came here to ask you a few simple questions. I know that you may not be able to answer them for me, but I only expect you to try."

Eleanor felt dizzy from the height and motion.

"The day of Jane's death Eleanor, do you remember it?" he posed carefully waiting for a response.

Eleanor managed a head-shake.

"You were standing in the cornfield, and had a view of the entire happening, yes?" he pursued. He was obviously awaiting another shake.

Spinning, barely she managed to carry this motion out.

"Yes? Winchester and Jane were there and they were arguing. Do you remember this scene?"

Another nod.

"Jane was only partly-clad. Is that correct?"

A nod.

"They were yelling at each other, but you were too far to actually hear what transpired. Correct or not?"

Nod.

"And then they were in front of the well. He had already beaten my Jane up some, correct?"

Nod.

"They were both before the well. Do you remember this scene?"

Nod.

"Did he then proceed to push her in? Did he murder my little girl? Next, you saw this happen?"

No response.

"Eleanor, Eleanor, stay with me. This is my question to you. I must know. Please. Please. Did you see this happen?! Eleanor, concentrate! I must know this. For a one-time scholar, why are you so unable to respond?! I have given you enough time to recover. I only ask you this. You are the only one who can answer me. Please."

The shadow before Eleanor begged. She could see the face of the pleader. It was not the man before her. This man who pleaded before her now hadn't pleaded for a long, long time. In fact, he had forgotten how.

"Eleanor, Eleanor!" the drum's booming was rising in magnitude.

"Yes, yes, now I remember," she muttered, unable to hear her own voice. "I remember all."

"Yes! Yes! Of course you do. He pushed her, didn't he?! That monster pushed my little girl into the well, didn't he? He did, didn't he, Eleanor?! He did!"

"No sir, you did," Eleanor smiled. The booming stopped.

Seizing her, he screamed something directly into her face, but she could no longer hear his words. The room had oddly lightened. The darkness of his form was contained in its own shadow. By this time her grandmother had swung open the doors, and was uncharacteristically shrieking at him, pointing adamantly toward the front door, with one protruding finger. Then, the oddly-handsome, Cimmerian figure vanished into the obscurity of his own dark night.

CVIII

I could have taught her a thing or two, he thought to himself. She would have cried out in pain, then begged for more. He had seen that look in her eyes before. She wasn't any different from the rest. She would have loved it, and he would have come so hard. It had been quite awhile, and he was grievously wretched doing nothing but cattle.

"Nothing but a two-bit hussy!" he murmured to himself, as he jerked on the end of the protrusion, the road winding out before him. He needed to hoist her atop his cock 'til the tip turned purple and numbed, and she bled. That was his favourite lastingness when they would beg him to stop and he would only respond by thrusting all the harder.

If he did stop, however, there was always a high price for mercy, as he would rock, rock, rock along their upper palate until after thrice swallowing each would always choke violently on their own regurgitant, making him come all the harder.

Desire in him had grown huge, large, like a living, breathing thing that desperately needed tending. Night having long set-in, when the headlamps illuminated the outline of a disfigured and limping beast, obviously making its way homeward along the flooded back road, he recognized its curious coloring at once.

With his lamed eyes full of cataracts, the approaching lamp's dispersion seemed an odd sprinkling of stardust. Then, it passed momentarily and nothing but darkness remained. His body now ached continually, and just the daily journey from house to field tired him so. Somehow he knew that the light would again return. Weary from the journey, he hadn't even energy to lie down. The time had come. Motionless, he shivered anxiously.

Agamemnon had finally resurfaced to collect him.

It was Orestes. It had to be. That damn girl and all her fancy games! He missed them more than anything though. He had wondered where the thing had got off to. No other creature could look just that way. He loped to one side, unsure in his gait. Bumping over a deep rut in the road, he braked heavily coming to a full and screeching halt.

Revving the engine fiercely, he tugged on it all the more wildly. The thing had stopped dead and was cowering stupidly. Swinging the shaft into reverse, he aimed, simultaneously accelerating backwards. Feeling the burst beneath him, collectively experienced as a yelp, thud, and pop, he struck Orestes down, as an explosion of bone and cartilage sprayed the soft, pliable earth, leaving tiny indentations everywhere in the soil.

Satiation having arrived, he continued the duration of the road's meandering, his pants again buttoned, his hand wiped clean, the only residual indication being the effluence covering the inner side of his windshield. Irritated now by the sight of it, he thought how need-lessly messy life was as he continued slopping through the dingy, dreary puddles.

CIX

She knew. It had only taken a day or two before the worry of where could he have gone overwhelmed her to the point of exhaustion and she had set-out, and found him, or at least what remained of him by the roadside ditch. That very morning, she had put on her new leather shoes, supple and black with tiny cut-out flowers atop of the arches. She had thought of Jane then, and how bare and fine her graceful arch-es were as they curved in mid-flight, as a dove's wing might, before the image dissipated into the shadow from which it had arisen.

There wasn't much of Beast left. There wasn't much left at all. He seemed so beyond vulnerability, everything so reduced somehow, but she didn't want to focus too astutely on this sadness, this percep-tion, this truth. It was too grave, and pointless, but a part of her mind couldn't help but remember, and cherishing that memory, the tears began to flow freely, now stinging and drying her shaded orbs.

She wanted something from him though, and she wanted it quick-

ly so that she wouldn't be required to stay and smell this stench of cadaver which invariably arose. A tiny, darkened velveteen lappet seemed
the appropriate memento, as she delicately stroked it, placing it into
the pocket of her petticoat.

Now, it waited only to be adorned by the vermilion ribbon which
she had been saving for a special occasion. Somehow, it would be
perfect.

CX

Amongst the buttercups Bast lay. She could just see her frame, dig-
ging, now squatting in the long, green blades, from the tiny, latticed
window burrowed deep into the recessed walls of the attic, green eyes
full of spry delight.

She had found her grandmother's saffron way at the back of the
kitchen cupboard. Mixing it with the white paste, it formed a soft,
lemon yellow. The pale antiquity of the shade mellowed her, like fine
Italian lace. The aromatic scent was wonderful. It filled her nostrils,
redolent of plenty. She had often wished her grandmother would use
this spice, this essence, this fragrance as its heat soothed her like the
cooling rain of a storm's outpouring. A little crimson and she became
ochre, the heat and depth of this hue like the amber pin her grandmother often wore. Next, the squeeze and force of the indigo paste was
like a relief, as waves of pure consciousness... of definition... of quintessence awashed her active psyche. Now nearly emerald, but the tone
defied this simple hue, she, primal, vital, had become a creeper of the
tropical climes, writhing and falling, analogous to her kind.

The shade, so dark and luscious like the peel of a fruit formed by
an act of her own rendering: Her own rendering... just the thought
of which made her ravenous; ravenous for more, plenty, something.
Forcing the admixture into her pores, the pappy brushstrokes careened
easily over her epidermis, much more gracefully than the cerebral one
which moved only when it desired.

The scents in the attic were antiquated and dusty, like most of its
predecessors as well as successors. As she applied the blended strokes,
it lay untouched in the shoebox beside her shed clothing, waiting for

the manifestation. Last but not least, she arched the jungle cream deep into the folds of her closed lids, now a bodhisattva, back erect, crossed-legged, palms cupped upward to receive all that was for the offering.

The light in the room was low and slanting, but she could not, would not, ignore the image forming, always forming, forever formed in her mind. She could finally recognize the form her heart had taken. It was no longer blood, nor flesh, nor tissue, but crystal, pure and green. In its clarity it contained all, every seed of beating hope or bleeding gratitude had been stolen by the very same thief who had replaced it with a faceted stone, green and pure, like the loss of a divine treasure.

Sacred, secret, secretion, she cut deep, but not too, into the fleshy part of her upper thigh where it met her groin. It ran fast and pure in its red course. Surprised that it too was not the chosen color of redemption, she began to pull, or rather, yank on the mons pubis until each hair was uprooted by the follicle at the papillae. Rendered bare as a child, the depilatory tactic was now complete.

Then lying down supine on the wooden planks of the floor's boarding, she placed the decorated structure at her feet to avoid the mounting current of blood. With her legs splayed, she became the chloroplast-producing, protein-starved organism which could and would deceive any interloper who deemed it necessary to tarry a little too long upon her bristle-hinged-blades.

Mr. John Skeaping would hardly have agreed, but this did not grieve her in any way. Her purpose being set, the progress was more than clear to her green crystalline-enclosed-heart.

CXI

The sunlight slanted moving from her dull brown shade graced with the achromatism which had been her mother's legacy. The rows upon rows of books, shelved and systematized by a hand that knew the feel of each cover, she could see still illuminated above the growing dimness.

The time had passed and the lunch crowd had come and gone in their habitual meanderings. Eleanor yawned, a silent, tired sough as she had often seen her grandmother do when she was still alive. The house had become hers after her passing, and she had lived there alone ever since.

Her father had visited once after a wild bout of gambling and drinking, only to accuse her of stealing something which was not rightfully hers in the first place. She hardly recognized him, and wouldn't have let him in, except for his persistent pleading. She was curious as to how her brothers and sisters had turned out as she had not inquired about them, nor they her in all these years. After she had let him in and asked this very question, his reply however was curt and more than a little obnoxious.

"What'd you care?! You up and left us all anyhow!" he growled menacingly.

"I don't remember it that way." Suddenly, Eleanor became irritated at herself for ever allowing this once-familiar man to enter her home.

The pause when it came was long. Finally, he cleared his throat, slurring, "I wouldn't know. The government came and took them all away. Said they wasn't getting enough to eat. Prob'ly not, but there wasn't much I could do 'bout it. Ended up way out in the old orphan's school, I think." Then, he took an extended draught on the bottle he was still holding in his right hand.

Eleanor had been the lucky one. She didn't know why or how. Deserved or undeserved she had been the one delivered into the arms of an old, sweet lady. She didn't know what to say to this bawdy, tired man before her. After all, that is what he was to her, almost as a stranger would be on the street.

"I'm sorry." She could think of nothing else to say, but he seemed to be waiting for some other response.

"Well, life is what it is. Not much more. The early days with your mother were good though. We were good to you."

Now, she knew he was waiting for her reply. Clearing her own parched throat she answered, "Yes, yes, you were. As good as you could be."

He seemed appeased by this rejoinder, yet continued, "I saw them pictures of yours in town. Quite a price on them too," he added with another swill.

"Yes, the exhibit's doing rather well, much better than I ever expected," Eleanor pondered for a moment this unexpected fortune.

An odd guttural sound emerged from his gullet, disapproving and profane.

Suddenly, Eleanor realized that he did in fact want something. She didn't know what that could be, but he definitely came here with a purpose in mind.

Piqued, yet still curious, she continued, "May I ask what you thought of them?"

Rousing him from his lengthy abstraction, he laughed, "What I think of them? I don't. Never had the chance to think like that. I guess, they're art like all the rest. Ugly as hell."

Well, at least his condemnation was comprehensive in its sweep. For a moment, she almost laughed, but something, she wasn't sure what, prevented her.

"Why, after all this time, have you come here?" she queried, not willing to remain silent any longer.

He just looked at her, and swigged with renewed vigor. "I was wondering when you'd ask that," he bawled.

"Want some?" he offered her the half-empty bottle.

The smell was enough to make her stomach lurch. "No, thanks. I don't like it," she replied, eager for him to remove the offensive odour.

"Yeah, I figured as much," he sneered. "You types never do."

"You must make quite a bit with all them pictures. Plenty to live on," he exclaimed, but the implication definitely fancied a response. She felt as if she were being ensnared, and resented the interrogation.

He continued, "I grew up in this place, you know. All my life, I lived here before the farm. Used to help a lot with the place. Knew all the neighbours, too," he expounded with a strange flourish about the mouth. When Eleanor's silence endured, he resumed, "I just want what's coming to me. Should have been mine to begin with. Would have been, if she hadn't taken such a fancy to you. Now, whadddaya think?" The bottle was still in his right hand. It was more than obvious that he tarried meaningfully, waiting for her retort.

"I suppose that would have been the case. But it was not, nor is it now to be," Eleanor enunciated firmly.

"That right? Y'even sound like her some. So you don't think you've had a free living long enough? You're not going to return to me what is rightfully mine to begin with?" His snarl was becoming all the time louder.

"We obviously do not see it from the same perspective," Eleanor declared, her tone still resolute.

"We're going to have to bring the law into it, I guess. Nothing else to do," he professed with that same flourish about the mouth that she had never before today seen.

"What has become of the farm? She gave you the property as a gift when you married mother," Eleanor again resumed.

He just looked at her, sneering and resentful, as he pulled on the bottle's contents. The dark rum glistened like pale amber in the subdued light.

"Gone. Long gone. 'Repossessed,' they called it."

He took another swig.

"Repossessed? It was your property."

Eleanor confused, blurted, "There was no mortgage!"

Suddenly outraged and bewildered by the idea of losing her house to a drunkard who wanted it to further his own interests, she did not empathize, nor even sympathize, as she marvelled at their predicament: How could this be?

Abruptly, she realized that a mortgage would have been foreclosed if the payments had lapsed, but she knew the bank must have stepped in for some reason or other.

"How did you accumulate it?" she murmured, at once enlightened.

"What?" he belched.

"The gaming debt." Her tone was sharp.

"Don't you take that tone with me, Missy!" the belligerent drunk hissed.

Wanting the confirmation she knew already, she promptly uttered, "I'm sorry," but it was too late. Drunk and past the point of bare civility, he pounced, striking her down as he belted her across the nose.

"You ungrateful, bitch! You haven't changed a wink!" he boomed, irate and fuming.

Eleanor wanted to laugh out loud at his antics, but instead got up, glared at him, and ran from the room to ring the police.

Picking up the shiny, black object, she hoped it would still work, as she used it on such rare occasions. As she dialed, she could hear objects hitting the adjoining wall, her grandmother's antiques smashed to oblivion.

"Yes, yes, there is a man on a drunken rampage in my home who just assaulted me, and I need you to come at once. Yes, yes, right away. Yes, thank-you." As she replaced it on its hook, she realized the noise from the adjacent room had extinguished. Proceeding cautiously with the stove stoker in hand, risen, and ready to strike at anything which moved, she crept from the kitchen into the ruin which awaited her in the parlour. Rum smeared the wall, where the bottle had exploded. Broken glass and bits of antediluvian treasure were strewn over the floor like the crushed shells of a shore, pounded and made priceless by its unmerciful surf. He, however, was nowhere to be seen, the front door left ajar.

Her shift now over, she couldn't wait to get home, put up her feet, have a hot cup of tea or two and feed the neighbourhood cat which she had recently befriended. First of all though, she wanted to stop by the post office before leaving town to walk the three, sweaty miles home.

CXII

As the afternoon sun now sat relatively low on the cusp of the horizon, Eleanor remembered reading something about an eclipse being forecast in the papers. The streets had resumed their usual dusty property with the changing of season. Again hoisting her leather pack over her left shoulder, she began her customary walk to the post office. Every Friday she would make this trip, if only to window-shop, and nod her head a few times in casual greeting. As the smell in the air was dry and acrid, Eleanor wondered how close they were to drought warnings.

This was the trip she had made so many times, each time with her precious cargo concealed within its covering. Already yellowing, and bent at the corners, it didn't seem much of a thing to behold, but it contained within its arcing curves and sloping characters her most precious possession: the illusions of her youth.

Each time she would come and go along this same beaten path, she questioned the reason she tortured herself so, but nevertheless, knew that somehow she had to walk this line, this course, that it was hers to tread. The warm air, although humid, felt good against her skin, even though she wished she could remove her silk scarf. Striding through the town's centre, she looked quite a figure of a woman with her long, slender legs, lengthy dark hair salted with white striations and tied back from her face in a bun, large, white pearl studs gracing slender lobes, pale skin, gray-green eyes obscured by the largeness of her glasses, and a nugget-coloured carrying-case to match. She would never have thought it herself, but many admirers had noticed her appeal, demure and classical in its timeless rendering. She often surmised that she mustn't be attractive to others, this being the only conceivable reason for never receiving formal invitations or even informal ones, but this wasn't it at all. Simply, people were intimidated by her aloofness and inapproachability, interested, even curious, yet still afraid of either offending or being upbraided by a face which could often seem severe in its conveyance of emotion.

Rehearsing the lines as she often did, it gave her a depraved sense of odd satisfaction to mentally replay the lilt and drop of them, the tune never tiring. If only she could translate such a resonance to the very palette which was her mode of choice:

"Your sustenance will be the very thing to steal your ever decreasing sanity and this is my sole comfort." She hummed the final bar. But she had tried and never could. It always manifested something other than this primal, elusive intention.

She had seen, passed, and left the vicinity of the post office, already making her way homeward along the dusty backroads. Taking off her scarf, she tucked it into her bag. She could hear a car approaching from behind and as it passed she could hardly miss either its color or occupant. Acknowledging her presence with a stiff nod of the head, she remembered the days when he would stop and offer her a ride home. She could still recollect the first day of her acceptance. Whenever she was in his presence, she noticed a protuberance of his trousers, large and very firm. She recalled the leering grins, and frequent shifting. That day, something dark and swarthy came over her, and she felt sly and more than a little cunning.

Running her tongue along the outer edges of her lips, she licked them carefully, making sure her observer was paying attention. When the bulge increased in surface diameter, she knew she possessed the totality of his focus. Quickly running her hand to the button of his trousers she began to unleash what lay beneath. Diving now, in word-lessness, her tongue a lapping mechanism, it took no time for the car to accelerate, swerve, make a screeching turn into her drive, and come to an abrupt halt as he moaned repeatedly in front of her entranceway.

Smiling and looking a little bewildered, he asked, "Can I come in, Eleanor?"

"No, not in the house," she replied softly. Continuing, "But thank-you for your participation."

He stared at her dumbfoundedly, not sure if he should offer her money in exchange for her services or inquire about the date he had wished to ask her on for the last ten years. Presently, he found his voice lacking and decided not to risk it further, nodding but saying nothing.

The weeks which followed spiced up the boredom of Eleanor's do-main. She would arrive at work, be called into his office, be requested in muted tones to lock the door behind her to which she would gladly accede, after which he would hurriedly unfasten his trousers, as she sat down on his lap, awkwardly attempting to stuff it in, eager to begin thrusting away.

It wasn't good; it wasn't even average, but it was sex, something Eleanor had hated going without for so long, the price for which she was required to listen to a counterfeit barrage of nonsensical gibberish: 'how I love you, and have always loved you'; 'You feel so good'; 'I'm coming, I'm coming, I'm coming,'; and lest we forget, 'I'm divorcing my wife honey, so we can make love all day long.' She wanted to guf-faw at his moronic tactics, but she was coming to enjoy her morning and afternoon breaks, as well as the little gifts that had already begun to arrive although she adamantly wished he would just say hump, screw, fuck, anything but that ridiculous phrase he so often employed, which she knew was not at all what they were doing.

"My wife is so fat, I am not aroused at all. If I can even get it up, a couple of plunges and I come. Very little satisfaction, I dare say, not at all like what we have," he blurted in the middle of it one day.

Eleanor thought, what about your poor wife? I bet her gratification is more than a little lacking, you rude pig. I could show her a thing or two myself.

Eleanor laughing, exclaimed, "Oh, Mr. Gaines, you're so strong and it feels sooo... good. I'm coming, I'm coming... yes, yes, yessss...." She loved to fake a loud orgasm, that is, for the benefit of the staff. Maybe he would be blackmailed.

It was all going splendid until one day Gaines came in, called her into his office as was customary, but this time he did not ask her to lock the door. She froze.

"Why not? What's the matter?" Eleanor didn't know what could possibly be the matter, unless Mrs. Gaines had been apprised of their activities, and cut it off after all.

"I've made it official, honey. Jean and I are getting a divorce and then, we can be married!" He watched for her reaction. When he couldn't detect any, he asked, "Aren't you thrilled?"

She never thought he had the balls to actually do it. "Yes, yes, of course. I am happy, just a little shocked that's all."

"I guess I can't help but being a little concerned for your wife and children." Eleanor eyed him wryly.

He fidgeted under such a scrutinizing gaze. "I thought you'd be happy! I did it for us! They'll be taken care of. Of course. What do you take me for?"

She didn't want to say. "I'm sorry. It's just that I got scared for a minute. I'm sure it will pass," Eleanor feigned.

"That's my Eleanor. Always concerned about the welfare of anyone besides herself," Mr. Gaines smiled now, his resentment having faded quickly away.

Eleanor, already tired from the day's turn of events, rose to leave the small, suddenly claustrophobic cavity.

"Now, wait a minute. Go lock the door. We haven't celebrated yet," Mr. Gaines grinned eagerly.

"I think I'd rather not. Not now. It doesn't seem right somehow," Eleanor replied.

"Come on now, don't be like that. We're both looking forward to it. I know I am, and I'm sure you must be, so come on, lock the door," he hissed.

"I need some fresh air just now. Excuse me, Mr... Mr...," she realized she didn't even know his first name, and even worse, than this, didn't want to.

Shoving her up against the wall, she could feel he was harder than ever. "Please, I don't want...." He couldn't hear her. He was already rapidly removing his trousers. "It'll just take a minute or two, honey. No time at all really."

Lifting her skirt, and pulling her underclothing aside, he forced it in, more excited than ever. Disgusted, and on the verge of crying and vomiting all at once, she knew what she had to do.

"Yes, yes, yes, oh you could always make me come," Eleanor simpered.

"Harder, harder, harder. That's it. Yes, I'm coming, I'm coming... oh, yes," she coyly repeated.

"I'm coming. I'm coming. I'm coming... Jane, Jane, yes Jane," she moaned meaningfully.

The desired effect had been achieved. Slipping out, the semen squirted onto her upper thigh.

S...E...M...E...N

The letters flew into and through her consciousness, forming, conforming, reconforming... each a singular entity...

M...E...N...E...S

The Pharaoh would not be pleased.

"What did you say?" his voice was severe but reduced to a whisper.

Eleanor did not answer.

"Who is Jane?" Mr. Gaines boomed.

"My child lover. Sometimes it just slips out," she smiled knowingly.

"That's disgusting! You're a filthy, dirty woman!" Mr. Gaines ejaculated.

"I believe that's your come on my thigh. And by the way, you're one lousy fuck, if I ever had one," Eleanor seethed.

He stepped away, suddenly afraid of the creature who stood before him.

A few weeks passed and Eleanor learned that he had 'cleared up the misunderstanding' with his wife, and they were reconciled, apparently happier than ever, planning a trip to Bermuda the following summer.

The day was ending in a display of such magnificent splendor, the dust of the road seemed a trivial nuisance. For the remainder of the walk home, she took off her shoes and knee-highs, feeling the dusty grit slide effortlessly between her toes. Eleanor stared off into the empyreum, the empyreum that was her own, and she couldn't help but thinking of the feet whose customary filth always made her smile in spite of herself.

CXIII

The doorknocker sounded. She could hear its resonation throughout the house. Eleanor hadn't been expecting anyone. A pang of foreboding all at once sent a shiver down her spine and legs, and oddly she could feel it converge in her Achilles tendon. Debating whether or not she should actually answer, since she hadn't been expecting anyone, it was probably one of two things, her irate father returning to berate her even further, or a lone traveler, lost and broken down on these backroads. If the former were going to pursue the matter with any real intention, she wished he would just take it up with her lawyer, and quit bothering her with the gory details of a life which no longer, and had not for more than twenty years, significantly concerned her. At the possibility of the latter prospect, she decided to risk another wearing altercation, with the notion of the clandestine stranger, stranded and needing her masterful assistance, prompting her forward.

Opening the door slowly, she saw a small, pale face bordered by darker, yet still red, frizz. She knew who it was immediately and smiled in spite of herself. "Effie? Effie Black!" Her tone was welcoming. "Come in, come in!"

"Eleanor, I wasn't sure if you'd recognize me after all these years. But as I was in the area visiting my cousins, I had to come. I had to come to see and say hello to an old, dear friend, myself." Her tone was warm and sincere, the years having softened the lines of hardness around her eyes and mouth.

Her face, still distinct, was furrowed with lines like a withering, dried apple, but not lines of rancor, no, lines of kindness, and something else, yes something like... like... hardship.

"Effie, let me take your wet coat and hat. Would you like a warm cup of tea? I've got the kettle on already," Eleanor smiled, eager for a visitor.

"Thank-you. Thank-you. If it isn't any trouble, I'd love a cup," Effie smiled, the lines nearly swallowing up her face.

In the entrance hall, in the light of a white and dreary afternoon, Eleanor suddenly found herself considering what could have become of this star-pupil, whom she had not often thought of since their final meeting.

Effie, suddenly nervous, abruptly uttered, "I'm sorry to have heard of your grandmother's passing. She was such a good woman."

"Thank-you. Yes, she had a good life, and extended the same privilege to me. I was very fortunate to know and have her." For a minute they both smiled and looked down.

"I am sorry though to admit that I am not apprised of your fortunes in the same manner as you are of mine," Eleanor expressed.

"Well, it has been a very long time," Effie conceded.

As abruptly as Effie had offered her condolences, Eleanor now asked, "Did you marry, Effie?"

"Me? Why heavens, yes!" Effie laughed, and it was obvious by her response that it conveyed a good-natured frankness.

"Yes, my surname is now Akcorn, and has been for nearly twenty years," Effie feigned a weak, tired smile.

"Akcorn, Akcorn? That sounds familiar," Eleanor ruminated aloud.

"Peter Akcorn?" Effie hinted.

"Jane's Peter? The one and same Peter you were so infatuated with when we were children?" Eleanor was flabbergasted.

When Effie turned quite pink, she realized that she had indeed flawed in referring to Peter in the possessive case.

"I mean, I didn't mean... I'm sorry. That must have sounded terrible." Now it was Eleanor's turn to go red.

Effie sighed. "Maybe, that should have been my warning, but I was too busy worshipping to take heed of warnings. I won't exaggerate, it has been a very trying existence. I gave up a prestigious scholarship to get married, and it has been an uphill battle ever since. He's not a bad man. It's just that... I don't know. You know that Biblical saying that goes, 'Cast thy bread upon thy water, and thou shalt find it after many days'? Well, I'm still waiting for it to come back to me." With those words, Effie smiled humbly again.

Eleanor couldn't help herself, "Oh Effie, I'm sorry life has been so hard for you."

"Well, maybe I complain too much. Perhaps, I never truly learned what gratitude is."

"I don't think so, Effie. I don't think that at all," Eleanor stated plainly. Suddenly, they both smiled at each other.

They still hadn't left the entranceway.

"What about you? Did you ever marry? I remember you liked that young man. Wasn't his name, Winchester?"

Again Eleanor suffused with crimson. "No. No. He didn't have eyes for me. He was another of Jane's possessions. Unfortunately, he ended up going to jail. I don't know if you would recall all that. It was so long ago. All so long ago." She repeated the final line more for her own benefit than Effie's, but Effie nodded just as well.

"That's right. What an awfully sad mess. Sad indeed." Now, they were both nodding together slowly, but not really to each other.

"Peter still claims that if he had been given half the chance he would have swept her up. I think he has always loved her." Now it was Effie's turn to ruminate aloud.

But Eleanor couldn't hear her. Her mind had turned instead to his face, the darkness of the shade, when they were both interrupted from their private abstractions by the blare of honking outside.

"What's that?" Eleanor asked.

"Oh, damn! It's my ride. I told them to pick me up on their way back. I didn't think an hour could have gone by already! I have to go, Eleanor. I'm sorry. I shouldn't keep them waiting," Effie was already breathless.

"Will we see each other again, then?" Eleanor had wanted to ask, but didn't know what she'd say to such an inquiry.

"I was hoping you'd ask that. I'd love to," Effie smiled a wider smile now, and Eleanor could even see the frizziness of her locks sticking out of the hat she had hastily clad upon her dainty head.

Grabbing her overcoat, she just as hastily ran out into the pouring rain, waving in retreat. The shade of the sky had darkened, and Eleanor wondered if there would be a storm. This shade had always made her think of him and for a moment Eleanor pondered how things would have been, had they gone differently. As Eleanor started to ruminate this futile conundrum afresh, a clap of thunder broke her from her reverie, and quickly she thought to do a charcoal sketching. It had been a long, long time since she had done one. The mood was perfect for a rendering of the tiny fairy-like face, although wizened with age, which had just graced her presence.

CXIV

"This one is interesting. The movement. It's rather unusual that this artist began with a white canvas and darkened accordingly. It is definitely an overall Neoclassical impression, the intensive layering creating an attention to brush detail that portrays a kind of movement, but one which is always obscure somehow... yet, even though the images are rarely defined there is a kind of compulsion to deconstruct the image itself."

Hope's eyes glittered in the darkness of the room.

Yet, the curator stammered on. "The orange flowers in this one convey a kind of clarity in their dark rendering, seeming to suggest perhaps an Oriental theme." The small group fixed on the image in question unanimously observing the profound nature of the deep cracks in the painting. The curator resumed, "Their life-like quality in line and form as well as the way the image seems to speak to one by this luminescent contrast of dark and light is really quite wonderful in a way. Yes..." the curator trailed off.

Hope's focus easily discerned the deep fissures through the painting's marrow, and she blinked to steady her eyes. The flowers in all of their luminosity seemed to pale and through the cracks Hope could almost see something other.

"Some of the images in these pieces suggest submerged figures, this figure here being employed rather often. The tendrils seem to be the distinguishing feature of this recurrent figure even though we're never quite permitted to see its face. Stalks are used throughout the paintings. Their ever-present lines and structure are a break from the monotonous coldness of the images reflected not only in the obscure renderings but also in the choice of colour which is usually dark, lugubrious hues, serving to give all of the works a submerged, subconscious aspect. One is forced to notice when she chooses a bright colour like this gold, even though it has been muted by various brown hues. With her use of glazes, it almost becomes the colour of honey. One cannot help but feel that this is how a wheat field would be apprehended by the senses in the darkness of night. The conveyance of texture allows one to step into the image. Its three dimensional nature is truly arresting from a distance. If this image were not bound in this way but put on the wall, by its very size, if one were to walk into the room, looking at it in its proper perspective in the distance, of course it being enhanced by placement, mood, and lighting, one would indeed be fooled into believing that they were indeed on the threshold of a field of wheat - trompe l'oeil... positively trompe l'oeil!"

The curator resumed on a heavier note. "Of course, for some utterly incomprehensible reason, the artist chose to add a mix of wax to her oils and the images are all in a very sad state. Yes, as you can see, the cracks are becoming all the time more pronounced."

But Hope had ceased to hear.

Three beings could only just be distinguished, frolicking in those golden fields chill with morning dew, the sun's warm, golden beams not yet having awakened those quiet, sleeping houses. Hand-in-hand they circled a centre full of infinite possibility and bliss. Now she could hear their unfettered peals. The sound became like a heralding to her tiny canals and the child at once recognized the source.